Other Works by M. Katherine Clark

The Greene and Shields Files:
    Blood is Thicker Than Water
    Once Upon a Midnight Dreary
    Old Sins Cast Long Shadows
    Tales from the Heart, Novelettes

Soundless Silence a Sherlock Holmes Novel

The Rest is Silence, an Edmond Holmes Novel – Coming Soon

Love Among the Shamrocks Collection:
    Under the Irish Sky
    Across the Irish Sea
    On the River Shannon
    The Land Across the Sea, an Emmet O'Quinn Short

Love Among the Shamrocks Collection,
The Next Generation:
    In Dublin Fair City
    The Song of Heart's Desire
    Chasing After Moonbeams – Coming Soon

The Wolf's Bane Saga:
    Wolf's Bane
    Lonely Moon
    Midnight Sky
    Star Crossed
    Moon Rise
    Moon Song, a Companion Guide

Silent Whispers, a Scottish Ghost Story

Dragon Fire
    Heart of Fire
    Will of Fire – Coming Soon

The Greene and Shields Files

Book One

BLOOD IS THICKER THAN WATER

M. KATHERINE CLARK

For my family:

Thank you for your support, love, and help throughout the years! And supporting me for this second edition!

Dad, for all the nights you stayed up listening and for your love and support! I love you, Papa!

Mama, my best friend! Thank you for introducing me to the world of mysteries and for all the times you sat and listened to this story, helping me through the tough parts and laughing with me during the good times! Without your constant love and inspiration, this novel would not have been written! I love you, Mama!

Cameron, my incredible big brother! Thank you for all the laughs and encouragement! I love you, Brubby!

If all the world hated you, and believed you wicked,
while your own conscience approved you, and absolved you
from guilt, you would not be without friends.

Jane Eyre, Charlotte Bronte

Prologue

On an Early May Morning

A man sat at a table in the outside Café Gijon in Madrid, Spain, listening to the live music that played. His face had been altered by a closely trimmed goatee. His hair, usually dyed dark brown, was now naturally salt and pepper.

Watching the tourists as they walked by, he thought of the events that led him there. The storm had finally calmed and, as he sat drinking espresso, he finally relaxed.

He was a man with a past. He was a man who had a family who loved him, a man with friends who would die for him. He was a marine, and he was in hiding.

Chapter One

"And once again, ladies and gentlemen, we want to thank you for choosing *Aer Lingus*, and welcome to New York City," the flight attendant announced.

The man sitting in row D stood as soon as the seatbelt light turned off. Stretching his back, after the long flight from Dublin, he opened the overhead compartment and pulled out his second carry-on. Reaching for his computer bag from under the seat in front of him, he wrapped the strap around his neck. The older woman sitting beside him looked up and smiled.

"Which one is yours, love?" the man asked her.

"Oh, thank you so much!" she gushed. "It's the paisley one."

As he pulled the overnight roller suitcase out, he looked through the window. He had never been to New York and, as he handed the older woman her carryon, he grinned.

"Thank you." She said. "What's your name again?"

"Aeron," he replied, proud he didn't hesitate.

"And what school did you say you were attending?"

"NYU," he went on.

"My granddaughter is a junior there." She smiled and pulled out her purse to show him a picture. He feigned interest

2

again. "Her name is Kelly. She's studying communications. You should look her up. She's dating this boy and we don't like him."

Having heard this story from her five times already, he smiled, shook his head and helped her stand.

"Oh these old bones of mine," she said as a few of them popped. "Thank you, dear."

"No worries, Mrs. Johnson," he replied.

"But you go ahead and go, this old lady takes her time," she teased.

"Well, it was a pleasure to sit beside such a beautiful lady."

"Oh listen to you, charmer," she laughed. "Enjoy New York!"

"I intend to," he replied.

He walked off the plane and looked around JFK before going to customs and pulling out his fake passport.

Four Months Later

The butterflies needed to go away, Courtney Shields thought as she returned to her apartment after her weekend shopping trip with her mom. Taking her spoils up the flight of stairs inside her apartment, she dropped them by the bar stools and went to the kitchen. Pouring a large glass of Sauvignon Blanc, she stood before the open door and debated on what to fix. Nothing was thawed and she was pretty sure lettuce wasn't supposed to have brown and black slimy bits all over it.

Huffing a sigh, she took a drink and shut the door. Fortunately, she had done all of the laundry and dishes before she left three days ago, but that didn't help her. She needed something to do to get her mind off Monday.

Taking the bags to her room, she meticulously hung up the blouses and dress pants. Took her new high heels and flats out of their boxes and set them on the floor of her closet in a neat line. Once that was done, she pulled out the vacuum cleaner and did a once over of her nearly nine hundred square foot one bedroom apartment. Changing out of her jeans and into a comfortable pair of grey cut-off loungers and a ripped t-shirt, she took her glass of wine back to the kitchen and refilled it.

The little bit of exercise had done her nerves a world of good. She sat on her chaise and pulled out her laptop. Turning on the TV, she flipped through the channels only to realize nothing was on. She left it on an HGTV house flip show and turned her attention to the Internet browser open on her computer screen. She had received her secured login the other day and was asked to try and remotely sign on to the Police Database. As Indianapolis Metropolitan Police Department stared back at her on the screen, those darn butterflies started up again. Taking a deep breath and letting it out slowly, she entered her assigned user name and temporary password.

She was in. Sending a quick email back to the HR person who sent her the message to begin with, she logged out and then went to Facebook.

Tomorrow I start my new job… she typed in her status. *Thank you to my mentor, Dave who always helped me, pushed me and made me the best I could be. I am very excited to start this new adventure. Please say a quick prayer, or send good thoughts for protection and favor, I truly appreciate it!*

Two o'clock in the morning glared at Jonathan Mitchell Greene as he sat in his study on the phone.

"Keelan, Keelan, I don't care, man, just do what you think is best," he said rubbing his eyes. "I trust you. I wouldn't have you as my steward if I didn't."

"You had no choice in the matter, Jon," Keelan replied with his tired Irish accent. "But I needed to run both options by you."

"I get it, but do what you think is right," Jon replied. "If you feel like tearing down that north wall is best for the sheep, then do it. There's not much I can inspect over here in Indiana."

"True," he answered. "But when you were here last, didn't you see it?"

"I saw it, Kee," he stated. Huffing a sigh, he went on. "What are you worried about?"

"If we knock that wall down, then what happens to the border? You know old O'Brien is a stickler. But it needs to be done."

"How long are we anticipating the wall to be down?" Jon asked.

"Possibly, if we do it in sections, then no more than a couple of weeks."

"So do it in sections and place a barrier in the parts we're working on. Double the shepherds to keep watch, and get the dogs out there. Keep the herd away from the section they're working on. O'Brien can't tell us not to work on our land and as I see it we're helping him out by keeping up our mutual wall."

Keelan was quiet for a moment then agreed. "Aye, well that's a good idea."

Jon's ear tuned to the garage door opening and looked back at the clock; two-fifteen.

"Is that it, man? I'm beat. I gotta get up early."

"Yeah sorry," Keelan answered. "I appreciate it."

"No worries," Jon said as the door connecting to the garage opened. "Talk soon."

Hanging up, he walked out of his study and down the hall to see his son, Scott walking in, his suit jacket slung over his arm and one hand in his pocket. He set his keys down on the washroom ledge and looked up.

"Dad, what are you doing up? You didn't wait up for me, did you?" Scott asked.

"Nah, got a call from Ireland," he explained. "Did you have a good date?"

"Yeah, ended well," Scott smirked.

Jon chuckled. "I know you're twenty-seven but be careful."

"Always," Scott replied as he yawned. "I'm heading to bed, I'm exhausted."

"Me too, I have to be in early," Jon said.

"Oh yeah," Scott teased as they went up the back stairs. "The rookie."

"Don't remind me," Jon grumbled.

"Might be a good thing," Scott said.

"How so?"

"She might be hot," Scott winked.

"And younger than you," Jon replied.

"So? You're still youngish and kinda still in shape," he poked his dad's hard sides.

"Yeah, yeah, just because you're on a sex high doesn't mean the rest of us are starving for it," Jon replied.

"If you've had sex since mom died that's a new one for me," Scott answered.

"I'm fifty-three years old, Scottie, I've realized there's more to life than that," he said.

"Damn, I hope I'm never that cynical," he laughed.

"Go take a shower, you smell like a brothel and you have a hickey," Jon pushed his son's shoulder.

Laughing as he walked to his wing of the house, Scott threw over his shoulder, "Love ya, Dad. I just want you happy."

Jon didn't reply. As soon as Scott shut the double French doors closing off his wing of the house, he took a deep breath.

"Eleven years, Carol," he whispered. "What the hell am I going to do with a new partner?" Turning to see her portrait hanging on the wall, he kissed his finger and gently touched it to the painting. "Love you, baby. Miss you."

Chapter Two

Stupid butterflies again, Courtney thought as she opened her eyes to her alarm going off. She was lucky if she slept more than three hours. The pizza she had broken down and had delivered last night, didn't sit well in her stomach. Standing, she ran a hot shower and stepped in. She shouldn't be nervous. She was meeting her future; her new precinct, her new partner, a new life, new adventure. The shower felt good, melting away her nerves and calming her heartbeat.

All of the sudden, her water turned ice cold, her shower sputtered and the water stopped. Gasping as the shock wore off, she seized her towel and wrapped it around her. Fully awake, she grabbed her phone and dialed the emergency maintenance line.

"Please state the nature of your emergency," the disembodied recorded voice said.

"Water heater," she answered going into the kitchen to turn on her coffee pot and pulled out an egg white and sausage-flatbread breakfast sandwich from the freezer.

"Good morning, what can I help you with?" the maintenance man answered.

"Hi Courtney Shields, apartment 2501, just wanted to double check, my shower water went ice cold this morning and then the spout stopped."

"Hmm, sounds like something with the water heater," he said. "I'll have to take a look at it. I don't have an opening until next Monday."

"Next Monday?" she questioned. "What am I supposed to do between now and then?"

"Not take a shower?" he offered.

"Funny," sarcasm was always her downfall. "I need this fixed by Wednesday, no later."

"I don't have any openings, sorry," he said. "I'll put you down for Monday."

Courtney was shocked when he hung up. If she could get to the water heater in the closet on her balcony, she would fix the damn thing herself. Her coffee finished and her microwave dinged. Pouring a cup and taking the breakfast sandwich out, she went back to her bathroom and started getting ready for work.

Jon knocked on the adjoining door to his captain's office and listened for his call to come in. Mateo Bernardo looked up as Jon walked in and leaned back in his chair.

"What's that dirt on your face?" he teased.

"Shut up," Jon replied. "I always had this scruff."

"Not so much of it," he answered. "Trying to impress the ladies, Jonny boy?"

"Oh absolutely, you know our old Mrs. Lindsey in reception… definitely had my eye on her for a while."

Mat laughed. "God, that's a visual I don't need." Jon chuckled and handed him a file folder.

"The Sloan case has taken a turn."

"Good, any news on the Miller one?" Matt asked.

"Nothing yet," Jon answered.

"Maybe Detective Shields will have some insights into it," Mat said.

Jon leaned against the side of the desk next to Mat and snatched the Nolan Ryan signed Texas Rangers' baseball off the desk.

"I gotta talk to you, Mat," Jon said staring straight ahead not looking at him as he tossed the ball into the air. "This new partner idea," Jon began. "It's insane."

Mat watched as his prized possession flew into the air and back into Jon's hands.

"There's nothing to talk about, Jon," Mat said. "It's been decided."

"But you can assign her to someone else," Jon reasoned, flinging the ball into the air again. "She's a rookie, Mat, a child. She's young enough to be my daughter. She's younger than Scott, for God's sake!"

Mat couldn't stand it anymore. He snatched the ball from Jon's hands and placed it back under its glass. Jon watched amused.

"I bought you that for your fiftieth, the least you can do is let me toss it into the air," Jon stated.

"No," Mat answered.

"Damn. If I knew you'd be so possessive of it, I'd've gotten you a bottle of whiskey instead."

"You know I have no stomach for that," Mat answered. "And there's nothing I can do. Dave called in a favor."

"What, is she sleeping with him or something?" Jon asked.

"Not that I'm aware of," Mat replied. "Like you said, she's a kid."

"Old enough," Jon shrugged. "What the hell does she know about being a detective? When I go out into the field, I need a partner I can trust to have my back," Jon said. "Like Carol did," he looked away.

"You don't like having a partner at all," Mat said softly.

"Not since she died."

"It's not helping, man," Jon looked back at his friend. "Why me? Why her? Why now?"

"Because Dave asked for you specifically. Why her? I don't know. And why now? Because it's been eleven years and I can't keep putting the chief off when he asks why you're the only cop on my payroll that doesn't have a partner."

"I could talk to the mayor," Jon threatened.

"Don't go over my head, Jon," Mat replied. "You will regret it."

"Love you too."

"You and I may be best friends," Mat went on. "We may even be brothers thanks to war and my sister, but I am still your captain."

"Aye, I get it," Jon answered.

"Talked to your folks in Ireland last night, I see," Mat said. When Jon looked at him confused, he laughed. "Your accent is always stronger after a call."

"I lost my accent when I was ten," Jon replied.

"Not entirely," Mat winked. "Besides I think old Mrs. Lindsey enjoys a man with an accent."

"Well then maybe I should put one on when I talk to the wee darlin'," Jon laughed thickening his Irish brogue.

"But seriously, Detective Shields has passed all the tests and has gotten this job early because she deserves it. Have a little faith in our old friend. He needed us to do this."

Jon stood and walked around the desk and towards the framed map of Indianapolis. "I'd like to know why."

"She graduated at the top of her class at the academy," Mat said.

"Save it," Jon stopped him. "I don't need a résumé on her. I'll figure it out myself."

Mat sighed. "Fine. Now straighten your tie and put on

your jacket. She's here." Jon looked out the glass wall of Mat's office to see a young woman in a suit and high heels enter the bullpen. She looked up and locked eyes with Jon. He gasped softly. "Dear God. Carol, what are you doing to me?"

———≫◦≪———

Courtney wanted nothing more than to find the captain's office and be done with the flirtatious twenty-something cop in uniform. Like most women, she enjoyed a little flirtatious banter, but she was there to work and not hook-up. Not that she would ever do that anyway. She was old school and wouldn't give *it* up unless there was a ring involved. Justin, the cop beside her, was still talking as she entered the bullpen.

"Oh, and one more thing," Justin, the cop beside her, said. "If Cap starts spouting off Spanish, don't worry about it. The man is from Madrid, and there are many times he starts speaking it without realizing. Our Lieutenant can speak it fluently, as can some of our other detectives but the rest… it's all Greek to us."

"Good to know," she answered. Her eyes scanned the area and landed on a man standing behind the glass wall of an office. He was older, probably the captain, but he was far too handsome for his own good. When his green eyes widened seeing her then a frown marred his face, she looked down and smoothed her short blazer. Maybe she should have worn the other one.

"There's the captain's office," Justin said indicating the glass wall in front of them. "Well, we'll be working together soon, I guess, so let me be the first to say welcome."

"Thanks," she answered but did not wait around to hear any more. Knocking on the office door, it was opened by the same man she had seen earlier, the frown still on his face making his handsome features harsh. "Detective Courtney Shields," she introduced. "I believe you are expecting me, Captain?"

Chapter Three

What the hell is going on? Jon wanted to scream. His eyes shot to Mat who was as dumbstruck as he was.

"I'm not the bloody captain," Jon spat, then turned and walked back, leaving the door open. His head was pounding and his heart was honest-to-goodness racing. *What the hell is going on?* His hands shook so much, he clutched them into a fist. *Damn you, Dave.*

"You must be Detective Shields," Mat stated from behind his desk. The damn wimp hadn't even let go of the chair; he was trying to keep himself upright.

"Yes, sir," the woman said. "Courtney Shields, you must be the captain." She stepped forward extended her hand.

"I am," he answered accepting her handshake. "Forgive my Lieutenant's reaction, he's stressed recently, which is why he needs someone to help him."

"Oh, hell no," Jon didn't realize that he had spoken out loud until Mat looked over and cleared his throat.

"I appreciate this opportunity, sir," the woman spoke again. "And I am sure the lieutenant and I will work well together. May I know your name, sir?"

Jon looked back at her, then at Mat. "*This* is not

happening," Jon replied and stalked out of the office, through the adjoining door and out his office door. He had to get the hell out of there.

———————

"That could have gone better," Courtney shrugged.

The captain laughed. "Forgive his reaction. You... have a very striking resemblance to my sister, his wife."

"And does he hate his wife?" Courtney questioned.

"No," Mat answered. "She died eleven years ago on the job. They were partners. She was the last partner he's had until now."

"Oh," Courtney breathed. "I'm sorry for his loss. And yours."

"Thank you," Mat replied. "Please sit." Courtney thanked him, took a seat opposite and handed over her portfolio. "Thank you, I will look at that in a moment. I wanted to speak with you, Detective. About Jon."

"Jon?" she questioned.

"I'm sorry. Jonathan Greene, my lieutenant," Mat said. "He's a tough nut to crack. He doesn't show his emotion and he hardly ever does anything like that. But with your resemblance... what I want you to know is that it wasn't you. He's an excellent cop and an even greater friend. Please don't let his behavior today affect you."

"I would like to speak with him," she replied. "Where would I find him?"

"When he gets like this? Probably the gym."

———————

Jon's hands ached as he punched the bag again and again. Having left Mat's office with that woman's face still in his mind, he decided a good long work out was what he needed. Since it was so early, there was only a couple people in the gym and neither was interested in talking. A fast seven minute mile run on the treadmill, then bench-pressing, followed by punching the bag. As usual, an undefined face held Jon's sole attention. The mastermind behind the gang who had shot his wife had never been found.

Again and again he punched the bag, had he not taped his knuckles they would have bled. Out of the corner of his eye, he saw someone approach but paid them no heed. When that woman stepped behind his punching bag and held it, he stopped.

"What the hell are you doing here?" he demanded.

"That all you got?" she asked. "Doesn't feel too powerful, old man."

"What do you want, Shields?" he questioned.

"I wanted to talk, but now I think a sparring session would warm us both up," she said.

"Find someone else, I'm busy," he replied and then went back to the bag.

"No can do, buddy," she answered. "Whether you like it or not, we're partners and partners talk. So talk."

"You're not my partner," Jon punched the bag with a low uppercut making Courtney grunt as she held the bag.

"Sorry to disappoint," she replied. "But I just signed the paperwork. Nice to meet you, Partner."

Jon struck the bag again then walked away. Sweat trickled down his face and his grey shirt had a visible sweat V. Courtney tried not to look when he raised the hem of the shirt to wipe the sweat from his forehead, but she couldn't stop herself. Solid muscle and defined abs showed Jon spent a lot of time in the gym. Knowing his age, as she had seen his birthdate on the form, she was surprised he was in such great shape.

"Sparring, now," Jon replied.

"Yes, sir," she answered sarcastically.

"Drop the sir," he ordered. "I may outrank you but it

makes me feel old."

"We wouldn't want that," she replied walking over to the sparring mats.

———————

"Where did you go to school?" Courtney asked as she dodged his right hook.

"New York," he answered. "You?"

"Indy," she replied throwing a jab into his side. "Family?"

"Son and nephew," he stated catching her punch with his left and spinning to knock her feet out from under her. She let out a grunt as her back hit the floor. "You?"

"Mom, dad and brother," she answered swinging her leg to knock him down. "Why the hell did you react that way when you met me?"

"Because I don't want a partner," Jon replied locking his arm around her leg in a wrestler's pose.

"No shit, Sherlock," she answered kicking his thigh and forcing him to release her. "But why?" They both stood and faced each other.

"Read my file," he replied throwing a few punches which she blocked and threw some of her own.

"It's because of your wife," she said, he blinked and she took it to her advantage, throwing a punch connecting with his jaw.

"Dammit," he shouted, backing away and massaging his jaw.

"I'm not your wife," she replied swiping her leg at his ankles, catching one and knocking him down. Immediately she was on him.

"Clearly," he answered. "My wife wouldn't leave herself open, like this," he threw a punch into her side. She yelled as Jon twisted her onto her back.

"I can imagine your sparring would wind up a little

heated," she replied twisting in his grip.

"She was fiery," he answered locking her wrists above her head.

"But one thing she probably never did," she panted, struggling against his vise-like grip. "Because she must have liked this part of you." Raising her knee, she struck him in the groin. Jon immediately cried out, let her go, cupped himself and rolled to his side.

"Dammit," he groaned. "What the hell was that for?"

"Like I said, I'm not your wife," she replied sitting up. "Now, are we good?"

Eventually Jon unrolled and leaned up, resting his arms on his knees beside her, taking a deep breath.

"Yeah, Shields," he answered. "You kneed me in the bollocks but we're good."

"Good," she replied. Offering her hand to him to shake, he took it. "Courtney."

"Jon," he said.

"Nice to meet you," she replied.

"And you, though my balls don't like you right now," he said slowly standing and taking a deep breath.

"Hey, a girl's gotta use whatever she can."

"Right," he answered offering his hand to help her up. "Lunch? On me? It's the least I can do."

"Sounds good," she said. "I'm gonna shower first."

"Me too."

Courtney unlocked her apartment door and immediately set the alarm. Her body ached from sparring with Jon but she was glad she did it. Lunch with him was interesting. She had found out that he was an English and History major at NYU and had come over to America from Ireland when he was ten years old, with his father, brother and sister. He was fluent in Irish and

Spanish and could understand Italian thanks to his sister marrying a man from Florence. Serving in the late years of the Vietnam War, he met the captain and soon the captain's younger sister Carol, his wife.

Heading up the stairs of her apartment, she stripped out of her suit and found her loungers. Then into the kitchen, she pulled out the ground turkey she had thawing and some chili beans. It was early fall in Indiana and she wanted nothing more than to have a pot of chili and a glass of red wine.

As the turkey fried in the pan, she popped the cork of her wine bottle and poured a glass. Her phone rang just as she turned back to the meat. Her mom's ringtone echoed in the kitchen. Answering it and shouldering the device, she spoke.

"Hey, Mama," she said. "I'm cooking dinner."

"Oh good, sweetie," her mom replied. "How did it go?"

"Well, do you want the good news or the bad?" she asked.

"Uh oh, the bad first," she said.

"The bad is my partner is a damaged widower who says he doesn't need a partner and when he first saw me he freaked because apparently I look like his dead wife."

"O…kay," was all her mom said.

"But the good news is, I beat him in sparring and now he looks at me as an equal and I think any weirdness is behind us."

"Just be careful, sweetie," she replied. "I don't want you to get hurt."

"I'll be fine, Mama," she said. "But hey, he's definitely eye candy."

"Oh is he?"

"Completely," she giggled. "A sexy silver fox."

Her mom laughed. "Oh, don't tell your father that."

"But honestly I think I'm safe from him. He's not interested in anything," she replied.

"How old is this guy?" her mom asked.

"Oh, in his fifties," she waved her off. "So way too old."

"Well, just be careful, sweetie," she replied.

"I will, promise, oh my turkey is done, I'm gonna have to call you later."

"That's fine, sweetheart, your dad and I are going out to dinner."

"Fancy," Courtney grinned. "Enjoy. Love you!"

"Love you too, Courtney," she said as they both hung up.

Chapter
Four

Jon pulled into his garage seeing his son's car already in one of the bays. Scott was inside playing the piano. The windows were open and Jon could hear his son's tenor voice singing Danny Boy. Stopping just inside the house, Jon listened.

Flashes of home raced through Jon's head, his father, his mother, his friends, his land. He missed it. Scott's voice caressed the notes as he sang and accompanied himself on the piano.

When the music ended, Jon waited to hear if he would sing again.

"Are you gonna come in or loiter in the hallway?" Scott called. Jon chuckled and pulled out of his suit coat, walking through the house to the music room.

Scott still sat at the black grand piano looking toward the door.

"That was beautiful," Jon said leaning against the door frame. "What made you sing that one?"

"Don't know," Scott shrugged. "It was in my head all day and I thought it'd be nice."

"It was," Jon answered. "Hungry?"

"Always," Scott said.

"Call Ryan and see if he's free. Mass Ave?"

"Bazbeaux?" Scott offered.

"Sounds good to me," Jon said. "Let me change."

"I'll call Ry," Scott replied.

Courtney sat at her small desk after dinner and checked her computer. Several notifications shown on her Facebook feed. Friends wishing her luck on her first day and even Dave, with all his computer illiteracy, commented on her status. Sipping on her wine, she commented so they all knew how it went. She left out the sparring session but said; *after a rocky start, my partner and I have come to a mutual understanding and I am excited to see where this goes.*

Her best friend was the first one to like her comment and then her phone was ringing.

"Hello, Chelsea," she answered and leaned back in her chair.

"Girl," she heard. "So spill the dets. I need to know. Who is it? What's their name? Man or woman? Hot or not? Come on come on."

"Okay jeez, give me a chance to answer you," she laughed. "His name is Jonathan Greene, he's the Lieutenant. As for hot, yeah, I guess, he's fit and handsome."

"Okay... I'm waiting for more here," she said.

"What more?" Courtney teased.

"Age?"

"Fifty-five," she answered.

"Damn," Chelsea sounded disappointed.

Courtney laughed and shook her head. "You're incorrigible."

"Hey, I'm just trying to get you a man," she said. "You haven't liked any of the doctors I've set you up with."

"That's because they're way too busy for a relationship and they're surrounded by all those pretty and easy nurses."

"Who you calling easy?"

"Oh please," Courtney said.

"Okay maybe true, but still," Chelsea replied. "There's this new one. A fellow just out of residency."

"No," Courtney stated. "I'm very happy single and I work such odd hours I can't commit."

"That doesn't stop you from all the times you go on stage," Chelsea said.

"Theater is different," Courtney admitted. "It's community service."

"Your boss can't honestly think that's community service," Chelsea replied.

"Sure," Courtney said biting her lower lip. "It makes the community better."

"Whatever, oh, speaking of theatre, did you hear that Michael is holding auditions for Jane Eyre?"

Courtney froze. "Don't tease me," she said.

"I'm not, honestly," Chelsea defended. "Michael's directing it. It's on the website and everything. Auditions are Tuesday and Thursday with possible call backs on Friday. I'm going tomorrow night. I have always loved the song by Blanche Ingram."

"You know my unhealthy obsession with Jane Eyre," Courtney replied.

"You can say that again. Look, I know it's late but how about drinks? You can come over or we can go out."

Courtney debated, it was only seven thirty. "Maybe one drink."

"Out it is then," Chelsea said.

"Sounds great," Courtney replied. "I'll meet you in about thirty minutes?"

"Perfect," Chelsea answered. "See you soon."

21

A woman sat in her hospital room, rocking back and forth. She held her hands up to her ears just wanting the voices to stop. She couldn't take it anymore and let out a long, blood-curdling scream, making the orderlies come running.

"It's all right, Hannah," the doctor said. "It'll all be all right soon." He injected the syringe into her arm.

She fell limp in the orderly's arms. The doctor nodded to him and the nurse set her back on her cot.

"I was hoping she was getting better," the doctor said to his nurse as they walked back out the door.

"Sir," the orderly said. "Should we put her in confinement again?"

"No, Dan." He sighed and patted the nurse's shoulder. "I don't think that'll be necessary. She just needs her rest. Add another session with me to her list, would you?"

"Yes, sir," Dan replied. "It's sad to see someone like that."

The doctor nodded. "I just wish I could help her," he said.

"What is she in here for?" Dan asked.

"She's delusional, schizophrenic and violent," the doctor explained.

"There's got to have been a reason," Dan said, stopping with the doctor at the nurses' station.

"She won't tell me yet. She just said it was something to do with her brother in the military," the doctor replied. "I can't divulge anything else, and I honestly shouldn't have said that much."

"You can trust me, sir," Dan replied.

The doctor smiled. "I know I can, Dan. Thanks," the doctor answered. "I'll be in my office, should anyone need me."

"Yes, sir," Dan replied watching the doctor walk down the hall.

Chapter
Five

Courtney knocked on the door to her captain's office early that next morning. Jon had texted her saying he would be a little late and to check in with Mat when she arrived. But she had her own reasons for speaking with the captain.

"Come in," Mat called. Courtney opened the door and stepped in.

"Sir," she nodded.

"Ah, good morning," he leaned back in his chair. "So Jon didn't scare you away? Good."

"It takes more than a broody alpha male to scare me away, sir," she answered.

"I like your fire," Mat said gesturing to a chair.

"Jon texted me earlier letting me know he was going to be late," Courtney said.

"Yeah his son needed the SUV for some heavy lifting. Jon's helping him out," Mat explained.

"He also asked me to check in with you," she replied.

"Good," Mat said. "We didn't get a chance to really talk earlier. I wanted to see how you found your first day and that broody alpha male partner of yours."

"He'll be a challenge, but I don't walk away from a

challenge," she answered.

"No, I wouldn't imagine you would," he replied. "Word of advice? Don't let his attitude affect you. He wasn't always like this. When my sister was alive he was less angry, more... free."

"Could I beg a confidence?" she asked.

"Depends on the confidence," Mat replied.

"I respect that," she answered. "Do I really look like his wife?"

"Yes," he said and turned the picture frame around on his desk. Courtney froze it was like looking into a mirror with a Spaniard flare. Instead of Courtney's Scots-Irish freckles and blue eyes, the woman in the picture had an olive tint to her tanned skin and deep brown eyes. She was looking up at the camera with what could only be described as a sisterly smirk, the spark in her eyes was one of mischief and laugher. "Not in every way as you can see," Mat's voice shook her from her thoughts. "She had brown eyes, not your blue and she was a little shorter than you. But in the bone structure, yes very much."

"I can't change my bone structure," she sighed.

"No and nor do we ask that," Mat chuckled. "Let him get over the shock of you looking so much like Carol. Let him warm up to the idea that he has a new partner, and I promise you, he will be the best friend you will ever have. He will lay down his life for you, be there for you at a moment's notice, drop anything if you need him. Trust me."

Courtney nodded slowly letting his words seep in. "I will give it time, sir," she promised. "Besides he's a challenge."

"And you never walk away from a challenge," Mat grinned.

"Exactly," she answered. "Oh, there was one other thing, sir."

"Namely?"

"There is something I enjoy doing that my previous boss

classified as Community Service," she said.

"Oh yes, the theatre," Mat answered.

"You know?"

"We've been in contact," Mat replied. "Is there a show you want to do?"

"Only if it's convenient," she said.

"What's the show?"

"Jane Eyre," she replied.

A smile tugged the sides of Mat's lips. "Well, now, I think we can allow that. I'll put it on the schedule."

"Thank you, I know with me being so new I didn't want to overstep. But please be assured that my first priority is to the citizens of this city and should you need, you may rely on me."

"Not to worry," Mat said. "But I do have one stipulation."

"Yes?"

"You get me a ticket for opening night," he replied.

"I think I can do that," she answered.

That evening, Courtney grabbed the song she chose to sing for the audition and headed out, dressed in a little black dress and heels. When she got to the venue, she saw Michael, who had directed her in several shows. He said hello but was too busy to stop and talk. Getting her number and the audition paperwork, she sat down in one of the half-moon benches under the mirrors and filled out the form.

After handing the paper to Michael's mother who helped with the shows, she sat back down and waited. Reviewing her music again, Courtney focused on the words and the meaning behind the story.

Looking up and waving when Chelsea checked in, she watched as her friend said hello to one of the other girls and walked over to sit with Courtney.

"Nervous?" Courtney asked making conversation.

"Not really," Chelsea answered. "More looking forward to it. Haven't been on stage in forever. Did you get this sorted with the new boss?"

"Yeah, he said he'll put it down on the schedule and wished me the best," Courtney replied.

"How's the partner?"

"Still a bit rough around the edges," she answered. "I caught him staring at me and it was a little awkward. But the captain said that might happen."

"It's eerie, huh?" Chelsea said. "You looking like his dead wife and all. Gives me the creeps."

"Gee thanks," Courtney said.

Chelsea couldn't answer as Michael stood before everyone and began.

The next morning, Courtney arrived at work early. After a good morning run and stopping at the coffee shop near her, she walked into the office. Jon was sitting at the desk looking at the computer.

"Good morning, Lieutenant," she said.

"Shields," he replied, nodding.

She set one of the coffee cups on Jon's desk. Surprised, he looked up at her.

"Extra shot, half caf, hazelnut latte?" she asked.

He raised an eyebrow. "Thanks," he said.

"You're welcome," she replied. "Enjoy."

She sat down at her desk and turned on her computer, humming a song from Jane Eyre as she waited for the computer to boot up.

As Courtney drove home that Friday, her windows down and heater on, the crisp October air cleansed her mind. Singing along with a song on the radio, she almost didn't hear her phone ringing. She pulled off the road to answer it.

"Courtney?" a man's voice said.

"Yes?" she replied.

"It's Michael," he answered.

"Oh. Hi, Michael! How are you?" she asked.

"I'm doing well, doing well. Thanks," he replied.

"What can I do for you?" she went on.

"Well, I wanted to tell you that we were so impressed with your audition, that I would like to offer you the role of Jane in Jane Eyre," he said.

Inside, Courtney was screaming, but she remained calm. "I would be very happy to accept that. Thank you," she said.

"Wonderful!" Michael replied. "Rehearsals start Monday night at seven thirty. We'll see you then?"

"Wouldn't miss it," she answered.

Chapter Six

Monday evening, Courtney went straight from work to dinner with Chelsea, who had gotten the role she wanted as Blanche Ingram, and then off to rehearsal. They were early, but the doors were unlocked. As they went in, Michael's mom greeted them both and offered copies of the script.

Courtney munched on an apple as she studied her lines and the other actors who were walking through the front door. Looking up to see if she could spot the man who was to play opposite her as Edward Rochester, she observed the faces of the men but none of them really looked the part; at least to her.

At two minutes 'til, the door opened and a man hurried in. He went straight to Michael and shook his hand apologizing for being almost late but saying he had gotten caught at work. Courtney didn't realize her jaw had dropped until she felt her mouth drying.

"Who is that?" Chelsea asked sitting beside her. The man accepted his script and a bottled water, turned and locked eyes with her.

"That is my new partner," Courtney finally said.

———

Jon's face was frozen in a stunned and confused gaze.

Courtney was staring back at him, a script on her lap and a look of near terror in her eyes. Thinking back to his Thursday audition, he hadn't seen her but then he remembered her humming a song Wednesday morning.

Shite, he thought. *This could be dangerous.*

"Come on, Jon, let me introduce you," Michael slapped him on the back.

"Ehm," Jon muttered. "Okay."

Michael was walking straight for her.

"Courtney, let me introduce you to Jon Greene. He's playing Rochester. Jon, this is Courtney Shields. She'll be playing Jane," Michael explained. Courtney closed her eyes for a brief second, no doubt thinking the same string of expletives he was.

"We know each other, Mike," Jon forced his voice to remain cordial.

"Oh good, wait not through Scott right?" Michael asked.

Jon let out a nervous laugh. "No, fortunately not."

"Then there isn't an issue, right?" Michael said.

"Not at all," Courtney forced. "It'll be nice working with you."

"And you," Jon replied.

"Great! Then let's get started. I'd like you guys to sit together if you would. Welcome everyone!" Michael called as he turned back to the actors.

As rehearsal went on, Courtney read through her lines trying to convey the emotion she felt but her stomach was sour. Her passion, the role of her dreams, everything was now bittersweet with her partner sat beside her. Begrudgingly, she did admit that Jon played his part well. But when they reached the part where Rochester conveyed his love for Jane, Courtney's eyes froze on the stage directions. *They kiss.*

"Oh hell no," she muttered.

At intermission, Michael gave everyone a ten-minute break and Courtney couldn't get up quickly enough. Jon leaned back in his seat but she didn't wait around to find out what he was doing.

"Courtney," Chelsea called as she filled her water bottle. "You lucky duck. You didn't tell me how hot he was."

Courtney glanced over at Jon. His black wavy hair, grey at the temples, and his green eyes did make him highly attractive. "I told you he was fit and handsome," she said.

"Not enough, girl," she replied. "Mm, lucky woman." Courtney followed her best friend's eyes and saw an older lady walk over to Jon, give him a kiss on the cheek and hug him.

"I really think you guys will be great together," Chelsea went on.

"Chels, we talked about this," Courtney replied. "Don't start playing matchmaker."

Chelsea laughed. "Oh no, he might be hot, but he's a little old for you."

"Exactly," Courtney answered.

"But not for me," she replied, her eyes scanning every inch of his six-foot two-inch frame.

"Oh my God," Courtney said. "Chels, get a grip."

"I intend to," she replied smirking as her eyes landed on his ass.

"Seriously? I have to work with the guy, please curb your enthusiasm. I don't need to think of you two rolling in the hay. Besides, don't you have a golden rule against sleeping with men who are over twenty years older than you?" Courtney asked.

"Ah," Chelsea waved it off. "Rules are meant to be broken, especially when a fine male specimen is right in front of you."

"Chels," Courtney stopped her friend. "Keep it for the stage."

Jon was heartily trying to listen to what his acquaintance was saying but he had caught some of Courtney's and Chelsea's conversation. At first he wasn't sure if they were talking about him, but when he felt Chelsea's eyes on him, he looked over. She was tall with milk chocolate skin and dark eyes. As her eyes trailed over him and landed on his ass, he smirked and winked. The woman literally groaned and he couldn't help himself.

"I'm so sorry, but I need to talk with Courtney for a moment," he said to his friend. She smiled and nodded. Heading over to his partner and her friend, he stuck out his hand. "Jon Greene."

"Chelsea Taylor," her friend said taking his hand. "Courtney's best friend. She's told me a lot about you."

"Probably all true, honestly. I made a bloody terrible first impression," Jon replied.

"I would say so," she answered.

"Chels," Courtney cautioned her.

"In all fairness, she did knee me in the ballocks in retribution," he admitted.

Chelsea whipped her head around to her friend. "You didn't tell me that!"

"It was in the heat of sparring," Courtney justified.

"Aren't there rules against that sort of thing?" Chelsea asked.

"Technically," Jon answered. "But not when I've been a bloody arse and treated my new partner badly. It was a painful wakeup call."

"But she looks like your wife, right? That's why you were shocked."

Courtney looked over at her best friend, murder in her eyes. Jon's gaze flipped to hers.

"Yeah," he answered. "If you don't mind, Chelsea, could I

have a second with Courtney?"

"Sure," she replied. "She's going to kill me later anyway."

"That's for sure," Courtney said.

———

Once they were alone, Courtney finally looked over at him. "I didn't know you'd be here."

"Yeah," Jon replied. "I audition for nearly everything Michael does."

"Really?" she asked. "I wonder why I've not worked with you before."

"Not sure," he said. "Why did you audition?"

"Jane Eyre is my favorite book," she replied. "I know the musical practically by heart."

"Did you see it on Broadway?" Jon asked.

She shook her head. "I didn't really know about it until it was closed," she replied.

"It was great," he said. "A friend and I went."

Courtney couldn't think of anything else to say and just took another drink from her water bottle.

Finally, Jon turned back to her. "This isn't going to make things strange at work, is it?" Jon asked.

"Of course it is," she said. "But it won't affect our work."

"Good," Jon answered. He smiled slightly to her as Michael called everyone back.

Chapter
Seven

Two Weeks Later

"I'm going to need Jon and Courtney on stage, please," Michael called after a dance number had just ended. "We're going to run through your proposal scene. Jon?" Jon stepped into the light so Michael could see him. "Good. Courtney?"

"Here," she called and stepped forward.

"Great," Michael smiled. "Now, I know you guys only went through the song yesterday, and it's not perfect, but just do your best. Let's start. Courtney, I want you on the opposite side of the stage. Jon, Rochester actually starts off-stage for and comes on when lights go up. Now, you both know what's happened between them, but this is the first time they actually admit they love each other. So, Jon, you cross to center stage and stand. That's all I'm going to say. I want this scene to be as natural as possible, so I'd like to see what you guys do instinctively."

So far their relationship had grown past the initial awkwardness and they began enjoying working together both on and off stage. Occasionally they would catch each other humming the songs while doing some paperwork. Jon would turn the musical soundtrack on softly and they would sing their parts together quietly while they worked, only to have Mat bang on the wall and tell them to shut up, followed by Jon shouting something back in Spanish.

"Let's start," Michael said. "Now, it's going to be dark on stage since this scene takes place at night. Jon," Michael called stopping him from walking backstage. "Give me all you got." Nodding, Jon disappeared behind the partition. "And, action!" Michael yelled.

Throughout the scene, all Courtney could think of was what they would have to do at the end. The stage directions resounded in her ears: *they kiss.* Pushing those thoughts aside, she acted the scene.

He stood in front of her and held her shoulders firmly toward the end of the song. Following his direction, they knelt together and she said her one line on her cue.

He leaned in and she could feel his breath on her lips. Closing her eyes, she felt the barest of touches then nothing. Confused, she opened her eyes and looked up at him. She had been kissed before and she was fairly certain stage kisses were supposed to be real. That felt pretty… disappointing.

"No, no, no, no!" She heard Michael yell from his chair in the audience. Jon sat back on his heels away from her and sighed. Michael walked up to the edge of the stage.

"Jon, for goodness' sake, you have this amazing build up to the climax where she agrees to marry you and you kiss her like that?" Michael scolded. Jon shrugged. "I wonder now how Scott was even born." Jon rolled his eyes. "Come on, man, she doesn't have the plague. I need you to plant a good one on her. You know about passion. Show me some of that. I know you wouldn't kiss your wife like that."

"I'm not his wife," she defended him.

"For all intents and purposes here on this stage you are," Michael replied. "If you don't like her, at least act for the sake of the show."

"It's not that I don't like her, Mike," Jon replied. "It's

just..."

"What?" Michael asked.

"He's trying not to make it awkward, that's all," Courtney said.

"Then you grab him," Michael replied. "I need a satisfying kiss here."

Courtney turned to him and saw the indecision in his eyes. The thought struck her out of nowhere and nearly floored her. He hadn't kissed anyone since his wife died. That seemed unlikely but there it was, written all over his face.

"Jon," she said softly.

"I need a minute," he replied standing and walking off stage. Courtney looked over at Michael's confused gaze, said nothing but followed Jon out of the stage door.

"Jon," she called when she saw him outside gulping in some fresh air. He didn't turn to her as she walked up to him. "What's wrong?"

"It's not you," he said.

"I know that," she answered.

"I just need a minute," he replied.

"Is it your wife?" she asked. "Is this too difficult for you? I know I look like her and if that's too much, then maybe we can ask Michael to just let us hug and that's it."

"No, he's right, the audience wants a kiss, I just..."

"I know," she placed a hand on his arm. "Would it help if I stepped down from rehearsing this scene with you? Maybe have someone else stand in?"

"No," Jon replied. "That won't work." Rolling his neck, he took a deep breath. "I'm not worried or upset it's just... I haven't... kissed anyone since Carol died and my last kiss was when she was dying in my arms." Courtney swallowed the lump in her throat that formed immediately at his words. He cleared his. "Well, I'll have to put that behind me, won't I?"

"You don't have too," she said.

"Yeah I do," he answered. "It's not fair to you."

"Me?"

"You love this role, it's a role of a lifetime, and here I am messing it up for you."

"You are not messing it up, Jon, in fact, I'm very glad it's you. Give me a chance? I don't want to be your wife. I know I look like her, but all I'm asking is that you see me. Not her."

"It's difficult, but I will try," he said.

"Good," she answered. "Now let's get back in there, partner."

"Wait," he caught her arm gently. She looked down at his hand and then up into his dark green eyes. "I need to try this." She nodded and slowly he stood before her looking about as skittish as a newborn puppy. Taking a deep breath, he moved his hand slowly up her arm and captured the back of her head. Lowering his lips before he could think any more about it, he slid his lips over hers tasting the peppermint gum she had chewed after dinner and just a hint of the red wine they had shared over their salads. She slanted her lips over his but kept the kiss innocent. After a moment, he broke away and pulled back. She smiled up at him and his heart began to melt. He had not realized he had kept the organ encased in ice until that moment.

"Thank you," he whispered.

"You are welcome," she answered. "And that is the perfect type of stage kiss. Now let's get back inside and repeat that."

"Probably going to need to be more than that," Jon countered.

"Probably, but hey, the first kiss awkwardness is over," she winked. "Come on let's go."

———

Aeron sat outside on the patio at Starbucks, reading a book, listening to his iPod, drinking his coffee. He had gotten off work earlier than he expected and decided to pass the time. But, as the story turned sappy, he closed the novel, sat back and took his coffee. His plan was finally coming together. Watching as Jon's son, Scott, stood in line waiting for his drink, with his girlfriend by his side, Aeron pulled out his book and took down the time.

He looked with pride over his previous entries. It had been almost a year since he landed in America, and he was still planning, carefully planning. He watched Scott tip the barista and walk back toward his office building, giving his girlfriend a heated kiss in the parking lot. Aeron thought about following him but decided against it. He would finish his drink and go back to his apartment.

He jumped and looked up as an older man stood in front of him with another cup of coffee. The man sat opposite and Aeron took out his earbuds.

"Can I help you?" Aeron asked the man.

"My name is Rob," the stranger said. "And I think you and I need to talk."

"Oh?" he replied. "And why is that?"

"Because I know why you're over here, and I think we could benefit from each other," Rob said calmly, drinking his coffee.

"And how would that be exactly?" he asked.

"Well, first of all, I can teach you a proper American accent, cover up that Irish. Secondly, I already have a plan to take down Jonathan Greene. It started when I orchestrated his wife's death."

"You killed Carol?" Aeron asked.

"My people did," Rob replied. "But it was good, wasn't it? I know you have a plan too. I think I could help you with it."

Aeron was quiet for a little bit. "I'm listening," he finally said, leaning back and drinking the coffee Rob had placed in front of him.

———◦———

"Wait," Jon said to Carol as she reached for the door.

They were about to go into a warehouse where a credible but anonymous source had said there was a gang of drug dealers.

"I'll go in first."

She nodded and pulled back. They both held their guns tightly. Backup was on its way, but they couldn't wait any longer. Jon slowly opened the door and peered in. It was their twentieth drug bust. They knew what they were doing.

He motioned her to follow. Just as he stepped into the warehouse, a gun went off and a bullet struck his knee. It shattered his kneecap instantly. He fell to the concrete and cried out in pain, clutching his leg.

Carol immediately jumped into action, firing her weapon in the general vicinity of the other shot. She grabbed her husband under the shoulders and dragged him to another location behind stacks of crates.

"Officer down! Officer down! We need an ambulance," Carol yelled into her walkie.

Jon tossed his gun to his wife. "Here," he said through clenched teeth. "I can't shoot it."

Carol's training as a nurse kicked in and she tore off her jacket, wrapping it gently around his knee. She pulled off his belt and looped it around his thigh as a tourniquet. Looking into his eyes, she waited until he nodded. Without another thought or look, she tightened the belt. Jon bucked in pain and cried out. Tying the belt off, she leaned forward and kissed him quickly then attempted to peer over the boxes.

"There's two," she said. "Straight out. I'm going to try and make the shot."

"No. Stay down. Don't move. Wait for backup," he ordered.

"No. I can make it, Jonny," she argued.

"Carol, stay down," he yelled over the gunshots.

She ignored him. As soon as the bullets stopped, she stood and took two shots taking the two men down.

But she hadn't seen the third.

As the two were shot, the third took over the machine gun and swept across the warehouse.

Carol buckled and looked down. She looked back at Jon, whose eyes were wide with fear and anger. She reached for him and fell backward. Blood seeped through her white shirt.

"No!" Jon screamed. He took his gun she had dropped and, not realizing the pain through his adrenaline, stood up and cleared his clip into the man. Jon stood with his gun still aimed. The smoke and cocaine dust kicked up by the gunshots cleared and he heard his wife's voice behind him.

She was pale. "I'm so sorry," she said as he reached her. A tear escaped her eyes. "I should have listened to you."

"Shh. You're strong, baby. You're going to be okay," he pulled off his jacket and pressed it to her abdomen. Her blood coated his hands, she groaned in pain.

"Jonny," she looked up at him. "I'm not going to make it."

"Yes, you are," he said. "Don't say that. You are. You'll be fine."
He wasn't sure if it was for her or his own sanity he said the words. He had seen that sort of wound before on the battlefield. It was fatal.

"Jonny," she said. "Take care of Scott. Tell him I love him and I'm sorry. I wanted to be there for him. I wanted to see his wedding. I wanted to hold his children in my arms."

"Baby, you will. You're going to make it," he said. "Please... make it."

"Shh," she said, reaching up, stroking his face and wiping his tears away. Her body was still. "I know it's going to be hard for you. You're going to be alone. I wanted to grow old with you and have grandchildren with you..."

Jon couldn't say anything. He was watching the life fade from the eyes of the woman he loved. A tear slipped down his cheek. She brushed it away.

"I love you, Jonny, and I'm so sorry. I know you hate being alone, but I'll always be with you." She reached up and tangled her hand in his hair. With all the strength she had left, she pulled him down to her and kissed him for the last time. Her eyes closed, and he felt her heart stop.

"No," he breathed. "No, Carol. Come back, baby! Please! Please, Care, come back. Don't leave me. Don't leave me. Baby, I need you. Please," he kissed her lips, which were still warm, but there was no kiss back. "Carol!" Only then, did he feel the overwhelming pain and he screamed.

The last thing he remembered before he collapsed over her was a pair of brown Italian leather shoes on a man standing in front of him.

Sirens blared in the distance.

Jon gasped awake, cold sweat trickling down his neck. Looking around the room, the darkness only made the dream more vivid. Reaching over, he turned on the lamp by his bed. Three o'clock shown on the alarm clock on his nightstand. Taking a deep breath, he rubbed his hands down his face and swung his legs off the bed. As soon as he tried to stand, his knee gave out.

"Dammit," he cried out. The replacement surgery had kept him down for months but occasionally he still had pain and at times the strength in his knee vanished. As he raised himself back up using the bed as leverage, he was grateful Scott was a heavy sleeper.

Testing the movement of his knee, he limped to the bathroom and splashed cold water on his face. Gripping the sides of the sink, he looked up at his reflection. His bloodshot, heavy rimmed eyes looked back at him. Ever since he met Courtney, the dreams had returned and ever since they started to perform together in a role he always considered his life, the nightmares intensified.

"Dad?"

Cursing silently, "be out in a second," Jon called and grabbed an extra pair of sweats from the closet. Pulling them on carefully, he walked out with a plastered expression on his face. "Hey, what are you doing up?"

"I thought I heard something," Scott answered. "You okay?"

"Yeah," Jon said. "What did you hear?"

"I thought I heard you cry out," he replied. "Are you okay?"

"Oh yeah," Jon smiled. "Just woke and thought I'd go down for a glass of water."

"You look pretty tired, Dad," Scott said.

"It's work and this bloody show," Jon replied. "Running me ragged."

"You sure it's nothing else?"

"Nah," he answered. "Just the usual stuff. I'm fine, Scottie, promise."

"Uncle Mat called me the other day," he revealed. "He said that your new partner is pretty... similar to Mom."

Jon didn't say anything at first. Then, taking a deep breath, he nodded. "She is," he admitted. "She's a lot like your mom."

"Are you okay?" Scott asked.

"I'm fine, Scott," Jon replied a little harsher than he meant. "Look, I know you're only trying to help, but I just don't want to deal with it okay?"

"I just wish you felt like you could talk to me," Scott said. "I'm here."

"Talk about what?" Jon asked. "We always talk about your mom."

"What you're going through," Scott replied. "I know you

41

want to keep it all close and closed off, but I'm here."

"What do you want me to say, Scott?" Jon asked. "That I'm lonely? I miss her? I want nothing more than to have her here? You know that. I'm not going to bring you down with me."

"She was my mom," Scott argued.

"Scott," Jon replied. "And as much as I'm hurting I refuse to bring you down too. Come on, lad you know me."

"Why have you never cried in front of me?" Scott demanded. "I hear you crying in here, why not in front of me?"

"I don't have to justify myself to you," Jon answered. "I love you but I won't do that to you."

"Why?"

"Scott," Jon's deep tone warned him not to proceed.

"Did you even love her?" Scott whispered. Jon's face went blank and Scott looked down. Jon said nothing only grabbed a shirt from the chair and pulled it on. "Dad," Scott called. "I'm sorry."

"Enough," Jon replied as he trotted down the stairs. He grabbed his phone and keys off the ledge and headed out to the garage.

"Dad," Scott called again as he followed him. "I'm sorry."

Jon didn't turn, he couldn't. He felt the tears on his cheeks and he could not let him see it. Opening his car door, he pulled out of the garage and down the long driveway. He had to leave. Scott stood inside the garage, his stance making him look like a little kid again.

Jon drove down the road and struck the steering wheel hard. As soon as he turned out onto the main street and away from the neighborhood, he rolled his windows down and shouted. The pain had built up so much that he couldn't breathe. Knowing his son didn't mean anything by it and it was said in anger, didn't help him. Gasping for breath, he still drove. Where, he didn't know, but he couldn't stay. It was barely three-fifteen but he still had to get away.

———

After driving around for an hour, he returned home. Scott sat on the living room sofa, waiting.

"Dad," he stood and tried again.

"Scott, no, stop," he said. "I know you didn't mean it, but that does not change the fact that you said it. I'm very tired, I have to work and then have rehearsal tonight. I'm going to go upstairs and take a shower then I'm going to go into work. I will see you late tonight. I love you, but I can't talk about this right now, okay?"

Scott pressed his lips together and nodded.

"Now go up and get some sleep, I'm fine, we're fine, okay?" Scott said nothing only looked down and nodded again. Watching his son walk up the stairs, Jon took a deep breath and closed his eyes. The pain was manageable now but occasional twinges stole his breath. The hot water from his shower helped ease the pain and after he dressed, he grabbed the script off the floor. When he walked downstairs, the smell of his espresso filled the air. Scott stood, holding a cup of tea, watching the machine drip the coffee.

"Scott, what are you doing?" Jon asked.

"I just wanted to make your coffee for you," he said.

"Look, you don't have to do that," Jon replied. "I know you didn't mean it."

"I didn't," he promised. "I know you loved mom. I was just angry that you don't talk to me."

"I know," Jon answered. "And the reason is, if I go down that path, I don't know if I'll survive. You can always talk about your mom to me, and how you're feeling but I just can't give in to that."

"I want you happy again," Scott looked down. "You're different."

"Of course I'm different. Your mother died in my arms," Jon answered then took a deep breath. "I pray you never have to experience that. But I have not changed towards you, have I?"

Scott shook his head. "I just miss her. And you, the way you used to be."

"I can't change that," Jon admitted. "But let's go on from here, hmm?"

Looking up at his dad, Scott smiled slightly. "Okay."

"Good, now give me that espresso before I turn into the Hulk. I'll make us some omelets."

Chapter Eight

Opening night of the show had finally arrived. After that kiss they shared, though Courtney knew it was nothing, she had grown to care for him. They worked well together both on and off stage. Courtney had yet to meet his family but Jon had told her a lot about his son, nephew, and best friend.

Jon had invited everyone back to his house for an Opening Night After-Party and she was looking forward to finally meeting his family. When she arrived, she went down to the women's dressing rooms and to her reserved mirror. Sitting on her counter were two dozen red roses. Some of the women gathered around, having admired them before she came in. Courtney smiled. They had to be from her parents, she thought then, taking the card she opened it.

To my Jane,
From your own, Rochester

Courtney grinned and ignored the conversation around her about how sweet Jon was. She wanted to thank him.

Crossing the green room, she went to the men's dressing room and knocked on the open door. Jon sat at his reserved station by the door, stripped to the waist, applying stage makeup.

"Hi," she said, not immediately looking away from his

45

chiseled abdomen.

"Hey," he smiled, stood and pulled on the white t-shirt that hung on his chair behind him.

"I just wanted to say thanks," she replied. "For the roses."

"Oh, you got them? Good," he said. "I asked them to bring it down when they saw you come in."

"It was really sweet of you."

"No worries," he answered. "Honestly, I do about one show a year and I'm really glad I did this one."

"Me too," she replied.

"Did I tell you Scott actually told me about it? He wanted to audition but he couldn't get the time."

"I'm kinda glad he didn't, though I am looking forward to meeting him."

"Yeah, both my lads are in the audience tonight," Jon smiled.

"And the captain," she reminded him.

"Yeah, I know, he texted me," he answered.

"He made me promise to get him a ticket to opening night," Courtney said.

"When did he do that?"

"When I asked him for permission. That Tuesday morning you were helping Scott," she admitted.

"Really? I had talked to him over the weekend about it," Jon replied.

"You mean he knew?" Courtney asked.

"Yeah," Jon nodded.

"That little…" Courtney thought better of her choice words. "No wonder he had a devilish smirk."

"Bloody waster likes to tease me about my hobby."

"Well, tell him from me, women find it hot," winking she walked back out as the other men in the room ooh'ed. Jon's face had lit with a grin and he shook his head.

"All right, all right, calm down, lads," she heard him tease then the door shut and their voices muffled.

———•———

Ryan Marcellino walked into the auditorium with his program and ticket in hand. Finding his cousin, Mat, and their friends already seated, he climbed over a couple people at the aisle and sat beside Scott.

"Hey, man, glad you could make it," Scott smiled and slapped his shoulder.

"Uncle Jon playing Rochester?" Ryan teased. "Wouldn't miss it. How's things?"

"Better," Scott replied. "Dad's starting to thaw a little."

"I doubt that has much to do with this new girl," Ryan winked at Beth sitting beside Mat.

"I think she's been good for him," Beth said.

"Aren't you jealous?" Scott nudged.

"Scott, your father and I have known each other for decades. No, I'm not," she laughed. "Besides we're just best friends."

"Mmhmm, keep telling yourself that," Scott replied.

"Should I hit him for you, Mama?" Kim asked.

"Please do," Beth teased. Kim smacked Scott's stomach causing him to laugh and rub the spot.

"Damn woman, what are you trying to do?" he asked.

Ryan shook his head as he watched them. Beth and Kim were staples in their lives since before Ryan was lived with them. Beth and Jon were childhood sweethearts back in New York but went their separate ways only to meet up when Scott and Kim went to school together. As the conversation turned to Scott's British girlfriend, Ryan looked over next to him as an older couple in their late fifties scooted down the row to the two seats next to him.

"Hello," they greeted him. Ryan smiled back and looked

at the woman's husband holding two dozen red roses.

"Do you know someone in the show?" Ryan asked.

"Our daughter is playing Jane," the wife answered.

"Really?" Ryan asked. "That's great."

"What about you?" she asked him.

"My uncle is Rochester," Ryan replied.

"Oh, Jon Greene," Courtney's mom said.

"Yeah, that's right."

"My daughter has told me a lot about him."

"Oh, I'm sure," Ryan chuckled. "Uncle Jon can be a little rough around the edges at times. He doesn't like working with partners, especially young partners. But he did tell me that he was really impressed with her."

Mrs. Shields smiled. "Well, she has told me that he is one of the best cops she's worked with. Her promotion came as a surprise to all of us," she explained.

"I'm sorry, where are my manners? Ryan Marcellino," he introduced himself. Scott wasn't paying attention but he introduced him anyway. "This is my cousin, Scott Greene."

"Isabella and this is my husband, William," she said.

"It's nice to meet to you," he said.

"And you," she replied. "What do you do, Ryan?"

"I'm a doctor in residence," he explained.

"That's wonderful! Where are you studying?" she asked.

"St. Vincent's in Carmel," Ryan replied. "And you?" he asked.

"Well, my husband and my son are in real estate and insurance, but I work as a consultant event planner," she said.

"Wow," he answered. "That's great. Busy, I bet."

"In May and June and holidays, but I love the down times," she smiled.

Ryan chuckled. "I don't know what that's like," he teased. "I feel like I'm on call twenty-four-seven."

She laughed. "I think that's expected when you're in residency."

"Yeah," Ryan sighed. "I'll be glad when I am out of it."

The lights dimmed and Michael stepped out onto the stage to welcome everyone.

———

"You are amazing," Jon praised as the curtain fell after the final call and everyone was running down the stairs to change and greet their audience.

"Thanks," she said. "But I think, Partner, they're clapping for both of us."

He couldn't answer her as everyone pushed them apart to get to the dressing rooms. Jon nodded across the room to her and she smiled slightly.

Once she had changed back into street clothes, but still sporting heavy stage makeup, Courtney went upstairs to find her parents. The audience greeted her saying what a great job she had done. Thanking them, she made her way to her mom.

"Oh, sweetie!" Her mom greeted her with a hug. "You were incredible! How many shows are there? I have to come to all of them!"

Courtney smiled at her mom, her number one fan and best friend.

After Courtney hugged her dad and accepted the roses, her mom pulled her close and whispered, "There is a guy I want you to meet," she said. "His name is Ryan Marcellino, he is Jon's nephew. Honey, he is so handsome! I really want you to meet him."

Courtney giggled. "Okay," she said. "Where is he?".

Her mom looked around. "Oh. Where is he? He should be with Jon," Isabella said.

"Courtney!" She heard her partner call to her.

Courtney turned toward Jon and saw a man standing

beside him. Jon Junior, she dubbed him, though he had brown eyes, he looked identical to his father. Recognizing Scott from the picture on Jon's desk, she walked over.

"Courtney," Jon smiled. "I'd like you to meet my son."

"It's nice to meet you, Scott. Jon's told me a lot about you," she said.

"It's all lies, I promise," he joked.

She giggled. Her mom had excellent choice in men for her, but Scott was mesmerizing with his dark brown eyes and Armani model-like appearance.

"Did you enjoy the show?" she asked.

"I did," Scott answered. "I liked the stage kiss." He side-glanced over at his dad.

A woman in her early fifties walked up beside Jon. "Stop teasing your father," she said as Jon slid his arm around her waist.

"He does it all the time," Jon said. "This is Beth, my rock," he introduced, pulling her into his side and kissing her temple. "She keeps me sane."

"Or you keep me insane," she teased, touching his chest.

"There's always that," he answered.

"It's so nice to meet you," Courtney said.

"And her daughter, Kim," Jon explained as a woman walked up and stood between Jon and Scott. "Kim, this is Courtney, my partner."

Kim smiled a brilliant smile. "Oh my goodness! Jon mentioned you. You are amazing! You should be on Broadway."

"Oh, thank you," Courtney replied.

"It's good to meet you," Kim hugged her.

"Likewise," Courtney replied just as Jon's eyes rose above Courtney's head and she felt someone walk up behind her.

"Ryan," Jon called. "I wanted you to meet Courtney. This is my nephew."

She turned to see who he was talking to and the man her

mother had mentioned locked eyes with her. She couldn't breathe and when he broke into a smile, her legs felt like jelly.

"It's nice to meet you, Courtney," Ryan said, his eyes not leaving hers.

"Uh," she answered. "Yeah, you too."

"Well, let's head out, I want to get back to my place before everyone gets there," Jon said. Courtney's mom walked up beside her.

"Oh, sorry. Jon," she called he looked back. "I wanted you to meet my parents."

"Oh grand," he replied smiling at her mother and extending his hand to Courtney's father. Even though they were right beside her, Courtney couldn't hear their conversation. Her eyes never left Ryan's.

Chapter
Nine

Two Years Later

Jon gazed at the picture on his dresser of he and Courtney in costume on their final night of Jane Eyre. Smiling as he pulled on a fresh t-shirt, he remembered how strong of a kinship he had to the character he portrayed. Edward Rochester, a broody alpha male who was trapped in his own grief meets a woman who draws it out of him and helps him live again. Not that he cared for Courtney that way, she was far too young for him, but the way she cared broke down his barriers.

Jon had to admit he was overjoyed when she and Ryan had started dating. For the first time in a long time, Jon looked forward to the future.

It was a cool Saturday morning in February and he usually reserved his chores for that day. Laundry and vacuuming were weekly rituals, but as he walked downstairs, he wanted nothing more than to make some breakfast, coffee and read Beth's latest book.

Scott was in his room, working and would be busy all morning. After he made his breakfast, Jon took the book to the sunroom, the windows overlooking the garden and stone walkway down to the pool. Turning on the gas fireplace and putting on a CD, Jon sat in the chair and read.

Losing track of time, his eyes burned and his stomach growled when he closed his book and looked at his watch. Scott's form walked to the door and he knocked. Jon smiled and waved him through. Sliding the door open, Scott leaned against the frame.

"Get your work done?" Jon asked.

"Mostly," Scott replied. "Needed a break."

"Me too," Jon answered. "It's past lunchtime." Standing he stretched his back and walked to the fireplace turning it off. "Hungry?"

"Always," Scott winked.

"Raid the kitchen and see what sounds good, I'm going to go out and get the mail."

It was freezing outside and the clouds threatened snow, but Jon loved the weather. Flipping through the mail on his way back into the house, he collected the junk mail and put it in the trashcan. The bill and letter he was expecting from Ireland he put on his desk in the study and the third he opened immediately. Walking into the kitchen to see Scott bending at the refrigerator, he called to him.

"You busy this Tuesday night?" Jon asked.

Scott looked back at his dad and straightened with a package of summer sausage in his hand. "No," he answered. "Why?"

"The monthly meeting is Tuesday the nineteenth at seven. Didn't know if you wanted to go." Jon tapped the invitation.

"Yeah, definitely," Scott replied.

"Great, I'll call Billy and let him know." Jon pulled out his cell phone and dialed the well-worn number.

"Yello?" Billy answered.

"What's up, brother?" Jon asked.

"Jon," Billy stated. "How have you been?"

"Pretty good," Jon answered. "You?"

"Can't complain."

"I got your invite."

"And? You comin' again?" Billy asked.

"I think I can fit you guys in," Jon teased.

"Haha. Very funny," Billy said dryly. "Got a date to it?"

"Yeah, actually," Jon paused for effect. "Scott."

"Ugh," Billy replied. "Come on, Jon. You need to find yourself a woman."

"I have two," Jon teased.

"I don't mean your partner, although she's a nice little piece from the pictures you've shown me," Billy said. "How about Beth?"

"How about her?" Jon asked.

"Oh come on you can't fool me," Billy replied.

"Ah, come on, you know I don't want that right now."

"You always did have better restraint than I did," Billy teased. "Seriously though, she's good for you."

"I know that's why I don't want to mess with something good," he answered. "I gotta go, brother, but it was good to talk to you. We'll be there, six o'clock."

"Sounds good," Billy said. "I'll put you on the list."

"Good," Jon replied.

"Call me. Let's do dinner."

"Will do," Jon answered.

"I'll hold you to that," Billy said. "See you Tuesday. You know it's at Jake's place, right?"

"Oh was that what was bolded and underlined on the invite?" Jon goaded.

"Well," Billy replied. "You never know, Eagle Eyes. You might have gone blind. You would have been in good company."

Billy had been blinded in his left eye after a chemical spill in an American-operated Vietnam laboratory.

"I definitely would be," Jon chuckled. "I gotta go man, but I'll talk to you later and see you soon."

Jon hung up and turned to Scott who was chopping an onion and already had some garlic ready to go into a pan with olive oil.

Aeron lowered his camera and watched Jon and Scott working together in the kitchen, laughing and joking. Looking down at the camera display, he scrolled through the photos he had just taken; Jon getting the mail, looking through the mail, throwing some stuff away, on the phone, and working with Scott.

Oh, this is going to be fun.

Scott carried Jon's slow cooker with his mother's recipe for Chili con Queso as they walked up the driveway. Carol used to go with Jon to these events, but since her death and up until a few years ago, Jon would go alone. The first time Scott with him, he thought he'd be miserable, but wound up thoroughly enjoying himself; the food, the company, the old stories. His eyes glanced over at Jon, his medals hung pinned to his blazer giving him a sense of pride in his father.

The door opened as they approached and Dave Weston stood before them. "Hey hey!" he called.

"How are ya, Dave?" Jon asked.

"Good," he answered. "How about you two?" He patted Scott's shoulder.

"Can't complain," Jon replied.

"Come on in," Weston said. Scott, seeing his uncle, excused himself from the conversation, and walked towards him. After greeting him, Mat stood close and looked over at Jon talking to Billy.

"How's he doing, Scott?" Mat asked.

Scott sighed. "He's been a little melancholy."

Jon's and Carol's wedding anniversary was coming up, they would have been married thirty-one years. Every year, Jon tried to leave town but this year he was tied down with a case.

"I just wish I had never assigned that case to him," Mat said taking a drink of his beer. "If he could just go to Texas and see mom and dad it might help him."

"I was thinking about them the other day," Scott replied. "Called Abuelita but didn't get a hold of them."

"They were out on the Mesa," Mat said. "I called too."

"I'll get him out of here, don't worry," Scott promised.

"I hope so," Mat said his eyes not leaving Jon. "Now," he sighed and turned to his nephew. "What'll you have?"

"Beer's good for me," Scott said.

Walking around the room, he greeted the people he knew and headed towards his father speaking with an old Army Commander. The monthly get together for all those who served in Vietnam and were living in the greater Indianapolis area was something Mat had stumbled on when he moved to Indiana. Once Jon and Carol had made the move as well, he invited Jon along.

"How have things been at the hospital?" Jon asked the Army CO.

"It's been interesting," Commander Albert replied.

"How so?" Jon asked.

"There's just something that is bothering me, I'll get over it," he smiled.

"Albert, I'm here, talk to me," Jon offered.

"You first," Albert replied.

"Touché," Jon said.

"I just get the feeling that I'm being watched. It's nothing. Just an old army man's super sensitivities."

"Well, we knew you were sensitive," Mat teased walking

up beside them.

After a good chuckle, Albert shook his head. "One of my patients left without us knowing."

"You mean escaped?" Mat asked.

"We're not a prison," Albert replied. "Our patients are not confined, unless it's for their own good. But she... she's dangerous."

"Have you told us?" Mat asked. "Are the police looking for her?"

"The hospital's private security is out looking for her," Albert said. "We have no reason to involve the police. She hasn't killed anyone she's more a danger to herself than others. But so far, they haven't found her."

"I'm sorry," Jon replied.

"Ah." Commander Albert waved it off. "How are things with you, Mat?"

"Not too bad," Mat said. "Been pretty quiet for a little while."

"Deep breath before the storm?" Albert asked.

Mat looked at him. "I hope not. If it is, it'll be one hell of a storm," Mat answered.

"I agree," he answered.

"What do you mean?" Mat asked.

"Forget it," Albert waved him off. "Come on, let's get some food."

Courtney ordered her coffee and one for Jon after she got his text that he was running late. His alarm did not go off and he overslept. The man woke at five o'clock every morning, Courtney was fairly certain he was allowed a lie in, as he called it. Once her name was called she accepted the coffees and headed out the door.

Someone was following her. Her instincts told her she wasn't safe. Taking a deep breath, she pulled out her car keys and unlocked her jeep. Setting the coffees down on the hood, she waited. Someone walked up behind her and just as she was going to turn to confront them, a voice cried *boo* and grabbed her shoulders. Turning, she came face-to-face with Justin Harding, the uniform officer who escorted her up to the captain's office her first day two years ago.

"Justin, what the hell?" she panted. "I could have hurt you."

"Nah," he replied. "I knew you wouldn't."

"Still, not cool," she said. "What are you doing here? I thought you switched to Lawrence or something."

"You've been keeping tabs on me?" Justin grinned. "If I had known you wanted a little of this, I would have kept in touch."

"Justin, I'm serious," she replied. "What are you doing so far out here?"

"It's not that far and, if you must know, I was meeting a friend," he said.

"A friend?" she asked.

"Mmhmm," he nodded giving her a once over. "Have you missed me? Tell me you've missed me."

Courtney laughed. "You are desperate."

"For you? Hell yeah," he said.

"Sorry, but I have a boyfriend," she replied.

"Who?" his forehead creased.

"His name is Ryan," she answered.

"Is it serious?" he asked.

"Fairly," she replied. "Been two years."

"That's okay, I don't mind being your boy on the side," he winked.

"I've gotta get to work," she said. "It's been… interesting catching up. Next time don't sneak up on me."

"So you do want to see me again?" he asked.

"God, you're desperate. Goodbye, Justin," she grabbed the coffees and got into her jeep.

Without another glance, she drove away. That man was definitely odd. She hadn't seen him for a long time and sometimes she was sure she caught a different accent hidden in his Midwest American. Shaking her head, she drove to Police Headquarters.

Chapter Ten

It was nearly nine when Jon strolled in. Courtney sat at her desk, replying to an e-mail and drinking her coffee. Greeting her, he took off his jacket and hung it up on the coat hanger they had in the corner of their office. Jon smiled when he saw his cup of coffee on his desk with her nickname for him in black sharpie written across the lid: Edward's, with a heart shaped apostrophe. Taking the drink, he walked over to her and leaned against her desk.

"Thanks for the coffee," he said.

"You're welcome," she replied. "You look rested."

"I feel rested," he answered. "Though I didn't go to the gym today."

She laughed. "I won't tell," she teased as she pulled out her phone and pretended to enter a status on Facebook. "My partner couldn't get his lazy ass up this morning."

"Yeah, yeah, I can still take you down in sparring."

"And I'll still knee you in the balls," she teased.

"Cheater," he winked.

"Winner," she countered.

"Jon, get in here," Mat called.

"Back to the grind," Jon replied standing.

Ryan was pulling an all-nighter, so Jon invited Courtney over for dinner. She eagerly accepted, always enjoying their dinners together. As they said good-bye in the parking garage, they planned on meeting at Jon's house in two hours, giving them both a chance to get home to change and giving Jon a chance to figure out what he was going to cook.

Waiting in his car, Jon pulled out his phone.

"Hello?" Beth answered.

"Book not going well?" he questioned.

He could almost see her lean back at her desk, cross her arm over her chest, and sigh.

"How did you know?" she asked.

"You answered on the second ring, hardly time enough for you to finish the paragraph if you were furiously typing," he answered.

"How are you?" she asked.

"Better now," he replied.

Her giggle made him smile. "Easy there, handsome. May give a girl false hope."

"Not my girl," he said.

"And I love being your girl," she replied. "Just miss being completely your girl."

"I know," he answered. "Not that I don't want to."

"I know," she said. "Any way, what's up?"

"Courtney's coming over tonight and I haven't a clue what I'm going to make."

"You're a good cook. You don't need me," Beth replied.

"That's not the point, babe," he said. "It's more a matter of if I want to cook or not."

"You did invite her for dinner," she reminded him.

"Yeah, yeah, I know," he sighed. "I wasn't thinking about how I felt and how much work will be going into this."

"Then let me help you figure it out. Tell me what meats you have."

"Uh… hamburger, chicken, steak…" He racked his brain.

"I see. Well, you could make your famous pizza."

"Too much work," Jon replied.

"If you want something a little less work, there's always hamburgers or baked or grilled chicken or spaghetti and meatballs."

"Oh," he answered. "Your spaghetti and meatballs sounds great!"

"*My* spaghetti and meatballs?" She chuckled at his subtle wording.

"Well, yeah," he answered.

"Are you asking me to come over and make the dinner for you?" she asked.

"I have the wine," he answered.

"You got me with the wine. I'm leaving now," she replied.

———

Aeron sat in his car up the road from Jon's house. Beth was waiting in her car looking at her phone. Pulling out his binoculars to take a closer look, she was just as he remembered her, about five foot seven and blonde. Though not as fit as he recalled, she was still somewhat thin and though not as vibrantly blonde with grey buried in the depths, it was still silky. He noted the time in his book and glanced in his backseat to see the old Vietnam M40 rifle tucked under the sweatshirt. Mat didn't even know he had been there.

"Oh what fun we will have," he said to the rifle. "You will be Aeron's weapon of justice. His life falls down around him by his own friend's figurative hand."

Chapter Eleven

Beth looked in the rearview mirror when she saw Jon's car pull up the long driveway. Grabbing her purse, she got out and went up to him as he pulled into the garage.

"Hey, sorry I'm late," he said, smiling, walking around the car and kissing her on the cheek. "Hit some traffic and," he pulled out what he was hiding behind his back, "a thank-you gift."

"Oh, Jon," she smiled as she took the bouquet of roses and lilacs. "They're beautiful!"

"I had to thank you for taking time out of your busy writing schedule to help me."

"Oh hush, you know I'm having writer's block."

Jon grinned and kissed her cheek again. "Let's get some wine that might help you out."

"Sounds good to me."

Jon grabbed some groceries from the backseat and they went into the house. He set the groceries on the counter and went down to the wine cellar. Picking the bottle he wanted, he grabbed two wine glasses from the bar.

Beth had already started unpacking the groceries and was putting them away before he got upstairs. Popping the cork, he poured them both a healthy portion and handed her the glass.

Toasting each other, Beth went to work. Jon put on some music and told her he'd be right back. He needed to get out of his suit. Taking a quick shower, he threw on some jeans and a black t-shirt.

He could smell garlic filling the house and inhaled deeply. Barefoot, he walked into the kitchen and leaned against the doorway, arms crossed over his chest. He watched Beth as she juggled three different pans on the stove, bread baking in the oven, and brownie batter in the bowl behind her. She looked like a ringleader with a very unusual but mouthwatering circus.

"Are you going to help me or just stand there, staring?" she asked without turning around.

"I think I'll just stand here staring," he answered. Rolling her eyes, she threw a look over her shoulder. "Damn, you're beautiful."

"Oh, stop it," she waved him off.

"I'm serious," he said. "I've always thought that."

"You know how I've always felt about you, even at sixteen I was in love with you."

"And I with you," he replied. "God, I should never have gone to war."

Turning, she walked toward him slowly. "If you hadn't, you would never have met Mat who would never have invited you to Texas and you would never have met Carol and you would never have had Scott. As much as I wish we could have been together, and knowing my life would have been so much better with you, I could never deny you your life."

Pulling her into him, he threaded their fingers together and placed her head on his chest. She took a deep breath and let it out slowly. Jon started to sway with the music. After two songs, she pulled away from him and looked up. Cupping his jaw, she loved how his stubble caressed the palm of his hand. He hadn't had that at eighteen and even though they had been close again for over two decades, she couldn't get enough of how it made him even more handsome and rugged.

She slowly leaned up and felt the slight resistance he gave.

"What are ye doin'?" he asked softly, his occasional Irish accent breaking through.

"Nothing you don't want," she replied and kissed his cheek. "I know my boundaries when it comes to you, Jon."

Pulling back, she felt the loss of his heat immediately but turned back to the stove. Jon took his wine glass and sat at one of the bar stools. It was different with Courtney. It was a stage kiss, a kiss to break the spell Carol had weaved over him. It meant nothing. Beth's kiss would be that of a lover and he was fairly certain he would not be able to stop himself after he gave into her erotic taste.

"How's Scott?" Beth asked, breaking the silence.

"Uh… fine, I guess. He's working late again tonight," he answered.

"Kim's told me that he's been working on this case for two weeks now," Beth explained.

"It doesn't help that he's been out late every night. He comes home around midnight or later and he's up with me at five," Jon answered.

"It's a difficult case?" she asked.

"I know he's going up against the seasoned DA, and he knows his client is innocent. When he wants something he knows is right, he fights for it."

"Like his father," she said quietly.

"He gets that more from his mother," Jon replied.

"Do you think he will ever settle down?" Beth asked, checking the bread.

"He'd better," Jon answered. "He needs an heir. I'm not planning on living forever."

"How is the estate?" Beth asked.

"Good," he replied. "Keelan's happy with the updates to the north wall, the riding school is going well, and tourism is up twenty percent. There's even been a film crew out recently scouting locations for a movie."

"That's outstanding," Beth replied.

"I'm planning on going for St. Patrick's Day. You coming with us again this year?"

"Definitely," Beth replied. "I could use Ireland's beauty to jump start my writing."

"Yeah, what's up with that?" Jon asked.

"Not sure, just haven't been inspired recently."

Jon absentmindedly played with some pretzels in a bowl on the bar counter. "I remember when you said something like that the opening night of that musical my senior year. Do you remember?" Jon started. "We drove to Central Park?"

"Please," she interrupted. "Don't bring that up."

Jon felt the sharp pang of grief in her words. "I just thought…"

"What? You think I wouldn't remember?" she said, turning to him. "Do you expect me not to remember the time you told me you were going to Vietnam, or the time you proposed to me, our last…" Her voice cracked. "Our last night together," she finished, tears finally streaming down her cheeks. "Do you expect me not to remember the most important day of my life?"

Jon stared at her and was silent for a few moments. He had loved her then, and he loved her now. Their physical love ended many, many years ago, but he carried the imprint that their love left with him.

Standing from the stool, he walked over to her. She turned away from him, but he pulled on her arm.

"No," she said.

"Come here," he ordered pulling on her arm again. She finally turned and allowed him to engulf her in his arms. "Don't cry," he whispered. "I didn't bring it up to make you cry."

Looking up, she felt his breath on her lips, slow and steady, teasing. Just as she felt the lightest touch, he pulled back.

"Why?" she begged.

"You know why," he replied.

"She's gone, Jon," Beth said. "She's been gone for nearly thirteen years."

He pulled away from her and turned his back, the sharp rise and fall told her he was struggling. "I know," he answered.

"Then why?" she asked again.

"I'm not... ready yet,"

"Then when will you be ready?" she questioned.

"I don't know," he answered. "I can't put a time frame on it. If you love me, you'll know that I can't be with you yet."

"I do love you, Jon. I always have," she replied. "But I just don't understand why you can't let yourself love me too. Do you feel she wouldn't approve?"

He didn't speak for a moment. "My wife knew everything I did before I met her. Everything," he stressed turning back to her. "When we met again after all those years, I was worried. The two women I had loved were going to meet. I was scared Carol would see me differently through your eyes. I was a right bastard to you when I returned. But, she told me that she wanted to start your friendship. She wanted to get to know the one woman I had loved before I loved her.

"Every time I see you, Beth, all of our times together are overshadowed by the fact that you were my wife's best friend. I need you to understand that... I want to feel your touch again, dear God I crave it, but, you deserve more than I can give you. I want you with everything inside me. But you have to know... it's been too long I just," he cleared his throat. "I'm not the same man you fell in love with."

"I do love you, Jon," Beth said. "And I'm sorry. I didn't

mean to ruin a perfect evening. You are a wonderful man and any woman would be lucky to have you."

"I am the lucky one to have had two of the most beautiful women love me."

"True," she nodded and bit her lower lip. Jon's eyes were drawn to the movement and the corner of his mouth ticked up. "You know," she sauntered toward him and ran her hands up his arms to his chest then over his shoulders until her fingers buried in the hair at the back of his head. "When she and I used to go out every Thursday for breakfast, we used to talk about you."

"Oh?" he replied. "What about me?"

Locking eyes with him, she allowed them to turn hooded as memories of their entwined bodies flashed through her mind.

"No you didn't," he breathed.

"A few times, we compared notes," she answered. "Especially when she was running late and looked flushed."

"And?" he pressed.

She laughed. "All good," she replied.

"Just good?" he asked, raising an eyebrow. Heat tinged her cheeks but she held his gaze.

"Never just good with you, Jon," she breathed. Jon's gaze landed on her lips again. Pulling away from him before she allowed him to do something he would later regret, she turned back to the stove.

"I think I should go now before I do or say something I'll regret. I put the brownies in the oven. They should be done in twenty minutes, fifteen if she likes them gooey. Keep an eye on them."

"Will do," he answered.

"Great," kissing him on the cheek again she got her things and headed to the front door. "Have fun tonight."

She got her keys out of her purse, and he walked her to the door.

"Thank you for everything, Beth. I appreciate it more than you know," he said.

She smiled. "You're very welcome. And I'll always take payment in the form of wine," she replied walking out the door and to her car.

Chuckling Jon stayed in the doorway and watched her leave. He waved good-bye and closed the door, setting the alarm as he went back into the kitchen.

Washing up, he corked the bottle and took it down to the basement, unlocked the wine cellar, and added it back to the collection then grabbed a new bottle for Courtney.

Once back upstairs, he set the dining room table and put everything on low. Courtney would be there any minute so he turned on the TV to a national news network and sat in his chair.

"Hmm," Aeron said, pulling out his binoculars again as Courtney's Jeep pulled up to Jon's house. "Oh Courtney, you do it for me every time," he whispered.

Courtney got out of the car, her cell phone to her ear. She was giggling at whatever the person on the other end of the phone had said.

"Nice, Jon." He adjusted his binoculars and focused on how her jeans hugged her ass until the door opened and Jon ushered her inside. "You old dog." He smirked and pulled out his book to make a note of the time.

Chapter
Twelve

Jon switched off the news and turned on some music as Courtney followed him into the living room.

"Would you like a glass of wine?" Jon asked.

"Do you even have to ask?" she answered.

"You like Italian, right?" he called over his shoulder as he went into the kitchen.

She trailed behind, seeing the door to his personal study off to her left. The double smoky glass doors were shut. The formal dining room off the kitchen was set for dinner for two.

"Let's think about that for a second, Jon," she smiled back as she looked at the pictures framed on the hallway wall.

"Food, Italian food. I know you like Italian boys," Jon teased speaking of Ryan's paternal homeland.

"I love Italian food," she replied. Jon reappeared with two glasses of a deep red wine and clinked his glass to hers.

"Sláinte," he toasted.

"Cheers," she replied. "I don't recognize this picture," she said gesturing to the wall. "Is that Scott?"

"Yeah," Jon replied. "He was about five. It was his first Little League match."

"And there's proud daddy." She pointed Jon out in the

picture. "Nice outfit, Jon."

"Hey," he teased back. "I was in style back then."

"I bet you were." Courtney smiled.

"I helped coach," he answered.

She looked at another picture. "Where was this one taken?" She pointed to one of the three of them, Jon, Carol, and Scott.

"That was at her parents' ranch in El Paso. It was Scott's thirteenth birthday, and he wanted to go back home for it," Jon explained. "I change the pictures on this wall every few months."

She nodded realizing why she had never seen those pictures before. "Scott was born in El Paso, right?" she asked.

"Yep. His mother and I met there, and I basically never left. Come on. Let's go eat while everything's hot."

⸻

They sat at the dining room table talking and laughing so hard their sides ached. Finally, when they pushed back from the table, Jon took a deep breath.

"Oh, I haven't laughed that hard in a while."

"Me neither," she answered. "I love these dinners with you."

"Well, you know," he said. "When Ryan's busy we both have to eat, so why not together?"

"And you have amazing wine," she teased, toasting him. "That's mainly the reason I come over."

"Oh, is it?" He smirked back. "And here I thought it was my movie star good looks."

"Well, that too," she grinned. "Gotta have something pretty to look at."

"Pretty?" Jon teased.

"Mmhmm," she bit her lower lip and grinned. "Beth is a very lucky lady."

"Is she?" he replied.

"Yep," she answered. "I can say that because I have firsthand knowledge of how good of a kisser you are."

"Make it awkward, go ahead," he teased.

"Thanks for your permission," she took another gulp of wine.

"I'm changing the subject," he replied.

"Oh, but I was having so much fun making you blush," Courtney laughed.

"I don't blush," he answered. "Anyway, I wanted to talk to you. Mat said something to me today."

"I was wondering when you were going to fill me in. Was it man-talk or something else?"

"Not sure," he admitted. "So every month, those of us who served in Vietnam and their families get together for a pitch-in dinner. This month, Mat and I went as usual. One of the men in the group said he thinks something might be brewing, something big."

"Good or bad?" Courtney asked.

"The way he said it? Bad," Jon replied. "I normally wouldn't be this concerned over that, but he's a psychologist, and he's pretty in tune with things going on and it bothered Mat. Just... promise me you'll watch your back. Okay?"

"I don't need to," she said. "I've got the best partner in the world to watch it for me."

Jon chuckled. "I'm not with you twenty-four-seven," he said. "Just be careful."

"Will do. So, tell me, how's Scott?" She asked changing the subject again.

"He's doing fine. Been working a lot."

"Is he and... oh what's-her-name still together? Angie? The ballerina from England."

"Angela, yeah," Jon replied. "They're still together."

"And Dad doesn't approve?" she stated.

"Dad is partial to someone else," he admitted.

"He's in love with Kim, we all know that, he's just sowing his wild oats," she said.

"He's been sowing them for far too long."

"He'll come 'round," she said. "But really, his father has no room to talk."

"Meaning?" Jon asked.

"How long has Beth been back in your life?" she offered. When he didn't say anything, she went on. "Oh come on, we all know. Why haven't you made it official?"

"Because, I'm not over my wife's death."

"Jon," Courtney leaned forward and covered his hand with hers. "Carol would want you to be happy."

"I know, I know. You're going to say the same thing that Scott and Ryan say, 'It's time to move on.'"

"No, I wasn't going to say that," she replied. "I was going to say it's time for you to get a dog."

"A dog, huh?" he asked.

"Yes," she replied. "Every bachelor needs a dog."

"Not a bad idea," he answered.

"Something manly like a poodle," she teased.

Jon shook his head and laughed.

"Come here," he stood and pulled her into a hug. "I love these dinners and thank you for making me laugh."

"That's what I'm here for. Oh, and make sure you tell Beth I enjoyed her cooking."

"Okay. Now how did you guess that?" he asked, looking down at her.

She sniffed his shirt. "Chanel Number Five isn't your scent, Jon," she answered.

Chapter Thirteen

Jon lay awake in bed reading. Even though Scott told him numerous times not to wait up for him, he always did, no matter how late it was. He sighed with relief when he heard Scott's familiar step. Getting up, Jon went to the landing.

"Scottie," he called.

Scott looked up, his dark brown eyes bloodshot and heavy lidded. "Dad?" he asked. "Have you been up this whole time? I told you not to."

"That doesn't matter," Jon said. "You look exhausted."

"I am," his son replied nearly missing the step.

"You've worked too much. You need to sleep."

Scott shook his head. "I'm not ready for later this month, Dad," he answered. "The trial is set for the end of March and if we're going to Ireland I need to be ready before so I can enjoy myself."

"Scott," Jon's fatherly tone made him pause. "You have time. If you face a judge or your colleague looking like this, you will not be taken seriously. You need your rest in order to make sense of everything. I know you believe your client is innocent. Doesn't he deserve a lawyer who is at the top of his game?"

"You're right," he finally said as he reached the top of the stairs.

"Get some sleep, Scottie," Jon placed a hand on his son's shoulder and pulled him into a hug.

"I'm so tired," he said.

"Try to sleep in a little bit tomorrow," Jon replied. "Tomorrow is a new day."

"Things will be looking up," Scott finished as he pulled back. "Mom used to say that."

"Yes, she did, and she also made me promise to take care of you. So if that means I'll have to lock you in your room in order for you to sleep, I'll do it."

"I know you would," Scott chuckled. "I'm going, I'm going."

"I love you," Jon called after him.

"Love you too, Dad," he said.

Jon watched as his son walked to his part of the house and turned back to his empty room. Crawling into bed, he took his book from the mattress and flipped it back open.

"Turn the light off, Jonny, and come to bed," he could almost hear Carol's voice.

The memory made his chest ache. He sighed softly, turned off his reading light and lay in complete darkness for a while waiting for sleep to overtake him. Though he didn't remember falling asleep, he heard Carol's voice again.

"Jonny," she called. "Jonny, wake up."

Opening his eyes to complete darkness apart from the sliver of moon light breaking through the curtains, he felt her familiar presence.

"Baby?" he said softly. "Where are you?" Carol stepped toward him and sat on the bed next to him. "This is a dream," he said.

"Yes," she replied. "But I had to come to you. Baby, it's time."

"Shh," Jon answered, stroking her face and moving the bedsheets for her to lie down with him. She slid underneath them and into Jon's arms. He closed his eyes tightly against the familiar pain. "I don't want to talk about that."

"Jonny," she said. "It's time. You have to move on. I wouldn't want you like this. If it were you, I know you would want me to move on."

"It should have been me," Jon said softly.

"No," she answered. "The only thing I would change if I could, is for you not to be lonely."

"I'm not," he replied leaning down to kiss her. When he felt her soft lips on his, he deepened the kiss and turned them both to hover over her. Even though he knew it would be a mere memory and not actually her, he let his body take over. He always craved her and as she responded to him, he let go of the hesitancy he felt and made love to his wife.

Jon reveled in the feel of her head on his bare chest and how her fingers played with the black hair that dusted his torso. He remembered when they lay like that before, but he did not want to break the spell by knowing it didn't truly happen.

"I love you," he breathed. Her fingers stopped playing and she looked up, her cheeks still vibrantly flushed and her eyes shone with love.

"I love you," she answered. "But Jonny it's time. You must move on."

"Why?" he asked. "I've lived thirteen years without you, why couldn't I keep on as I am?"

"Because it breaks my heart to see you like this," she replied.

"How can I move on? How," he asked. "When I see you every day, reflected in the eyes of our son?"

"Scott will always be a part of me, Jonny, but you need to

be happy. You need to let yourself love again," Carol said.

"I can't. I love you," he replied.

"I will be gone in the morning, Jonny," she said. "You will get up alone again. I can't let another morning go by where you do not smile. She will be here for you. Beth will help fill the gap I left in your heart." She touched his chest and his heart beat beneath her fingers. "I give you my permission. You would not be cheating on me if you let yourself love her."

Jon lowered his head to kiss his wife. Carol pulled back and locked eyes with him.

"Love her," she said. "She will not take my place you know that. But I need you to be happy. For me, baby, please."

"I can't, Care," he replied. "I love you."

"Please just try," she begged.

Jon opened his eyes but everything was black. He hadn't moved from his position on his side, his wife was not there and his chest hurt. Tears stung his eyes. He shut them tightly, took Carol's pillow, clutched it to him, and finally fell into a deep sleep.

———

Jon sat at his desk that next morning, trying not to let his dream of Carol affect him. It did little good. He couldn't concentrate on the work and could only remember the days he and Carol had shared that office. The room was fundamentally the same, only Carol's old desk had been replace by Courtney's and instead of the desks facing each other, they were now in an L shape. The walls had been redone into a dark chocolate, replacing the old, late eighties wallpaper. He caught himself staring at her picture on his desk and shook himself to regain his senses.

He checked his watch. Courtney was twenty minutes late. She had texted him earlier telling him that she was running behind but should have been there ten minutes ago. He debated calling her, when she rushed in, breathless.

"I am so sorry," she said, trying to catch her breath. Her

cheeks were flushed and her eyes were bright. After the dream the night before, Jon's breathing stopped for a moment then instinctively, he stood and walked toward her.

"It's all right," he said gently. "Are you okay?"

"Yeah," she replied. "Just been a crazy morning. My stupid heater broke down last night, so I spent the night at my parents' house. My phone alarm didn't wake me up in time, and I forgot my shoes at my apartment."

Jon chuckled. "That's all right. You're here now. Did you get some coffee?" he asked.

"Are you kidding?" she stated.

"Let's go get you something. I want to go over a couple things with you. I was going over a case file from my cabinet and I want you to read it," he replied.

Knocking on the adjoining door he opened it when he heard Mat's call.

"Hey," he said. "Courtney and I are heading out."

Mat simply nodded, not looking up from the computer. "Be safe," Mat answered.

"Always," Jon replied.

Chapter Fourteen

Jon and Courtney walked down the street to the coffee place nearest their office. Courtney got a table outside while Jon ordered.

"Thanks," Courtney said when Jon returned with their coffees and breakfast.

"You're welcome," Jon replied as he sat beside her. They were content to say nothing as they ate their breakfast and people-watched.

"Are you okay?" Courtney finally asked. Jon turned to her and smiled softly.

"Yeah, why?" he asked.

"You seem tense.

"I'm all right, didn't get much sleep last night."

"Oh? Why?" Courtney asked.

"Probably because of a dream I had," Jon replied.

"A dream?"

"Yeah," he answered. "It doesn't matter though."

"It matters," Courtney said. "Talk to me, what was the dream?"

"It wasn't anything important now, have you talked to your landlord?" he asked.

"Nice dodge. I'm not going to let it drop. But since you obviously don't want to talk about it now, no, I have a maintenance guy who works on our complex," she answered. "I called him this morning."

"And?" he asked.

"He said he wouldn't be able to fix it until Tuesday," she replied. "I swear the things I have to put up with this guy!"

"That's ridiculous!" Jon said. "It's his problem. He should be out there today."

"Yeah. I agree, but he just won't do it, Jon. It took him two weeks to fix my water heater once."

"Listen," Jon said quietly. "I know a guy, a good friend of mine. He'd be there today, tomorrow at the latest. Let me give him a call."

"Thanks," she said. "If I let him do it, it's part of the complex insurance. I don't have to pay for it."

"As it would be with my friend. He wouldn't charge you so long as you let him flirt with you a little," Jon winked.

"I wouldn't want to take advantage of you or your friends. I'll be all right."

"Courtney, I'm serious," he said.

She thought a moment. "Okay," she finally answered. "Okay. I'll give in."

There was a smile that Jon gave her occasionally and she had to remind herself how old he was. That smile became one she wanted to see more often and as he gave it to her as they sat at the coffee shop, Courtney couldn't help but love it.

Jon pulled out his phone and scrolled through his contacts. When he found the right one, he put the phone to his ear.

"Could I speak with William Simpson please?" he asked into the receiver.

There was a pause while the phone changed from the answerer to the one Jon needed.

"This is William," the man said on the other end.

"Hey, Billy."

"Jon!" Billy replied. "How've you been, brother? Long time no see." He laughed. "What can I do for you?"

"My partner's heater broke down last night, and her maintenance man—"

"Let me guess, says a week until he can get it done?" Billy asked.

"Basically," Jon replied.

"Well, I've got an opening tonight at five. Would that work?" Billy asked.

Jon turned to Courtney. "Five o'clock tonight?" he asked. She nodded. "Sounds great, Billy."

"And this partner," Billy started. "I'll get to meet her?"

"Yes and I've warned her about you," Jon answered.

"Awe where's the love, Devil Dog?"

"You know I love you," Jon teased. "But she's spoken for."

"Oh yeah?" his salacious question made Jon laugh.

"And young enough to be your grand-daughter."

"I'm not that old," Billy grumbled. "But, fine. I'll be there at five. Send me the address."

"I'll text it to you," Jon replied.

Jon hung up his cell and looked over at Courtney. "Vietnam," he offered.

"Really?" she replied sarcastically. "I would never have guessed. But thanks."

"Of course," he replied. "What are partners for? We were both injured in the Easter Offensive, nineteen seventy-two," Jon stated. "Shrapnel blew into his leg, tore it up pretty badly. They had to amputate," he explained. "And he lost his sight in one eye from a chemical exposure. But he is one of the most brilliant men

I've ever met."

"Well, I'm looking forward to meeting him."

———

It was a quarter to eleven when Scott stepped off the elevator to his law firm. As usual, he thought back to when the idea of creating his own firm took shape. Jon, Ryan and Scott were walking around his college campus after his graduation ceremony.

"I can't do it, Dad," he had said. "I've seen what Tom has gone through and I don't think I could be managed by a slave master."

"Then why not start your own, Scottie?" Jon had replied with a shrug.

He had graduated in the top percentile of his class at Northwestern University School of Law in Chicago. He graduated with two offers from law firms in Chicago and three in Indianapolis.

He had come into his own part of the Greene Family fortune when he turned twenty-one and had put it in secured investments. When he decided to sell them, he had doubled the small fortune, allowing him to set up his own law firm. Tom Roberts, the lawyer Scott had worked for during his internship was his first acquisition. He offered a partnership and Tom accepted.

Scott smiled as he walked through the glass doors of Greene, Roberts and Moore Attorneys at Law and headed toward his corner office.

Before he reached the door, Tom's voice came from the open door of his office.

"Scott," he called. Scott stopped and peeked in.

"Hey, Tom," he said. "Sorry I'm late to our meeting. Give me ten minutes to get settled?"

"Actually, I was wondering if I could speak with you

about something else," Tom stood. "Can I come to your office?"

"Of course," Scott replied. "Give me five minutes?"

Tom nodded and sat back down. Walking on to his office, his assistant walked up to him.

"Good morning, sir," he said.

"Morning, Jay," he answered accepting his tea.

"I did that research you asked me to do last night," Jay replied, following Scott into his office.

"Remind me, what research? I was half asleep last night," Scott said.

"You asked me to dive into the corporate accounts and see if anything struck me as odd or out of place," he explained.

"Right, but I hope you took my advice and went home. You needed as much sleep as I did."

"Oh yes, sir, I did this this morning," Jay answered.

"Good, did anything pop out at you?" Scott asked, setting his shoulder bag down, taking a sip of tea and turning on his computer.

"Yes, sir," Jay replied, grinning and handing him a file folder.

The twenty-three-year-old had just graduated from IU last May and Scott saw a little of himself in his fresh approach and keen eye. Scott took him as his own junior instead of a much older and perhaps, more experienced, candidate.

Scott sat at his desk, leaned forward and took the file. "My, my," he said, flipping through the papers. "What did you find, Jay?" Scott stated the question as he saw exactly what it was that struck him as interesting. "This was all obtained legally, correct?" Scott asked looking up.

"Oh yes, sir," he replied. "The police had served a warrant on the company before, and they didn't want to risk a subpoena. So I just very nicely asked for the accounts, and the CEO signed a receipt for me."

"Paper trail. Good thinking," Scott replied, his eyes looking over the files.

"Thank you," he answered.

"You said the police served a warrant on them already?" Scott asked.

Jay walked back to Scott's desk. "Yes, sir. A couple years ago, there was enough evidence for probable cause. But the police served a warrant to confiscate and search the account history."

"Did you get the name of the officer in charge?" Scott asked.

"It was a Detective Henderson," he replied.

Scott turned that name over and over, but he didn't remember his dad ever mentioning him. He wrote it down on his Post-It notes.

"The forensic accountant found an unexplainable one-hundred-thousand-dollar office supply purchase. Turns out the CFO was having an affair with the CEO's wife, and they went to New York for a weekend on the company. The CFO has since been sacked and indicted for fraud. The CEO and his wife divorced and are in a custody battle for their three kids."

"Tough break," Scott replied.

"Yeah, especially when it's your brother whose sleeping with your wife and stealing from your company," Jay replied.

"Yeah," Scott answered tightly, an old wound raising its head. "Even worse. Good job, Jay."

"Thank you, sir."

"How did you get all that other info?" Scott asked.

"Well, ya see, there is this really pretty receptionist, and she and I kinda got talking, and—"

"Okay, okay." Scott chuckled. "I get it. Did you at least get her number?"

"Of course," he winked. "We're going out Friday. Anything else, sir?"

"Not right now. Thank you," Scott answered. "Thanks for the tea too."

"You're welcome, sir," Jay said then turned to leave. "Oh, excuse me, Mr. Roberts," he apologized as he almost collided with Scott's firm partner standing in the doorway.

"Can I come in?" Tom asked.

"Of course." Scott waved him in, setting the file behind him on his filing cabinet. "What's up?"

"I need a favor," he said without preamble.

"All right," Scott said slowly then offered a seat. "What's going on?"

"It's my nephew. He's gotten into some trouble," Tom said as he shut the door behind him and walked over to Scott's chairs.

Aeron was sitting in the white sedan outside Courtney's apartment. He pulled out his binoculars again and watched Jon and Courtney walk in and open the curtains. Could they really be that clueless? He'd been following them since Delaware Street and they never even noticed. He waited and made a note of the time.

A FedEx truck stopped in front of Courtney's apartment and he gazed at the M40 rifle begging to be used.

How about a little test run? See if he remembers me. He reached for the rifle and got out of the car.

The doorbell rang throughout the apartment and Courtney looked up while pouring them both a glass of wine.

"Could you get that?" she asked.

"Sure," Jon answered trotting down the stairs to the front door.

Opening it, thinking it would be Billy a few minutes early, a FedEx driver looked up at him.

"I've got a package for Courtney Shields," he said.

"I'll sign for it," Jon offered. The delivery guy looked him in the eye. "I'm her husband," he said.

"Of course," he answered and handed Jon the electronic clipboard.

"Honey," Jon called up to her as he shut the door. "Your package is here."

Too easy, Aeron thought at he walked back to the truck. The body of the delivery guy lay in the back. He jumped into the driver's seat and drove away, needing to dump the body somewhere. The White River came into view. He pulled into an alley, grabbed the body and forced it into the driver's seat. He ignored the picture of a young woman and a baby on the dashboard as he dug the bullet out of the head rest and grabbed his rifle. Putting the truck into neutral, he watched it slowly ease into the river.

The rifle was in his hands, ready to be used again. He checked his book and added the driver to the list and crossed him out. Rob reviewed the list of names every week and he needed a valid reason to have killed the man. Looking on the list to the next name; Billy Simpson, Aeron needed to hurry if he was to greet the old war hero before Jon got to the door.

Chapter
Fifteen

"Jon, I was curious about something," Courtney started as they sat together drinking their wine. "I've never been to Ireland. Ryan talks about it all the time. I know you own land over there, but can you tell me a little more about it?"

"Sure, what do you want to know?" Jon asked.

"I'm fascinated by the history. Are you related to one of the High Kings of Ireland?"

"No," Jon answered. "But I can trace my lineage back to before the Crusades. I have five thousand acres of rich farm land and sheep. There's a whiskey distillery on the grounds too."

"Are you a lord or something?" she asked, intrigued.

Jon chuckled. "I am, but I don't use the title," he replied. "We haven't for generations, except on very rare occasions."

"Such as?"

"At the celebration when the Lord's heir takes over for him. In my case, my title will be passed to Scott, and he will be named the next."

"The next what?"

"Baron Caiseal of County Clare," he answered. "I am the thirty-eighth lord. Scott will be the thirty-ninth."

"Is Ryan a lord too?" she asked. "How does that work?"

"Not technically," he answered. "Being my sister's son, he would have the title of sir if we were still in the old regime. He does have his mother's portion of the capital, though. But, because she was a woman and he was her second-born child, he inherits nothing of the main estate. Now, obviously, he does have some portion of the land through my decree, and I've helped him maintain stocks. I found a loophole where he could own the distillery just not the land it's on. But if, God forbid, something would happen to me and my son, the structure is such that my steward's family would get a large settlement, and Ryan would be forced to partition the acres off and sell them."

"How much would your steward get?"

"About ten million euro," Jon replied.

"That's a strong motive for your steward. Do you trust him?" she asked.

"Keelan and I grew up together. I dated his sister, Siobhan, for a time," Jon said. "Yes, I trust him. I trust him with my life. He's a good friend. His youngest son will succeed him when Scott succeeds me."

"When will that be?" she asked.

"When Scott gets married and has a son of his own," Jon explained. "Or in my case since my father died before Scott was born, it would pass to my steward in trust until Scott's son is born."

Courtney nodded. "I've always wondered why you work as a cop," she said. "It's not like you need the money."

"I like it," he answered. "Yes, it's taken a lot from me, but there's nothing I like more than finding a murderer and having the satisfaction of putting them away for good. I love putting a puzzle together."

Courtney nodded. "I can understand that," she replied. "But still, it's gotta be fun not having to worry about money."

"It is, I'll not deny it," he answered. "How are your

parents?" he asked changing the subject.

"They're good, planning a trip down to see family sometime next month," she answered.

There was a knock at the door before Jon answered. "That's gotta be Billy," Jon said standing. "It's five o'clock on the dot." As Jon reached the top of the stairs, a loud bang rang out. Courtney stood.

"What the hell?" she demanded.

"That was a gun shot," Jon said, then raced down the stairs flinging open the front door. Billy was in his wheelchair, blood seeping out of his mouth.

"Billy," Jon shouted and rushed toward him.

"Jon, he's back," Billy said and coughed. "You gotta run," he barely got out.

"Courtney, call an ambulance!" Jon yelled up. He got Billy out of his wheelchair and onto the ground. Billy fought against the blood pooling in his mouth, coughing and gagging. Jon ripped off his shirt and held it to the wound in Billy's back. "Billy, come on, man! You've been in worse scrapes than this! Keep breathing! Come on, Billy! Keep your eyes open!"

Courtney ran down the stairs with her cell phone to her ear. "They're on their way," she said.

"Where the hell are they?" Jon demanded of the ambulance. "Come on, Billy!"

Jon checked his pulse when his eyes fluttered closed and immediately started CPR. "Stay with me, brother, stay with me. Fight, dammit." Finally, the sirens blared as they entered the complex. Even though he knew the fight was over, he still tried to keep his friend alive.

The ambulance crew took over for Jon as he fell back and explained what had happened. Courtney helped him sit up and they watched as the EMTs loaded Billy onto a gurney, but as they shook their heads, Jon knew there was no hope. His friend was dead.

Aeron reveled in crossing Billy Simpson's name off his book. As Hannah, a former psychiatric patient and someone he met a couple years ago, poured their champagne, he put the M40 away. When he returned, Hannah wore a fur coat and her hair was down.

"It's fairly warm to wear something so heavy, babe," he said.

"Not when I'm chilled wearing this underneath," she replied opening the coat to reveal nothing but a matching pair of black lace and silk underwear and bra set.

Aeron sat down and watched as she grabbed the two glasses of champagne and walked towards him.

Sliding down on his lap, she wrapped her arms around his neck and licked his lips.

"I want you," she said.

"Good," he answered. "Give me my champagne I have some wicked ideas."

"I love wicked ideas," she replied standing and handing him his champagne glass.

Scott yawned as he pulled into the driveway, turned off his car, and groaned as he stretched his back. Gathering his briefcase, gym bag and computer case from the backseat, he walked into the house.

"Scott?" he heard from the living room.

"Uncle Mat?" he called back, smiling and walking into the room. "What are you doing—?"

He was cut short when he saw the look on his father's face. Mat sat with him on the couch but they both looked troubled.

"Dad? What's wrong?" he demanded going straight to him. Jon didn't answer.

"Your dad called me around six, informing me of an... accident," Mat explained.

"Oh, God. Is Ryan all right?" Scott asked, searching his dad's face.

"Yes, Ryan, Kim, and Beth are all safe. It was nothing to do with anyone like that," Mat answered.

"Then what happened?" Scott asked.

"Jon was at Courtney's apartment after work getting her heater fixed. He had called Billy Simpson, and while they were there," Mat explained. "Billy was fatally shot."

"What?" Scott breathed remembering the old man in the wheelchair. "Why?"

"We don't know yet," his uncle replied. "But Jon called me from the hospital. I met them there and we came back here. Courtney is upstairs taking a shower. She's staying the night."

"Dad, I'm so sorry. Are you all right?" Scott asked.

"He's barely said anything since I got him home," Mat answered. Scott noticed the whiskey bottle sitting on the table in front of them.

"Scott," Jon finally said. "I need you to take Courtney and stay with Ryan tonight."

"No," Scott replied. "No way. I'm staying with you."

"I need you, for me, to stay with your cousin," Jon said.

"I don't think so," Scott replied.

"Please, Scott." The tone of his father's voice cut off Scott's reply. "I know you want to stay, but I need you to go. I need to know you're safe. Courtney didn't want to leave me and I don't want her back at her place. You guys can take care of each other. I've already talked to her and we've called Ryan. He doesn't know why, but I've told him to expect you both. Your uncle will stay with me."

"Dad, no, what if something were to happen?"

"Nothing's going to happen, Scott," Jon replied. "Trust me." Jon pulled his son into him and hugged him tightly.

"I'm so sorry, Dad," Scott repeated.

"He was a good friend," Jon said. "Please, for me, stay with Ryan."

Scott nodded into his dad's shoulder. "Okay," he answered.

Chapter Sixteen

"Scott, what the hell happened?" were the first words out of Ryan's mouth as he walked into his apartment. Courtney looked up and Ryan rushed to his girlfriend. "Are you all right?"

"Yeah," she replied. "I'm good. Honest."

Ryan framed her face and read the truth in her eyes. Kissing her quickly, he turned back to his cousin.

"What happened?" Ryan shook out of his topcoat and hung it on the wall peg. He then took off his suit jacket and tie.

"One of Dad's service buddies was killed today." Scott continued with the story Mat had told him while Courtney made them all a sandwich.

Ryan stared at his cousin when he was finished. "Is Uncle Jon okay?" he asked.

"Yes," Scott answered.

"Is somebody with him tonight?" Ryan asked.

"Uncle Mat's with him, but I really wish he hadn't made us leave," Scott said taking a sandwich from Courtney and thanking her.

"I tried talking to him but he didn't say much after the hospital," Courtney explained. "They were pretty close. We both heard the gun shot."

"Why wouldn't Uncle Jon want us to stay?" Ryan asked.

"Probably because of what Billy said," Courtney replied. The men looked at her as she took a sandwich and a water bottle. "I was still inside the apartment but I heard it. He said 'Jon he's back, you gotta run.'"

"Who's back?" Ryan demanded.

"I'm not sure," she replied. "But Jon seemed to think about it. He kept saying it while we were at the hospital."

"Okay this is crazy," Scott said. "If dad thinks that we're just going to let it go then he doesn't know us."

"He wants you safe," Courtney replied. "Trust me, I don't like leaving my partner alone but I'm doing this for his sanity. If something happened to me, you or Ryan and he couldn't save us? It would drive him insane. I promise you that."

"But what does he think it'll do to us if something happens to him?" Scott demanded.

"He'll be all right," Courtney promised. "But if it makes you feel better, I am all for going back. Ryan, he'll listen to you."

"Why me?" Ryan asked.

"Because you're the only one who hasn't argued with him about staying," Courtney explained.

"You're pimping me out?" Ryan teased.

"And not even sorry," Courtney replied.

"Great," he chuckled. "Fine, okay I'll do it." Ryan took his phone and walked into his room.

———

Scott and Courtney sat together in the living room when Ryan came back out of his bedroom changed into jeans and a sweater.

"No. I know what you said," he spoke into the phone. "But I just think that maybe we should all be together... stop it. You and I both know that's not true... nothing would happen, and even if it did, wouldn't you rather us be there than here? No, I mean to us… don't you understand Scott, Courtney, and I want to be with you? We don't care about ourselves."

Ryan wrenched the phone away and winced as Jon's voice was loud enough for them to hear him yell, "but I do!"

"I just think," Ryan continued after a short pause. "That it would be best if we were all together as a family." They couldn't hear Jon's answer, but Ryan looked over at them and nodded. "Of course, it's my day off tomorrow anyway," he replied. "We'll leave in a couple minutes and be there soon… I think Scott could work from home tomorrow… no, it does make sense, Uncle Jon. I'm a doctor. How do you think I would feel if I couldn't help you, or Uncle Mat for that matter?"

Even though Mat wasn't technically Ryan's uncle, he gave him the title out of respect for his position in their family.

"We'll take the bikes, leave the cars here… see you in about fifteen to twenty minutes… okay? Yep, bye."

Scott and Courtney were already at the front door. "Thank you," Scott said.

"Give me a sec, let me pack an overnighter and we'll head out."

Courtney and Scott waited at the door for Ryan. As soon as he was ready, they walked out, let him lock up his apartment and walked to Ryan's detached garage. As the door went up, Scott and Ryan eyed their twin, Ducati motorcycles standing side-by-side. Scott sat on his black one while Ryan buffed out a smudge on his red one. Straddling the bike, he helped Courtney onto the back. She wrapped her arms around his waist as they started the engine.

"Ready?" Ryan asked.

"Yep," Scott answered, slinging his bag on his back and pulling on his leather gloves and his helmet, visor up. Ryan and Courtney followed suit and the boys kicked their bikes into gear. Scott pulled out first and Ryan closed the garage.

Aeron's phone rang an alert. Easing Hannah off his shoulder, he reached for the cell phone.

Rob: They're heading over to JG's. Have our girl text Mat and tell him she wants to see him.

Aeron: Will do. I'll be there in twenty minutes.

Rubbing his eyes, trying to wake up, he got out of bed and pulled on a shirt and jeans. He brushed some cat hair off his clothes as Hannah moaned a little and turned over, drawing the sheet closer around her. They were in this for mutual gain nothing more. Sex was just an added benefit though it meant nothing. Hannah had her own vendetta, but he was willing to use her obsession to get what he wanted. Leaning over to wake her, he explained what Rob wanted her to do.

Jon heard the bikes coming as they entered the subdivision and opened the garage door just as Scott and Ryan, with Courtney pulled up. Walking the bikes into the garage, they parked them next to Jon's weekend Ferrari.

"I don't like this," Jon said as they pulled off their helmets.

"But we do," Scott answered.

"And I'm not leaving my partner," Courtney replied. "Now shut it and let us in, it's bloody freezing and I need to pee. Or do I need to knee you in the balls again?"

Jon looked at his partner and finally laughed. Stepping aside, he let her in. Scott and Ryan looked at each other then back at Jon.

"Long story," Jon replied. "But don't think I'm all right with this."

"I know," Scott answered. "But I'm not leaving you alone, with or without Uncle Mat."

"We're family, Uncle Jon," Ryan said as they walked into the house. "Hey Uncle Mat." Mat looked up and greeted them.

"You lads hungry?" Jon asked, coming up behind them and putting his hands on their shoulders.

"No, not really," Scott answered.

"Courtney made us a sandwich," Ryan replied, pulling off his leather jacket.

"There's some of Beth's leftover spaghetti and meatballs," Jon answered, heading to the fridge.

"Oh, wait now I might be hungry," Scott replied.

"Me too," Ryan said as Courtney came out of the restroom and laughed.

"It is pretty amazing," she said.

"You want some, babe?" Ryan asked.

"No, I'm good," she replied sitting at the bar stools watching Ryan pull out the food and warm it up.

"Didn't you have a date last night, Uncle Mat?" Scott asked as he flopped down on the sofa.

"Yeah, I did," he answered.

"How did it go?" He asked.

"Eh," he answered. "It was okay. Probably no second date."

"Oh really?" Scott asked.

"Why?" Ryan asked.

"Because the woman lives with six cats and Mat's a dog... person," Jon winked.

"It's not that. A man can change," Mat replied. "It's just when she lets them all curl up on her, it's disturbing."

"I hate cats," Ryan said absently.

"Yeah," Mat answered. "Me too."

Chapter Seventeen

Ryan couldn't sleep at all that night. He tossed and turned, trying to get comfortable in the basement guest room. He had given Courtney his room but no matter how hard he tried, there was just no position that helped him fall asleep. He finally had enough of the movie that was playing in the background and turned it off. Standing, he walked through the basement and up the stairs to the kitchen, leaving the lights off. A glass of milk sounded good and as he grabbed the carton from the bottom shelf of the refrigerator and a glass from the cupboard, lightning struck and the clouds finally let loose the rainfall that had threatened all day. He poured the milk and chugged it.

Just as he set the glass down on the island, the lights flipped on, blinding him. He blinked for a few seconds and then looked over at the light switch. Jon stood with his arms crossed over his chest wearing the same sweats he had on earlier.

"Did I wake you?" Ryan asked.

"No," Jon replied. "I was up." Turning slightly, he indicated the living room where Ryan saw a blanket and a pillow on the sofa. "Can't sleep?"

"Not so much," Ryan answered.

Jon pushed off the doorway and walked toward him.

"Come sit with me," he said.

Ryan sat down across from his uncle at the kitchen table. They were quiet for a moment then Jon leaned forward.

"You will never go against my direct order again. Do you understand me?" Jon said. All Ryan could do was nod. "With that said," Jon went on. "I am glad you are with me." Ryan exhaled. "But I don't appreciate you disobeying me. Especially in this. It's dangerous and I need to make sure my lads are safe. You are adults but you will always be my lads and if something happened to either of you... I need to be certain that when I tell you no, you will not go against me."

"If it's something I can help in I'm not going to agree, Uncle Jon. I'm a doctor. Granted, I'm no veteran or a cop but I have had my fair share of stressful situations."

"Understood, but I would rather have you safe than involved."

"I'm already involved."

"Fair enough. Now why can't you sleep?" Jon asked, leaning back.

"Don't know," Ryan replied. "Must be all the stress. I'm exhausted, but I've given up trying to fall asleep."

"I know the feeling."

"What about you?" Ryan asked.

"I never can sleep when my family is in danger," he answered.

"I'm really sorry about your friend, Uncle Jon," Ryan said.

"Thank you," he replied. "I've known Billy for nearly forty years. We served side by side in 'Nam. I was there when he got hit, and I would visit him in the hospital after the amputation."

"That's gotta be hard," Ryan replied.

"You get really attached, you know. Those who survive. You can talk to people about what happened, but the men you served with are the ones who really know what it's like. Everyone wants to know what happened. They want war stories, look at you as a hero. But to me the heroes were the ones who never returned."

"I can't even begin to imagine what it must have been like for you guys. I mean, what I heard about Vietnam, and all the protestors—"

"Yeah them, the ones we fought for, the ones we sacrificed for, the ones we were protecting and whose freedoms we were maintaining. They were the ones we had to be hidden from when we came home. They were the ones who, if you were caught in uniform, would attack you. I wondered why we even fought for them. I know it wasn't our war, but how I look at it is: if Communism was allowed to take hold in that country, how long would it be until America became like that?

"I fought for my future family. I fought for you and Scott. Even though I wasn't born in this country, I am a citizen of it. I love this country. We have the right, as all men are created equal, to help our fellow brother."

"People don't think like that anymore, Uncle Jon," Ryan replied.

Jon shook his head. "No. That's the problem. They do, subconsciously. But they don't know what it actually means, and they're afraid of what we're capable of," Jon replied. "We live in the greatest country on earth, Ryan. It's difficult for someone like me who has fought to preserve the freedoms of others to see our freedoms shrink before our very eyes. And good men like Billy Simpson are killed in cold blood."

It was a little while before Ryan spoke. "You'll solve this, Uncle Jon. You always do."

Jon sighed. "I don't know, Ryan," Jon replied. "I'm too close to this one."

"As true as that is," Ryan answered. "I really think you should stick with it. He was your friend, a fallen comrade. Who else will give him the respect that's due to him? You know what to do and Billy Simpson, the war hero, deserves someone who cares and respects him in life and in death."

Jon was quiet again. "You're right," he answered. "Thank you."

"And you know Scott and I love you," he said.

"I know," he replied. "I love you, too, so very much."

At that moment, thunder rolled and lightning struck. The window next to them shattered and Jon tackled Ryan to the floor, knocking the wind out of him.

"Don't move!" Jon ordered.

"Did lightning just strike the house?" Ryan asked as soon as he got his breath back.

"No," Jon answered. "That was a bullet. Stay down and get to the living room."

Ryan crawled. Jon inched his way to the door, looking out into the night, trying to decipher the weird shapes and shadows the rain had created. Nothing, even his sniper eyes couldn't see anything.

"What's all this?" a voice asked, smiling from the doorway. "Who started the party without me?" Scott rounded the corner and froze when he saw what happened.

———

That next morning, Jon and Scott were in the kitchen, vacuuming up the glass shards, while Ryan was outside on a ladder, drilling the boards into place to keep the rain and bugs out of the house until Jon could schedule a replacement. Courtney was out by the edge of the yard trying to see where the gunman would have been.

Mat walked down the stairs, still wearing his sweat pants and a white t-shirt. He yawned as he entered the kitchen and froze when he saw what was going on.

"What happened?" Mat asked.

Scott and Jon looked up from the floor where Scott was feeling around for more glass and Jon leaned up against the island, rolling a little metal misshapen ball in the palm of his hand.

"Ah, good morning, Rip Van Winkle," Scott said.

"What?" Mat asked.

"Where were you last night, Mat?" Jon asked.

"What are you talking about?" Mat asked. "I was in my room."

"Anyone who can sleep through a gunshot should earn a medal," Scott replied, standing.

"What?" Mat asked, concerned.

"Someone took a shot at us last night," Jon said.

"Who?" Mat demanded.

"That's what we're trying to figure out," Jon answered. "But first, I want to know where you were."

The drilling sound stopped and Ryan appeared at the doorway to the patio.

"That's done, Uncle Jon," he announced. "It should hold."

Jon nodded. "Thanks, Ryan," he said. He then turned back to Mat.

"I was in my room," Mat said again.

"Really?" Scott asked sarcastically.

"Scott," his dad said without dropping Mat's gaze. "This is between your uncle and me. Please go outside with Courtney and your cousin."

Scott frowned but did as his dad asked without replying. Once Scott was outside, Jon looked away from Mat.

"I know you're lying. I went upstairs to make sure you were okay at four thirty, and you weren't there," he said.

"If you must know, I went to go see someone last night and stayed for a few hours," Mat explained.

"Thank God," Jon sighed. Mat looked at him. "Not like that. I mean, I was just a little freaked when I found this." Jon handed his friend the small bullet he had found. "You recognize the grooves?" Jon asked.

Mat turned the bullet over and went pale. "My God," Mat said. "Someone tried to kill you with my gun?"

"Where's your old M40 rifle?" Jon asked.

"I don't know," Mat answered. "Honestly, I had it in my house, mounted in the basement. But... I haven't seen it for a while."

"And you didn't think to call me or the police?" Jon asked.

"I am the police," Mat said.

"You know what I mean," Jon replied.

"Jon, honestly, I thought it had been misplaced," Mat explained.

"When was the last time you saw it?" he asked.

"Uh... I don't know," Mat answered. "Two weeks ago, maybe."

"You know what this means?"

"Yeah," Mat replied. "This killer has been in my house."

"Who has been in your house recently? I would like to clear everyone surrounding you and... you yourself."

"Me? Do I need an alibi?" Mat asked.

"You're a cop, Mat. What do you think?" Jon said. They looked at each other for a while. "This woman you were with, what time did you leave?"

"I left here at around one and left her place at around five," Mat admitted.

"And she can vouch for you?" Jon asked.

Mat stared at Jon for a second. "Do you want an exact play by play?" Jon's face was stern. Mat finally sighed and pulled out his cell phone. They waited while it rang.

"Hey," Mat said. "Yeah, it's me... Listen. I need you to tell someone where I was between one and five. Yeah, yeah, fine just... ehm... tell them where I was. Thanks. I'm gonna hand you off to him."

Mat handed Jon the phone.

"Hello?" Jon said into the phone.

"I heard you needed to know where Mat was last night," a woman said.

"Yes," Jon answered.

"Well, he was with me," she said.

"And you are?" Jon asked.

"Hannah Turner," she replied. "Mat and I have been seeing each other off and on for a little while. He got to my place at about one fifteen and didn't leave until about four forty-five."

"Thank you, Ms. Turner," Jon said.

"Anything else?" she asked.

"No that's it, thanks." Jon handed Mat the phone back.

"Thanks," Mat said into the phone, and he turned a little away from Jon as he spoke. "Yeah, yeah. Everything's fine… no, probably not tonight… I'll see… I'll call you again soon," Mat and Jon looked at each other when Mat hung up the phone. "I'm sorry I wasn't here, Jon," Mat said.

"It's all right," Jon replied. "It's probably for the best anyway. Who knows who might have been killed last night?"

Jon looked out the window to see his son on the phone and his nephew talking with Courtney by the edge of the pool.

———

Jon and Mat sat in the living room, flipping through the channels on TV.

"How did you meet this new woman?" Jon asked.

"We met at church, is that what you want me to say?" Mat replied.

"I'm serious, Mat," Jon said. "She's not a hooker is she?"

"Are you being serious right now?" Mat demanded.

"I don't know, you've never mentioned her before," Jon replied.

"She's not a hooker," Mat said. "And after that one time after 'Nam I've never used them again. I don't have to pay for sex."

"So how did you meet her?"

"At a club," Mat replied.

"That's not so bad," Jon answered. "Why the third degree?"

"Because I don't want to deal with your holier-than-thou attitude towards casual sex, okay? Just because you're not getting any doesn't mean the rest of us need to be monks."

"I never asked that," Jon said. "And I'm far from a monk."

"No? So you've had a one night stand after Carol died?" Mat asked.

Jon sucked his teeth and looked away. "There's more to life than sex."

"True, but not much," Mat replied. "Have you and Beth sealed the deal yet?"

"Excuse me?" Jon asked.

"Oh come on," Mat said. "It's obvious to anyone with eyes."

"If you're asking if Beth and I are dating, then the answer is no," Jon answered.

"That's not what I was asking," Mat replied.

"That's all there is to it," Jon said standing. "I'm going for a swim."

Heading up the stairs, Jon calmed his anger. Mat was starting to piss him off. The conversation had started innocently enough, Jon merely wanted to know more about the woman he was shagging, but Mat took it out of context. Changing into his swim trunks, Jon grabbed a towel and headed to the stairs. Scott came out of his rooms wearing his workout clothes.

"Hey, you okay?" Scott asked.

"Your uncle is pissing me off," he replied.

"Oh," Scott said. "Well it's a good thing you've got us

then."

Jon laughed humorlessly. "I guess," he said. "I'm going for a swim."

"You sure you should be alone?" Scott asked.

"He won't be," Courtney stepped out of Ryan's room in a swimsuit cover-up. "Don't even try to say anything." She raised her hand when Jon opened his mouth.

"I was going to say, okay, so long as you can handle the water so cold," Jon said.

"It's heated, Jon, don't even pretend that I don't know that," she replied.

"Okay, okay, I've been married to a stubborn, headstrong lass, I know to pick my battles," Jon admitted.

"Good," she answered. "Besides there's something I need to talk to you about."

"Okay," he replied. "Let's go."

Listening to the recent exchange between Jon and Courtney, Aeron sat outside Jon's house in a white sedan and cursed. He hadn't thought about bugging the pool. It was bloody March, who the hell swam in March? Turning up the headphones, to maximum, he tried to focus in on the intercom in the sunroom. He could hear the splash as Jon dived in and Courtney's gasp as she felt the water, even though it was heated it was still bloody freezing.

Huffing, Aeron turned to plan B. Getting out of the car, he pulled on his reflective vest and hardhat. He was getting near enough to listen to their conversation even if it killed him.

Chapter
Eighteen

Courtney thought better of swimming in the cold and sat by the pool wrapped in a towel. She watched Jon power through the water but her eyes caught movement near a utility poll. Someone was watching them but as Jon hoisted himself out of the pool and padded over to where he left his towel, she spoke softly.

"We need to go somewhere we can't be heard," she said.

Catching her tone, he dried his chest and casually looked around the pool. "There is something I want to do. Meet me on the main floor in half an hour?"

She nodded and they both went into the house without another word.

Thirty minutes later, Jon walked down the stairs and heard his phone ring. Heading into his study, he sat at the desk chair and answered it.

"Jonathan Greene," he said.

"Jonny, Rick, howya?" His brother's voice made him smile.

"Rick, good, man, it's good to hear from you," Jon said.

"Aye and you," he replied.

"How are you doing?"

"Grand, grand," Rick replied. "Hadn't heard from you in a while; just wanted to call and say hello, like."

"I'm glad you did," Jon answered.

"Been wanting to know if you, Scott, and Ryan are still planning on your trip to Ireland. Jenny and Sarah have been nagging me to call and confirm."

"Yeah, we're still planning on it," Jon replied.

"Good," Rick said. "How you doing? You sound a little tired."

Jon leaned back in his chair and sighed. "I'm all right," he answered.

"Uh huh," Rick replied. "You know I'm your brother, right? Half or otherwise."

"Yeah," Jon answered.

"Good. Then you know that I know that there's something you're not telling me," Rick replied.

Jon was quiet for a moment. "I'm working on this case. It's dangerous. That's all."

"How dangerous?" he asked.

"Very," Jon answered.

"Are you all right?" Rick asked. Jon didn't say anything. "Jon, what's going on?" Again, Jon was quiet contemplating telling his brother. "Look you can tell me or I can call Scott and be on the next flight out of Tampa International. See ya in three hours."

Jon sighed. "Fine, I'll tell you. I just need you to stay there."

"Tell me," Rick said.

"A friend of mine was killed the other day and last night, someone took a shot at me," Jon answered.

There was silence for a minute then Rick yelled for his wife. "Jenny, could you pack me bag?"

"No, Rick. I can't have you here," Jon said. "Listen to me—"

"No. You listen to me," Rick interrupted. "You're my brother. I know I've been a shitty older brother to you in the past, but I'm not just going to sit here in Florida while some eejit is shooting at you!"

"Rick, I'm fine," Jon replied. "Everyone here is fine. It would help me to know that my brother and his family are safe. I can't have another distraction."

"I don't like this, Jon," Rick said. "I really don't." Rick's voice, heavily accented when he was agitated, reminded Jon of his father's voice.

"I know," Jon finally answered. "But listen to me. I need you to trust me. If I need you, I'll buy you the plane ticket."

"Fine," he finally agreed. "But you had better be calling me every day, telling me that you are okay."

"I will," he promised.

"Good, and you tell Scott and Ryan to be careful," Rick said.

"I'll let them know," Jon replied.

"And you had better take care of yourself, Jon. I swear if I find out that you got shot, I'll come up there and kill you myself."

"I know," Jon said, smiling. "I'll be fine."

"You'd better be," Rick demanded. Courtney walked into Jon's office and leaned against the doorframe.

"I gotta go, my partner and I have things to do," he said.

"Say hello to Courtney for me and tell her I'm looking forward to meeting her."

"Will do, talk to you later, Rick." When he hung up the phone, Courtney smiled.

"Your brother?" she asked.

"Yeah," he answered. "Pretty pissed off that I didn't tell him about what happened."

"As he should be," she replied. "But I know why you didn't."

"That makes one of you," he answered. "Oh, and he said he was looking forward to meeting you."

"I'm looking forward to meeting him too, he seems larger than life," she said.

"Oh, he's definitely a character."

"A family trait I see," she teased.

"Yeah, yeah, you'll meet him soon," he said. "But now, I have someone I want to see."

"I'm ready," she replied. "Let's go."

"I'll tell the lads," he answered going to the wall and pressing the intercom button. "Scott, Ryan," he called and Courtney heard him echoing throughout the house. A couple seconds later Ryan's voice came from the speaker.

"Yeah, Uncle Jon?"

"Courtney and I are heading out, we both have our mobile," Courtney looked at him and raised an eyebrow. He only used odd words when he had just spoken to his brother or his family in Ireland. "Call us if you need us."

"Check in when you can," Scott's muted voice came next as if he wasn't close enough to the intercom.

"Will do," Jon promised. "You lads be careful. Mat, take care. Not sure what's going on."

After Mat's affirmative reply, Jon turned back to Courtney and nodded once. They were ready to go.

———————

"Who is it you wanted to meet with, Jon?" Courtney asked as he drove.

"Billy's brother, Jake," Jon replied.

"Did he serve with you?" she asked.

"No, Desert Storm," Jon answered. "But we're friends and I want to talk to him and see if he knows something about Billy's death."

Courtney nodded. "I'm curious, Jon, is there a connection between his death and what happened last night? Someone was trying to kill you."

"Or Ryan," Jon replied. "He was right there and there isn't a way to know which of us they were targeting."

"And why the captain's gun?"

"Symbolic?" Jon offered.

"Of what?" her mind trailed off as she gazed out the window scenarios flashing through her mind. "Could it be that this person thought you saw something at my apartment, and whatever it was, was worth killing you? Maybe what Billy said would trigger something for you."

"Possibly," Jon said.

"Who did Billy mean when he said he's back? Who's back?"

"I don't know," Jon answered. "I've been wracking my brain to figure it out and I have nothing. I don't know who he meant."

"Was there something in your past that you haven't told me?" She asked.

"If there was, I would tell you, but no," he said.

"Well if you do remember something—"

"You'll be the first to know," he promised.

She looked out the window again as they pulled into a small neighborhood. The houses were cookie-cutter American but the setting was quaint. Pulling up to a house with a cop car in front, Jon and Courtney walked up the driveway and to the front door. Jon rang the doorbell and a uniformed cop answered.

"Good afternoon, Lieutenant, Detective," she said. "I got your message. The family is waiting for you in the living room."

"Thank you," Jon replied.

She shut the door behind them, and they followed her to

the room.

Three people greeted them, a man in his early forties with
the same blue eyes Courtney had only glimpsed in Billy earlier, his
wife and their daughter, clearly going through a Goth phase. The
man's eyes flashed with recognition and relief when he saw Jon.

"Jon," he said. "Oh, thank God it's you looking into this."
He walked up to Jon and shook his hand.

"Jake," Jon started. "Accept my deepest condolences."

"Thank you," Jake replied. "Do you have any idea who did
this?"

"We're still looking into it. I wanted to talk to you and see
if you could tell me anything about Billy's work or personal life,
something that he maybe knew or something that could have
gotten him killed?" Jon asked.

His daughter's eyes jerked up. "No!" she cried. "Everyone
loved Uncle Billy! If you really knew him, you would know that!"

"Audra!" her father scolded. "Jon feels this just as much as
we do. Billy was his good friend. They've known each other since
I was younger than you. He's just as upset by Billy's death as we
are."

Audra looked at her dad. "Then how could he ask that?"

"It's his job to ask. He wants to know if Billy could have
kept anything from him," Jake explained. He turned back to Jon.
"No, I don't know anything. He was as open with you as he was
with me."

"If he cared about Uncle Billy at all," Audra started.
"Then how could he let him die?"

Jon gasped as if he was verbally punched in the gut.
Covering by coughing, Courtney watched him. His lips had gone
a slight shade whiter and his body weaved for a second before he
righted himself. Jake told his daughter to leave the room and
when Audra was gone, Jake spoke softly.

"I'm so sorry. She was really close to her uncle."

"I understand." To anyone but those who knew him, Jon's voice sounded the same, but Courtney could hear the strain he was trying to cover. "Tell her it's all right. If you can think of anything else, give me a call or have the police family liaison call me."

"I don't know if it will help," Jake's wife spoke. "But he mentioned meeting a woman last week. Not unusual for Billy and you know he flirted harmlessly, but said afterwards he had a weird feeling. He said something about her reminded him of someone he knew once, long ago. He didn't tell me who but I know he said he needed to talk to you or Commander Albert."

Jon nodded, his lips still pale. "Thank you," Jon said and turned to leave.

"Jon," Jake called him back. "You'll find whatever son-of-a-bitch killed my big brother, right?"

"Semper Fi," Jon promised.

It took Jon a little while to start the car and Courtney didn't say anything. His color had yet to return and as she waited, resisting the urge to take his hand.

"Courtney," he finally said. "Would you mind if we take a side trip?"

"Of course not," she answered.

"Thank you," he replied.

Chapter Nineteen

When Jon pulled into a parking lot and headed to the florists, Courtney knew the destination. She watched him pick out red roses, greenery, and baby's breath and the florist wrapped it all together to create an exquisite bouquet. While Jon waited at the counter, Courtney walked around the store, pretending to look around but watched her partner. His eyes were shadowed and his body was almost folded in on itself as if he carried the weight of the world on his shoulders.

He didn't speak to her and as they drove again Courtney listened to the silence. Finally, he pulled into Crown Hill Cemetery and weaved his way through the winding roads. When he parked, he looked over at her.

"You don't have to come with me if you don't want to," he said softly.

"I want to," she said.

Again, he said nothing, took the flowers and got out of the car. Jon walked towards a headstone near a stone bench. Focusing on him, Courtney watched as he sighed softly, bent down to be eye-level with the headstone, and set the flowers down. He brushed off the dead leaves.

"Hey, baby," he said softly. "Happy Anniversary. Thirty-one years, that's a record, huh? I miss you so much. Every day I think of you and I wonder what you would look like, would you still give me shit for leaving the dishes out or not ironing my shirt right," he chuckled and looked down. "God, I miss you. Scott's doing well. He's um... he's doing well." Taking a deep breath, he looked up at Courtney. "I wanted you to meet my partner. This is Courtney, though you probably already know that.

"I need you to do something for me, baby, a friend of mine died yesterday; Billy. You know Billy. I need you to greet him show him around, tell him that we'll get whoever killed him. I made you a promise to look after myself, after Scott, and I don't know if I've done a good job but what I did, I did thinking of you." He let out a heavy sigh and looked up at the sky. Taking a couple deep breaths, he went on.

"Billy's niece asked me something today. She said if I really cared about him, how could I let him die and all I could think of was Scott saying those same words to me. I loved you, how could I let you die?" Courtney placed a hand on his shoulder. "I ask myself that every day and I still have no answer. All I know is, I wish every moment that it was me instead of you. You were stronger than me, always were. You would have raised our son better. You would never have allowed the estrangement that we had when he was a teenager. God, babe," he sighed. "I don't know what to do. I can't keep living this way. This half-death. I miss you." His voice choked and he cleared his throat but his tears spilled over and streamed down his cheeks.

"It hurts so much. Every day I feel we were robbed. Robbed of a life we could have had, robbed of a future that will never be. Robbed of our baby you carried. I can't do this anymore, Care. I have to let you go. I don't want to, but I have to. I'll go mad if I don't. You will always be in my heart and I will always love you. But I'm tired of being alone, being sad, being tired..." he kissed his fingers and rubbed her name. "What I wouldn't give for one more day, an hour, a minute with you. I need you to show me that you're all right, and that you want me to move on. Today of all days I need to know." He closed his eyes for a long moment and took a deep breath. After a beat, he opened his eyes and stared straight ahead. He let out a short laugh and his eyes flooded with tears. Smiling and laughing he sighed and looked up. "Thank you," he said then laughed again. "Thank you," he whispered, his eyes once more locking on the object that held his attention.

Courtney followed his gaze only to see a daisy defying the cold and growing near a tree.

"I love you," he said once more to the headstone, kissed his fingers again and pressed them to the name. Standing he turned back to Courtney and wiped the track of tears on his cheeks. "I'm sorry."

"Don't apologize, Jon. You loved her a lot," Courtney said.

"Yeah, I did," he answered. "I do. But it's time."

"Time?" Courtney asked.

"Time to move on," he answered. "I'm in love."

"Oh?" she asked. "Well Beth is a very fortunate woman."

Jon smiled slightly. "Yeah? Don't know what I have to offer but it's hers if she wants it."

"Don't you think you should be telling her this?"

"Yeah probably best, huh?" he teased.

"I mean it's all beautiful and such but I'm taken," Courtney winked.

Chuckling Jon shook his head. "Pity. Come on, let's go."

He took Courtney's hand and walked toward the car. They said nothing and as he walked around to the driver's side, his eyes turned to a white sedan parked a little ways away from him, the driver obscured by the tinted windows. Getting in, Jon adjusted the rearview mirror to watch the car. It didn't move, but as soon as Jon put his car in gear, the white sedan slowly eased forward.

———◦———

When Scott finished his shower and got dressed, he walked back down to the basement in search of Ryan and his uncle. Ryan was in the guest bathroom shower and Mat was sitting on the couch watching a game.

"Hey," Scott said.

Mat looked up. "Hey," he answered apathetically.

"So, are you and Dad okay?" he asked.

Mat sat still, not looking up at him. "Your father and I have known each other for a long time, Scott. I doubt in all these years we were ever not okay."

"What kind of an answer is that?" Scott asked.

"Scott, I will not be questioned by you. I already had this with Jon. I just wish everyone in this family would let me be and leave me to my own damn business," Mat replied.

"What's wrong, Uncle Mat?" Scott asked.

Mat stood and looked up at Scott. "I don't think you have the right to lecture me on how to treat your father," Mat replied coldly. Stunned, Scott blinked a few times and took a deep breath before answering.

"I did not mean to lecture you, I merely wanted to know what was going on," Scott replied. "I don't want us to fight."

"We're already fighting," Mat spat. "You know, why don't you stop always taking your dad's side and step back for once? Be the lawyer and see both sides here, Scott. Stop living in your daddy's shadow. He's not as pearly white as you might think."

"I know Dad's history," Scott replied.

"Oh really? Did he ever tell you that he never fully fell out of love with Beth, even when he was married to your mom? You know, I've always wondered if every time he and Carol were together, he really saw her or some other woman."

"Shut the hell up! Dad loved Mom, he still does! I am proof of that! I know today is tough for everyone, being their anniversary, but have a little respect for the man who saved your life and loved your sister so much that he was willing to put his own happiness on hold for thirteen years to mourn her. If dad wants Beth, then I'm all for it. You should be too. Dear God, what is wrong with you?"

Mat let out a roar and tackled Scott to the ground breaking a table behind them as they crashed to the ground. Scott threw punches into his uncle's side but Mat caught him on the side of the face and Scott lay stunned for a moment but then, with all the strength he could muster, he kicked Mat in the stomach forcing him off and gaining the advantage. Straddling his uncle, he threw punch after punch not stopping until he felt someone wrap their arms around his and pin him. Struggling to free himself, he was about to pull the other person off him when he heard Ryan's voice in his ear.

"Don't. It's not worth it."

Scott trembled in Ryan's grasp but he came to his senses and looked down at his uncle's bloodied face.

"Get out," he spat. "I want you out. Now."

Crawling to his feet, Mat stood and without another word, limped his way up the stairs and out of the house.

Once they were alone, Ryan helped him sit and started taking in his injuries.

"I don't know what happened to him," Scott said. "It's like he was possessed. He just tackled me. I know we were shouting but he deserved it. God, what he said about dad pissed me off."

"Let me take a look," Ryan offered. "Where does it hurt the most?"

"I have a bloody terrible headache, he caught me on the temple, and my ribs and back hurt but I don't think anything's broken," Scott explained.

Ryan nodded and walked over to the bar to pour a shot glass of tequila. He handed the drink to his cousin and watched him throw it back and swallow.

"My bag is upstairs. I'll be right back. Don't lay down," Ryan ordered. Scott mock saluted and watched him run up the steps.

His whole body ached but he cast his mind back to see if he could remember physically attacking him. He was defending his father but never laid a finger on his uncle. Mat had never raised his hand to him in the past. He still had no answers when Ryan came back down.

Taping the cut above his brow, Ryan checked his nose for any breaks and stuffed some cotton up Scott's nostrils when there wasn't a fracture but it was still bleeding. Checking the dilation of his eyes, Scott blinked at the bright light. His body was relaxing thanks to the tequila and all he wanted to do was sleep when Ryan began prodding his side.

"Nothing broken," Ryan said. "Good."

"Can I sleep now?" Scott asked.

"Yes," Ryan replied. "You don't have a concussion."

"Call dad and let him know what happened," Scott asked.

"Oh no, that's on you, man," Ryan replied.

"Wuss," Scott stated. Ryan rolled his eyes and almost immediately Scott's phone rang. "Shit," he said. "That's Dad."

Aeron cursed and hit his hand against the steering wheel. That was exactly what they did not want to happen. What the hell is Mat playing at? He pulled out his cell phone.

"What?" Rob answered.

"Mat left," he said.

There was a long pause.

"I thought you understood he was supposed to stay with Jon," Rob's low voice made him clench his fist.

"Yes, I know," he answered. "But there is only so much I can do. At least he hasn't left Hannah. What do you want me to tell her?"

"She needs to keep him close," he answered. "We now have to make sure Mat doesn't talk to Jon. He could warn him somehow."

"How?"

"They're old friends and marines. They have codes," the man said. "Trust me, I know them."

"Okay," he answered. "Do you want me follow him?"

"No," he answered. "Have Hannah pick him up. You stay with Scott and Ryan. Jon should be home soon. Then go to Commander Albert and fulfill his words that something bad is coming. Do what you do best. Then we'll talk about Dave Weston next. He's always been too close."

"And he's a good friend of Jon's," Aeron said. "And Courtney's."

"Exactly," Rob answered.

"Done," he answered.

They hung up as Aeron pulled off to the side of the road when Jon and Courtney drove into the garage.

Chapter Twenty

"Scott," Jon called as he walked down the stairs.

Scott and Ryan hadn't moved from the basement since the fight and as Jon appeared at the foot of the stairs, Scott woke from his doze and slowly sat up. His face had bruised and his body was stiff but Ryan had some medicine on the end table for him. "What happened?" Jon asked hurrying to his son's side.

"I'm sorry, Dad," Scott said. "But he pissed me off and when I yelled at him, he tackled me. We broke the table."

"Shh," Jon replied calmly taking his son's chin and looking at the damage. "That doesn't look terrible. Tell me what happened." Scott looked over at Courtney. She smiled sweetly and spoke low.

"Ryan," she said. "Could you help me make something for lunch? We're starving."

"Sure babe," he replied walking with her upstairs to the kitchen leaving Jon and Scott alone.

Scott had told Jon what had happened with Mat and it made his chest ache. He hoped Mat didn't truly believe his words. Jon had loved Carol more than his own life. Granted he was no pearly white virgin when he married her but with her and after her there had never been another nor any image of anyone but her. Wavering for a moment when he held his phone in his hand, he warred within his mind. He wanted Beth and Kim there so they would be safe, but then he wondered if it was the right time to tell her he loved her. Was this Carol's way of telling him to wait?

Courtney came around the bend in the hallway to his study on her phone saying she would see them soon and hung up.

"Who was that?" Jon asked.

"Kim," Courtney answered. "I know you weren't going to call them after what Ryan told me he overheard Mat say and let me say this, if he were here right now I'd do more than just yell at him. How dare he say that about you!"

"Easy," Jon replied. "He did it for a reason, I just don't know the reason yet."

"Well it had better be a damn good one," she said. "Don't you even think about turning back from telling Beth. She deserves it as much as you do."

"God you know me too well," he admitted.

"I do, now they'll be here soon. Ryan and I made BLTs. Come and eat."

<hr />

Beth and Kim reached Jon's house in record time and Beth immediately went to Jon. Hugging him tightly, she gazed into his green eyes to make sure he was all right.

"I'm fine," he answered reading her mind. "Truly."

"Oh, god," she cried and buried her head into his chest. "I was so worried when Kim told me what happened."

"It's okay," Jon said. "Everything is okay. Courtney and I are going to continue our investigation here and I want you all where I know it's safe."

Kim looked over at him. "Are you sure this guy isn't clever enough to get close to us?" she asked.

"From what we can see," Jon replied. "He wants to stay in

the shadows for now. If he wanted to get closer, he would have done it already."

"And firing a bullet at you as you sat at the kitchen table isn't close enough?" Beth demanded. "Kim told me what happened."

"Baby, I'm okay," Jon said. "And I need to talk to you... alone for a moment."

She gazed up at him confused but nodded. Jon looked back at Courtney, who smiled brightly. He then looked at Scott, whose eyes were dancing as he watched his dad.

They walked to another room and Jon shut the door.

"What's all this about, Jon?" Beth asked crossing her arms over her ample chest. The movement only drew Jon's eyes to the small dip in her shirt showing tantalizing cleavage.

"I needed to talk to you," Jon said.

"You said that," she replied. "Why?"

"Because I had something I need to tell you," he took a step closer to her. She dropped her arms and gazed up at him. He gently pushed a piece of her hair away from her eyes.

"Oh?" her breath hitched. "And what do you need to tell me?"

"Tell and show you," he said leaning even closer. Her breathing sped up but her hand came up to his chest and forced him to stop.

"Wait," she begged. "Don't do this if you can't follow through."

"Oh, I'll follow through," he promised. "Maybe not tonight, maybe not tomorrow night, but as soon as you are ready you will be mine."

"I'm ready," she answered. Without another word, Jon lowered his lips to hers and took her mouth in a strong kiss.

Chapter Twenty-One

Jon and Courtney sat in an unused room next to the workout room in Jon's basement. Scott had attempted to make it an office but left it unfinished several years ago. Luckily, the room had a whiteboard and a corkboard, two semi-comfortable chairs, and a table.

Jon stood at the whiteboard, a black dry erase marker in his hand. "Billy Simpson." He wrote the name out. "Me." He wrote his name and drew a connecting line between the two. "What's the connection?"

"Vietnam," Courtney offered.

"Right," Jon wrote above the line. "Mat." He scrawled Mat's name below and in the middle of the other two names and drew three lines, one to his name, one to Billy and one to Vietnam. On the line connecting Jon and Mat he wrote *Carol/Vietnam* and on the one connecting Billy and Mat he wrote *Vietnam*.

"It's pretty safe to say that the overarching connection is Vietnam," Courtney said. "Don't forget it was the captain's gun."

"Good point," Jon wrote M40 beside Mat's name.

"What camp were you guys stationed at in Vietnam?" she asked.

"Bearcat," Jon said. "Same camp, different barracks."

"There's a connection," she replied.

"A lot of guys were in that camp, Army, Airborne, MPs, it was a huge base. Why single the three of us out?"

Courtney was silent for a moment. Someone knocked on their door and Jon called for them to come in. Beth opened the door carrying a pitcher of lemonade and two glasses.

"I didn't mean to interrupt, but I thought you might be thirsty," she said. Jon grinned and walked over to her.

"Thank you," he said taking his glass after she poured. Looking up at him, Beth gently touched his chest. Not thinking about Courtney, he wrapped an arm around her waist and pulled her close, kissing her deeply.

When he pulled back, her deep flushed color made him puff his chest in triumph

"Play later, get back to work," Beth whispered. Winking at her, Jon released her, took his glass and drank, not breaking eye contact with her. Her flush increased and she turned away from him.

"Sorry to interrupt," she said again. "Kim and I were going to make some dinner in about two hours. Any requests?"

Jon's eyes went hooded as he watched her. Her eyes grew large and she shook her head at him. Courtney just laughed.

"Should I leave you guys alone?" she teased. "Because, man, it is getting hot in here."

The corner of Jon's mouth ticked up and he lowered his eyes. "As tempting as that is," he said. "We need to work. Whatever you guys want, babe, works for me."

"Maybe not chicken though?" Courtney asked. "I've had nothing but chicken for the last couple days and I'm tired of it."

"All right, no chicken," Beth smiled. "We'll think of something."

Beth squeezed Jon's hand and left the room.

"I am so happy for you, Jon," Courtney said. "Let's finish up in here so we can join the others."

"Gladly," Jon replied.

They both stared at the whiteboard as they drank their lemonade. "Jon," Courtney finally spoke. "What battle was Billy wounded in?"

"Easter Offensive in seventy-two," Jon replied.

"Were you and Mat there?" she asked.

"Yeah. We were nearly right next to him," Jon admitted.

"Okay. So maybe we're looking at this the wrong way round," Courtney said, taking the marker from him and turning toward the board. She wiped the line drawn from Vietnam to Billy and wrote, *Easter Offensive, 1972*, in big letters in the middle and drew three lines connecting the three names.

Turning back to him, Courtney could almost see his thoughts. "We were all wounded in that battle," Jon explained. "Billy's leg, Mat was shot in the arm and side, and I took a bullet to my thigh."

"I think we just found the connection," she said. "How many casualties and how many wounded?"

"I don't know offhand. It lasted months. Let me check." He pulled up the chair and clicked on the laptop.

Jon's body tensed as he sifted through pictures of the war. "How many of those men that died did you know?" she asked.

"I have no idea," he replied rubbing his face. "As much as I hate to say it, I think we need more information. We need to know what this person wants from us."

"What did Simpson's brother's wife mean when she said Billy met someone?" Courtney asked.

Jon turned to her and pulled out his phone. "More importantly," Jon went on. "Jake said he was going to talk to Albert."

"Who?"

"A Commander," Jon explained, putting the cell phone to his ear. "It's ringing." They waited. "He's not answering. I'm going to try the home phone." Just as Jon hung up the phone, Scott opened the door with such haste that Jon and Courtney jumped.

"Dad," Scott said. "Come quickly. You've gotta see what's on the news."

———

"We are reporting directly from Dr. George Albert's house, where an apparent home invasion has occurred. The psychiatrist was found dead on the floor of his kitchen earlier this evening. No apparent robbery was committed, but authorities are treating this as a targeted attack. The shooting was committed in broad daylight, but no one saw or heard anything except neighbors of the doctor said they did hear breaking glass and that is what prompted them to call 911. If anyone has any information, the Carmel Police ask that you call the number now shown on your screen for the tip line. Dr. Albert was a retired military commander who received the Purple Heart for his service and sacrifice in Vietnam. He worked at the Northwestern Psychiatric Facility for nearly twenty years. A spokesman for the hospital says that Albert's death is a tragedy and though they cannot hope to replace him, they will strive to fill his void as much as possible."

The TV jumped to a man speaking at the podium saying the exact words the anchor had just said and Ryan muted the TV.

"Dad, what's going on?" Scott asked.

"I don't know, Scottie," Jon admitted holding Beth closer. "But until I know, I want you all to be extra careful. This guy is after us. You ask me to watch my back every day. Now I'm asking you to watch yours."

"We will," Scott promised. "It might help if we all bounced ideas around."

"Do that here," Jon said. "Courtney and I need to talk

more about this case and even though it's silly, we can't do that with civilians."

"Understood," Ryan replied. "But if we think of anything we'll let you know."

"Come on, Jon," Courtney stepped forward. "Let's add this new information to the board."

Jon nodded and stepped away from Beth, following his partner back to their office.

———————

Beth and Kim worked in the basement kitchen area making pulled pork enchiladas while the boys watched TV. It was a couple of hours before Jon and Courtney came back out of the office.

"This is madness," Courtney said. "You cannot possibly think I would allow this."

"You are my partner, not my boss. You do not *allow* me to do anything," Jon replied.

"Not when it's insanity," she replied. "Think of us. Think of Beth. You want to make her your widow before she's even your wife?"

Beth gasped and looked over at them.

"What is between Beth and I is none of your concern," Jon answered.

"It is if it can help you see sense," she replied. "You are proposing a suicide mission."

"I am proposing the only logical thing to do," Jon answered. "Two people died and another could have been killed. Your own boyfriend could have died."

"Don't try to use Ryan against me, Jon," she said. "I love him, he knows that, but he's not planning some idiotic mission that will get him killed."

"What else is there?"

"Hey!" Scott shouted gaining their attention. They turned

to him as he stood stiffly from the couch. "What the hell is going on?" he demanded.

"Nothing that concerns you," Jon replied.

"If you're planning on making me an orphan then it most certainly does concern me," Scott placed his hands on his hips. "So talk."

"I'm tired of this," Jon started. "I just got off the phone with my former CO. I'm calling all the lads together tomorrow. We're all going to be in one place at one time. If this person wants us, they can come and get us. I'm done trying to hide just to save my own life when others are being killed."

"That's crazy, Dad!" Scott said. "I'm sorry but I'm with Courtney on this one."

"They're taking us out one by one. It's a power play, a message. Frankly, I'm tired of waiting to be next, of worrying about who might be hurt and not knowing what to do. I'm not going to hide anymore."

"So, you want to go and get yourself killed?" Scott demanded. "Think about us!"

"I am thinking about you, Scott," Jon replied. "That's why I have to do this."

There was a small sob from Beth still over by the kitchenette. Jon turned to her.

"Don't cry," he said. "There's no reason to cry."

She looked down and breathed deeply. "No tears," she said.

A reminiscent smile crossed Jon's lips as he pulled her into a hug. "No. No tears allowed," he replied.

She laid her head on his chest and breathed him in. "Don't go, not when I've just gotten you back. You promised."

Jon took a deep breath. "You're right. It was a stupid idea. I'm sorry. I just feel like a caged animal. I don't like it."

"So, you won't do it?" She asked.

Sighing, he shook his head. "No," Jon replied. "I won't do it."

"Thank God," she breathed and stood on her toes to kiss him.

"Good," Courtney crossed her arms. "God, that took a lot of energy." She looked over at Ryan. "You're not going to be this much trouble, are you?" Ryan shook his head. "Thank God. Now, I'm starving and could use a drink."

"Dinner is ready," Kim replied. "What can I get you?"

"I'll take a whiskey," Courtney said. "Then chase it with a red wine."

Kim laughed but poured everyone a whiskey. Jon took his glass, looked over at Ryan, and winked.

"Don't you have something important to tell everyone, Ryan?" Jon asked. Everyone looked over at him.

"Gee thanks, Uncle Jon," he said. Courtney looked at him and raised an eyebrow. "I guess the secret is out."

"Oh god, Courtney's pregnant," Scott teased.

"Haha," Courtney replied sarcastically.

"It seems so important," Scott shrugged.

"No," Ryan answered. "Courtney isn't pregnant. But it does affect our future. I have been asked to interview, just interview mind, I don't have the job yet. But I have been asked to interview Monday morning for assistant head of surgery."

Everyone applauded and wished him luck. Jon raised his glass to him.

"May good luck be your friend in whatever you do, and may trouble be always a stranger to you," Jon said. "Well done, Ryan. Sláinte."

"Thanks," Ryan replied as everyone downed their whiskey.

"Oh that's good," Scott praised.

"The best," Kim answered.

"What is it?" Courtney asked.

"Green Spot," Kim replied. "Didn't think Jon would mind us breaking into his good stuff."

"Not at all," Jon answered. "There's a couple cases in the wine cellar."

"Oh good, Mark's birthday is coming up and he asked for a good bottle of whiskey," Beth spoke about her second son.

"You're welcome to them," Jon replied. "But now we can break out the champagne. Kim, behind you in the cooler, could you pass it over? And that dinner smells divine."

She looked back inside the wine cooler and found the Dom Perignon. Handing it to Jon, Kim grabbed six glasses.

Hannah rushed out of Mat's house and down the three steps to Aeron's waiting arms. After kissing her, he pulled back.

"How's it going, baby?" he asked.

"Every time he touches me, I cringe inside."

"Don't think about him," he said. "Think about me."

"I already do that," Hannah replied kissing him lightly.

"You'd better go back in," he said.

"Anything I need to know?" she asked.

He shook his head. "Everything is under control."

She nodded. "Have you marked Dr. Albert off your list?" Pulling out his book, he showed her and she threw her arms around his neck.

"I miss you," she said. "I want you so much right now."

He grabbed her roughly to him and yanked her hair to lift her lips up to his. Groaning, she opened her mouth to him as he bent down. Only a breath away, he whispered, "later," and let her go. "Now go."

She walked away from him and back into the house. Aeron sighed and got back into the car. She played perfectly into his plan.

Chapter
Twenty-Two

Kim woke early and as everyone still slept, she slipped out of the guest room and tiptoed her way to the basement kitchenette. Smiling when she saw her mom wrapped protectively in Jon's arms on the pullout couch, her eyes drifted to Scott sleeping on the recliner, his bruised face hurt her heart.

Shaking her head knowing he would never see her as anything more than a friend, she slipped noiselessly into the kitchen. Jon had ground the coffee and gotten the pot ready last night, all she had to do was turn it on. As she pulled out the ingredients for blueberry muffins, she quickly measured out the correct amounts and stirred. As soon as the muffins were in the oven, she turned on the coffee. Courtney walked out of the other guest room and smiled at her.

"Anything I can do?" she whispered. Kim shook her head and thanked her silently. "Jon's already awake, he's just pretending," Courtney said a little louder. Both women looked over at Jon who was fighting a smirk.

"Shh," he said not opening his eyes. The women chuckled but said no more to him, got a cup of coffee and walked over to the bistro table and chairs beside the pool table.

"I bet you're happy with Ryan's news," Kim said as they

sat and drank their coffee.

"I am," Courtney replied. "He always promised that he'll propose after he's certain of his future."

"I'm surprised you guys haven't moved in together," Kim said.

"No," she answered. "I want him but I'm pretty old school. We actually haven't slept together yet."

"Seriously?" she asked.

"I know it's the thing to do but I don't want to until there's a ring involved," Courtney answered.

"I can definitely understand that," Kim replied. "I wish I had."

"Bad experience?"

"Good experience just wrong guy," she admitted.

"Can I ask why you haven't just told him?" Courtney asked glancing over at Scott.

"It's a lot more complicated," she explained. "We are best friends, always have been, but if I just come out and say it and he's not ready, I risk losing him not only as a potential lover but as my best friend."

Courtney sighed. "I can see that, but he loves you, he's just—"

"An idiot?" Kim offered.

Courtney laughed. "Something like that."

"I know," Kim's voice was soft as she looked back over at him. "But he's my idiot."

The timer beeped for the blueberry muffins causing the women to jump and laugh but Jon, Scott, and Beth woke with a start.

"Sorry," Kim apologized hurrying to turn the alarm off. Ryan walked out of the gym, a towel slung over his shoulder.

"Everything all right?" he asked. Courtney eyed her boyfriend up and down and bit her lower lip. He looked sexy in his gym shorts, black t-shirt and running shoes, a light sheen of sweat reflecting on his body.

"Definitely, baby," Courtney went over to him and tugged him into another room.

"Some men have all the luck," Scott replied.

"If you want a good make out session, let me know," Kim winked after she pulled out the muffins.

Scott laughed. "I'll keep that in mind. But for now, the only thing I want near my mouth is your blueberry muffins."

"And tea, don't forget your tea," she said gesturing to the pot on the stove.

"I knew I loved you," he teased kissing her cheek.

"Any chance of making that real anytime soon, lad?" Jon called then grunted as Beth elbowed his stomach. "Seriously, baby? The first time we sleep in the same bed since we were teenagers and you elbow me? What is it with the women in my life hitting me in sensitive places?"

"Love taps," Beth teased patting his face.

"Mmhmm," he answered then his face went soft. "Good morning."

"Morning," she whispered kissing him.

"Muffins?" Kim offered.

"Love some, sweetheart," Beth said, slowly peeling away from him and standing. Jon stood and began folding the sheets. Scott helped him collapse the pullout couch.

"How are you feeling?" Jon asked seeing his son's bruises.

"Better," he answered. "Still have a headache but it's better than it was yesterday."

"Good, and food will help," Jon said. "Ryan! Stop snogging your girlfriend or there won't be any food left for you."

"Not happening!" Ryan shouted back. Everyone laughed but eventually Ryan and Courtney came back out of the room holding hands. Courtney led Ryan to a chair and pressed him down into it with a wink. Walking back to the kitchenette, she got four muffins, two plates, and cups of coffee. Jon was already grinding more beans to make a second pot.

After everyone had some coffee and another batch of muffins were in the oven, the conversation turned to the case.

"You said you talked with your former CO, Jon. Do you trust him?"

"Yes," Jon answered. "And you do too."

"Me?" Courtney asked. "Do I know him?"

"Dave Weston," he replied.

"Wait… My Dave Weston?" Courtney asked.

"Dave Weston your trainer at the academy?" Ryan asked her. Jon nodded.

"Did he write to Mat to get me this position?" Courtney demanded.

"Your skills got you the position," Jon replied. "Dave just moved you along."

"Why didn't you ever tell me?"

"Because it wasn't important," Jon said.

"I guess not, but honestly I should have been told that my promotion was some back-room deal."

"No back-room deal," Jon replied. "Your merits were noticed. You interviewed. You got the job."

"I never interviewed with Mat," she revealed.

"No, the chief," Jon agreed. "But still."

"Putting that aside," Ryan said. "What were you thinking, babe?"

"Well, I wondered if you could call him back. I know you want to warn your friends, that's your main goal. But what if you don't know everyone? I know you said that you all get together every month, but can you honestly tell me you have all of their numbers?"

Jon shook his head. "You're right. I don't."

"But he might," she offered. "If we could get his help in contacting them it might expedite the process."

"Grand idea," Jon praised. "Do you want to join me?"

"No, and I don't want you to tell him you told me. I want him to sweat a little," she said. "I love him but he needs to know I don't appreciate him puppeteering my life."

"So, I don't know, Dave," Jon was saying as he sat alone in the office.

"I agree," he replied. "I don't think it's a wise decision to gather everyone and be in one place at one time. Courtney's right, the best thing to do is to call everyone we know and warn them about what is going on."

"And tell them what, exactly? Some lunatic is out for blood. Watch your back if you were in the Easter Offensive?"

"Maybe without the out for blood part," Dave replied.

"I'm serious," Jon said. "Think how it sounded to you earlier today? You didn't believe me."

"That's because I sit here in my ivory tower, untouchable," Dave teased.

"That ivory tower won't save you from a sniper's bullet." Jon was serious.

"I appreciate your concern, Jon but I'm fine. We have guards all over the place, I'm well protected. No one gets into the building without a thorough background check and security clearance. You need to worry about yourself and your family."

"I was wondering if you could do a check for me on all those who had been rejected or dishonorably discharged from the corps who wanted to be a sniper. This guy's good. Professionally trained."

"Can do," Dave answered.

"Also, cross reference any of those you find with fallen veterans at the Offensive. If it isn't retired military, it might be a relative." Jon asked.

"I'll do a quick check and get back to you." Dave promised. "Meanwhile, what are you going to do?"

"I'm going to start calling my contacts and warning them," Jon replied.

"I'll do the same on this end. You take care, Jon," Dave said. "That might also mean dropping this case and going to Ireland as planned."

"There's way too much to do, Dave. I can't just drop and go home," Jon replied.

"Yes, you can and you will," Dave answered. "I'm not making a suggestion."

"You're not my boss anymore," Jon said.

"Once a Marine, always a Marine," Dave stated.

"True," Jon answered. "If I see nothing happening for a little while I'll consider it."

"Strongly."

"Strongly," Jon acquiesced.

Chapter
Twenty-Three

Jon spent a couple hours on the phone with his old friends, explaining what was going on. They made plans to leave town and took precautions to warn their families. Courtney sat with Jon in their office going through the forensics report from the bullets used for the murders. Although Albert's case was Carmel PD's they shared their findings since the cases were similar and according to the forensics, the bullets were the same. Once Jon hung up, Courtney called him over to look at something.

The autopsy for Dr. Albert had not been completed but Billy's had. Cause of death was blood loss due to a bullet wound. And the bullet matched the one Jon found in his kitchen after the attack.

"Can you get his financials? I need to look something up," Jon spoke low.

"Sure, might take some time," Courtney replied.

"That's fine," Jon answered. "Both personal and the business. I'm going to request phone records, I want to see who he was talking to recently. If we can find that woman he met we might be able to figure out what it was about her that made him suspicious."

"Okay," Courtney agreed and went to work.

———————

Scott was out in the main area with Kim and Ryan. Beth had her laptop set up in a guest room so their movie didn't bother her as she wrote. Her writer's block had cleared and, after years of knowing what that meant, the three of them left her alone to work.

The action movie didn't hold his attention and he pulled out his phone to text his girlfriend. They had hit a rough patch in their relationship. He had missed two of her performances the last three months. They had a fight earlier in the month, she told him she thought he worked too much to really be there for her. As terrible as he felt, he was starting not to care but she was still his girlfriend and he wanted to try and make it work.

Scott: Hey baby, how was the show? Sorry, I couldn't make it, but someone tried to kill my dad yesterday.

It took her a minute to respond and when she did, Scott rolled his eyes.

Angie: Seriously? That's the best you can do? How stupid do you think I am? You could have just said you couldn't make it because you were too busy.

Scott: I wasn't too busy. Someone shot at him, but think what you want.

Angie: What's that supposed to mean?

Scott: Nothing, I shouldn't have even brought it up. I'm tired and wasn't thinking.

Angie: I'm getting tired of you not supporting me, Scott. Don't worry, Sean is supporting me.

Scott: Not supporting you? I always support you. And who the hell is Sean?

Angie: I can't talk about this right now. I'm about to go to warm up.

Scott: No, I think we need to talk about this. Who is

Sean?

When she didn't answer, he texted her again.

Scott: You answer me or I will call you every five minutes.

Finally, she texted him back.

Angie: Easy. He's just a dancer in the company.

Scott: Why haven't you mentioned him before?

Angie: Because he's not important. And he's new. We were just partnered.

Scott: I'm guessing he likes you since he's being 'so supportive'.

Angie: Grow up. At least he's here.

Scott: He's there because he's in the damn company.

Angie: Switch to decaf. Rehearsal is about to start.

Scott: We're not done talking about this.

Angie: Yes, we are. Look, this isn't working out for either of us.

Scott: Oh my God. Are breaking up with me over a TEXT?

Angie: You're never available to do anything else. I'm sorry to be so callous but I just can't do this anymore. I can't pretend like you not being there is okay. I'm tired of pretending that I'm okay with all of this. God, Scott we haven't had sex in weeks.

Scott: Okay, one, that's not true, it's only been nine days and you've been in a show. Two, you are too tired to do anything.

Scott: You know what? Fine. I'm not going to argue with you. I'm tired of pretending too. So if you want to end it, it's over.

Angie: Don't put this on me.

Scott: Well it sure as hell wasn't me who said this wasn't working out. But I will be the last to say it. Goodbye Angie, it was okay while it lasted. And the sex wasn't all that great. We're done.

Scott thought his phone might break because of how hard

he was typing and gripping it. Finally, he leaned back in his chair and sighed.

"Scott?" Kim's voice came from beside him on the couch. "Is everything okay?"

"No, it sure as hell isn't okay," he spat. "Angie just broke up with me."

"What?" Kim and Ryan asked together.

"Yeah over a damn text message," Scott replied.

"Everything all right?" Jon's voice came from the doorway of the office.

"No," Scott answered. "My girlfriend just broke up with me."

"Angie?"

"I don't have any other girlfriend, dad," Scott replied.

"No I know, but, really?" Jon asked.

"Yep, over a damn text message," he said.

"That's just cowardly," Jon replied.

"I gotta get out of here," Scott paced back and forth. "I can't stay here."

"You can't go outside, it's too dangerous," Courtney said. Beth came out of her room to see what was going on.

"To hell with that," Scott shouted. "I'm not staying here like a caged animal all while my ex-girlfriend is shagging someone else."

Scott tried to walk passed his father to the stairs but Jon stopped him with a hand on his chest.

"I'm not letting you go alone," Jon replied. "Get your coat."

Relief flashed in Scott's eyes. "Really?"

"Yes," Jon answered. "Now go." Turning back to everyone in the room, he locked eyes with Beth and said they would be back soon.

Finally, when they were alone, Courtney and Beth looked

at Kim and Ryan.

"What happened?" Beth asked.

"No clue," Ryan answered. "All we know is he was texting and then he got a little agitated typing angrily."

"I asked him if everything was all right, then he told us," Kim said.

"It sounded like she had someone on the side," Ryan admitted.

"Oh no," Beth covered her mouth. "Not again."

"Again?" Courtney asked.

"Yeah. It's a long story," Ryan said. "But Scott's ex-wife was unfaithful—"

"Wait, hold on, back up. Scott was married?"

"You have about forty-five minutes, Ryan, they went for a beer," Beth said looking at her phone and the text Jon just sent her. "Tell the story."

"Okay," Ryan took a deep breath. "Help me with some of the details, Kim?" She nodded. "After Aunt Carol died, Uncle Jon was unable to walk for weeks due to his knee and surgery. He was in therapy for a year. My parents and I moved over from Italy, my mom wanted to help and Dad was always pretty close to Uncle Jon. I was fourteen. Uncle Jon was unable to do simple things such as shower and dress himself, so Mom would cook and clean for him. Dad and Uncle Mat would help him with everything else.

"I remember they would get into terrible fights because Uncle Jon wanted to do everything on his own. My dad, who went to school for physical therapy, knew Uncle Jon couldn't do those things and tried to stop him but Uncle Jon was going through the mourning process and was at the angry stage. Since Scott was only sixteen, he didn't understand what had happened. All he knew was that in the morning his mom drove him to school and in the afternoon, he was being driven to the hospital where his dad was in surgery and his mom was dead. He believed it was Uncle Jon's fault Aunt Carol died."

"Jon just lost his wife, for God's sake!" Courtney said.

"Granted," Ryan replied. "We all know that. Scott was young and has since apologized for all the hurt he caused but it was during the time he hated Uncle Jon all of this happened. Life under this roof was a living hell when Scott was here. When Uncle Jon took me in after my parents' accident a year later, Scott hated me saying I was trying to take his place as Uncle Jon's son. He and Uncle Jon would get into major fights. It was scary. Scott would cuss him out calling him all sorts of names and Uncle Jon would slap him, saying he would not accept that language from his son. There were times when I thought Scott would punch him. The one time he almost did, Uncle Jon blocked it, grabbed Scott's shirt and held him against the wall with his arm across Scott's neck. I've never seen Uncle Jon use brute strength like that. He spoke so quietly to Scott, I couldn't hear what he said but it stopped Scott from ever doing that again.

"He went to college in Chicago, Northwestern Law School and met his math professor's graduate student. They eventually moved in together, and Scott married her. They had a daughter, Sarah. After the baby was born, Scott realized he was a family man and should stop partying and settle down. His wife didn't like that as it was the wild frat boy she wanted. It was on his twenty-first birthday, also the last day of first semester finals for them that Alex—"

"Scott's and my best friend since elementary," Kim interjected.

"I've met him," Courtney replied. "At the company Christmas party. He's one of Scott's partners."

"Yes," Ryan went on. "Well, Alex took him out to celebrate and got drunk. Alex started talking about this woman he had slept with earlier that day and when he was describing her,

Scott recognized something he said and—"

"Oh God, no," Courtney said.

"Yeah," Ryan replied. "Alex had slept with Scott's wife."

"Scott was furious," Kim went on. "He punched him and when the patrons pulled them apart, he left going straight back to his wife, demanding to know if it was true. When she didn't deny it and made it out like it was his fault, Scott left her, took his daughter and drove down here."

"We hadn't seen each other for about a year and a half," Ryan said. "You see, Alex wasn't the only one she tried to seduce. She tried it with Uncle Jon and me. Neither of us succumbed, but it wasn't a good situation and Jon told him she was not welcome in his house. Scott arrived home around five in the morning driving through the night. He shocked us both when he had a baby in his arms. We didn't know he was a father."

"But Scott doesn't have a child," Courtney said, looking around as if expecting to see an eight-year-old girl playing with Barbie's in the corner.

"Uncle Jon offered to take her in and raise her since Scott was going to law school and wouldn't be able to take care of a child. But then he was slapped with a lawsuit by his ex-wife. He counter-sued and won. He always wanted what was best for Sarah and with Uncle Jon still a cop and he was going to law school, the best opportunity for his daughter was with our Uncle Rick and Aunt Jenny, Uncle Jon's and my mom's older brother and his wife. They live in Tampa."

"Does she know?" Courtney asked.

"Sarah? No. They've agreed to tell her on her eighteenth birthday," Kim replied.

"Oh, what a nice birthday present," Courtney said sarcastically.

"I know," Kim answered.

"So, he's fully divorced, has now broken up with his

girlfriend, and he's a father," Courtney summed up what Ryan just explained. "And tell me, how is it I've been dating you for almost two years and you've never told me this."

"It wasn't my secret to tell," he said.

"Hmm," Courtney grunted. "Scott's led a very colorful life. But he and Alex talk now?"

"Alex has turned his life around. They both have never forgotten what Alex did, but he's apologized and is forgiven," Kim explained. "But he is never fully trusted."

"I can understand that," Courtney replied. "But he's single now so he has little to worry about."

"True," Kim answered. "But it won't take Scott long to find someone. The longest he was single was six months."

"One of those, huh?" Courtney teased. "Well hopefully it will all turn out well." She winked at Kim. Kim smiled sweetly but never got her hopes up.

Chapter
Twenty-Four

Aeron again sat in his car down the road from Jon's house. He had to admire the red Ferrari Jon pulled into the garage. Smiling as he thought about his next plan, he watched Jon and Scott walk back into the house.

Jon walked down the basement stairs, his phone to his ear. Scott trailed behind him and went to the couch, sitting next to Kim. The anger had faded from his eyes, but hurt had replaced it.

Jon waved Courtney over and they went into the office, shutting the door behind them.

"Can you tell me what was on the paper you found on the body? Was it a suicide note?" Jon asked putting the phone on speaker.

"In all my years, I've not seen a suicide note like this, if it is one." Courtney recognized the voice of the Carmel Department Coroner.

"What's written on the note, Doc?" Jon asked.

"You didn't get it from me, but it is strange," he said. "Part of it has been blotted out by the blood and, since it was written in pencil, our forensics team has little hope in restoring the words. It reads, *White Queen* and then it's blotted out. *Black*, and then something beginning with the letter k. *Four*, and under that, *It's time for the truth*. The rest is blotted out."

"That's not much to go on, but thanks, Miller," Jon said.

"I shouldn't even be talking to you. Officially, you're off this case," Dr. Miller said.

"So I heard. I got the run-around from the office," Jon answered.

"You take care of yourself, Jon," Miller said.

"I'll be careful. Thanks," Jon replied.

"We're off the case?" Courtney asked when he hung up his phone.

"Did you expect anything else?"

"No," she conceded. "That was for Albert I'm guessing."

"Yes, I worked with Dr. Miller for nearly ten years when he was coroner for Indianapolis. He was willing to give us some information. Mat took a side trip back to the precinct when he left here to take us off of this case. Now we both know the consequences of working a case without permission. I don't want you to deal with this. I've had a long career and can handle being suspended but you are just starting out."

"Jon," she said. "You're my partner. I'm with you."

"Then let's get down to business, partner."

———————

Later that evening, Scott and Jon were deep in a chess game while Kim and Courtney read. Beth had brought her laptop out and was sitting at the table furiously typing. Ryan broke the silence.

"Have you heard anything from Uncle Mat?" he asked.

"No," Jon replied. "I haven't heard anything."

"Should you call him?" Scott leaned forward.

"No," Jon answered, still focused on the chessboard. "He walked out on us. He can call if he wants."

"But I didn't give him much of a choice," Scott said.

"You gave him a chance. You couldn't make him leave if he didn't want to leave."

"But," Scott started. "He's my uncle. He's a part of Mom."

Jon paused for a moment. "I know. And I hate it as much as you do. But he made his choice. He knows where we are and he has our number. If he wanted to contact us, he would." Jon moved his remaining knight on the board. "Check," he said.

Scott's eyes lit up and he grinned. Moving his bishop, he spoke again. "Check and mate."

Everyone looked over. Scott very rarely beat Jon at chess. Leaning forward, studying the board, Jon laughed and sat back.

"Good game," he said flicking his king over.

"It was relatively simple," Scott teased.

"Yeah, yeah whatever," Jon waved him off.

"White queen's bishop to black king's knight four," Scott labeled the move.

Jon froze. "What did you say?" Jon whispered. Courtney walked over to him.

"What is it?" she asked.

"Scott," Jon turned. "Did you ever play chess with your uncle?"

"No," Scott replied. "I can barely beat you even when you let me. Do you honestly think I could play against his mastermind?"

"I played against him a couple times, Uncle Jon," Ryan stepped forward. "He was quick."

"In Vietnam, his code name was White Queen's Bishop," Jon answered. "Our CO was obsessed with chess. He would play all of us. Mat was White Queen's Bishop, and I was Black King's Knight."

"The note left at the crime scene," Courtney stated.

"Exactly, Mat's trying to get a message to me."

"But why Dr. Albert? Was he wounded in the Easter Offensive?" Courtney asked.

"Yes, Mat, Billy, Commander Albert, and I were wounded, but not on the same day," Jon said. "The offensive lasted from March to October."

"There's gotta be something specific," Scott said. "Something that could have stayed covered up until now, something that affected Uncle Mat."

Jon thought a moment. "I've got to talk with Jake Simpson again," he said.

"I understand why you feel you have to go, Dad," Scott was saying as he sat on the edge of his dad's bed while Jon tied his tie. "I just don't like the idea. Why can't you call someone else, like Dave to do the leg work?"

"He was wounded at the Offensive too, Scott," Jon replied. "And I wouldn't want to put him in that type of situation."

"Dad, Dave Weston is the king of this type of situation."

"He's well connected, I agree," Jon replied. "Look, I'll be the first one to praise my friend and former CO but he's not a miracle worker, he's just an average guy with an above average ability to make everyone think they're his best friend. But this time it's up to Courtney and me."

"But why?" Scott asked.

"I know you're worried," Jon said. "But you have to believe me. I promise you it will all be all right. We'll be home before you know it."

"It's not just worry, Dad, it's… Ryan got a call from the hospital and he's heading out. I'm gonna be here alone with Beth and Kim."

"That's not a bad thing." Jon smiled.

"No," Scott replied. "But I feel useless. My Celtic and

Spanish blood is boiling and I need to fight."

Jon chuckled. "I know. But I need someone to stay with the women. That's my commission for you."

"I have a case going to trial in less than a month. I've already had to reschedule a lot of consults. I need to go to my offices to make sure everything is running smoothly."

"Alex and Tom can do that," Jon replied.

"It's not the same."

"Scott," Jon sighed sitting beside him to pull on his shoes. "Ryan has the entire hospital to protect him. You're an easy target and I can't have anything happen to you."

Scott was quiet for a moment. "Okay, I won't argue but God I'll be glad when we go to Ireland. I need a break from the insanity."

"I know it," Jon replied standing and going to the door.

"Dad," Scott said called him back. "Am I totally crazy?"

"That depends," he answered, smiling.

"I think I'm in love with my best friend," Scott replied.

"Kim?" he asked.

"No, Alex," Scott rolled his eyes. "Of course Kim."

Jon chuckled. "You don't know where Alex has been, I'm glad," he winked.

"Shut up," Scott laughed. "I'm trying to be serious for once."

"You know I've always thought she was the one for you. But if I may, give it time, Scott," Jon counseled. "She doesn't deserve to be a rebound."

"I know," Scott admitted. "Am I really in love with her, or am I feeling insecure because of my breakup?"

"She loves you," he said. "Could you be realizing you've loved her all along and no other woman has measured up to her?" Scott said nothing as he listened to his father. "Think on it. Courtney and I will be back later."

Chapter
Twenty-Five

Following Jon and Courtney was easy. Aeron pulled out his phone and hit redial.

"Yeah?" Rob asked.

"I'm following them," Aeron answered.

"And?"

"I'll have a perfect shot on her," he said.

"Good," was the reply.

"How did you want it?"

"Two in the chest," he answered. "The others were sloppy. His wife was still alive when he got to her. Make sure he doesn't have a chance to say good-bye. And you sure as hell better not miss."

"You can trust me," Aeron replied.

"You know what will happen if I can't," Rob answered, and he hung up the phone.

Jon and Courtney walked up the driveway together and Jon knocked. Officer Harding opened the door and grinned.

"Lieutenant, Detective," he said. "It is good to see you. What are you doing so far out of your jurisdiction?"

"They're old friends of mine and I wanted to pay my

respects," Jon lied.

"Of course, sir. The captain's with them now. He says he knows them too."

"Yes, their brother served with us," Jon explained.

"Oh right, I'm sorry for your loss."

"Thank you."

Harding stepped aside allowing them to enter.

"You know, Courtney was telling me you were a high rank in your division on accuracy. Is that true?" Jon asked.

Courtney did not react. Jon was up to something.

"She talks about me?" Harding asked.

"All the time," Jon replied. She wanted to kick his shins.

"Well, I'm second right now. Working on getting better."

"My partner said she was very impressed with you," Jon went on. *Or maybe the balls... yeah, balls, definitely,* she thought.

"She did?" Harding asked, smirking.

"Yes," Jon answered. "Didn't you, Courtney?"

"Yes, of course," Courtney smiled tightly.

"Mmhmm," Jon replied. "I was wondering, Harding, if you could explain to my partner here about the way a gun backfires when you're firing rapid rounds and the instinctual reaction you have to close your eyes. She doesn't believe me."

"I would love to," Harding said. "Maybe we could talk in the kitchen."

"Great." She looked back at Jon after Harding turned. "You will regret this," she mouthed. Almost instinctually, Jon covered his lower region with his hands.

Once Courtney and Harding disappeared around the corner, Jon walked on toward the low, droning voices. Mat was talking to Jake. He turned slightly acknowledging that he knew Jon was there.

"Jon, thank god you're here," Jake greeted him with a hand shake. "Mat's just been asking some questions. You knew my brother very well. Maybe you could help answer some."

"I'll do what I can, Jake," Jon replied.

Mat looked at him and Jon noticed the bruises Mat had tried to hide with makeup. Going off of the state of Scott's hands, Mat's injuries were fairly severe.

"What are you doing here?" Mat's voice brought him back to the present.

"I came to pay my respects," Jon replied.

Mat stared at him but behind those cold dark eyes was a scared look he was doing an excellent job covering.

"Mat was asking if there was anything in Billy's past that might have been a catalyst for what happened," Jake explained.

Jon looked at Mat for a long moment. "I can't say I know of anything. He was a great guy," Jon replied.

Mat never dropped his gaze. "I was wondering if there could have been anything that happened in Vietnam that might have a bearing on this now," Mat said.

"Not to my knowledge," Jon answered. Mat stared into his eyes and Jon nodded once. "Wasn't there something during the Easter Offensive?" Jon offered. Relief flooded Mat's eyes. "Something he saw?" Jon tested.

"Like what?" Mat prompted.

"Something to do with the enemy?"

"No," Mat replied. "I don't think so."

"You're right," Jon picked up on his reply. "Something about friendly fire?" He offered.

Mat nodded slowly. "That sounds more like it."

"Right, I remember," Jon lied. "Something happened that Billy saw."

"Did you see it too?" Jake asked oblivious to their exchange.

"I don't think so," Jon replied.

"You must have," Mat answered.

"I don't remember," Jon said.

Mat finally looked away then turned to Jake. "Well, that's all I came for," Mat said. "Sorry to have bothered you, Jake. I'll see myself out."

After Mat left the room, Jon put a hand on Jake's shoulder. "I'll be right back," he said and followed Mat out of the house.

———

Mat quickly walked down the drive to his car when Jon called after him. He froze and turned as Jon jogged up. "What are you doing here?"

"What are you?" Mat asked harshly. "I took you off this case."

"Level with me, Mat," Jon started. "What's going on?"

"Nothing," Mat answered.

"I know you better than that," Jon replied.

Mat looked down, put his hands on his hips, and sighed. "I don't have anything to say to you, Jon," Mat said.

Jon watched him. "Whatever it is you're doing, I hope it's worth it," Jon replied. "You are my best friend. Scott and I love you. You're part of this family. You're part of Carol." Jon waited seeing his friend look away. "If you're in trouble, we can help. Just tell me."

"There's nothing to tell, Jon," Mat said. "You and me, we're like two pawns on a chess board, facing each other; neither one can be captured. And there's nothing more powerful behind you," Mat answered.

Jon's eyes widened for a split second as Mat looked directly at him. Jon nodded. "Well, I hope you know what you're doing," Jon said. "I hope it's worth it."

Mat said nothing for a moment then continued, "are you going to Ireland for St. Patrick's Day?"

"I always do," he replied.

"Scott, Ryan, and everyone going with you?" Mat asked.

Jon's brows furrowed. "I'm not sure."

"I think Scott could use some time away from work," Mat said.

"I'll tell him," he promised.

Mat nodded, paused a moment, and then looked down. "You'd better get inside," Mat said. "It's cold out here."

"You've got to keep both eyes open when you shoot. It gives you the best accuracy," Officer Harding explained to Courtney in the kitchen.

"Yeah," Courtney forced a smile, but when she saw Jon leaning against the door, she continued. "Did you need me, Jon?"

Jon smiled as Harding looked up and disappointment entered his eyes. "If you can be spared, I could use my partner," he said.

"I think I can," Courtney replied then turned back to Office Harding. "Thank you, Justin, for explaining some things to me."

"I enjoyed it, Courtney," he winked. "Sorry. Detective. Maybe we could get a coffee sometime?"

"No, I'm still dating someone," she answered.

"Awe, come on," he replied. "When are you going to leave him and run away with me?"

"Never," she answered and turned back to Jon. "Ready when you are." Jon nodded and left the room to say goodbye to Jake.

"Get down!" Justin cried as he pushed her forward, knocking her out of the way.

Glass shattered, someone screamed. There was another loud noise and then a thud. Courtney grabbed her gun and turned around. The window had shattered and Justin lay on his back, blood spilling out of his chest.

"Justin!" She screamed and hurried to him keeping her eyes fixed on the tree line outside. "Officer down!"

Jon ran back into the kitchen. "Courtney?"

"Officer down, call an ambulance," Courtney shouted.

Jon pulled out his cell phone and dialed as Courtney grabbed some kitchen towels and applied pressure to the wounds.

Chapter Twenty-Six

Ryan walked into the hospital's doctor's lounge and saw Fred, his mentor and boss during his residency, nursing a cup of coffee.

"Is it any good?" Ryan asked him.

"It's cold," Fred replied, grimacing. "But it's caffeine."

"How long have you been on call?" Ryan asked, pouring himself a cup.

"Forty hours, thirty-two minutes, and... six seconds," Fred replied. "I was at home, and then we had that pile-up on the highway and came in."

"Only seven and a half hours to go," Ryan said.

Fred grimaced at the cold coffee and nodded. "Yeah, thank god. I can't wait to have some real coffee."

"I'm sure you can have some when you get back home," Ryan replied.

"No, probably not," he replied. "I'll just want to sleep when I get home."

"I can imagine."

"How are you and Courtney?" Fred asked, changing the subject. "Do I hear wedding bells in the near future?"

"Soon," he replied. "With that new position I have an

interview for… not that I'm planning on an offer, but it would help."

"I'm sure you will have it, it's perfect for you. If I have anything to say about it," Fred winked. "It's yours."

"Thank you," Ryan said.

"It's well deserved."

"Dr. Marcellino, you have a phone call on line one. Dr. Marcellino, you have a phone call on line one," the voice over the intercom called.

Ryan nodded to his mentor, pulled out his cell phone and saw several missed calls from Courtney and his uncle.

"I gotta go," he said not looking up from his cell.

Fred nodded. Ryan downed his coffee and walked to the nurses' station.

Aeron's cell phone rang but he resisted answering it when he saw who it was. Expecting a torrent of curses and the third degree, he finally answered.

"Yes?" he said.

"Did I make a mistake?" Rob asked calmly.

"With what?"

"Don't play coy with me," his voice was low. "I expected more from you. You were in the IRA."

"I'm aware," Aeron replied.

"Then maybe you need some practice. Why is she still alive?" Rob asked.

"Because the idiot I shot pushed her out of the way," Aeron answered. "If you notice, he was standing right where she was when he was shot. So technically I didn't miss."

"Don't try and be cute," Rob replied. "You have one mission. We cannot have all of this collateral damage. First the FedEx guy to satisfy some deranged need of yours and now an officer. You need to get your mind back on track and get that sniper's eye of yours on the end game."

"He's running scared already," Aeron said. "What do you want to do next? Keep to the plan and move to the next or do you want me to try and get her?"

"Move to the next," Rob replied. "And pray you don't screw this one up."

———————

"This is getting ridiculous!" Ryan ran down to the basement. Racing to Courtney, he framed her face to make sure she was all right.

"I'm fine," she replied and gently pulled away from him. Grabbing her hand, he held it tightly.

"I completely understand your fear, Ryan," Jon said. "Fortunately, Courtney is all right. It's Justin Harding's family that needs your anger. They lost their son."

"And as much as I grieve for them, they're not my family," Ryan said. "You and Courtney are."

"I'm not a delicate flower, guys," Courtney replied. "I'm a cop. If you can't handle the risks that I may never come home then I'm sorry."

"Dammit, Courtney I can handle the risks," Ryan answered. "But it doesn't mean I have to stop caring about you. I will not stop worrying about you."

"We need to speak in private," Courtney said.

"I am not going to stop, love, don't even think about it," Ryan replied.

"I need to speak with you," Courtney pressed.

Ryan thrust a hand through his hair and nodded. Courtney led the way to one of the rooms and shut the door.

"I'm not going to let you tell me to stop," Ryan said. "I love you and I'm not going to—"

"Shut up and kiss me," Courtney ordered. Ryan blinked when she wrapped her arms around his neck and leaned up. "I love you. I love that you worry about me, but I need to keep a strong front with them," she nodded towards the door. "I was scared as hell and all I could think of was if I died I would never know you truly and that is something I refuse to give up. Our future, our love."

Ryan wrapped his arms around her waist. "I am ready whenever you are," he said softly kissing her nose.

"Don't tempt me," she replied. "I know it's old school and probably stupid but I've always waited. Though, I've never been tempted as much as I am with you."

"Me neither," he answered. "I love you and I want to start our life together."

"So do I," she said. "But can we wait until we're engaged?"

"We can wait for as long as you want," he replied. "But I'm not going to give up worrying about you."

"I love that about you," she said and closed the gap between them.

"Do you think they're all right?" Beth asked sliding her arm through Jon's.

"Yes," Jon answered. "She didn't want him to smother her in front of me. She thinks she still needs to prove something to me."

Nodding, Beth looked up at him. "What are you going to do?"

"I think I'm going to call Rick and talk things out with him. When Courtney's done, have her join me in the office?"

"Will do," Beth answered.

"Well, that's quite a tale," Rick said. "Have you thought about what Mat meant?"

"All the time," Jon replied. "I'm trying to consider if it was a message like the note or if it was simply him being... well, him."

"What does your gut tell you?" Rick asked.

"He's telling me something," Jon admitted.

"Okay so, looking at it like that, what are the facts? Mat's been a good friend to you. He's been your brother when I failed. He was with you in Vietnam, at your wedding, when Scott was born, at Carol's funeral and has continued to be with you during this whole time. In my opinion, that is no' the behavior of a man who is trying to hurt you. Look at it this way; he could have said anything to you but he chose to ask if you were going to Ireland and if everyone would be joining you. Why?"

"Something he knows? Something might happen or something connected with Ireland."

"Okay, let's go with that. So, he wanted you to think about Ireland. And he wanted to make sure you take everyone with you. A warning?"

"He said everyone but he focused on Scott."

"Grand, so what does that mean? Ireland and Scott."

Jon thought a moment before he answered. "Could this whole thing be to get Scott out of the country, away from work... but why? What's at work?"

"Is he working on a case that could be tied to this?"

"I'll have to ask him," Jon said. "Mat changed so drastically overnight it seemed."

"And what causes a man like that to change so drastically, so suddenly? When did he change?"

"The night Billy died, or the morning after, he was different. He told me he had a date and it was that next day he was different."

"Who did he meet that night?" Rick asked.

"There was a woman, but she seemed harmless. I remember she had cats," Jon said. "Mat hates cats."

"Were the lads there?" Rick asked.

"Aye," Jon answered. "I'll ask them. Maybe Mat said something more to them."

"Glad to help," Rick chuckled. There was a knock at the door and Jon looked up to see Courtney waiting for him.

"Thank you, Rick," Jon said. "I owe you a pint when we get to Ireland."

"I'll hold you to that," Rick replied. "See you soon. Give my love to everyone."

"And ours to Jenny and Sarah."

Chapter
Twenty-Seven

"Scott." Jon called opening the door without knocking.

Scott held up his hand to stop his dad from saying anything as he spoke into his work cell phone.

"Mmhmm," Scott stated. "No. I understand, Mr. Harrison and I agree entirely... No, I don't think it's out of the possibilities but we'll have to... Mmhmm, well, let me see what I can discover and I'll call you back, say, Friday same time? Excellent." Scott leaned over his black appointment book and wrote something. "Thank you, Mr. Harrison, and thank you for agreeing to meet like this, I apologize I could not meet with you in person. I appreciate it. Bye," Scott hung up his phone and looked at his dad.

"Sorry," Jon replied. "I should have knocked."

"No worries," Scott answered, smiling. "What's up?"

"Do you need a second to write anything down?" Jon asked.

"Got it all written up already and I always record the calls on my cell," Scott answered. "Everything all right?" His eyes drifted to Courtney standing behind Jon.

"You remember the day Billy died? Mat had come over and he talked about his date. You and he were talking for a little while."

"Yeah," Scott replied. "What about it?"

"Do you remember the name of the woman?" Jon asked.

"No, I don't," Scott apologized, standing and gathering his papers.

"Do you remember what he said about her?" Jon asked.

"I kinda tuned him out, I didn't want to hear about old man sex," Scott said.

"Old man sex?" Jon raised an eyebrow.

"Yeah, it's gross," Scott teased.

"Okay sure, we'll discuss this when you're in your fifties," Jon replied. "Anyway, you don't remember anything he said?"

"He said that it was okay but probably no second date," Ryan said from behind his uncle.

"What does that tell you?" Scott asked.

"He was talking about it before you both got home, trying to get my mind from what had happened with Billy. As you both know Mat is very physical with the women he dates. He said they didn't sleep together, but I remember seeing cat hair on the inside collar of his shirt."

"Didn't the woman live with a ton of cats? He was bound to get hair on his collar," Scott stated.

"True, but it was on his shirt collar, which means he would have needed to take his shirt off."

"So that means they slept together," Ryan said.

"Infers," Jon answered. "But why wouldn't he say that? He's never been shy telling me about his women. So why this one? What was it about her he wanted to hide? It was that next morning he changed. He was different. Angry, secretive. Why the change?"

"Could she have said or done something to him or known something about him?" Courtney offered.

"Possibly," Jon replied.

"What do you want to do?" Courtney asked.

"I want to find her and talk to her," Jon said. "I spoke with her and she told me her name but I can't remember it. Scott, did Mat tell you her name?"

"Hannah? Anna? Something like that," Scott said.

"Hannah Turner," Ryan answered.

They all looked at him. "What?" he asked. "I remember random stuff like that."

———————

Jon called in a favor from one of his friends at the precinct and had them to run a check on a Hannah Turner. They came up with ten in the general metropolitan area. They narrowed it down to five between the ages of twenty-six and sixty.

"I just don't think that the captain would date a twenty-six year old," Courtney stated as they drove.

Jon scoffed. "You don't know the captain, Courtney. He's dated younger than that."

"I just don't believe it," she replied.

"Well, believe it. I've gone out with him and his twenty-one year old girlfriend. Okay?" Jon said. "Awkward is too tame a word."

"Yeah but, no offense, how long ago was that?" she asked.

"Six months ago," he replied.

Courtney's eyes grew wide and she looked back at Ryan in the backseat, who simply nodded.

"Oh," she replied. "I guess… wow."

"Yeah," Jon sighed. "So every woman on that list, that's legal anyway, is of interest."

"Okay, the first Hannah that we're talking to is twenty-six years old and a journalist for Indy Nuvo magazine," Courtney explained.

"Journalist?" Jon asked.

"Yeah," she replied.

"We can safely skip that one. Mat's not going to date someone who could portray the precinct in a negative way if the breakup ends badly," Jon replied. "He at least has decent judgment on that."

"Okay," Courtney replied crossing that name off. "Then the next is a twenty-eight year old businesswoman, works for Liberty Mutual."

"That's a possibility," he said.

"It's Saturday. She's probably at home. North Meridian."

After speaking with Ms. Turner at her home, they thanked her for her time and left. She had no connection with Mat. Jon and Courtney did not get into the car and after Jon passed Ryan the keys, his nephew got in and turned the heater on.

"What are you thinking?" Courtney asked her partner.

"Let me see the list again," Jon said.

She handed him the names. "What are you doing?"

"I'm trying to get inside Mat's head," Jon explained.

"So think of every woman as a conquest," Courtney said.

"That shouldn't be too difficult since, before I was married, that's exactly what I did think," he replied. "Okay," he looked back at the papers and flipped through the driver's license pictures. Taking a pen from his lapel pocket, he began crossing out faces.

Courtney didn't interrupt but opened the car door and got in to warm her hands at the heater vent. Ryan took her hand in his to warm.

"I'm glad you came with us," Courtney said.

"Thought you might need a doctor, just in case," he replied.

"Never know," Courtney stated. "We could be dealing with someone in need of psychological help."

"Quite possibly," he answered.

"Very probable," Jon replied stepping closer. "I've narrowed it down. There's one on here that Albert spoke of last month. She was an inmate at Northwestern Psychiatric Facility. Apparently, she escaped, or I should say, left without permission or their knowledge. She lives on Pennsylvania Street."

"Pennsylvania?" Ryan asked.

"Yep," Jon replied.

"Is that important?" Courtney asked.

"Uncle Mat lives on Pennsylvania Street," Ryan replied.

"You drive, Ryan," Jon got in the backseat.

"Here they come," Aeron said to her over the phone. "You know what to do."

"Unchanged?" Hannah asked.

"Unchanged," he said. "You can do it?"

"Definitely."

He heard the determination in her voice.

"That's my girl," he said. "I'll be here for you when it's over."

"I love you," she said.

"I love you too, baby," he lied. "Now, they're parking down the road. Be ready."

Ryan pulled onto Pennsylvania and found the address on the driver's license three doors down from Mat's house.

"Drive on a bit," Jon said. "Mat's home, but he's not alone. I think she's with him."

Ryan drove on, pulled to the side of the narrow road and parked the car.

"How do you know he's not alone?" Courtney asked.

"As Police Captain, he has a system of notification. Cops patrol this area, watching out for him. His code is; if the door is open to the screen, he's home alone and willing to have people come over for a drink or coffee. The door closed and the light on in the front room means he's home but he's entertaining. The porch lights on and door shut, he's not home," Jon explained.

"So the door is closed and the light is not on, nor is the porch light," Courtney said.

"A warning," Jon replied. "He's asking for any patrol car to come and knock on the door. He needs help."

"How do you want to do this?" Courtney asked.

"I don't want to spook her," Jon said. "We approach as if we were in the area and ask for a coffee or drink or whatever. He'll know we got his message."

Jon reached over the backseat and pulled out three bulletproof vests.

"Put these on," he ordered. "Under your sweater, Ryan." Ryan nodded and tugged his sweater off. Courtney and Jon pulled off their suit jackets and strapped the Kevlar vest on.

"Let me do the talking. We get in, grab him if necessary and get out."

"Arrest him if we have to," Courtney said.

"Anything," Jon replied.

"Okay," Ryan replied. "Let's do this."

Chapter
Twenty-Eight

Scott sat on the couch, bored out of his mind. He looked over at Kim as she talked with her mom by the kitchenette. His chest ached and he didn't know why. He had the strangest urge to pull her into his arms and kiss her. Looking away, he listened to his head. She didn't deserve to be a rebound and he sure as hell wanted more than just a quick hookup with her. He thought about bolting to the door and heading down to Broadripple, the artsy and eclectic side of town just a stone's throw away from Butler University, but Jon would be worried sick about him.

Staying put, an idea occurred to him. He stood and went to the office. Shutting the door, he pulled out his phone and scrolled through the numbers. He stopped on a name, *Tio Mateo* and pressed call.

Jon pushed the doorbell and tapped on the screen. It was a few seconds before they heard anything. The bolt slid back and the knob turned. Slowly the door opened and Mat stood there. His eyes grew wide for a split second then his features relaxed.

"Jon," he stated. "What are you doing here?"

"We were in the neighborhood and thought we'd stop by for a drink," Jon said.

"I don't have anything to offer," Mat answered. "I'm afraid I'm a little busy at the moment. Maybe come back later?"

"I just thought we could talk," Jon replied, moving his jacket so Mat could see his gun and vest. Mat shook his head ever so slightly.

"Let them in, Mat," a woman's voice called from inside. "We just opened the wine."

Mat closed his eyes for a moment, then plastered a smile on his face.

"Sure, babe," he replied then unlocked the screen and opened the door. Jon buttoned up his coat to hide the vest as he walked in. Mat led the way into the living room. When they turned the corner, a forty year old, red haired, dark eyed woman greeted them as she sat on the couch.

"Is this Jon?" she asked Mat. Mat just nodded. "Well, it's a pleasure to meet you, Jon. I'm Hannah."

"It's nice to meet you, Hannah," Jon replied. "Sorry if we were interrupting anything, we were in the area and thought we'd pop over for a chinwag or whatever it is you Americans say." Courtney noticed how he thickened his slight Irish accent.

Hannah froze when she heard him but then stood and walked over to Mat, sliding her hand through his arm.

"You never told me he had a hot accent," she said.

"I didn't?" Mat replied. "Must have slipped my mind."

"One thing you did get right is that he would make any woman swoon," Hannah eyed Jon up and down. Jon hooded his eyes and took a step closer to her.

"I'm afraid Mat hasn't mentioned you," he said. "I can see why, he didn't want any competition. What are you doing with a guy like him? I would light up your world."

Even Courtney suppressed a shiver that ran up her spine at Jon's low, thick Irish voice. Hannah licked her lips and took a step forward.

"What can I do for you, Jon?" Hannah asked.

"Dangerous question to ask," Jon replied his voice still heavy.

"I mean, why are you here?" she clarified.

"I wanted to talk to my friend," he said. "And now you."

"You are handsome, but the accent doesn't do anything for me, I have my own Irishman," she revealed, then her eyes grew wide and she took several steps back.

Suddenly, she pulled out a gun and aimed it at Jon.

"Hannah," Mat cried. "What the hell are you doing?"

"Shut up," she replied. "You think I don't know what you're doing? Trying to distract me so I give you information? Trying to get Mat away from me? It may surprise you to know that your precious captain is up to his eyeballs in scandal. He was right there when Albert was killed. In fact, his prints are all over the kitchen."

"Hannah, please," Mat begged.

"Shut it, pretty boy," she replied.

Jon took a step closer to her. "You wanna shoot me? I know you or your lover boy tried ever since that night you killed Billy. Irish is he?" Her eyes flashed with fear. "Oh no, there's someone else. Someone you both are answerable to. You fear him."

"Shut up, shut up, shut up, shut up!" She screeched. Mat's cell phone rang a familiar song just as a gun went off.

Ryan watched the scene unfold. The woman was clearly disturbed. His Hippocratic Oath urged him to help her but when she pulled out the gun, his familial connection with Jon, Mat and Courtney overtook his instinct. When she started screaming, he raced forward and wrestled the gun away from her. There was a loud bang and pain like he had never experienced raced through his chest. The force threw him onto his back. He wasn't sure what had happened but it was hard to breathe.

"Ryan!" Courtney shrieked.

Hannah screamed and ran out of the room, yelling the name Chris. Courtney drew her gun and aimed. Mat stepped in front.

"Get out of the way," she shouted.

"No," Mat replied. "If you want to shoot her you need to shoot me first, Detective."

"Captain," she started.

"Trust me," Mat said.

"I hope you know what you're doing," Jon yelled from Ryan's side. "Courtney, help me!" Jon and Mat locked eyes and Mat raced after Hannah.

"Ryan, Ryan, talk to me," Courtney knelt beside him, his forearm draped across his eyes.

"I can't right now, baby," he answered between clenched teeth.

"What the hell were you thinking?" Jon demanded examining his chest. "Thank God, the vest caught it."

"I wasn't going to let her shoot you," Ryan said.

"So you jump in front and wrestle the damn gun?" Jon challenged.

"To save you? Yes," Ryan coughed then groaned. "Can't... breathe well."

"Is anything broken?" Jon asked.

Ryan breathed and groaned. "Not sure."

"Can you get up?" Jon asked.

Ryan nodded slowly and rolled to his side. Jon helped him up, but stopped when Ryan cried out in pain as he stood.

"Courtney, call an ambulance," Jon ordered.

Ryan shook his head. "No, no. Just get me to St. Vincent's," Ryan said. "If we call an ambulance, there will be too many questions."

"Put your arms around my neck," Jon said, getting into position to take all of Ryan's weight. Ryan did as Jon asked and groaned when his uncle lifted him.

"Where are the keys?" Courtney asked.

"In my pocket," Ryan replied. Courtney retrieved them and ran ahead to pull the car up to the curb. Ryan laid down in the backseat.

"Is Fred working today?" Courtney asked. Ryan nodded.

"Good," Jon replied taking his seat behind the wheel. "Courtney, get him on the phone and tell him what happened."

"Have them prepare a morphine drip," Ryan instructed. "I'll need an x-ray and an MRI to check for any internal bleeding."

Courtney said nothing, just took her boyfriend's phone from his pocket and dialed.

"Hey, buddy. How's it going?" Fred answered.

"Fred, it's Courtney," she said.

"Oh hey, Courtney. What's up?" he asked. "Is everything okay?"

"No, we're heading to the hospital now. Ryan needs you."

"What happened?" he asked, concerned.

"He says he needs you to set up a morphine drip, x-ray and MRI."

"Courtney, I need to know what I'm working with," Fred said. "Is he bleeding?"

"No," Courtney replied.

"What does he think is broken?"

"A rib," she said.

"Internal bleeding?"

"Not sure," she said.

"How did this happen?"

"Listen," she said. "We can't have any questions."

"I need to know what happened. Even if I don't report it, I need to know."

"Tell him," Ryan groaned when Jon swerved to avoid a pot hole.

Courtney glanced at Jon who nodded once. Listening to everything that happened, Fred said nothing until she finished.

"Okay. What's your ETA?" Fred asked.

"Five minutes," she answered.

"Okay," Fred replied. "I'm getting a room set up for him and a team of nurses with me to be ready for him. Come to the south entrance. I'll be keeping an eye out for the black Escalade."

Five minutes later, Jon pulled into the south entrance and the car was swarmed by nurses and Dr. Fred Sullivan. They pulled Ryan slowly out of the backseat and onto a gurney.

"It's all right, buddy," Fred said. "We gotcha. You're gonna be all right." They rolled Ryan's gurney into the hospital followed closely by Jon and Courtney. Jon pulled out his phone and dialed Scott's number.

―――――――

"I did shoot him!" she screamed. "But he had a vest on!"

"I believe you, baby," Aeron said, rubbing her arms, calming her down as she stood in front of him. She looked at Rob who took a deep slow breath.

"I ask both of you to do one thing, kill the people closest to Jonathan Greene, and you can't do that," Rob said. "I'm beginning to wonder if I picked the right people."

"You will not get in the way of my revenge," Aeron said, standing from his stool.

"Oh, no?" Rob stated. "And what about the end game? You want to give that up?"

Aeron walked over to Rob and stood face-to-face with him, staring him down.

"None of this would have happened if you had just let me do my thing. Jon would not be alive right now if I was in charge."

"And that's why you're not," Rob replied. "Do you want a

quick death for the man who cheated you out of your birthright?"

"I'm not some puppet you can pull the strings and move," Aeron said.

"No," Rob answered. "Perhaps not, but I am someone who would not hesitate to call the police to report illegal activity."

"Try it, we'll take you down with us," Aeron replied.

"Oh? And just how do you plan to do that? You don't honestly think I gave you my real name, do you?"

"I know where you work."

"And what an upstanding citizen I am," Rob grinned. "No one will believe you." His face went hard. "So do as I say."

Chapter
Twenty-Nine

One week later

"Are you sure it's safe for you to fly?" Courtney asked as she helped Ryan pack for the trip to Ireland.

"Yeah, Fred said nothing was broken," Ryan replied. "And as bruised as I am, I'm not missing our trip."

"Why are you so adamant to go?" Courtney asked pausing for a moment and looking over at him sitting on the bed.

"Because I love it over there," he answered.

"But we could go again any other time," Courtney sat down beside his knee. "I wish you would take better care of yourself."

Leaning forward slowly, he stroked her face. "I know, baby," he said. "But I want to go. There's a good reason, trust me," he smiled. "Besides you have never been and I'm not about to let you go without me."

"I wouldn't," she replied. "I'm just worried about you."

"Don't be," Ryan kissed her softly. "I promise I'm all right. Now, let's go out and get a drink. I want to spoil my girl. The flight will wear me out, I'll not lie but I would rather have a great night out on the town than lie here all night not moving."

Courtney smiled lightly. "Okay," she gave up. "I'll not argue with you anymore."

"Promise?" he teased.

"Don't push it, mister," she replied.

———————

Jon led the way through the Indianapolis airport terminal and through security. As they waited at their gate, Jon took orders for Starbucks as it was barely six thirty. Their flight to New York City was on time according to the screen above the desk. Courtney checked her boarding passes, they would land at JFK around ten. Jon had planned everything out so they would have a full day and a half in New York both going and coming back.

Looking up when she heard Jon and Scott laugh as they walked back carrying a couple drink carriers, her mom sat beside her.

"I'm so glad you and dad could come with us," Courtney said.

"I wasn't about to let you have all the fun, sweetie," her mom smiled. "As much as I want to visit Ireland, I can't wait to see Scotland."

"Don't worry, I'm not unbelievably jealous," Courtney replied.

"You said you couldn't get the time off," her mom winked. "We would love to have you and Ryan join us."

"I'll see what we can do," she bumped her shoulder to her mom's. "Besides I have a feeling Ryan and I will be a lot closer after this trip."

"You think he's going to propose?" her mom whispered excitedly.

"I think it's a possibility," she answered. "I tried to get him to tell me why he was so adamant about going considering his injury and he wouldn't tell me."

"Oh sweetie, I hope so!" her mom clutched her hand.

"So if we are, maybe we can join you at least for part of the time in Scotland. You're doing a chauffeured tour, right?"

"Yes, a friend of your brothers offered to drive us so there would be plenty of room for you two."

"If it happens, I'll talk to Jon and see if he could do without me at least for a few days."

"If what happens?" Jon startled her. Looking over, her partner was offering a coffee.

"If something happens with the case," Courtney covered, glancing over at her mom. "Mom and Dad are going on a tour of Scotland after Ireland. I would love to go with them but it depends on the case."

"What case?" Jon teased. "We were pulled from that one, remember? I don't think there's anything pressing currently."

***

Scott handed Beth and Kim their coffees. When Kim smiled brightly at him, he blinked at the feeling stirring inside him. Beth took her leave and walked back towards Jon. They were alone.

"Are you excited?" Kim asked.

"Yeah," Scott answered.

"Me too," she replied. "I love this time of year with you guys."

"So do I and hey it's your birthday in a few days."

"Glad you remembered," she winked. His hand grew sweaty around the paper cup and he swallowed his chai tea awkwardly.

"So I owe you a shot," Scott said.

"Maybe one," she grinned. "Wouldn't want to get frisky." Reaching out, she tickled his stomach.

"What?" his reply was strangled.

"What's up with you?" She pulled back. "You're normally not so jumpy. Are you feeling okay?"

"Fine," he answered.

"Okay," Kim drawled. "Well, I'm gonna go sit with

mom."

"You look great today, by the way," Scott said.

"Oh," her eyes clouded with confusion when she looked up at him. "Thanks."

"I like that, um… sweater-thing you're wearing," he stumbled.

"You've seen me in this a thousand times, but um… thanks," she replied.

Scott watched her walk away and locked eyes with his father. Huffing a sigh, he thrust a hand through his hair and went into one of the gift shops.

"You okay?" Jon asked as he and Scott strapped into their seats in First Class.

"Yeah," he answered, the awkwardness he had felt earlier had not quite disappeared.

"I noticed some awkwardness between you and Kim earlier."

"I don't know where that's coming from," Scott admitted.

"You're over thinking it. If what you told me last week is on your mind every time you look at her you'll think about that. Let it go and let it happen if it's supposed to happen."

"But how?" Scott asked.

"Don't let your feelings change how you treat her. You'll lose her. She hasn't let her feelings for you change how she treats you."

Scott sighed. "Yeah, you're right. What do I do?"

"Be yourself and if you start feeling those nerves or whatever it is you're feeling, think of something else."

"That's just it. All of my memories with her are now…" he glanced over to make sure she wasn't listening. "Erotic."

Jon chuckled. "Oh son, believe me when I tell you, you get that honestly."

"From you?"

"From your mother," he winked.

"How about you and Beth? Have you guys…"

"No, not yet," he answered.

"Maybe the romance of Ireland might jump start that little issue."

"What issue?" Jon asked.

"Well, I mean at your age…"

"Ha, yeah that's not an issue. Never has been."

"Glad to hear it, since it is hereditary," Scott teased.

Jon rolled his eyes but didn't respond as the flight attendant began speaking and demonstrating the safety features.

Chapter
Thirty

Courtney could not hold in her excitement as they boarded the early evening flight from JFK to Shannon airport. The fact that they had their own personal TVs in the seat in front of them and free drinks didn't help her excitement.

After choosing a movie to watch, she ordered a glass of champagne and settled into the seat. After a moment, her mother touched her arm and she looked over taking her earbuds out. Ryan stood in the aisle.

"I'm going to go sit with your dad, sweetheart," her mother said. Courtney nodded and watched Ryan and her mom switch places. Ryan settled into the seat beside her with his drink in hand. Resting her head on his shoulder she sighed.

"Happy, baby?" he asked resting his on top of hers.

"Very," she answered.

"Can I get you a refill?" the flight attendant offered as he came around.

"That would be great," Courtney replied. "Champagne, brut."

"And sir?"

"Godfather, neat," Ryan ordered. The attendant nodded and walked away to fill their order. Ryan wrapped his arm around

Courtney, pulled her closer to him and kissed her hair. "I love you."

She hummed happily. "I love you too," she said.

"When we get to Ireland, I want to take you to a place that's very dear to me."

"I would love that," she replied.

"It's a place my mother shared with me," he explained. "And it's a place I love and I want to share it with the one I love."

"Then I will be very happy to share it with you."

Jon walked back to his seat but paused a moment beside them. "Might want to get some sleep. The jetlag can be brutal if you let it."

Courtney couldn't help but giggle. Jon looked at her and raised an eyebrow. "What's so funny?"

"Your accent," she said. "It's a lot thicker."

"Not you too," he replied. "Scott thinks I have an accent as well."

"That's because you do," she answered. "But don't worry, most women find it hot."

"Most women?" he teased.

"Mmhmm," the champagne was relaxing her far too much but as she snuggled into Ryan's neck, she didn't care. "I like Ryan's."

"I don't have an accent," he protested.

"A faint one," she replied. "Now shush I want to watch my movie and enjoy my boyfriend's company."

Jon shook his head and walked back to his seat with Scott, only to find he and Beth had switched places. Kissing her, Jon leaned the seat back and closed his eyes.

Jon woke when they were on their final descent to Shannon Airport in County Clare, Jon's home. Looking beside him, Scott was asleep in the chair beside him. Catching Beth's eyes across the aisle from him, she winked and smiled brightly. They had switched sometime during the night.

Looking out the window, he could see the ocean crash against the rocks and the expanse below was covered in a green patchwork. It was one o'clock in the afternoon and the sun shone brightly, a rainbow welcomed them back.

"Ladies and gentlemen," the voice of the captain said. "I want to be the first to welcome you to Ireland and to thank you all for choosing to fly Aer Lingus today. The weather looks clear and brisk at seven degrees Celsius. Enjoy your stay, and I hope you fly with us next time."

After they landed and went through customs, they followed Jon and Scott down to the lower level of the Shannon airport to the baggage claim to pick up their luggage. Once outside, Courtney couldn't find the words to describe her first vision of Ireland at ground level. The airport sat on a field, surrounded by trees, with a road on one side, and a mountain range on the other. The parking lot was smaller than she thought it would be, but as they stood under the overhang, Jon pulled out his phone and sent a text. A small, black bus pulled out of a parking spot and drove up to them. A man a few years older than Jon, got out of the driver's seat and walked up to him. They shook hands and embraced. Ryan leaned down to her.

"That's Keelan O'Grady," he explained. "He's Uncle Jon's steward. He takes care of the land when he's not here. His family has been with us since the beginning."

"Jon's mentioned him," she replied.

"Just how large is this estate of his, Ryan?" Courtney's mom, Isabella asked.

"It's about five thousand acres," Ryan replied. "But that also includes the village near there."

"Oh my," Isabella said. "And how old is the house?"

"It's more like a manor house or castle," Ryan explained.

"The original structure was built in the early twelfth century, but there's very little from that site left any more, a few stones showing the original location, but the modern house was built in 1650, renovated in the Victorian era, and finally updated with modern conveniences in the 1960's."

"Jon's shown me pictures, I cannot wait to see it," Courtney replied.

"As soon as Uncle Jon stops talking with Keelan we'll be on our way," Ryan said.

"They're Irishmen, we'll be here all day," Courtney teased.

———

"God, it's good to see you, Kee," Jon said holding his friend at arm's length.

"And you, Jon," Keelan O'Grady replied. "It seems like it's been longer than usual."

"It has," he answered. "You have a few more grey hairs than I recall."

"That's all your fault by the way," Keelan replied. Jon laughed and clapped his friend on the arm when Scott walked up to them and greeted the steward. Jon motioned everyone to come over.

"Keelan, this is Courtney Shields, my partner on the police force, and her parents, Isabella and William," Jon introduced.

"It's a pleasure to meet you all," Keelan replied. "It's about twenty minutes to Alleen Caiseal. But they say the weather will hold."

"Keelan," Jon clasped his friend on the shoulder.

"Yes, my lord?" Keelan replied formally but grinned.

"Take me home," Jon said.

"With pleasure," Keelan replied.

———

"Iollan's been looking forward to seeing you," Keelan said as Jon sat up in the front seat.

"How is the lad? Is he back from Trinity?" Jon asked.

"No, not yet. He's coming to visit in two days," Keelan explained. "He asked me specifically to set an appointment with you. He has an idea about the outfield crops. He saw something while he was down for winter recess."

"Did he tell you about it?" Jon asked.

"Only slightly," he answered. "He wanted to tell us together."

"I am happy to listen. Scott should be there too, I think."

"I'll be there, tell me when and where," Scott piped up from the backseat.

"How's the rest of the family? How's Aislín?"

Keelan didn't answer immediately and Jon's brows furrowed.

"My wife has not spoken to me recently," he answered.

"No change?" Jon asked. "I was hoping you two had been able to reconcile."

"No, and it's been nearly five years since Riley died and Brendan disappeared." Keelan sighed. "Five years, Jon."

"I know," he replied. "Do you think divorce is her end goal?"

"I think it might be," he answered. "We've been separated for a while as you know. Kathleen has been a godsend letting me stay at the castle."

"Always," Jon replied. "You're always welcome."

"I appreciate it. But enough about that, I don't want to bring us down on your first day back."

"We're not done talking about this," Jon said. "I want you to know you can talk to me."

"I know that well, Jon thank you," he stated. "But now, I know Kathleen has something special planned for this evening.

She wouldn't tell me but she did ask me to tell you in case she forgot, be ready to go out by six."

"Six?" Jon

"Aye," he answered. "Whatever it is, she's very excited about it."

"Grand," he replied. "We'll be there."

As they turned down a road and stopped at a gate, Jon looked back at Courtney and Ryan. "We're here," he said. The gate keeper opened the gate and nodded a bow to Jon as they passed. "He's new," Jon looked over at Keelan.

"He is, yeah," Keelan answered. "Old Kelly immigrated." Jon said nothing more on it as they drove up the winding path and then, through the trees stood his home.

Hearing Courtney and her parents sigh "oh my God" made it all worth it. Keelan came to a stop in front of a line of servants at the door.

Everyone climbed out of the van and Keelan went around to help the porters with the bags. Jon waited for his son to be by his side and they both stepped forward to greet the servants lined up the path.

"Welcome home, my lord," his butler stepped forward.

"O'Connell," Jon smiled. "God, it's good to see you."

"And you sir, we are glad to see you well," O'Connell said.

"And you," he answered. "Mrs. O'Connell," he greeted the housekeeper who curtsied. Going down the line of servants, he greeted each of them by name except the last two who were the new stable lads and O'Connell introduced them as lads from Bunratty village, a ten minute drive from the gate.

Once introductions were made, the door opened and an older woman, elegantly dressed in a black dress stood at the top of the stairs.

"Jonathan," she said.

Jon's eyes shot up to the top of the stairs and a wide grin

spread across his face.

"Ma," he breathed and raced up the stairs to embrace his mother.

"Welcome home, lad," she said.

"I've missed you so!" he said.

"I've missed you, too," she replied. "It is wonderful to talk to you on the phone every day, but seeing you is so much better." Jon smiled, and the corners of his eyes crinkled. "Oh," she sighed, gently stroking his face. "You look more and more like your da' every time I see you."

Jon's bright smiled faded slightly. "I miss him," he replied.

"I know, love," she answered. "I miss him too, but seeing you makes it better." Scott walked up to them. "Oh, Scottie!" his grandmother cried.

"Hiya, Mam," he replied hugging her tightly.

After introductions were made, Kathleen turned to all of them. "I know you must all be exhausted, but I have something very special planned for this evening. It's lunchtime now, have you eaten?"

"We had something on the plane," Jon replied.

"Well, that's not real food," she teased.

"Not your food," Jon replied. "I stopped eating for a few days to be ready."

"Och, you always exaggerate," she laughed lightly tapping him on the arm in reproach.

"An Irishman's lot," Jon winked.

"Well, come in and let's get you settled, then we'll plan the rest of the day," Kathleen said.

Chapter Thirty-One

Jon and his mother walked to his room after getting everyone settled. The master suite was four rooms combined; the sleeping quarters, the library, the master bath, and an attached manservant's chamber. The walls were a deep forest green and as Jon stood in the doorway for a moment, he reveled in the memories that flooded back to him.

Kathleen walked past him and sat on the bed. Smiling, she patted the spot beside her.

"Oh, Ma," he sighed heavily as he sat beside her. "It's so good to be home."

"It's so good to have you home, love," she replied, rubbing her hand across his shoulders. "How are you doing?"

"That's a loaded question if ever there was one."

"Glad to know you recognized it," she laughed. "But truly, you look tired."

"I am," Jon replied.

She stood and went to the side table in the library and came back with two glasses of whiskey. She sat beside him and watched him sip the golden liquor.

"There's a lot on my mind," he finally admitted.

"Anything I can help with, my love?" she asked.

Shaking his head, he turned his attention to the glass and swirled its contents.

"There's a case I'm working on back in the States," he said. "It involves Mat."

"In a bad way?" she asked.

"Yes," he answered. "But I don't really want to talk about it. I'm home and I want to hear about you."

"Oh darling, not much to tell," she said. "We haven't changed much here."

"How are you feeling?" he asked. "I know you took a fall the other day."

"Keelan exaggerates," she replied. "I merely missed the last step and twisted my ankle. I am fine."

"Are you certain?" he asked.

"Yes," she answered. "Keelan called the doctor and he took a look at it. A sprain only."

"Good," he said. "What's going on with Keelan?"

"He's been staying here for a little while," she explained. "Things have gotten difficult with Aislín."

"I am sorry for it," he said.

"As am I," she replied. "But now, we should get you something to eat."

"What do you have planned tonight, Ma?" he asked.

"Never you mind," she answered. "But wear that gorgeous Aran sweater I bought you, hanging in the closet and your black slacks."

"All right," he said. "I'm going to unpack. I'm not tired. I slept on the plane. Maybe we can meet up in the drawing room later? I've missed you."

"If you're not tired, I can stay here while you unpack," she offered. "Mrs. O'Connell can handle the luncheon."

"Please do," he tossed back the rest of the whiskey and stood, unzipping his suitcase.

————◦————

Jon knocked on Beth's door about two hours later. Looking up from unpacking, she smiled at him.

"Hi," she replied.

"Damn, how did I get so lucky to get that breathy greeting?" he said.

"By being you," she answered, walking over to him and sliding her hands up around his neck. Going up on her toes, she kissed him.

"I'll take it," he teased, wrapping his arms around her and pulling her flush against him.

Stepping into the room, he kicked the door closed and lifted her. Instinctively, she wrapped her legs around him. Never breaking their kiss, Jon carried her to the bed and laid her down gently. Hovering over her, he finally broke the kiss only to latch on to her neck.

Impatiently, she tugged at his sweater until he rose up allowing her to pull it off him. Slipping his hand under her shirt, he held on to her, caressing her. No words passed between them, only a mutual need. Beth welcomed his touch but then, dread, like she had never experienced before, washed over her. The last time he had seen her naked, she was sixteen. That was decades ago and before she had three children.

"Jon," she panted. He didn't answer as he sucked on the most sensitive part of her neck. "Jon, please," she pushed gently on his shoulder. Tearing away from her, he looked down into her eyes.

"What is it?" he rasped.

"I—"

"Dad," Scott called knocking on the door. "Are you in there?"

"Shite," Jon replied and immediately rolled off her. "Yeah, hang on a second, Scott."

Beth pulled her shirt down and sat up. Jon sat on the edge of the bed, pulling on his sweater.

"I'm sorry," Beth finally said.

"Don't be," he replied. "But can I ask why you froze on me?"

"I don't know," she answered. "I guess... the last time was... It wasn't anything you did. I promise."

"You sure?" Jon asked. "I'm sorry. I shouldn't have done that."

"I wanted you to," she answered. "But maybe we can revisit this tomorrow?"

"We can revisit it whenever you want," Jon promised leaning forward to kiss her gently. Standing, he walked to the door. Opening it, he came face-to-face with his son.

"Am I interrupting anything?" Scott asked grinning.

"Possibly," Jon winked.

"Good," Scott teased. "Mam wanted us to gather, she said we should be getting ready to leave. We should head out in about forty-five minutes."

"We'll be right there," Jon promised. Scott walked down the hall and Jon turned back to Beth. "You all right?"

She nodded. "Let's go."

He wrapped his arms around her shoulders and pulled her into him, kissing her hair as they walked out of her room.

Aeron stepped out of Shannon airport and took a deep breath of Irish air. As much as he loved his home, it brought with it several unpleasant memories. This was supposed to be his legacy. He was supposed to have everything. But, Jon denied him. His first stop was to get another gun. He was forced to leave the M40 back in the States. As he got a cab from the airport terminal, he asked them to take him to the town of Moher. Someone would put him up for the night, but, he needed to get to Jon's estate.

Kim's birthday was coming up in a day or so and Aeron had a big surprise planned.

———◦———

The surprise Kathleen had planned was a Medieval Banquet at Bunratty Castle. They were greeted by hosts dressed in medieval attire and offered a glass of Mead, a honey liquor Courtney did not favor. After mingling and listening to music in the upper level, they were escorted through the halls to the large dining hall. They ate, drank and listened to traditional Irish music. At the end of the evening, they walked, or in some cases, due to the unlimited wine, stumbled to Durty Nelly's, one of Ireland's oldest pubs sitting in the shadow of the castle.

It was well past midnight when they all finally got into the small van that transported them there. Since Keelan was invited, O'Connell had volunteered to drive them and pick them up.

When they all returned to Jon's castle, Courtney was well and truly in love with Ireland. She didn't blame the wine swirling in her stomach, but it helped.

"I don't know if anyone is interested, but there's a hot tub, open bar and pool outside," Jon stated. "Beth and I are going, you are welcome to join if you brought your swimsuits. Sorry, no skinny dipping allowed."

"Pity," Beth said softly leaning into Jon. His wicked grin made Courtney laugh.

———◦———

Ten minutes later, they were outside. Scott and Kim waded in the pool and lounged at the joining wall that was cut to chest height next to the hot tub.

Courtney's dad joked saying, "Too bad I didn't know we would be doing this, Jon. I would have brought my Speedo."

"Ugh, Dad!" Courtney replied, stepping into the bubbling

hot water next to Ryan.

"You know," Jon laughed. "I think I might have an extra one upstairs."

"Don't encourage him," Courtney replied.

After a bit, Courtney's mom spoke up. "It's so beautiful here, Jon."

"It is yeah, cheers," Jon replied his Irish accent coming through strongly; Courtney blamed the alcohol and the location. "It's absolutely stunning in late spring."

"Do you allow tours?" Isabella asked.

"Absolutely! Tourism is up, what is it, Keelan twenty percent?"

"About that," Keelan answered pulling off his shirt and stepping into the hot tub.

"We only open the east wing, though," Jon replied. "We keep the family quarters private."

"What's in the east wing?" Courtney asked.

"Just a lot of paintings and furniture," Jon replied. "I'd be happy to show you, maybe tomorrow."

"Would love to," Courtney said.

Chapter Thirty-Two

Courtney joined Jon as he waded in the main pool about a half an hour later. "I don't understand how you could leave such a beautiful place," she said. "Why did your family leave?"

"Because my brother couldn't keep his pants on. You'll meet him tomorrow, though much more settled now than when he was eighteen. He got into some trouble with several of the town's leaders by sleeping with their wives and daughters."

"Oh," Courtney answered.

"Yeah, I still remember that day. The lynch mob had dragged Rick from one of the town counsel's wife's bed. Dad calmed them down to where they didn't hang him but he made a deal with them. He would take Rick away and go to America. They didn't want Dad to leave for the sake of the land, but he wouldn't let his son go alone. We left soon after."

"How old were you?" Courtney asked.

"Ten," Jon answered.

"And your brother?" she asked.

"Eight years," Jon agreed.

"So why didn't he inherit the land and castle?" Courtney asked.

"It's a long story," he answered. "Rick didn't want it. My

father and his mother married when Dad was eighteen, and my brother came two years later."

"Your father and his mother?" she clarified.

Jon's eyes drifted over to Kathleen, who sat on one of the poolside chairs.

"My father and my mother were childhood sweethearts. When her father found out about their love affair, he quickly put an end to it by betrothing her to another man. She married Liam, a good man but not her love. When my father found out, he went that day and enlisted in World War II. He didn't want to live without her but he knew he needed an heir. He was forced to marry the week before he left. He told me once, after one too many whiskeys, he had tried to get shot down several times, going on some of the most dangerous missions but he always saw her face, and once, he saw me. I wasn't even born yet, but he said he could see me and I told him to please come home.

"When the war ended, Liam had been killed at Normandy and a few years later my father went to say how sorry he was, and how he still loved her. He was still married but they loved each other so much and it was only once but once was enough. Here I am. He was overjoyed at the idea that the love of his life would give him his heir. You see there's a prophesy in our family that the lord of the manor would know his heir by the color of his hair. Black. Rick, as you will see tomorrow was strawberry blonde. I had an impressive head of black hair when I was born. My father knew then that I was his heir. Just as I knew Scott was mine."

"What is the prophesy?"

"It blesses our line, saying that as long as the lord marries the love of his life, the one God ordained for him, his son would always be first born. My father's wife would not grant divorce even though my father took the blame for the affair. She said she would not be shamed. When we moved to America, she would not let Ma come with us. Da' tried everything. When his wife did finally file in New York, Da' signed the papers right away and went back to Ireland to bring Ma back. We all lived together for a while. When Da' died, Ma went back to Ireland asking me to come with her, but my life was in America, I was engaged to Carol and I wasn't going to take her from her family. I promised I would visit and here we are now."

"Did your dad marry Kathleen?" Courtney asked.

"Yes," Jon replied. "In a small protestant service, since he was a Catholic and they would not recognize divorce nor sanction him marrying the woman he had an affair with."

"But at least they were married."

"Aye, thank goodness," Jon answered.

"Ryan's mentioned his grandmother in passing," she said. "He never really spoke fondly of her."

"She died in the nineties I think," Jon answered. "She loved his mother, my sister, but Ryan's loyalty to me is stronger and he saw how she would treat me. Not that I couldn't handle it, she's nothing to me, but he was at an impressionable age. Ma has always been a grandmother to him though she's not blood."

"Hey, Dad!" Scott called.

Jon swam over to the ledge that joined the hot tub and the pool. "What's up, Scottie?"

"William had a great idea," Scott said.

"What's that?" Jon asked.

"My buzz is wearing off, so how about a round of Guinness and some music?" Scott offered.

"We can't have the buzz wearing off, now can we?" Jon teased. "But that does sound good. O'Connell," Jon called. His butler walked over. "A round of Guinness for us, and could you turn on some music?"

"With pleasure, sir," he replied.

That next morning, Jon woke with a slight headache. The unlimited wine at the banquet, followed by a couple of rounds at Durty Nelly's and then a Guinness at the pool had given him a hangover. Reaching for the glass of water and two Tylenols he had set out the night before, he downed the pills and the water tasted good, washing away the dryness on his tongue.

The drapes had been closed but the sun shone brightly that morning breaking through and casting beams of light around the bedchamber. Surprised, though not concerned to see Beth had not joined him, he stretched and swung his legs over the edge to stand. Walking over to the massive window, he opened the drapes, winced and looked out. The sky was blue and the forest trees were green and healthy.

Tomorrow was Kim's birthday and the day after that was St. Patrick's Day. The visit was originally going to be a short one, but with the fact they were not officially on the case and Mat told him to stay away, he had extended the plan to two weeks. Courtney and Ryan would join her parents touring Scotland in a few days and Jon would get back to work. There was much that needed his attention and he could still work on the case while he was in Ireland.

As always, the thought of retiring from the police force and moving back to Ireland entered his mind. Beth could write from anywhere and Scott would come with him, he had no doubt. There wasn't anything in America for him anymore. He would miss his friends, but with his mother getting on in years, his heart hurt with the thought he may not have spent enough time with her.

One more case. As usual his thirst for problem solving trumped his ability to retire. Once this case was over, he would retire. Promising himself this time it was true, he turned when there was a knock at the door. Pulling on his sweat pants, he told the person to enter. Beth popped her head in.

"I thought you'd be awake by now," she whispered. "No one else is up yet and I was getting bored."

Jon chuckled and pulled her close, kissing her gently. "Book still not going well?"

"It will be if you keep that up," she answered kissing him back.

"You didn't join me last night," he said.

"I wasn't sure you wanted me to," she replied. "After I froze on you earlier and this is your room. The room you and Carol shared. I never want to take that from you."

"Thank you," he answered lightly kissing her nose. "But I want you here."

She laid her head on his chest and sighed. "Right where I want to be."

"What are your plans for the day?" Jon asked.

"I wrote for about an hour this morning so I'm open. Aren't Rick, Jenny and Sarah arriving today?"

"They should be here any minute," Jon replied. "So maybe we can have breakfast in the morning room and drive down to the Cliffs?"

"That sounds perfect," she said.

He pulled her face up to his and kissed her once more. Suddenly, Scott knocked excitedly on his door.

"Dad," he called. "They're here!"

"Be right there, son," he answered then looked down at Beth and smiled softly. "Let's go?"

"Let's go greet your brother and granddaughter," she said.

"If only I could claim her as such," Jon sighed.

"It's for the best," she answered. "Scott is handling it well."

"Not that well, but better," pulling on a sweater and changing out of his sweats into jeans, Jon took her hand and slipped it through the crook of his arm as they left his room.

Chapter
Thirty-Three

Detective Shields, her email read.

In answer to your recent questions regarding Hannah Turner, she was released from Northwestern Psychiatric Hospital in Indiana. Her doctor was the late Dr. Albert, formally of the US Army, Commanding Officer of the 38th Infantry Division. As you may already know, Dr. Albert was recently killed in an apparent home invasion shooting. She has not checked in with the hospital and they now believe she may have suffered from a second psychotic break. Reports say she was fixated on her late brother, formerly of Oklahoma.

Courtney jumped when Ryan knocked on her door.

"Hey," he said.

"Hi," she replied a little too quickly and closed her laptop.

"Did I interrupt something?"

"No," she answered. "Just taking care of a few things."

"Anything fun?" he asked.

"Some girls asking me if my romantic boyfriend is going to propose to me on this trip," she teased.

"Well, they're just going to have to wait and see," he replied, leaning over and kissing her. "As will you."

"Waiting... not exactly my forte," she replied.

"It'll be worth it," he promised.

"I have no doubt," she answered kissing him deeply. He pulled away from her when she started to lean back pulling him down on top of her.

"Not yet," he whispered just as Scott raced down the hall and past the open door. "They're here," Ryan said.

Scott threw open the front doors and ran out to greet his Uncle, Aunt and daughter. Sarah squealed his name and raced to him. His heart hammered in his chest as he saw her. She looked so much like him with her sparkling large brown eyes and dark hair. They met halfway and Scott scooped her up in his arms, kissing her cheek and holding her tightly.

"I've missed you so much, sweetie," he said.

"I missed you too," she replied. "I gotta show you something. I made something for you."

"For me?" he asked.

"Uh huh," she nodded. "I made it at school."

"I love it already," he answered.

"You don't know what it is yet," she said.

"You made it for me, that's all I need to know," he replied. "How's school?"

"Boring," she answered.

"Boring, huh?"

"Yeah, I told Mrs. Dixon the other day that I didn't need to go to school because I was going to be a lawyer like my cousin, she didn't agree with me."

"I went to school for a long time," Scott answered. "School is needed to be a lawyer."

"But you could teach me everything I need, right?"

"I wish I could, sweetie," he said. "But you be what you want to be."

"I want to be a lawyer," she stated.

"Then I will help you," he agreed.

"See, Mommy? I don't need to go to school," she turned to her mother. Jenny smiled sweetly at her.

"That's not what Scott said, honey," she said.

Sarah huffed then wiggled out of Scott's hold when Rick pulled her suitcase out of the car and held up her teddy bear.

"Teddy stays with me," she called indignantly. Scott laughed but went to greet his aunt and uncle.

Jon walked up and embraced his brother, slapping him on the back affectionately.

"It's good to see you, Jon," Rick said.

"It's been too long," Jon replied. Jenny stood next to her husband. "How've you been, Jenny?" Jon asked as he hugged his sister-in-law.

"Can't complain," she answered. "You look well."

"You do," Rick replied. "There's a twinkle in your eye."

"There's a reason for that," Jon smiled.

"Is that *reason* the gorgeous blonde standing behind you?" Rick grinned. "How are you, Beth?"

"You're such a tease," she answered hugging Rick.

"It's true though," Jon replied. "You are the reason I smile now."

"Oh, stop it," she lightly slapped his chest.

"Where's my girl?" Jon looked around only to see Sarah standing beside Scott with her hands on her small hips.

"I'm waiting for my hug, Uncle Jon," she said crossly.

"Well you were hiding from me," Jon replied walking over to her slowly.

"I was standing right here," she answered.

"Well maybe I was blinded by how beautiful you are and didn't recognize you since you've grown. But I bet you're still ticklish," Jon lunged towards her, tickling her sides. She squealed and giggled then threw her arms around Jon's neck and held on. "Guess what, sweetheart," Jon went on.

201

"What?" she asked.

"I brought you something from New York," he said.

"You did?" she replied. "What is it? What is it?"

"It's in my room," he answered. "Go with Scott, he'll take you."

She kissed Jon's cheek. "Thank you," she said.

"You're welcome," Jon replied setting her down.

"Come on, beautiful," Scott said, taking her hand. "Come with me."

He walked with her through the open door and up the stairs to Jon's room.

Everyone stood in the grand entry as Jon called Courtney over to introduce his brother. Rick's smile was the same as Jon's, the little bad boy smirk that crinkled his eyes.

"I'm so happy to finally meet you, Courtney," he said, his accent making her smile. "Jon hasn't told me nearly enough about his work, but I have heard a lot about you. I enjoyed the musical the two of you were in. I couldn't make it up to Indiana, but Jon bought me a copy and sent me the DVD. Jenny and I loved your performance."

"Thank you," Courtney smiled. "And it's so wonderful to meet you too. I've heard about you from both my boys. I've anticipated meeting you to make sure it's all true."

"Oh, I'm sure it's all true," he laughed. "I was a heartbreaker in my youth."

"Fortunately, that is something age has knocked out of you, babe," his wife said from beside him. The petite blonde was no older than forty with the bluest eyes Courtney had ever seen.

"It's not age, darlin', it's you," he wrapped his arm around her waist and pulled her into him.

"Good to know," she winked then turned back to Courtney. "We are so happy to meet you, Courtney. And we are excited for Ryan. He's a wonderful catch."

"He is that," Courtney agreed.

"From where I'm standing it's Ryan that's the fortunate one," Rick answered.

"Can't argue there," Courtney said.

"Are you guys tired?" Jon asked. "I've got tonight planned, but I had a surprise for lunch-time after you got settled."

"I slept most of the way, so I'm fine. But I can't speak for the girls. Jenny?"

"I'm fine, and Sarah slept most of the way so she should be all right too," Jenny explained.

"Grand," Jon answered. "I wanted to go to the cliffs."

"Done," Rick replied. "I'm in the mood for a good Irish stew. Though there's nothing like Kathleen's."

"She promised to make it for us tomorrow," Jon revealed.

"Excellent."

"We'll have to dress warmer for the cliffs," Jenny said. "It's freezing."

"It's not Florida that's for sure," Rick replied. "It's better."

"I agree," Courtney said. "Perfect. And I cannot wait to see The Cliffs of Moher."

"I had a feeling since I saw them as your background on your laptop," Jon replied.

Chapter
Thirty-Four

Courtney walked up the steep incline, Ryan by her side and her parents walking behind her. A man sat on the side playing the pennywhistle, selling his CDs. The welcome center was to her right, but she had one goal in mind. The path split into two directions but she didn't care. As she crested the incline, all she saw was the view before her. A half wall just below chest height stopped her but as she gazed, four large cliffs spread out into the ocean before her.

The mist of an earlier downpour still hung to the third and fourth cliff. The sky was overcast and the wind bit sharply, but all she saw and felt was the sheer majesty of the cliffs before her. The stone had been chipped away and layered in a rugged image of what the Atlantic Ocean could do. The white caps of the water hitting the rocks below contrasted the dark brown-black of the stone.

Tears gathered in her eyes at the sheer magnificence of the view before her. Ryan's arm came around her shoulders and he whispered in her ear.

"I want a picture of my two favorite things," he said. "You and this view."

Looking over at him, she smiled and kissed him lightly. "I

think I can make that happen."

Courtney posed as Ryan took a couple quick snaps then lowered the camera. "Let's go a little further up to the observation area. Then to O'Brien's Tower."

"Lead the way," she said.

"Ryan's a lucky man," Rick spoke low to his brother as they watched the two walk on to the observation area.

"He is," Jon replied. "As am I. I learn much from her daily."

"Such as?" Rick asked. When Jon didn't answer, Rick nodded. "You have become much more your old self, Jon. I am glad to see you looking so well and happy."

"The happy stems from Beth," Jon admitted.

"I have no doubt," Rick replied. "But what about this case you are working on?"

"I tried to discourage Courtney from working on it any more but I know she has. She thinks I didn't see her sending emails from her tablet in the airport," Jon stated. "I worry this may catch up with us."

"Here?" Rick asked.

"Possibly," Jon replied. "Hannah Turner said that she had her own Irishman. That made me think, who could possibly be behind it?"

"It couldn't be from your eejit stunt in the IRA could it?" Rick asked.

"It could very well be that," Jon admitted. "But I don't know. This doesn't look like an IRA hit. It's a single perpetrator but I have a feeling Hannah and this man she mentioned are actually doing the dirty work for someone else."

"And you don't know who that is?" Rick asked.

"No," Jon answered. "But I have a feeling that they will reveal themselves soon."

"Keep me informed," Rick said. "I will help in any way I can."

"I appreciate it," Jon replied.

"You're my brother," Rick stated. "You're family. You're blood."

––––––––––––––

Patience is a virtue, Aeron kept repeating as he watched the castle from the woods. His eyes drifted to the rifle leaning against the tree next to him. When he saw Keelan through his binoculars, he clenched his jaw. *Soon,* he thought. *Soon, it will all turn out the way it should have.*

––––––––––––––

Kim woke the next morning to a brilliant sun warming her through the drapes. Smiling brightly as she stood and walked to the window, she threw the curtains open. The immediate temperature drop caused her to shiver and wrap her arms around herself. The mountains stood in the distance and she once again hoped she and Scott could be happy. After a minute of hoping and wishing, she pushed those feelings aside and opened the window to let in the fresh air.

Though the sun was warm, the air held a bit of a bite and she wrapped her arms tighter around her. The thin sleep tank top did little to cover her from exposure but wanting to enjoy the fresh air longer, she turned and pulled on an oversized sweatshirt. Once warm, she gazed back out to the woods and the mountains.

Four shadows of men riding massive horses caught her attention. They ambled out of the row of trees to her right, two black horses and two brown. Jon, Scott, Keelan, and another young man she had never met, sat atop the magnificent beasts. Her eyes went immediately to Scott, and they wouldn't move. Sitting tall on his horse, wearing a red sweater and tight tan pants with black knee-high riding boots, he was laughing at something the young man had said, his black hair glistened in the sun. Biting her lower lip to prevent a groan escaping, she clenched her hands into fists. She wanted him with every fiber.

Scott looked up to her window as they approached the house. His eyes lit up when he saw her and her heart jumped. Scott dismounted his horse and handed the reins to the young man beside him. He took the back steps two at a time and called up to her window.

"Oh fair maiden with the golden hair," he started.

"Maiden?" she questioned.

His eyes sparked for a split second then he continued. "Wouldst thou do me the honor of letting down thy silky tresses so that I may come up to thine bedchamber and gift to thou my present for the anniversary of thy birth?"

"Oh good and noble knight," she answered. "You mistake me for another. For no maiden linger here only one eager to be thy lover."

A grin spread across his face and for the first time since college, Kim actually blushed.

"I wanted to be the first one to say happy birthday," he went on.

Kim smiled, thankful he did not ask any embarrassing questions. "And you are. Thank you," she replied.

"Come down?" Scott asked. "I want you to meet Iollan." Kim's eyes drifted to the man still on his horse. She had heard of him. He was being groomed to take Keelan's place as steward when Scott took over for Jon. Saying the name in her mind so she would say it correctly, she nodded and disappeared from the window.

"Ool-lan," she said softly as she raced about her room. Anything was better than remembering Scott's heated look when she admitted she was no maiden. Paying no heed to his sparkling eyes or the way it heated her from head to toe, she pulled out a purple sweater and skinny jeans. Once dressed, she headed to the bathroom and brushed her teeth.

Thanking her lucky stars she had her mother's complexion, she applied light makeup and twisted her thick, golden hair up into a messy bun. Spraying some body spray, Scott's favorite, she left the room and raced down the back stairs to the terrace.

"Damn," Scott breathed. At her raised eyebrow he grinned. "I mean, fair lady you take my breath away and I do not intend to need it back."

"Is that your way of saying I look good?"

"Damn good," he answered. "Happy birthday."

"Thanks," she replied. "You don't look too bad yourself, though I think Alex would laugh his ass off if he saw you."

"Probably, but it's oddly comfortable," he winked. "Come on, I want you to meet Iollan."

She smiled and nodded. They walked down the terrace stairs and toward Scott's black war horse. The sheer size of the creature made Kim's heart skip a beat. She barely came to the shoulder of the animal and at five-nine that was a feat.

Before Scott introduced her, he gently took her hand and guided it to the horse's snout. "Easy, Devil," Scott soothed when the horse lifted its head.

"Devil?" Kim asked. Almost as if the animal understood, he dipped his head in a nod. "It's a pleasure to meet you, Devil."

The animal's ear twitched and he bowed his head to her.

"You've bewitched him, my lady," the young man said from atop his brown horse. "Horses very rarely bow, only to their masters and the most beautiful women."

"You must be Iollan," she turned to him.

"What gave me away?" Iollan asked.

"Your father's charm," she gave a sidelong glance at Keelan who chuckled.

"I am indeed, Ms. Anderson and it is a pleasure to finally meet you," he swung his right leg over to the other side and slipped down off the horse. "Iollan O'Grady."

"Kim," she corrected. "And it is nice to meet you. I've heard about you as well."

"All lies, I promise," he laughed.

"I doubt that," she replied taking in his twenty-five-year-old face, blondish-brown hair and light sea-green eyes. He wasn't as tall as Scott, but his bearing lent him an intimidating presence.

Jon walked up and engulfed her in a hug. "Happy birthday, honey," he said.

"Thanks," she mumbled into his shoulder.

"Your mother and I have something very special planned for tonight," Jon explained.

"Oh?" She smiled. "Sounds like fun. I have a feeling this will be the best birthday ever."

"With any luck," Jon replied and she didn't miss his subtle glance at Scott.

"Have you ever ridden 'round the grounds, Kim?" Iollan asked holding the reins and petting his horse's snout.

"No," she replied. "I haven't. But I can't ride."

"What?" Iollan pretended shock. Kim laughed and looked up at Scott. "Well," Iollan went on and mounted his horse in one swift movement. "That is something we will have to remedy. Would you do me the honor?" He offered his hand with a wink.

"Oh, I don't know," she answered.

"Nothin' bad will happen to you. Lucky here has always been safe, haven't ya, lad?" He stroked the horse's neck as Lucky huffed in agreement. "I promise."

Kim looked back at Scott and he stepped forward. "Actually, Iollan," Scott said. "I would like to take Kim," he locked eyes with her. "If you want, that is."

"I would," she answered then turned to Iollan. "Not that I

don't appreciate you offering."

"Knocked out by the lord of the manor, eh? I think my ego can handle it," Iollan winked.

Scott walked over to Devil and swung up on the back of the horse. Jon offered his hand as a low stirrup for Kim. She slipped her Sketcher clad foot into the foothold and took Scott's hand. Scott didn't let her go until she settled behind him and wrapped her arms around his waist. As soon as she was ready, he clucked to his horse and Devil started out at a slow canter.

Once they were out of earshot, Keelan slapped Jon on the back. "It's about damn time," he teased.

"Right? Thanks for your help Iollan," Jon said.

"My pleasure, milord," Iollan grinned. "It's time he settles down."

"You're one to talk," his father replied.

"I know who I'm going to marry," he answered. "I just haven't asked her yet."

"Be sure you do before someone else catches her eye," Jon said.

"No one can catch her eye when she's blinded by me," Iollan teased.

"Cocky sod," Jon laughed.

"And proud of it."

"Must be O'Grady blood," Jon laughed. "Breakfast?"

"Starving," Keelan agreed.

"Save me a few slices of bacon, I'll take the horses," Iollan offered.

"Since it's such a generous offer, we will save you some eggs too," Keelan stated.

"Appreciate it," Iollan called over his shoulder as he took the reins of the two other horses and moved them towards the stables.

Chapter
Thirty-Five

"Are you really not a virgin?" Scott asked Kim as they rode slowly through the forest.

"Does it bother you?" Kim countered.

"No," he answered swiftly. "Just surprised, I guess. I didn't know. Who was it?"

"That question is on the same line as how much do you weigh and what's your age. You don't ask it of a woman," she replied.

"I just want to know who I'm competing against," Scott answered.

"Why would you think you were competing?" she asked.

He shrugged when he answered. "I know we're best friends and I don't want to ruin our friendship, but I…"

"Go on," she prompted.

"I feel things for you, Kim," he said. "And not just friends. I think of us in a different way now."

"Why now?"

"I don't know," he admitted. "Maybe it's this threat hanging over us, or maybe it's time. I don't know."

"What are you asking?" she questioned.

He said nothing but navigated his horse to the small

stream deep in the woods. Offering his arm for her to slide down, she took it and landed wobbly on her feet. Scott followed and led Devil to water. Kim followed without a word. It took him a second to form the right words and when he spoke, he prayed he didn't screw it up.

"I'm asking for you to give us a chance," he said. "Not as friends, but as something more. Something romantic. I think the reason none of my previous relationships have worked is because I measure every woman I'm with against you and none compare. You love my family and I love yours. I've said I love you in passing and never flinched when I said it, that's because I truly do." He raised his eyes to hers. "I love you, Kim. I know I'm throwing a lot at you right now, but I…" Kim pressed a finger to his lips to stop him.

"I'm willing to give us a try if you are," she said. "I've loved you for so long, Scott. I've wanted you for so long. But, you have to tell me this is real because I've had dreams like this. Don't tease me if you aren't ready. It's not fair to me."

Pulling her hand down from his lips, he wrapped his arms around her and crashed his mouth to hers. Before either of them knew what was happening, they had torn at each other's clothes and as the sun shone down on them, they made love for the first time.

Detective Shields,

In regards to your email, Captain Bernardo it has been rumored, is on intimate terms with Hannah Turner. According to my sources, he will be asked to step down no later than the end of this week. If you or your partner know what is going on, I highly suggest you contact my superior and tell her everything. I hope you know what you're doing, Courtney. This is political now. Steer clear.

The warning was clear, stay away from the case. But why? Mat would be blacklisted and probably imprisoned for simply being in the wrong place at the wrong time. Replying, Courtney stated that she and Jon had no intention of staying away and that the captain was innocent. Just as she hit send, someone knocked at her door. Looking over, she called for them to enter, surprised when Jon's mother walked in.

"I'm sorry, my dear," Kathleen said. "Were you busy?"

"No," she answered closing her laptop. "Is everything okay?"

"Oh, yes. Jon just asked me to find you and see if you could join him in his study."

"Oh," Courtney checked the time. "Crap, is it after ten?"

"It is, we didn't want to disturb you in case you were tired," she said.

"No, I've been up. I didn't realize it was so late," she stood and pulled out a pair of jeans and a sweater.

"I was hoping to speak with you too, my dear," Kathleen said.

"Oh, I'd like that, please stay. I'll go to the bathroom."

"I don't wish to intrude," she replied.

"Not an intrusion at all," Courtney confirmed with a smile as she gathered her things and headed to the bathroom. "What did you want to talk about?"

"Jon. Is he happy?" she asked.

"I'm not sure, honestly," she answered.

"I worry about him," Kathleen replied.

"I think that's a mother's prerogative," she called.

"True," she said. "I appreciate you taking care of him."

"I haven't really done much," she admitted.

"You have," Kathleen said. "I've seen a different Jon these past two years. He's almost like he was when Carol was alive. I know that's because you've brought him out of his shell."

"We've been good for each other," Courtney replied.

"I like your bluntness," Kathleen said. "It's refreshing."

"I've learned as a cop you don't have time to be nice most of the time," she said.

"Well, I thank you for your candor," Kathleen answered as Courtney came out of the bathroom dressed in jeans and a sweater. "And he's right. You do look like her."

"I know sometimes that's difficult for him."

"It is, but he knows you're not her," she confirmed. "He's a good man and he would never take advantage."

"Oh, I know, he's a wonderful man. You raised him well."

"He takes after his father in many ways," she answered. "But tell me, you love Ryan?"

"Yes," Courtney answered. "Completely."

"Even though he is not my blood, I love him like he is," she answered. "I just want to make sure. Jon has talked about you but I have never met you until now and I needed to see the truth in your eyes."

"I love Ryan more than anything. I want to make him happy."

"I know he loves you," Kathleen said.

"I think so," Courtney agreed as they started down the hall.

"I do want you to know, no matter how much I see the truth in your eyes, I love him as my own grandson," Kathleen paused and turned to her. "If you break his heart, I will take yours out."

Courtney blinked. "I promise you," Courtney started. "I want nothing more than to be his wife. I love him and want to spend the rest of my life with him."

Kathleen broke into a smile. "Yes, I can see that," she replied. "That is how I felt for Jon's father. Now, Jon is waiting for you," Kathleen turned to a door and knocked.

"Come in," they heard Jon call. Kathleen opened the door and Jon looked up. "Ah, thank you, Ma," he smiled.

The room was exactly what Courtney expected for the lord of the manor; dark mahogany furniture, forest green walls, bookshelves lined the back wall from floor to ceiling, many old titles, well-worn beneath the glass panels on one side. The large painting of a man on a horse, one of Jon's ancestors, hung on the wall directly behind him.

Jon and Keelan stood from their seats across from each other when the women came in.

"I will check on those and get back with you," Keelan spoke to Jon after greeting her.

"Please do," Jon answered. "And if you can, get me the project itinerary and the job orders so I can read over them and sign off?"

"They'll be on your desk before we leave for Kim's party," Keelan promised.

"I'll be right with you, Courtney," Jon said after Keelan and Kathleen left and he sat back down. Courtney took Keelan's seat and waited as Jon looked over something on the computer.

Finally, he turned to her as she set up her laptop.

"So," he started. "What have you found out?"

"I'm sorry?" she asked.

"About the case, what have you found out?" Jon asked again.

"What makes you think I've found anything out?" she replied.

"Because you're a good cop and nothing, not even a direct order, would stop you when you have a mission. You've been working on this and I want to know what you've discovered. We're partners."

"Okay," she answered and turned her laptop around so he can read the emails.

"Interesting," he spoke after reading. "I would like to know more about Hannah Turner while she was at Northwestern.

Have we gotten those financials yet?"

"No," Courtney answered. "I don't know what's taking so long."

"Mat," Jon replied. "He's put up roadblocks. I haven't gotten the phone records either."

"If he really is in trouble and not a part of this, why isn't he helping us?"

"It could reach deeper than we know. He may have done this to protect us. Let's continue with the information from the hospital. If we could get a list of names of orderlies, doctors, and nurses we could cross-reference them with the names Dave comes up with."

"I'll have a friend of mine help us out."

"Who? Can you trust her?"

"Chelsea," Courtney replied.

"Oh okay," Jon nodded. "If she could get us a list we could start with that."

"Sounds good," Courtney started typing up notes.

"Also see if you can't—" Jon was cut off by the phone on his desk ringing. Jon's brows furrowed. "Keelan just left. Who would be calling me?" Without another word, Jon picked up the phone. "Jonathan Greene," he said, then his jaw clenched. Courtney watched his face change as he pressed a button on the handset and mouthed to Courtney; *record*. She took out her phone and opened the record app.

"You're on speaker," Jon said.

"Oh good," a voice replied. "How are you, Courtney?"

"Who are you?" Courtney asked.

"Not yet, niceties first," the voice answered. "I have to say that certain shade of pink looks beautiful on you." Jon's eyes went sharply to the window. "That's right Jonny-boy I'm watching you." Jon stood and pulled the drapes.

"Oh, now that's not very fair," the voice continued.

"Who are you?" Courtney asked again. "What do you want from us?"

"You can call me Aeron," the voice said. "And to answer what I want from you, well, you'll just have to wait and see. But don't worry, I can't do anything here. My orders are to observe and report."

"What do you mean 'observe and report'?" Courtney asked.

"Beauty but no brains..." Aeron sighed. "I'm disappointed. Maybe that's why Ryan loves you."

"Well, at least I run my own life and I don't have to answer to anyone telling me to just 'observe and report.'" Courtney replied.

"Ooh, feisty," Aeron answered. "You're right. Your life is perfect. Perfect job, perfect family, perfect boyfriend, perfect partner... well, almost perfect, right, Jonny-boy?"

"Why do you keep calling me that?" Jon asked.

"That's your name, isn't it?" Aeron asked. "That's what everyone called you while you were here."

"Not everyone," he answered. "Who are you?"

"No one you need to know yet," he explained.

"Are you that pathetic you can't even show yourself? Oh, that's right you can't go against your orders. Do not engage, right? Are you so afraid of your commander you can't face me?" Jon demanded.

"Ooh," Aeron replied. "You're gonna regret that. By the way, did you know Scott and Kim just had sex? They thought they were alone," he laughed and Courtney shivered. "But I do have a birthday present for her. Doesn't she look pretty on Scott's horse?"

Jon raced to the door and ran outside, Courtney was right on his heels. Kim and Scott were riding up to the house, laughing and smiling at each other. They shared a soft kiss just as Jon shouted.

"Scott! Get her down!" They broke the kiss and looked over at him confused. "Drop!" Jon bellowed.

"Go," Scott ordered Kim when he saw the look on Jon's face. Both dismounted just as a shot rang out. They dropped to their stomachs. Devil whinnied and reared up as Scott covered Kim and rolled away from the horse's pounding hooves.

"Devil!" Scott yelled. Jon ran towards them and grabbed Devil's reins just as a second shot rang out. "Dad!"

"I'm fine," Jon called back. Iollan ran outside and took the reins from Jon. "Get inside away from any windows," Jon ordered and took off running towards the woods.

"Jon!" Courtney yelled after him. "Don't be stupid!"

Rick ran outside to see what was going on just as Scott rushed Kim up the steps.

"Dad!" Scott shouted.

"Scott, get inside," Courtney ordered. "I'll go after him." Scott locked eyes with her and nodded once. Rick grabbed Scott's arm pulling him into the house and glanced back to see Iollan safe inside the stables with Devil.

Chapter Thirty-Six

Courtney ran after Jon seeing him duck into the woods.

Dear God, don't be stupid, Jon, she thought. She ran faster but froze midstride and ducked when she heard another shot. Reaching the edge of the forest, she rushed into the woods.

"Jon," she called quietly. "Jon? Where are you?"

A twig cracked behind her; she jumped. Her heart was pounding in her ears. The forest was dense and dark.

"Jon?" she called again. Still no answer. As the leaves rustled behind her, she shook her head. "Stop it, Courtney," she said so softly it was almost inaudible. "Focus."

She swore she heard giggling behind her and took off running, stumbling on a root sticking out in the ground. Lying on the forest floor for a moment getting her air back, she heard rustling in the trees. Standing, she looked around and to her horror she had lost her sense of direction.

"Jon?" Courtney could barely call out. A hand came up behind her, covered her mouth, and pulled her into the undergrowth. Her scream was muffled but she instinctually bit the hand and kicked the shins of the person behind her.

"Ow, Dammit Courtney, it's me!" She heard the voice of her partner in her ear. She relaxed and he removed his hand.

"Damn you, Jon," she turned and punched his chest. "Don't do that! Where is he?"

Jon lifted a hoodie in his hand. "All I know is that he was here, but I don't know when."

"New York Yankees?" She asked looking at the insignia. "He didn't sound like he was from New York."

Jon shook his head. "No, he's from Ireland. That much I know," he said. "How are Kim and Scott?"

"They're fine," Courtney answered.

"Let's get back to the house. The last thing Kim needs is a recap of this. Let's go ahead with the party as planned. You and I have to figure this out."

"I agree," she said. "This guy is really starting to get on my nerves."

"And when I find him…" Jon was saying taking the hoodie back. "I'm going to kill him."

"I'm going after them," Scott paced.

"Why?" Rick asked.

"Because he's my dad and he's in danger," Scott said.

"Scott, I understand you want to, but think clearly," Rick replied.

"This bastard shot at Kim. I'm not letting him get away with it!" Scott shouted.

"Scott," Kim tried to calm him. "Please."

Scott turned to her, sitting on the couch next to her mother. She looked up at him and he saw the fear in her eyes. Rushing over, he sat beside her and pulled her into his arms. She rested her head on his chest and sighed.

"I'm sorry," Scott said softly. "Are you all right?"

She nodded and looked up at him. Gently brushing her lips across his, she held him close just as Jon and Courtney walked back in.

"Are you okay?" Jon asked immediately looking at his son and Kim.

"Shaken," Scott answered. "But fine."

"Good," Jon replied. "And Devil?"

"The bullet struck the cantle of the saddle," Iollan stepped forward. "It didn't hit him."

"Thank God," Jon replied.

"What happened?" Scott asked.

"Later," Jon said. "I promise. But now I need to make sure you are well."

"I'm fine, Da'," Scott replied.

"Was it a hunting accident or something?" Beth asked.

"Something," Jon answered.

"Can someone please just tell me what's going on?" Kim cried. "Someone just tried to kill Scott and me and after everything that's happened today," she glanced at Scott with a mixture of emotions. "I need to know what's going on."

"It's okay," Scott soothed rubbing his hand up and down her arm.

"It's not okay," Kim sobbed. "What the hell is going on?"

Looking over at Courtney, she agreed and sat down in one of the chairs near Jon as he began.

Jon closed the door to his study after he invited Scott in for a talk. Scott stayed standing even after Jon sat at his desk.

"Whatever it is, Dad, can we hurry up? I need to get back to Kim," Scott said.

"What happened during your ride around the grounds, Scott?" Jon asked.

"It's perfectly obvious you already know," Scott answered.

"Don't play coy with me, lad. I'm not in the mood," Jon stated.

Scott looked down. "Sorry, Dad," he apologized. "Just a

lot of stuff has happened."

"Did you have sex with her?"

Scott looked away. "Yeah, I know what you said and I respect your opinion, but… god it was just…"

"Natural?" Jon offered.

"Yeah," he sighed. "I never thought it would feel like this."

"Like what?"

"Like… I'm home," Scott replied. "I know we've known each other for so long but honestly, I've never felt this way with anyone. It was like one second we were friends, best friends and the next we are best friends and lovers. It was just a natural transition and dear god, it was amazing."

"When it's love, Scott, it is natural," Jon explained. "I don't think you've ever been in love before."

"Not if this is the way it feels," Scott agreed. "And when I heard that shot ring out… the thought of losing her." He shook his head.

"Trust me, I know," Jon answered.

"I can't imagine what you went through, Dad," he said. "But now… I understand why you closed yourself off." Jon looked up at his son standing before him across the desk. "Forgive me for what I put you through."

"Scottie, forgiven and forgotten long ago," he stood and embraced his son. "Now, I want you to spend some time with her. Help her calm down from today's events. We're still going to the pub later tonight and I want her to enjoy herself. Maybe go out to the village for a little shopping or spoil her with a hot bath." At Scott's salacious grin, Jon knew precisely what his son would be doing as soon as he left the study.

"I will do my best," Scott replied.

"I'm sure you will," Jon laughed. "Now go, but have Courtney come in, would you?"

That evening they caravanned to the village pub where the publican greeted Jon by name.

"Good evenin', milord, glad to have you back," he said. "How are you?"

"McGriffit! Good evening, how about you? How's young Sean doing?"

"Not so young anymore, sir," McGriffit answered. "He's eighteen now and a foot taller than me."

"Is he really?" Jon asked. "Ha! Your wife snuck the postman into her bed, eh?" Jon laughed.

"Very possibly," his barrel laugh shook his belly. "And is this the birthday girl?"

"Indeed," Jon answered pulling Kim into his side.

"Many happy returns of the day, miss," he said.

"Thank you," she replied and smiled at the funny looking man.

Scott was with her all day making her laugh and stealing a couple kisses, but as Scott held his daughter while they waited, Kim's eyes shown with love.

"Everything is set up, if you'd follow me," McGriffit explained.

McGriffit escorted them to another room and when he opened the door, Kim looked inside. Sitting there at one of the tables was Mark, Kim's older, middle of the three, brother. She squealed and rushed to him.

"Oh my god!" she cried hugging him. "What are you doing here?"

"You didn't think I'd miss your birthday, did you, baby sis?" he asked calling her his pet name. "Mom and Jon explained what they were planning and I had to be a part of it."

"I'm so glad to see you!" she said. "You won't get in trouble at the hospital?"

"Nah, the kids will hardly know I'm gone," he replied.

"Oh good," she said, hugging him again. "I'm so glad you're here. I know you hate flying."

"Who, me?" He chuckled. "Never. They had a great open bar to calm my nerves." Beth stepped forward, and he kissed her cheek. "Hey, Mom."

"I'm glad you made it," Beth said.

"Yeah," he answered. "Me too."

Scott passed Sarah to Jenny and was at Kim's side in a moment when she looked for him. "Mark," she said softly. "I have some news."

"What's up, baby sis?" Mark asked glancing at Scott then back to Kim and dropping his eyes to their intertwined hands.

"Scott and I are officially together."

He looked up sharply and his brows furrowed. "I see."

"I love her, Mark," he said. "I know I've had some issues in the past that you've seen. I ask you to let me prove to you I'm a changed man."

"We'll see," he replied. "I'm the easy brother. What do you think Steven will say?"

"I don't care," Kim answered. "I'm happy."

"Then, baby sis, if you're happy, I'm happy," he kissed her cheek and offered his hand to Scott. "You hurt her, I'll kill you."

"I would expect nothing less, but I have no intention of hurting her," Scott promised.

Everyone sat at the tables while McGriffit and a couple other workers served dinner and drinks.

"I thought Ireland didn't have table service," Kim teased.

"For your birthday, Miss," McGriffit replied. "We will do anything for you."

"Awe," she smiled at him. "Thank you for making it so special."

"Our pleasure."

Dinner was cleared and a birthday cake was brought out. Everyone sang "Happy Birthday," as Kim blew out the candles. The cake was cut and as everyone enjoyed a slice, McGriffit and three young men brought in some equipment. A large TV, a microphone, a DJ set, and lots of wiring.

Jon leaned over to her and whispered. "Your mom and I thought a little karaoke is always fun," he said.

"Love it," she giggled.

Scott was the first one to sing and he dedicated it to Kim. The words were a tribute to their new found love stemming from friendship and tears gathered in her eyes. Scott claimed a kiss after he finished and everyone cheered.

Mark watched the entire exchange between his sister and Scott. He took a drink of his beer and listened as Kim finished a song. He would have to have a talk with his older brother, Steven. They both knew how much Kim cared for Scott. But they also knew Scott's playboy history. No matter what Scott asked, Mark was hesitant.

Chapter
Thirty-Seven

CIA Special Agent Steven Anderson, Kim's eldest brother, stood in the shower in a flat in London, England, letting the hot water soothe his back while the steam rose and condensed on the mirror. His blue eyes were closed as he concentrated on something else to get his mind off what he was in the middle of.

He was tired, tired of this case, tired of keeping up a British accent, tired of whole situation. He had already done his job; he infiltrated the suspected terrorist cell through a female cousin. This was the time he hated, pretending that he cared about her and having to watch his every word and action. In his past experience, the women became possessive now. All he needed was to know where the plans were for the bomb they intended to use.

Russia gave them the intel and although Steven was skeptical of its origin, he wasn't about to allow World War III to begin under his nose. It was times like these he wished he was like other men with a normal job and not one he had to look over his shoulder and carry a gun everywhere he went. He could be over in Ireland for his sister's birthday instead of having to play Casanova in London.

There was a knock at the bathroom door followed by a

whiney accented voice. "Craig?" she called. "Aren't you coming to bed?"

"Be there in a sec, babe. Don't worry."

This was what he was good at, getting women to talk and to tell him whatever he needed. In fact, he was better than good. He was the best.

"Casanova," he heard over his ear bud. "Come in, Casanova." He turned on the exhaust fan to drown out his voice.

"I read ya, Mac," he replied softly. "Loud and clear."

"The info you supplied was hot. Flash says good job, but we need more," Mac, the computer geek of the team, replied speaking of his handler; Gordon, codename *Flash Gordon*.

"Yeah, I know," Steven answered. "Tell him to stop breathing down my neck. I can't do my job with you watching my every move." He closed his eyes as soon as the words were out of his mouth, he knew exactly how that would be taken.

"And damn do you have moves, Cas." Exactly what he expected. "Keep up the great work."

He took the ear bud out without replying, knowing they had cameras everywhere in the flat. His phone buzzed by the sink with a text from his mother reminding him of his sister's birthday and, if he could, to call Kim as they were out and available. He erased the text quickly and debated on calling. It could be dangerous. He took his ear bud and put it in his ear again.

"Mac, I need a secure line on my phone for five minutes. Make it happen," he ordered.

"Oh, okay," Mac said sarcastically.

"Sorry. I need a secure line for five minutes. Make it happen, *please*," Steven mocked.

"Yeah, yeah give me a second," Mac replied. "Done."

Steven took his phone and called his sister.

"Hey!" Kim answered on the third ring. "I didn't think you'd be able to call."

"You don't think I would let the day go by without wishing you happy birthday, do ya, baby sis?" he asked. Knowing his sister would understand he was undercover, he kept his fake British accent.

"I hoped not," she replied. "But I didn't want it to be a problem."

"No problem. What time is it over there?" he asked.

"About seven," she answered. "What about you? Where are you? Or can you say?"

"Can't, sorry," he replied. "What's the plan for tonight?"

"We're at a pub. Jon and Mom planned it. It's been a lot of fun. There's your favorite thing… karaoke," she teased.

"Oh really?" he asked. "That sounds like fun."

"Yeah," she replied. "It is."

He hated it, but every time Jon's name was mentioned, a knot grew in the pit of his stomach. The question of his paternity was a sore subject with him. Jon had never really taken an interest in him or his career, but he grudgingly admitted that the man was always there for him and his family. Beth loved him and Kim and Mark looked at him as a surrogate father, but Steven never could. When he was a young, reckless agent, early in his career, he looked up Jon and had found out more than he wished to know.

"That's great, sweetie," he answered.

"Craig?" He heard the voice in the other room whine.

"Coming," he called back. "Hey, baby sis, I gotta get going. Have a great birthday and a safe flight home, okay?"

"Okay. Thanks. And we will. You be careful," she answered. "Love you."

"Love you too," he replied.

He hung up the phone and Mac came over the ear bud.

"Secure line is now dropped. Any other calls can and will be monitored."

"Thanks, Mac," Steven replied. "I owe you one."

"You better believe it," Mac answered. "You're taking the heat from Flash on this one."

Steven took out the ear bud and put it in the soil of one of the potted plants in the bathroom. Taking his phone, he walked out and into the main bedroom.

"I thought you'd never get out of that shower," the woman said.

He smirked, shrugged off the door frame, and let the towel drop from around his hips.

———

Scott and Kim sat together on the couch back at the castle as Kim opened her presents. As the last ones were opened, she thanked everyone for all the thoughtful gifts. A round of Bailey's on-the-rocks passed and they sat comfortably in the living area. Kim's head rested on Scott's shoulder, the excitement of the day catching up with her. When Scott felt her body relax against him, he looked up at Jon who was telling a story.

"Is she out?" Jon asked.

"Yeah, she's exhausted," Scott answered.

"I'll take her up," Mark offered.

"I got it," Scott replied. "Could you help me maneuver so I don't wake her? She's had a crazy day."

Mark nodded but watched as Scott gently cradled Kim in his arms and lifted her.

"I'll help you upstairs," Mark said.

"Mark, sweetheart," Beth called. "I know you're trying to protect your sister's honor, but let Scott be. He's taking care of her."

Mark looked between them both and huffed a sigh. "Fine."

"Good night," Scott whispered as he carried Kim out of the room and up the stairs.

"How long?" Mark asked.

"Today," Jon replied.

"It seems like it's been going on longer than that," he started. "He's…"

"Devoted," Beth offered.

"Yeah," Mark answered. "Oddly so."

"He loves her," Jon replied. "He truly loves her."

"I see that," Mark sighed. "He has changed."

"Very much," Jon stated.

"I'm still skeptical about how Steven will react to the news," Mark replied.

They were quiet for a moment then Courtney spoke up. "Well, it's been a long day, perhaps we should all follow Kim's example and go to bed?"

"Agreed," Jon replied and drained his glass. Courtney waited until everyone was heading out of the room to stand.

"You going upstairs?" Ryan asked.

"Yeah in a moment," she smiled. He looked between Jon and Courtney and nodded.

"What's up?" Jon asked once they were alone.

"I got an email back from Chelsea," she answered. "Didn't know if you wanted to work on it a little."

"Not tonight," he replied. "Let's visit it fresh in the morning."

"It's St. Patrick's Day tomorrow," she said.

"Then the day after," Jon replied. "We need all of our focus on this. I won't have anyone threatened."

"Okay," she answered. "Sleep well." Looking up at Ryan waiting on the stair, she wished Jon a good night and walked towards her boyfriend.

Chapter
Thirty-Eight

Jon lay restless in his bed. He was hot then cold then hot again, not from the fluctuation of the heater, but from the fluctuation of his emotions. Whenever he saw Mark, he thought of Steven and that brought on hot and cold chills. He always tried to be there for all three of Beth's children, but when he came into the picture, Steven was a surly teenager who never had a father and the one he had, beat him. But the mere thought of Steven created an unbearable knot in his stomach not knowing the truth.

He had to know. He needed to know and the only person to tell him the truth called out to him in the darkness.

"Jon," Beth whispered. "Are you asleep?"

"No," he answered. "I'm up. You okay?"

"Yes," she replied, finding the bed and crawling up into his arms. "I'm fine, just couldn't sleep and I wanted you. You're tense. What is it?"

"Nothing," he sighed.

"Tell me," Beth said.

"I'll be all right."

"Is it something I did?"

"No, not at all," he tightened his arm around her.

"Then tell me what is bothering you," she prompted.

"Is Steven mine?" he blurted out.

"Is that what's troubling you?" she asked.

"I need to know," he answered turning on the lamp beside his bed and pulling away to look at her.

"I know," she nodded. Taking a deep breath, she continued. "I suppose it's time I tell you the truth." Jon said nothing as he waited for the answer he had wanted for thirty-six years. "Before I say anything could you kiss me once more, in case this answer changes how you see me?" His brows furrowed but he leaned towards her and brushed his lips against hers. "You know about Paul Anderson," she began.

"Your ex-husband," Jon supplied.

"Yes, but do you know what he would... do to me," she said.

"He was abusive," he answered. She nodded.

"It was a week after you left for Vietnam," she began. "My parents were pleased you were gone, they never liked you. They knew about us and thought it unsuitable. You remember what they are like. My father had this friend; Paul. He was much older than me but Father always had him over, even when you and I were together. They would play pool and drink, a lot. Mother would have me take their drinks out to them and Father would ask Paul if he thought I was beautiful," she shut her eyes. "Paul would say I was and make lewd comments about me and what he would like to do to me. Father laughed it off and when I talked to Mother about it, she told me to encourage his attentions. He was far more suitable to our *way of life*.

"One night, a week after you left, we were having a party and I missed you so much I thought I might die. I went into the billiard room, the only room the party was to stay out of, just to collect my thoughts and he followed me. He shut the door and locked it, then stalked towards me like a predator. He told me that he always fancied me and wanted to see me out of my dress. I refused and tried to get around him to the door, he wouldn't let me. He grabbed me so tightly. I was seventeen, he was thirty-two and so much stronger than me. He ripped my dress open to my bra and grabbed me so tightly he left bruises. I cried out. I screamed for help but the music was too loud. He picked me up and threw me on my back on top of the pool table and before I knew what to do, he raped me. When he was... finished... all I wanted to do was run away but he told me he wasn't finished with me yet. I fought him but he raped me two more times, beating me as he did but never striking me where bruises were seen.

"Finally, he was done. I lay there limp, violated and tears streaming down my cheeks. My parents came in and found him... on top of me. My mother called me a whore and my father demanded we marry. I tried to tell them what he did and even showed the bruises but Paul convinced Father I had asked him to be rough, that I liked it and Father believed him. Mother hauled me out of the room and up into my bedroom. My Au Pair saw me and tried to convince Mother what I said was true. She smacked Olga to the ground and locked us both in the room.

"Olga held me all night as I cried. I told her what had happened and she promised to take me to the police in the morning. Olga woke me early and told me we needed to hurry. We were getting into the car when my parents came out along with Paul. They grabbed me, threw me into my rapist's arms and dismissed Olga on the spot. I never saw her again. Paul and I were married by a magistrate friend of my father's that day. That was my life; married to the man who raped and beat me. He even hit me once in front of my father but he did nothing.

"When I found out I was pregnant, I hoped against hope my baby was yours, but in my heart I knew he wasn't. I knew he was Paul's. I hated my husband but I could never hate my baby. So no, Steven isn't yours, Jon, at least, I don't think so."

Jon said nothing for a long time. He had always known

Paul was abusive. The maniac would track her down and Jon and Carol would receive a call late at night begging for help. But never in all his dreams did he know or guess the origin of the story. As much as he knew she needed him, he couldn't handle the anger that flowed through him. Standing, he turned to open the balcony doors letting the cold air calm his anger. He wanted to kill Paul Anderson.

He didn't turn until he heard the door to his room close. Only then did he realize Beth had left. Cursing, he grabbed his shirt and raced to her room. Without knocking, he barged in only to find her on the bed crying.

"Why did you leave?" he demanded.

"Because you didn't want me there."

"That's not true," he replied.

"Then why did you turn away from me?"

"Because I am this close to tracking the bastard down and killing him myself. And if I ever see your parents again I swear to God." Jon's anger was near to exploding. But when Beth turned back to look at him, he saw the sixteen-year-old young woman he had loved peek out and his anger melted. He rushed to her side. "I'm sorry." He held her tightly. "I'm so sorry." For what he did or for going to war and leaving her alone, he wasn't sure. "No matter what happened, we found each other again."

"Paul will never stop," she sobbed. "And this new case worries me. He swore he would come after you. He promised me he would see you dead. I worry he's using every one of us against you."

"He will stop when I have my hands around his throat," Jon answered. "You don't hurt what's mine and you are mine." His lips crashed on hers and she eagerly accepted him, anxious to rid her mind of unpleasant thoughts. Jon moved them both until he hovered over her. Removing his lips from hers for a moment, he gazed down at her. "That's why you froze yesterday. The last time you had a man make love to you he raped you."

She bit her lip and looked down. Jon gently slid a hand under her chin and forced her to look up at him. She nodded.

"I love you, Beth," he said keeping his anger in check. "I want you, but if you don't want to or can't do this, I understand."

"I want you, Jon," she replied. "Just understand I may have strong and unpleasant memories. And I'm... not the same."

"Of course you're not," he replied.

"No, I mean," she looked away. "I have stretchmarks, flab and wrinkles."

"You honestly think I care about all that?" he asked. "I love you. All of you, just the way you are."

"Could you just..." she started.

"What?" he asked kissing her nose.

When she didn't answer, he pulled back and looked down at her. They locked eyes and as usual, he read her mind.

Reaching over, he turned out the light on the nightstand. He felt her relax into the bed, but the full moon gave him just enough light to see her eyes glowing as she looked up at him. Raising his shirt, she slowly raked her nails down his stomach.

"Baby," he groaned. "It's been a while."

"Yeah, same here," she replied. "We'll take things slow."

"Not so sure about that," he said.

She framed his face and kissed him lightly.

"I love you," she said. "I love you so much."

"I love you too," he replied. "So damn much it hurts."

"Then prove it to me," she said. "Make love to me, Jon."

"With pleasure," he answered kissing her again and running his hand down her leg.

Chapter Thirty-Nine

It was past midnight but Courtney opened her email again and reread Chelsea's message.

Hey Courtney,

Has Ryan proposed yet? I just checked my references and I have attached the staff list for Northwestern Hospital from a year ago, six months ago, and the current listing. I found most of it on their website so it was pretty much easy-peasy. The rest was from a guy I knew there. Due to the economic struggles facing non-profit organizations these days, they have not hired any other staff members so what you see from six months ago should match the current listing. They did have to let some people go, though. Hopefully you find what you need. Let me know if you need any more help.

Courtney quickly opened the attached documents and skimmed through the two hundred names from six months ago and the one hundred and fifty from the current list. She opened both documents side by side. Sighing in relief when they were in alphabetical order, she highlighted the fifty names on the one from six months ago that did not show up on the current listing in one color and the names from the current list that were not on the one from six months ago in a different color.

Checking the time, she sighed and thought about going

to Jon's room to tell him what she had found but quickly rejected the idea, thinking Beth might be there.

Wanting to print the pages so Jon could see them with their detailed colors, she unplugged her laptop, threw on one of Ryan's sweatshirts she had commandeered and tiptoed quietly down the stairs.

At the door to Jon's study, she yelped when she heard a voice in the darkness.

"Courtney, what are you doing?" It was Rick.

"Oh, you startled me," she said then, taking in his appearance and jacket he wore, she asked, "were you outside?"

Rick pulled his coat around him tighter but spoke again. "You didn't answer my question. What are you doing?"

"I need to print something off and I'm sure Jon wouldn't mind," she answered.

"Does it have anything to do with the pot shot at Kim this morning?" Rick asked.

"I'm afraid I can't speak about open cases," Courtney stated.

"I'll take that as a yes," Rick answered.

"Take it however you wish, Rick," she replied. "But I am not saying anything more. What are you doing out so late?"

"Are you interrogating me?"

"Are you evading the question for a reason?" she asked.

"Don't you know? I always prowl around late at night," he spoke heatedly. "I have every right to prowl, it's my house, dammit."

"Why the anger?"

"Why the third degree?" Rick replied.

"What's going on here?" Keelan's voice came from the stairs. Rick looked up and headed to the steps.

"Don't show up in the middle of the night," he turned back to Courtney. "You might get cross-examined." He disappeared down the hall and Keelan came down the stairs.

"Are you all right?" he asked.

"Yeah, that was weird, wasn't it? I mean I'm not crazy, right?" she asked.

"Very strange," he answered. "Not sure what's wrong with him. Is there something I can help you with?"

"No, I just wanted to print something out. Jon showed me his printer earlier and told me I could use it. I couldn't sleep and thought I'd work a little."

"All right, well if you need my help, I can't sleep either. I'll be in the kitchen getting a glass of milk," Keelan offered.

"Thanks," Courtney answered and thanked him again when he opened the door for her.

As the lists printed, Courtney wondered how to approach Jon with his brother's odd behavior in the morning.

St. Patrick's Day morning, Courtney woke to the sound of raindrops hitting her windowpane. Getting up, she pulled on the same sweatshirt from the previous night and went to the window. She gazed out and smiled to see an almost eerie haze over the ground and a light drizzle wetting the earth. It felt like Thornfield Hall and her Rochester was knocking at her door.

"Can I come in?" Jon asked outside.

"Yes, Edward," she called.

Jon chuckled as he opened the door. "Good morning, Jane," he teased.

"Good morning," she replied, then, looking him up and down she smiled. "Did you and Beth have a good night?"

He blinked but didn't answer, instead he cleared his throat and asked, "did you sleep well?" He was already dressed in an emerald green sweater and jeans.

"Fairly," she replied. "It got cold."

"It'll do that," Jon answered, smiling.

"But I bet you were warm all night," she teased.

"Okay, how do you know?" Jon asked.

"Because a woman knows," she answered. "And you look different."

"I guess I am different," he replied.

"I'm so happy for you," she said. "I just hope she doesn't break your heart."

"My heart has been shattered many times but never more so than when I held Carol's body in my arms. Nothing can compare to that," Jon answered.

"No, I would imagine not," she replied turning back to the window. "Jon," she started. He walked up beside her. "Can I ask you something without issue?"

"Of course," he stated.

"I went down to your study last night to print something, it was around one in the morning and… Rick was there in a coat. He stopped me for a moment and we talked but when I asked him what he was doing he became frustrated and told me 'this is my house I have every right to prowl'. I thought it was a little odd. Is there something I don't know about him?"

Jon thought a moment. "I don't know why he would be upset. Did you see him doing anything?"

"It was so dark I didn't, but he was agitated and angry," she said. "Keelan was there too. Well, he came down the stairs when he heard him. He was going to the kitchen but told me it was odd behavior."

"Hmm," Jon's brow furrowed. "I'll talk to him. See what's going on."

"Thanks," she replied. They were quiet again and gazed out the window. Their eyes caught three people standing around a specific grave in the family graveyard she had seen earlier. "Is that Keelan?" She asked.

"Aye," he answered. "Keelan, his wife, and Iollan."

"Why are they there?" she asked.

"Today is the anniversary of Riley's death," Jon replied. "He was Keelan's middle son. He died in a boating accident four years ago today. His body wasn't found for another six weeks."

"Oh that's terrible," she said, seeing Aislín dry her eyes as she placed flowers at the grave. "How old was he?"

"Thirty-two," Jon replied. "Brendan, his older brother by three years, disappeared that day too."

"Do you know what happened to him?" she asked.

"No," Jon replied. "Keelan has five sons; Colman, Brendan, Riley, Sean and Iollan." Jon shook his head, watching Keelan reach for his wife as she cried, only to have her push him away and walk towards the side of the house and the pathway to the front. Iollan looked down but gripped his father's shoulder. Keelan nodded and they both walked into the house.

"Do they know what happened to cause the boating accident?" Courtney asked.

"He went out early one morning fishing and never returned. The boat was found washed up on the shore battered on the rocks. When Brendan disappeared, we found a note in his room saying something about going to France," Jon explained. "But he's not been in contact with anyone. After Keelan's money ran out, he begged me to hire investigators to find him. I would do anything for my friend and I cared for Brendan. When the first three investigators I hired found nothing, I went myself."

"And?" Courtney asked.

"No one had heard of Brendan," Jon replied. "And he's never been heard from since."

"To lose one child is bad enough but to lose two at one time is terrible."

After a moment, he continued. "I'm sorry, I didn't tell you why I came into your room this early."

She turned to him and smiled. "Why?" she asked.

"I bought this for you," he said. "And I was hoping you'd wear it today."

He offered a rectangular box that fit in the palm of his hand.

"What is it?" she asked, taking it.

"Open it," he said.

She looked up at him slyly and opened the lid. "Oh my God," she said. She looked up at him.

"Do you like it?" he asked.

"It's too much," she said.

"But do you like it?" he pressed.

"I love it." She took the emerald drop necklace cut in a four-leaf clover out of the box.

He walked around her to help her with the clasp as she pulled her hair up off her neck. Once the necklace was secure, she let her hair fall.

"Ryan and I picked it out. We both saw it and thought of you," he said, walking around to face her. "It's beautiful on you."

"Thank you," she hugged him.

"You're very welcome," he said. "Since I don't have a daughter I can spoil, I hope you don't mind me spoiling you."

"Jewelry is a woman's best friend," she smiled, pulling away from him. "You can spoil me all you want."

He chuckled. "Your first St. Patrick's Day in Ireland needed to be special. Now get dressed and come on down. Breakfast will be ready in about thirty minutes."

"And you'll talk to Rick?"

"I will," Jon promised.

"Oh, before I forget," she walked over to the nightstand beside her bed. "I looked at what Chelsea sent and highlighted who was there and who is new so we can go through it with Dave's list you asked for."

"Grand idea," Jon looked at the lists for a moment.

"Daniel Howard... why does that name sound familiar?"

"Do you know him?"

"Don't think so, but something," he focused on it then shook his head. "Old age, it'll come to me. When we get back to the office, let's get a background and current whereabouts for these," Jon said.

"I can order them from here," she offered. "That way they'll be waiting for us."

"Aren't you going to Scotland with your parents for a couple days?"

"Crap," she sighed. "Yeah. Well, then they'll be waiting for you."

"Listen, today," Jon started. "We're not going to think about the case. One day won't hurt us."

"True, okay. Then get out of my room so I can get dressed," she replied.

Scott and Kim walked down the hall and passed the door holding hands. Peeking in, Scott smiled and said good morning.

"I'm going," Jon replied once his son and Kim walked on. "Come down to the morning room."

"I'll be there in about twenty minutes," Courtney promised.

When she was alone, she grabbed a pair of jeans and a green sweater she had brought specifically for that day. Just as she was searching for her boots, she glanced out the window again and stopped. A man she had never seen before tiptoed out of the barn. Looking closer, she watched him look to his right and left then run towards the woods. He stopped briefly at Riley's grave and laughed, then disappeared into the forest.

She promised Jon she wouldn't look into the case, but she could look into the forest. She wanted to know just who was sneaking around and why, in the pit of her stomach, she hoped Rick wasn't involved.

Chapter
Forty

Jon and Rick stood outside the church waiting to greet the parishioners before mass. As usual, the service would reflect on who St. Patrick was and the brothers were expected to greet their villagers. Stealing a couple of minutes to themselves Ryan escorted everyone inside showing them the architecture of the four hundred year old church.

"What were you doing outside last night, Rick?" Jon finally asked.

"Courtney told you, didn't she?" Jon nodded and Rick sighed. "The business is failing," he admitted.

"What do you mean?" Jon asked.

"I mean we have been in the red for a while," Rick answered. "I can't keep the doors open for much more than... three months."

"Why didn't you tell me?" Jon asked.

"And have you sink another few thousand into it?" Rick demanded. "No, it's time to close up."

"Does Jenny know?"

"No," Rick replied. "She thinks it's only a few hundred."

"How much is it?"

"That I'm in debt for?" Rick clarified. Jon nodded.

"Twenty thousand."

"Jaysus, Rick," Jon breathed.

"I know I know," he answered. "How do you think I feel? We've been living off Jenny's teacher income and I've dipped into the retirement fund."

"And you were outside because?" Jon prompted.

Rick looked down but put his hand in his coat pocket and pulled out a pack of cigarettes. "I can't smoke in front of Jenny, she'll know something is up. So I go out in the middle of the night."

"Rick," Jon breathed.

"I know," Rick shook his head and gripped the pack as if ashamed. "I know what you're going to say. Da' made us both swear to drop it when he found out about the lung cancer but it's not that easy. I've been clean for forty years but it's…"

"Stress," Jon offered.

"Yeah," he answered. "So I was worried last night Courtney would find out and tell you and I sorta lost it. I didn't mean it. It was a stressful day and it's so hard to keep up appearances. My smoke break is the only time I can let it out. She got the brunt of it. I'm sorry."

"It's not good to keep it all inside, man," Jon said. "You need to tell Jenny. I can see she's worried."

"I will," Rick answered. "I just feel like such a failure."

"The economy is not kind to small businesses at the moment," Jon replied. "But you know you have me. I would see you back in the black if you wanted."

"You can't pay my debts for me, Jon," Rick shook his head. "I appreciate it but I won't have my baby brother solve my money problems."

"We're family," Jon replied. "Blood is thicker than water, Rick. I want to help. If you have to, consider it a loan and pay me back when you get your head above water."

"You'll never take repayment," Rick said.

"True but you don't have to tell yourself that," he answered. Just then, the first few parishioners came through the old gate.

"I'll think on it," Rick promised as they smiled at the older couple coming forward.

———

After mass, everyone walked to Bunratty town for the parade and celebrated at Durty Nelly's with Irish dancing and music. After a couple of drinks, Courtney felt Ryan's hand slip into hers. Looking up, she smiled at him and he nodded towards the door. She agreed and after telling her parents where she was going, she followed Ryan outside. The patio was just as busy and there were people in the streets laughing and singing along with the music.

Ryan led her down the street between the pub and the castle. Bunratty Castle loomed beside them and Courtney took a moment to enjoy the view. Eventually Ryan stopped on a small stone bridge overlooking a pond, with the castle at their backs. The trees had grown around the bridge but there was an opening through the limbs and Courtney saw the moon beginning to rise and the last of the sun's rays reflecting on the pond. A gander and his mate rested on the still water, their heads together.

"This was the view I wanted to share with you," Ryan whispered.

"It's breathtaking," she said and leaned back into his chest. His arms came around her and he rested his chin on her shoulder.

"I love you," Ryan breathed.

"I love you too," she answered reaching up and stroking his face.

"Thank you," he said.

"For what?" she turned in his arms and looked up at his

shining blue eyes.

"For loving me, for giving me a family. I never thought I'd have anyone else care for me, but you and your family have accepted me and care for me. I never dared hope for anything after my parents died."

"I love you, Ryan," she said. "You are my family."

"You have always been there for me, helped me through tough times and laughed with me through good times. I want more of that. I want you by my side, in my bed, and with me until we grow old and die together." Courtney's breath caught when he released her and lowered to one knee. Pulling out a jewelry box, he opened the lid. The engagement ring she had fallen in love with two months ago at Tiffany's, stared back at her. "Courtney Shields, I have brought you to the place I love. I have shared with you the one thing I have not shared with anyone and I want to share many more with you. Will you make me the happiest man on earth? Will you marry me?"

Covering her mouth with her hands as tears gathered in her eyes, she nodded. "Yes," she confidently said. "Yes, Ryan. Yes, I will marry you."

Ryan's eyes lit and his face glowed in the late light. He took out the ring and slid it onto her finger. When he stood, she threw her arms around his neck and he picked her up, twirling her around. They kissed in the shadow of the castle. Finally pulling away, Courtney heard cheers and applause. She didn't realize their family had followed them out of the pub and were taking pictures.

Laughing, she leaned into Ryan's chest. Her mother ran up to her and hugged her tightly as her dad shook hands with Ryan and pulled him into a hug. Jon walked up to them and hugged them both. After pictures were taken and shared, Jon announced there was cold champagne back at the castle and they all piled into the van.

Chapter
Forty-One

"Anything?" Rob asked as soon as Aeron arrived back in the States.

"Nothing," Aeron lied. "It was quiet."

"You know what to do," he said.

"Oh yes," he answered. "I've been looking forward to this for years."

With the new list of names, Courtney decided to get back to the States and work on the case instead of heading to Scotland. After they solved the mystery, she would treat herself and maybe Chelsea and her mom to another trip. But, Monday morning she and Jon arrived back at their office to go over the lists she had color coded.

After about three hours, Jon rubbed his eyes. "Any luck?" He asked as soon as Courtney hung up her call. She shook her head.

"They are all legit," she answered.

"Same here," he replied rolling his neck and standing. "I'm gonna run across the street and get a coffee. You want one?"

"That'd be great, thank you," she replied.

"Your usual?" he asked.

"Actually," she answered. "Could you get me a small one of yours? Jet lag is catching up with me."

"Sure, be back in a sec," he replied as he pulled on his suit jacket and left the room. Courtney turned to the next name on the list:

Daniel Howard, RN

"All right, Daniel," Courtney said. "What's your story? And how does Jon know your name?"

"I'm in position, but they're in the basement," Aeron said over his earpiece.

"They'll have to come up some time," Rob promised. "Oh, how was your conversation with Detective Shields?"

"I pulled off the Dan Howard, RN pretty convincingly," he answered. "She has no idea who I am."

"Let's keep it that way," Rob replied. "Why did they think they knew your name?"

"Are you bugging my phone?" Aeron demanded.

"Of course I am," Rob answered. "Now tell me why."

Aeron sighed. "I used middle names from my family. Daniel is my original middle name and Howard is my brother's."

"How could you be so stupid?" Rob asked. "Don't you think he would recognize them?"

"No, I never used my middle in Ireland," Aeron answered. "It's nothing."

"She would not have mentioned it if it was nothing."

"I think I've earned a little of your trust after everything."

"Trust? Like you wouldn't stab me in the back at the first opportunity? Spare me," Rob stated. "Now do your job."

Jon, Scott, and Ryan watched a movie downstairs in the basement finishing Jon's famous pizza. As the credits rolled on the new action movie, Jon stood up and took the dishes to the small kitchenette.

Scott stretched out on the couch. "Dad, I think your pizza is the only one I eat like ten slices."

"I'm glad you liked it," Jon laughed. "I always like cooking for my lads but aren't you supposed to be over at Kim's place?"

"She's having girl night with Courtney and Chelsea wedding planning, so I've been kicked to the curb for the evening," he explained.

"And our usual guy nights will have to be moved around to fit your schedule, huh?" Ryan teased.

"You're one to talk," Scott laughed. "Besides Kim told me as long as we don't have strippers and a pole come up out of the floor she'll be fine."

"Damn, I'll have to call Destiny and Desirae and cancel our usual dances," Jon pretended to pull out his phone and dial as the lads rolled with laughter.

After a little while, Scott turned to his cousin. "So," he started. "How does it feel?"

"How does what feel?" Ryan asked.

"Being off the market?" Scott replied.

"I've been off the market for a while now," Ryan smiled. "But it's pretty incredible to be engaged. And you? You and Kim seem... serious."

"Never thought I could be this happy," Scott said. "What do you think, Dad? Both your lads found women to love."

"I wanted nothing more," Jon replied cleaning up the kitchen.

"When's your time, Uncle Jon?" Ryan asked.

"Oh, don't let him fool you," Scott laughed. "He and Beth are... well let me just say I saw more of both of them than I ever intended to see."

"If you had knocked and waited for me to reply before you

barged in then maybe you wouldn't have," Jon replied.

"So you're official?" Ryan asked.

"Yes," Jon answered. Before Scott could say anything, Ryan's phone rang.

"Excuse me, gentlemen," he said, standing and taking his beer. "My future wife is calling."

"What about the girl night?" Scott called after him.

"How are things really?" Jon asked after he finished with the dishes and walked over to Scott.

"Honestly," Scott shook his head as Jon sat beside him. "I never thought it could be this good. Why didn't I see it before? She's funny and brilliant and so damn sexy."

"Have you thought about the future?" Jon asked.

"Yes, I have," Scott admitted.

"And?"

"I want to marry her," he answered. "I know it's crazy we've only been together as a couple for two weeks but I don't want to lose her. I love her and I want her by my side."

Jon smiled and squeezed his son's shoulder. "I'm glad. Wait here, there's something I want to give you." Jon stood and headed for the stairs. Once up in his bedroom, he opened his armoire and rummaged around. Finally finding the small box, his eyes caught Carol's picture. "You told me to give it to him when he's ready, baby, and I don't want it on anyone else's finger but hers. I know you loved her for our son." Kissing his finger, he placed it over her lips in the photo and smiled.

Trotting down the stairs, he stopped short when he saw Scott in the kitchen bending over the fridge.

Pulling up, Scott looked over and indicated the bottle of coke in his hand. "We were out downstairs and I wanted a whiskey coke."

Just as he said that, the window shattered and the coke bottle exploded. Jon collided with his son, tackling him to the floor just as rapid firing bullets ricocheted around them.

Grabbing a gun from under the cabinet, Jon didn't think, he leopard crawled to the back door. "Ryan, stay down there," Jon shouted when he heard his step on the basement stair. Looking out the door's window, he pulled back and ducked as a bullet whizzed past his cheek and lodged into the wall.

It was so quiet.

A couple seconds later, tires squealed away and faded into the distance. Jon took a deep breath.

"Sound off," he shouted.

"I'm fine," Ryan called back.

Then nothing. "Scott?" Jon called. Nothing. "Dammit, Scott, answer me." Nothing. A sick feeling overcame him and he looked down. His shirt had blood on it.

He raced to his son's prone figure still lying on his stomach in the kitchen. "Scott!" he shouted. Turning him over, Jon froze. Scott's eyes were closed and blood covered his face and shirt.

"Ryan!" Jon shouted. Ryan raced up the stairs and to his uncle. Checking for a pulse, Ryan's face was grim. Jon's body shook when he saw the bullet wound in his son's left shoulder.

Ryan let out a breath. "Thank God," he sighed. "He's alive. We need to get him to the hospital." Ryan dialed 911 and spoke quickly to the dispatcher. Jon held Scott in his arms and didn't realize he was rocking him back and forth until Ryan's hand landed on his shoulder. "He's alive."

Jon nodded quickly but that didn't stop the image of his son, bloodied and unconscious. Whoever it was that shot him, Jon would kill, slowly.

Chapter
Forty-Two

"Is he dead?" Rob asked.

"Yes," Aeron confirmed.

"Good. Get on the phone with Hannah. It's time for her to do her bit."

Aeron nodded, but when Rob left the room, he pulled out his book, noted the time and crossed Scott's name off the list.

Ryan instructed the ambulance driver to take them to St. Vincent's Carmel, ten minutes from Jon's house. As they rushed Scott's gurney into the hospital, Ryan went with the doctors, giving Scott's blood pressure, heart rate and telling them what happened.

The nurses stopped Jon from following them. Had they been men, Jon would have knocked them down and forced his way in, but since two women nodded at him trying to convey that his son would be all right, he just thrust his hands through his hair and pulled out his phone.

Ryan walked to the waiting room to see his uncle on the phone. Walking towards him, he heard him say, "Ryan's back. I'll see you soon." Hanging up, Jon looked over at him. "Well?"

"He's in emergency surgery. It shouldn't take more than a couple of hours," Ryan answered.

"Who's the surgeon?"

"Fred," Ryan replied.

"Thank god, so what now? I can't just wait around here for an hour while my son's in surgery."

"You need to calm down, Uncle Jon," Ryan said. "You'll do neither yourself nor Scott any good if you work yourself up."

Jon walked away from him, thrusting his hands through his thick black hair, and closed his eyes. Ryan waited. His uncle turned back to him.

"Beth and Kim are on their way," Jon spoke low. "I've sent Courtney to the house to claim the crime scene."

"Maybe you should go with her," Ryan replied.

"If you think for one second I'm leaving this hospital then you don't know me at all," Jon spat.

"I'm trying to get you to calm down," Ryan replied.

"My son is fighting for his life," Jon shouted.

"And the man I would trust with anyone's life is operating on him," Ryan said calmly. "He will be all right."

———————

Jon paced the waiting area. Beth held her daughter as Kim cried silently. There had been no news and even Ryan was starting to worry. Four hours after they had arrived, the buzzer they had been given buzzed in Kim's hand. She let out a dry little cry and looked down as if she held a snake. Everyone froze. Finally, Ryan stepped forward and extended his hand to take the object. Turning, he locked eyes with his uncle and nodded once. Walking over to the station, Ryan led them all to a private waiting room.

Another ten minutes ticked by as they waited for the doctor. Finally, Fred walked in, his face a mask of cool confidence.

"He's alive," Fred said. Kim let out a small screech and Jon let out a sigh, bent at the waist and put his hands on his knees as if he was about to pass out.

"What took so long?" Ryan asked.

"We nearly lost him twice," Fred explained. "The bullet was clamping his subclavian artery and when we removed it, he lost a substantial amount of blood. We were able to clamp it and revived him, but as we were trying to stabilize him, he began bleeding internally and again flat-lined. We got him back but we wanted to make sure he stayed that way before we let him out of the OR. He's in recovery now."

"Can we see him?" Jon asked.

"For a short time," Fred replied. "He needs to be watched constantly. His heart is beating but he's not out of the woods yet."

As Jon nodded and helped Beth and Kim to their feet, Ryan walked over to his mentor.

"Thank you," he said. "If it had been anyone else operating on him..." he shook his head. "I doubt the outcome would have been the same."

"I never lost faith in you when you were rushed into my ER over a decade ago after your parent's accident," Fred replied. "I wasn't about to let another family member be taken from you."

Ryan clapped him on the upper arm. "I know, thank you."

"You're welcome," Fred smiled. "Now, Scott's in room 310."

"I'll take them," Ryan said.

Chapter
Forty-Three

A dull ache was all Scott could feel and comprehend. He was in pain, a massive amount of pain. Groaning, he moved his head as much as he could. His shoulder hurt like hell but he couldn't move.

"Scott," he heard faintly, his ears ringing. "Scottie?"

Unable to reply, he merely groaned and moved his head toward the voice. Finally, he opened his eyes to slits and his father's face came into view.

"Hey," Jon breathed and stroked Scott's hair off his forehead. "How are you feeling?"

It took Scott a second to reply, his throat and mouth were so dry. When he finally mustered the strength to speak, his voice was raw.

"Okay," he answered. "Could I have some water?"

"I don't know," Jon replied. "Let me call the nurse." Jon reached over him to push the nurse call button.

"Nurse? What happened?"

"What do you remember?" Jon asked.

"I was talking to you, then the window shattered and there was just this pain, then nothing."

"You were shot," Jon stated.

"Shot?" Scott asked. "How? What happened? Is everyone else okay? Where's Kim?"

"Shh shh shh," he soothed. "She hasn't left your side. I told her to go rest for a moment, get some coffee. She'll be back up. We're not sure how or why, but it has to do with this case."

"Are you okay?" Scott asked.

"Now that you're awake? Yes," Jon said. "You scared the shit out of me, Scottie."

"I'm sorry," Scott replied.

"It's not your fault," Jon stated. "But I will kill the man who did this to you."

"Did I... die?" Scott asked.

"Why do you ask?" Jon replied.

"I don't know," Scott tried to shrug but immediately grimaced and groaned. "I do remember something. I... saw mom."

Jon swallowed and took a deep breath before answering. "You did?"

"Yeah, I opened my eyes and saw the doctor and nurses working around me, but I didn't hear what they were saying, and I wasn't in any pain. I saw this brilliantly bright white light. I walked toward it, but before I could reach it, it dimmed and I could see someone standing there. It was mom. She was dressed in a beautiful white gown. I ran to her and she hugged me, but the weird thing was I didn't feel like a little kid like I do when I dream about her. I actually felt my age. It felt so real.

"She kissed my cheek and stroked my face. I asked her if I was dead and she told me that for a short time, I was. But I had to go back for your sake. She said you couldn't lose me too.

"I told her how much I missed her and she told me how much she loved me. She said Kim and I will have a wonderful life together and told me not to be afraid to ask her. She also asked me to tell you something."

Jon waited, trying to swallow around the lump in his throat.

"She made me promise to tell you something. She said to tell you to start living again and that she loves you forever and a day."

Jon closed his eyes. The lump in his throat won and his tears ran down his cheeks. He remembered those words. She had whispered them to him on their wedding night just as he was falling asleep.

"She also said you must remember October twentieth," Scott said.

Jon's brows pulled together. "October twentieth?" he repeated. "Are you sure?"

"Positive," Scott promised. "She made me say it back to her. What does it mean?"

"I don't know," Jon admitted.

"I don't remember much else except she kissed my cheek and then I woke up here."

"You scared me, son," Jon said.

"I'm sorry," Scott answered.

"I love you, you know that, right?"

"Yeah, I do, Dad and I love you too. I have been very blessed. You and Mom have been the best parents to me."

"We love you," Jon said.

"I know and you have put your life on hold to help me," Scott answered. "I want you to promise me you will pick your life up again. You and Beth are great. I know you will never stop loving mom but you deserve to be happy."

"I promise I will try," Jon said. "I will always love your mother, but yes I am in love with Beth."

"Good," Scott answered.

A sharp knock came from the door and Jon and Scott turned to look. Ryan and a nurse walked in.

"You're awake," Ryan smiled. "Good, how are you doing?" The nurse went over to the machine to take vitals.

"A bit stiff and thirsty," Scott said.

"Ice wouldn't hurt, but not a lot," Ryan cautioned.

"When can I head home?" Scott asked.

"We need to keep you here a couple more days. There was a complication during surgery. The bullet nicked your subclavian artery, so you lost a lot of blood."

"I know I flat lined," Scott said.

"Twice, according to Fred," Ryan answered. "What's blood pressure reading?" He asked the nurse.

"One hundred over sixty," the nurse said.

"Okay but low," Ryan pulled out his stethoscope and, with the nurse's help, elevated the bed so Scott could sit up. Untying his gown, Ryan instructed him to take as deep a breath as he could without pain and listened. After a moment, Ryan pulled back and wrapped the instrument around his neck. "Lungs sound clear and heartbeat's strong. Low BP isn't unusual after surgery but we definitely want to monitor it."

"Anything I can do to help?" Scott asked.

"Focus on getting healthy," Ryan said. "I'll get you that ice." After they left, Scott looked around the room.

"Who sent the flowers?" he asked.

"Your firm sent you the largest one," Jon said. "Alex and his parents, Tom, Courtney and her parents. Rick and Jenny sent you this one," Jon said, gesturing. "They're in the cafeteria too, by the way, with Sarah."

"They came?" Scott asked.

"They got the first flight out," Jon said. "I called them before you went into surgery. Want me to go get them? I know they'll want to make sure you're okay."

"How long have I been out?"

"Three days."

"What?" Scott breathed just as Ryan walked back into the room with Kim. One look around Ryan, she gasped and raced to him.

"Hey, baby," Scott reached for her with his good arm. She gently but quickly wrapped her arms around him. "I'm okay." She was crying into his shoulder. Jon took his leave and stepped out into the hallway.

As soon as he shut the door, giving them privacy, Jon turned and headed down the hallway. "Jon?" a voice called to him. Jon froze and turned. Mat stood in the shadows. Without a second thought, Jon walked towards him. "Is he okay?"

"He's awake," Jon said.

"Oh, thank god," Mat breathed. "I was sick when she told me."

"What's going on, Mat?" Jon demanded. "This son-of-a-bitch just shot my son."

"I know," Mat replied. "And if I could tell you without unknown consequences I would, I promise. I'm so close, Jon I am so close to taking it down."

"Let me help you. You can't do this on your own."

"I have to."

"Dammit, Mat, I won't let you."

"You don't have a choice," Mat said. "Now listen, I can't stay long."

Aeron unlocked his front door and walked up the stairs with his groceries. When he flipped on the light, he jumped when he saw Rob sitting in the chair waiting for him.

"Jaysus," he breathed. "You scared the life out of me. What are you doing here?"

"He's still alive," Rob's voice was calm but Aeron heard the tense undertone.

Aeron was quiet for a moment. "Are you sure?" he finally

asked.

"Yes," Rob replied. "And Mat went to the hospital. Where is Hannah?"

"Not sure," he replied setting the bags down on the counter. "She's supposed to come over tonight."

"Not until this is settled," Rob stood in a movement similar to a cat and walked toward him. "You screwed up. Fix it."

"How?" Aeron asked.

"Use your head," he said walking towards the stairs. "Who did I first meet two years ago?"

As he left the apartment, Aeron began putting his groceries away. Rob was asking him to become Dan Howard, RN again. The disguise was only good as long as Jon didn't see him. Scott would be too high to recognize him and it had been over four years since they had seen him. He texted Hannah to cancel their evening and went to the bathroom pulling out his actor's makeup. Dan had a scar that Aeron was rather fond of but it took time and precision. Setting the makeup on the counter he got to work altering his face.

Jon walked back into his son's hospital room, pausing in the doorway when he saw Scott and Kim snuggled on the hospital bed.

"Was that Mat I saw leaving?" Beth asked walking up beside him.

Jon turned, pressing a finger to his lips and ushered them both out of the room. Shutting the door behind him, he pulled Beth into his arms and slowly leaned down to kiss her.

"Don't think about distracting me," Beth said.

"Never," his wicked grin successfully distracted her for a moment. Shaking away the thoughts his grin caused her to have, she asked him her question again. "Yes," Jon answered. "That was Mat. He came to make sure Scott was okay."

"Okay?" Beth asked angrily. "He is part of the reason he's in here."

Jon placed both hands gently on her arms. "He's told me somethings that I need to tell Courtney. Will you stay here until I get back?"

"You have to ask?" she said.

Kissing her lightly, thanking her, he promised to be back soon and headed out.

"Just be careful," she called after him. "One Greene in the hospital is enough."

"I will. I promise," he replied.

Chapter
Forty-Four

Courtney stood as soon as Jon walked into the office. Just as he was about to say something, she stopped him.

"We have a problem, sir," she stressed. Jon said nothing and soon heard the voice coming from Mat's office.

"Mr. Mayor, sir I understand our best man is on the job, but I should have been notified and not have to hear about this on the news. Do you know the kind of accusations that are being thrown at this division?"

"Let me handle it," Jon whispered. Courtney nodded and walked with him to the door. Knocking sharply, Jon waited until he heard the approval to come in. Opening the door, Jon stepped through. "Mr. Mayor, Deputy Chief," Jon greeted.

"Ah, good, Lieutenant," the mayor said and stood, offering his hand for Jon to shake. "Detective," he addressed Courtney and offered his hand to her.

"Mayor Balton," she greeted.

"Did you fail to notify me of this, Lieutenant?" The Deputy Chief demanded.

"Lieutenant Greene and Detective Shields were working for me and I instructed them to keep a tight lid on things," Mayor Balton stated. "Your fight is with me, not them. Now I appreciate your concern and trust me when I say that when you are needed, if you are needed, to make an arrest, you will be the first to hear of it. Until then, I ask you to leave this very delicate case to me and my hand chosen team. Trust me, Tim." Huffing a sigh, the deputy chief finally nodded. "Now, if you would, I will need to speak with the Lieutenant and Detective." Tim left the room and once the door was shut, silence lasted about ten seconds until the mayor turned to Jon and fell into Mat's chair. "This is a shit show, Jon."

"Believe me, sir, we know," Jon answered. Mayor Balton offered them both a seat and continued.

"I received this letter from Mat earlier today," he said and tossed the paper to Jon and Courtney. "How the news media got a hold of it, I'm not sure."

> *Mr. Mayor,*
>
> *I hereby tender my resignation. I have become involved too deeply in an ongoing investigation and I can no longer place my colleagues and my friends in the danger that surrounds me. I have kept a case file, number WQB2BKK4 in my safe in my office. Lieutenant Greene knows the combination. Everything I have garnered is in there. Please accept my apology for putting the force, my family, friends and even you, sir in danger. I ask you to give me twenty-four hours upon receipt of this letter and I will turn myself in, if I do not, you may safely assume I am dead.*
>
> *Thank you for all of your support over the years. It has been my highest honor to serve you as Captain of the greatest police force.*
>
> *Mateo Bernardo*
> *Former Captain IMPD*

"Where's this case file he's talking about?" the mayor asked.

"Sir, he may have said that I know a combination, but he never told me," Jon admitted.

"Then he clearly thought you could figure it out."

"The safe is behind you, sir, in that wall behind the painting," Jon explained. The mayor stood and turned to look at the painting. Removing it from the wall, he studied the wall safe. "This is an original of the building. The combination would have to be in the files somewhere."

"Forgive me, sir," Courtney stood and walked to the safe. "This is a Liberty safe, it's one of the hardest safes to crack."

"Didn't you excel at safe cracking in the academy, Shields?"

"I did, sir," she answered. "I would be happy to work on this for you, but I will need absolute silence."

"Go work on it and let me know when you have it open."

Once Jon and Courtney were alone, she turned to him. "It will take too long for me to crack this. It would probably be best if I knew more about him. Something personal. You probably know the combination, we need to think," she said.

"All right," Jon replied. "Liberty safes have a four-digit combination, right?" Courtney nodded.

"If we look at it objectively," she continued. "It should be something he treasured, a numeric code of a name or a favorite date or a lucky number. Most of the time, as odd as it is, it's a birthday. Try his birthday, month, day, and block the year to two numbers like nineteen then sixty-five or whatever," she said.

Jon side glanced at her. "He will love you for that." Reaching for the spin dial, he spun it as he said the numbers aloud.

"Eight, twenty-three, nineteen, forty-nine," Jon said.

"Nineteen forty-nine?" Courtney asked.

"Like I said, he will love you for that."

"Wow. He definitely doesn't look his age," she replied.

"Or act it," Jon said then tried the handle. "That's not the right combo."

"Is there another date he would have used?" Courtney asked. "Something important to him? Come on, Jon. You know him better than anyone."

Thinking a moment, he reached for the dial again. "Twelve, twenty-three, nineteen, fifty-six," he tried. Still nothing. "Damn. I was hoping that was it."

"A birthday?" Courtney asked.

"No, it's the day they arrived in the US as immigrants," Jon replied.

"Was there a woman in his life? I mean, besides the one right now," Courtney said.

Jon shook his head. "Mat isn't exactly the monogamous type."

"What about when he was deployed to Vietnam?" she asked. Jon tried the date. Still nothing. "What about when you saved his life, when he was wounded?" she asked.

"Oh hell, I don't remember the specific date," Jon replied.

"You said in your text to me he met you at the hospital, did he mention anything, something that could be used?" Courtney asked.

"Maybe," Jon replied. "He said he was sorry it had gotten this far and that he wouldn't let it go on. He's ending it all soon."

"There's got to be something else," Courtney said. "Something personal."

"He said he envied me," he admitted. "Scott and me, our relationship. He said he missed his chance to be happy and have the same type of relationship with a son or daughter. He said ever since Carol died, he's seen our relationship grow stronger and he knows I still love her—"

"That's it!" Courtney interrupted. "Jon, what day has impacted all three of your lives in such a way none of you will ever forget? What day was your life turned upside down? Try the day Carol died."

Without another word, Jon reached for the dial and spun it to the date. The bolt clicked and the safe opened. The file lay before them.

"Courtney," Jon said softly reaching for the file. "Lock the doors."

Courtney nodded and locked both doors as Jon sat at Mat's desk. Coming back to stand behind him, she watched as he opened the file.

There was nothing but several blank pages of computer paper, nothing was written on the document.

"I don't understand," Courtney said. "Why would he go through all that trouble to hide something that's empty?"

"Because he's sending me a message," Jon replied.

"What message?" she asked.

"I wish to God I knew," he answered. "He gave me the clue to unlock the safe. He knew the Deputy Chief would be on this case and he knew the mayor would stonewall him enough to give us some time. But in case he didn't or someone else cracked the safe, he added another layer of security. I don't want to get any of these pages out of order," opening the desk's drawers he pulled out a large clip and clipped the pages together.

"What are you thinking?" she asked.

"Not sure, but there is a lot of ways an old Marine can communicate," Jon replied as his eyes drifted to the Remington statue Mat had on his desk. "Mat always treasured this. His father bought it for him after he got home from Vietnam. He always teased me saying it should have been mine since my code name was knight and his was bishop. This isn't going to be easy. Mat is a math genius. It could be anything."

"But how do you even know it's a code?" Courtney asked.

"Because it's Mat. And what else could it be? He's given

us at least that much," he answered. Grabbing the Remington statue, the heavy, bronze, cowboy on a bucking horse, he turned it over and paused. A key was taped to the bottom with the letter J written in black sharpie.

"A safety deposit box key?" Courtney asked.

"I'm going to hold on to it," Jon said, pocketing the key and turning back to the file. "Count with me," Jon asked as he began to flip through the pages.

"Sixty?" she asked after they finished. "Is that important?"

"I hope so," he said pulling out his phone and dialing a number. "Hey baby, listen is Scott awake? I need to talk to him."

"Let me check," Beth said and after a moment heard muffled voices. "Yeah, he's awake but he's tired."

"Understood, I just need his help on something," Jon replied. After a second, his son's voice came over the phone. "Hey lad, how are you feeling?"

"I've been better," Scott replied. "But the pain is manageable. What's up?"

"Good, I had an emergency at work but I know the women are keeping an eye on you."

"Mmhmm," Scott replied.

"I won't keep you long, I know you need to rest. But I have a puzzle. Does the number sixty mean anything to you?"

"In what context?" Scott's sleepy voice asked.

"Mainly your uncle," Jon said.

"Then yeah, it means something."

"So what did he say?" Courtney asked after Jon hung up the phone twenty minutes later.

"Sixty is a very interesting number to mathematicians. It's the only number between one and fifty-nine that has the largest amount of divisors. These," Jon pointed out the list of numbers he wrote down. "Are twelve divisors. If you take away sixty and have only the unitary divisors of one, three, four, five, twelve, fifteen, and twenty and add those, you get sixty."

"I'm guessing that's unique to the number?" she asked.

Nodding, Jon continued. "According to Scott, unitary divisors are numbers that divide into the number it divides. If the number five, which is a divisor of sixty, is placed in the divisor of an equation and sixty is the dividend, twelve, which is another divisor of sixty, would be the answer or quotient. Because five and sixty have only one, besides the number one, common factor, then it is a unitary divisor, as are one, three, four, twelve, fifteen, and twenty, they're interchangeable. That is what makes it so fascinating."

"What does all of this have to do with the captain?" Courtney asked.

"I'm not sure yet but there's more," Jon replied. "The number sixty is between two primes, fifty-nine and sixty-one and it is the sum of two primes, twenty-nine and thirty-one, the same style of numbers ending in nine and one, as well as the sum of four primes; eleven, thirteen, seventeen, and nineteen. The Roman numeral for sixty is LX."

"Was the captain into numbers?"

"Yes," Jon answered. "Very much so. He was the one who got Scott interested in math at a very young age."

"So, he knew you'd call Scott? And he knew Scott would know all of this?" Courtney paused a moment.

"What are you thinking?" Jon asked.

"What if you didn't call Scott?" she asked. "I mean, what if you hadn't counted the papers?"

"With Mat? Always count the papers," Jon said.

"No matter what, you would have counted them. You would have called Scott. So... let's think about what, in all of the information given, would be important to real life. It's not like this guy Aeron is a mathematician. At least, I doubt it. You and I are not either. So what would make sense?" After a beat, she continued. "What's the Roman numeral for sixty?"

"LX," Jon answered.

"Okay so what could that mean?" Courtney sat across from him. "LAX California airport... Luxury, Lux, light... Lexus..."

"Lexus LX," Jon said.

"It's the car," they both said at the same time.

"Brilliant," Jon praised. "Let's go."

Chapter
Forty-Five

Kim looked toward the door as it slowly opened and someone knocked gently. When Rick popped his head in, she relaxed.

"How is he?" Rick whispered.

"He's fitful," she answered. "His shoulder hurts him. I've tried to move away but he keeps holding me too tightly."

Rick smiled gently. "He doesn't want you to leave."

"I wouldn't, but he needs to rest comfortably," she replied.

"Aye, but I think I can safely say he would not sleep comfortably if you left. But that's not why I'm here. Jon called and let me know he's heading back to the house to get some things but didn't know if Scott requested anything specific?"

"I don't think so," Kim said. "Not to me at least."

"I'll call him back," Rick smiled. "Is there anything I can get you?"

"I'm good, thank you," she answered. "I just want him healed."

"I know, we all do. Sarah is so worried about him, but I know she'll want to crawl on the bed and I don't want her to hurt him. Once he wakes up I'll bring her."

"He'll like that," she said. Another knock drew their

attention. A nurse walked in and looked from one to the other.

"Oh, I'm sorry," he said. "I was called to help Mr. Greene shower."

"He's asleep at the moment," Kim answered. "Thank you, Mister…?"

"Dan Howard, Mrs. Greene," the nurse said.

"Ms. Anderson, we're not married."

"Yet," Rick supplied.

"My apologizes," Dan answered. "When Mr. Greene is ready, please don't hesitate to give one of the nurses a call. If he would prefer a male nurse bathe him, I'm the one on duty at the moment, but there's another coming in later. Just ask for me and they'll get the right person."

"Thank you, I will," Kim replied. Dan nodded to them both and as he headed for the door, Rick spoke up.

"Have we met before?" he said.

Dan stopped and turned to him. "I don't think so, sir," he said. "It's possible, though. Do you come to the hospital a lot?"

"No, I'm not from here," Rick replied.

"Well, I do a work rotation at a couple other hospitals in the area. I'm helping out here today."

"No, no, it wasn't here," Rick said. Then after studying him for a moment waved it off and turned. "Sorry, must be me old mind playing tricks on me."

"Well, if you do remember, let me know, there's nothing I like more than meeting old friends again." With that, Dan smiled at Kim and walked out of the room.

"Are you all right?" Kim asked.

"Something's off," Rick replied. "I know I've seen that man before but I don't know where." Rick shook it off and turned back to Kim. "I'll call Jon."

———— ◦ ————

Jon pulled into the driveway of his house and parked the

car outside the garage.

"I'm going to grab a couple things for Scott. Won't be a second."

"I'll come in with you, I could use a water," she said.

"Sure," he answered opening his car door. Walking in together, Courtney was silent for a moment, then as Jon unlocked the garage door to the house, she spoke.

"There must be a thousand Lexus LX cars in the general metropolitan area. How do we know which one we're looking for?"

"Before we left, I sent a text to Dave. He's running a trace on Mat's phone and hopefully when it's found, we will search security cameras in that area and see if there's a car matching that description."

"Smart."

"Yeah, yeah," he waved off. "I'll be right back."

"Take your time," she answered going to the fridge. "I'm going to raid your fridge by the way. I'm starving."

When he didn't answer, she looked over at him. His eyes were on the floor of the kitchen beside the fridge. Scott's blood still stained the cherry wood, cordoned off by the police line tape. Slipping her hand over his forearm, Courtney squeezed.

"Come on, partner, let's get out of here quickly and go see your son."

Taking a deep breath, he nodded and stepped around the police tape to run up the back stairs. As her partner disappeared up the stairs, Courtney opened the fridge and pulled out a water bottle and a slice of cold pizza. Looking around the kitchen as she ate over the sink, the bullet holes that marred the cherry cabinets were concentrated near the fridge. Scott was the target.

With that revelation, she finished her pizza and walked toward Jon's study. She needed to use his computer to log in to the Police database. As much as it would be an intrusion of her partner's privacy, she needed to run a background on Scott. Someone wanted him dead.

Hoping to have the background check ordered before Jon finished upstairs, she opened the door to the study and froze.

"Jon," she called.

———————

Scott slowly opened his eyes. The pain in his shoulder was manageable but his head ached. Groaning softly, he felt someone shift beside him.

"Scott?" Kim said softly making him smile.

"Mm," he moaned.

"How are you feeling?" he opened his eyes to see her leaning over him and feeling her body pressed to his.

"Better now," he answered. "Kiss me?"

Stroking his hair off his forehead, she leaned down slowly and kissed him lightly. When she pulled back his eyes were still closed

"I missed you," he said. "You were in my dreams but every time I tried to reach out for you, you pulled away."

"I'm right here," she answered. "Maybe it's because real life is better than a dream."

"It is now," he replied. "I love you."

"I love you," she said. "Don't scare me like that again. Do you understand me?"

"Yes, ma'am," he teased his Texan drawl, which only came out on occasion, caressed the moniker.

"Good," she kissed him again. "You have two options," she went on. "One, see your family now or two, have a shower. Which will it be?"

"Do I need a shower?" he asked.

"You could use one," she teased. "But I think more for your comfort than anything else."

"Then I'll take a shower, love," he replied.

Chapter
Forty-Six

Everything except Jon's desk lamp was thrown on the floor. The papers, books, and knickknacks he had on his desk were scattered everywhere. One thing sat in the center of the mahogany desk. The white queen from the chess set he had in the corner of the room, sat alone on the surface. Looking back at the chessboard, only two other pieces were in play, the rest were pushed to the floor.

As Jon's eyes took in the scene, he saw his picture of Carol had been picked up and placed on the mantelpiece behind the desk. That subtle move told him who had been in the room. Mat was trying to tell him something.

"There was something about that letter from Mat that still bothers me and I can't quite put my finger on," he said.

"What was it?"

Jon said nothing for a while but as he walked to the chessboard, he paused.

"The file, do you have it?" he asked.

"Yeah," Courtney went back out to the car and grabbed it from the side pouch. Once again, she walked to the study to see her partner sitting at his desk studying the white queen. Handing him the file, she spoke. "Didn't you tell me that Mat's code name was white queen's bishop?"

"I did," he said taking a pen he had picked up off the floor and a notepad. "That's one of the reasons I needed to see the file name again."

WQB2BKK4

"What if it's an anagram?" she asked. "Then the number two would equal to as a place to go."

"Do you play chess?" Jon asked.

"Not really," she replied. "Occasionally. I know the basics."

"Could you go to the board and tell me if the bishop in play is on a black space four spaces out from the king's knight?"

"The black king is on a white space right?"

"Right," Jon confirmed.

"Then yes," Courtney replied. "The white bishop is on a black space four rows from where the knight is."

"And the other piece is a black knight?" he asked.

"Yes," Courtney answered.

"White queen's bishop to black king's knight four," he said.

"And a white queen on your desk," she replied. "He's warning you."

"He is, yeah," Jon answered. "But he should know I will never give up."

———✳———

After Dan Howard had helped Scott into the shower and got him back to his bed, Ryan came in to change the dressing. Kim stepped out of the room, unable to see the wound. She walked down the hall to where their family waited. Rick stood when he saw her coming.

"Hey," he said. "Ryan told us he was awake. But I didn't want to disturb him if he was tired."

"He needed to take a shower and they're changing the

dressing," Kim replied. "He didn't want *someone* to see him like that," she stressed looking down at Sarah where she colored in a Disney coloring book.

"I thought so," Jenny answered. "How is he doing?"

"He's still in pain but the nurse is with him," she said. "Have you figured out where you've seen him?"

"No," Rick replied. "Nothing yet. But I keep thinking it's... ah, well it can't be that important."

"Is there anything you need, sweetie?" her mom asked.

"I was just going to get a coke," she answered. "It's so dry in there. Water's not helping."

"I'll get it for you," Rick offered. "Unless you need a walk."

"I could do with a walk," she admitted.

"I'm going to go sit with him, then," Rick squeezed his wife's shoulder and she smiled.

Sarah looked up from her coloring book. "Can I see him?"

"Sweetie, Scott's not feeling well. He's resting right now, but soon we can go see him," Jenny said.

"I just want to hug him and tell him I colored this for him. And Ryan gave me some of this white stuff for Teddy. He's hurt just like Scott. I didn't know if he wanted Teddy with him. He always makes me feel better."

Kim's eyes watered as she listened to his daughter. Even though the young girl did not know the true familial bond she shared with him, she loved him deeply. For a moment, Kim let herself hope for the future with him. Unconsciously, her hand pressed to her abdomen where she hoped one day to carry his child.

"Are you all right, sweetheart?" her mother asked. Shaking herself out of her thoughts, she forced a smile.

"Yeah, sorry," she said and realized she was sniffling the tears back. Beth and Jenny shared a glance but Kim bent down next to the little girl. "I know Scott will want to see you soon, sweetie," Kim said gently. "He even told me to tell you he loves you and as soon as the doctors are done with whatever they're doing, he wants to see you."

"Really?" Sarah's eyes grew big.

"Yes, but you'll have to be careful. Like Teddy, he can't move his shoulder very well," Kim cautioned.

Sarah's little face screwed up into a frown. "Then, could you give this to him?" She asked holding up a coloring book page. "I colored it just for him."

"He would much rather it come from you," Kim answered. "I promise as soon as he's done, I'll come back and get you."

"Could you tell him I love him?" she asked.

Kim bit the inside of her cheek to prevent the tears from spilling. "Of course, sweetheart. I'll tell him."

Rick walked into the room just as Dan helped Scott to lie down.

"Easy there," Dan coaxed. "That's better. Let's get these IVs out from under you." Moving to his right side, the nurse eased the tubes out from under Scott's arm.

"Hey, Uncle Rick," Scott called seeing him at the doorway.

The nurse turned and smiled, the scar on the apple of his cheek crinkling. "Nearly done, sir."

"That's fine," Rick said. "I'll stay over here out of the way."

Once Scott was settled, Dan checked the chart and went to the cabinets. "It looks like the doctor asked for you to be given another shot of anti-inflammatory."

"He's on morphine, will that interact?" Rick asked stepping forward.

"No, sir," he answered. "Morphine has no anti-inflammatory properties it's merely a pain reliever. This is to help the inflammation around the area." As Dan found a syringe, he retrieved a small bottle from his pocket and pulled on some plastic gloves. Filling the syringe, he went to the IV and injected the medicine into the tube. "There, now, you should feel a little drowsy." Removing his gloves, he marked something on the chart and patted Scott's good shoulder. "Give us a buzz if something doesn't feel quite right."

"Thank you," Scott said. As soon as Dan left, Rick sat down beside his bed.

"How you feeling, lad?" Rick asked.

"I've been better," he said. "But feel better after a shower."

"Good. Your dad should be here soon," Rick replied. "He stopped at the house to pick up some things."

"Great," he answered and blinked hard. "Sorry," his speech slurred. "I'm not feeling all that great."

"Should I call a nurse?" Rick asked.

"No, it's probably the medicine," Scott said. "How's Sarah?"

"She's worried about you."

"I…" his eyes closed and his voice slurred. "I… mmm…"

"Scott?" Rick asked concerned.

Scott didn't reply. His eyes closed and his body went limp. Rick's eyes shot up to the monitor. His blood pressure was dropping and his heart rate was slowing. Lunging for the button, he pressed the nurse call button just as the machine began beeping and nurses, along with Ryan, raced into the room.

"Code blue! We need a crash cart in here!" Ryan shouted. Ripping Scott's gown open, he began CPR.

Jon and Courtney walked to his car in the driveway when his cell phone rang.

"Hey, Rick," he answered. "What?" he shouted. Courtney looked over at him and watched his face go pale. "I'm on my way."

"What happened?" she asked.

"Scott flat lined again."

Chapter
Forty-Seven

It was like a yell from a mile away; the voice was soft but intense. He didn't want to open his eyes, but the voice sounded so afraid.

"Scott, can you hear me?" it said. It was getting louder and louder, as if coming right at him.

He couldn't move. His body was limp and he had an annoying itch on his right forearm he couldn't reach to scratch.

"Scottie," the voice asked, a little louder and less intense. "Can you hear me, son?" He wanted to nod, but his body wouldn't let him. He tried to open his eyes, but they would only open into slits. "Scott," his dad's voice said again. "It's me. Can you hear me?"

He tried to turn his head, but it would only go a little bit. His shoulder ached horribly.

"Dad?" he finally groaned. Jon sat next to his hospital bed with his hand in his. He was not in the same room as before and his dad looked horrified. "What happened?"

"How do you feel?" Jon asked, stroking his son's forehead.

"Terrible," he answered. "Why can't I move?"

"Do you remember anything?" Jon asked.

Scott shook his head. "No, what happened?"

"First, let me call the nurse," Jon said. "And Kim and Rick need to know you're okay."

"Where are they?" he asked.

"Just outside," he said reaching over for the buzzer. Once the nurse was called, Jon went to the door and called to the two of them. Kim raced to the door. Seeing Scott awake, she let out a small groan and ran to his side.

"Hey, baby," he breathed. "I don't know what happened. But I think I'm okay."

"Thank God, oh thank God," she cried. Tears streamed down her face when she pulled away to look at him.

"Could someone tell me what happened?" Scott asked as he cupped her cheek.

"Someone messed with your meds," Ryan's voice said from the door. "Someone tried to kill you."

"Dan Howard," Rick replied. "Jon, it's the nurse I know it is. I've seen him somewhere before but I couldn't place him."

"Who?" Ryan asked.

"The nurse that was in here when you changed his bandage," Rick replied. "Blonde, about five-ten, thirties, had a scar on his cheek."

Ryan shook his head. "Must be new, I've not seen him before and I was more focused on changing Scott's bandages."

"I promise you, Jon," Rick turned to his brother. "Something about him I didn't like. Trust me."

"I do," Jon replied putting a hand on his brother's shoulder. "We've put a guard at the door. No one gets in without Ryan, Fred or one of us. Can you stay with him? I need to talk with Courtney."

"I am not leaving," Kim swore. "No matter what happens."

Scott nuzzled her hand as she stroked his cheek. "Wait, Dad," Scott called. "Can you ask Beth to come in too and don't leave yet?"

Jon looked at his son and saw a look in his eyes he had never seen before. In that moment, he knew what his son was planning. "Kim, Rick, could you get Beth? I need to tell Scott something."

"I want to stay with you," Kim said.

"Please, baby? Just a moment with my dad."

"Okay," Kim finally agreed. Rick and Kim left the room and Jon walked over to his son.

"Are you sure?" He asked.

"One hundred percent," Scott answered.

"Then you'll need this," Jon took the small box he had carried with him since the night Scott was shot and handed it to him.

"Mom's ring?" Scott asked. Jon nodded. "Are you sure?"

"She would not want it on anyone else's finger," Jon promised. Scott swallowed and accepted it just as Kim knocked on the door. Jon took a step back as Kim, Rick and Beth walked in. Beth went to Jon and wrapped an arm around his waist as Kim went directly to Scott. Rick hung back by the door.

"There's something I wanted y'all to share," Scott said. He looked up at Kim. "I love you. I have loved you for so long but I didn't know it. Everyone I have looked at in the past has been compared to you and I didn't realize it. You are the most amazing, beautiful and loving woman I have ever known. Kim, you have saved me from myself, you have saved me from a life of loneliness and I love you for it. There is not much I need or want in life, but you are at the top of the list. And I want you by my side for the rest of my days. I want you as my own." Opening the box, he gazed up at her. "Kim, I know it's only been a short time, but... will you marry me?"

Kim covered her mouth as she looked at Carol's ring inside the box. The beautiful five and a half carat circular cut diamond in a platinum setting with smaller diamonds lining the band took her breath away. Looking back up at Scott she nodded. "Yes!"

"Why would they screw up his meds?" Courtney asked as she and Jon left the hospital intent on heading back to the precinct.

"To finish what they started," Jon said coolly. "This isn't about Vietnam anymore. That was just to get my attention. This person is after me. It has always been a personal attack. Their end goal is me. And if Rick is right, it has something to do with Ireland."

Jon pulled out his keys and beeped his car.

"Does he remember where he's seen that guy before?" Courtney asked.

"No," he answered. "I've asked for CCTV cameras maybe we can see him."

"What was the name again?"

"Dan Howard," Jon replied. She opened her mouth to say something but he cut her off. "I know, same one that worked at Northwestern when Hannah Turner was a patient. And I still don't know why I know the name."

"You know the name and Rick knows the face," she said. "We need the security footage."

"Agreed," Jon replied. "We have to go back to the precinct and get a warrant." Jon pressed the button on the keys to start his car when they were a few feet away from the Escalade. Just as he did, the car exploded throwing Jon and Courtney across the parking lot. The last thing she saw was Jon's bloodied face as he lay on his back beside her.

Aeron answered the phone as he drove down Meridian

Street. He had seen the explosion from the side road near the hospital.

"It's done," he said.

"Like hell it is," Rob replied. "Scott's still alive."

"What?" Aeron demanded. He had given him enough liquid tranquilizer to kill a horse.

"It's over," Rob said. "I made a mistake trusting you. I'll do it myself now."

"Don't you even think about shutting me out."

"You screwed up," Rob shouted. "This is on you. Don't get in my way again."

Aeron was about to respond when Rob hung up. Cursing, Aeron threw the phone down on the passenger seat and nearly stood on the gas pedal. If Rob shut him out, that was fine with him. He wasn't about to stop. He had put too much into his revenge to stop now. Without Rob pulling the strings, he was free to do it his way. The explosion gave him some satisfaction, but Scott, Ryan and Rick were still alive. Now that Kim was sleeping with Scott, he would have to kill her too. She could be pregnant. Yet another heir he would have to get rid of. He was tired of not having his due.

Taking his phone again, he dialed Hannah's number.

"Hey," she answered.

"Plans have changed," he replied. "Meet me at my apartment. Ten minutes."

"I'll be there," she said.

Chapter
Forty-Eight

CIA Special Agent Steven Anderson unlocked the front door of the three-bedroom apartment he shared with his brother Mark. Lugging his suitcase and laptop through the door, he was greeted by their huge German Shepherd. Barking and trying to jump on him, the sixty-pound pup demanded attention.

"Hi, Ada," Steven cooed. "Did you miss me, baby?" At her bark, he smiled. The pup would not let him take another step. Setting his case on the floor, he got down on his knees and framed his dog's face giving her a good scratch behind the ears.

"She's been sulking since you left," Mark called from the kitchen as he walked out to greet his brother.

"You missed daddy, baby," Steven said giving her a good belly rub.

"Does that make me mommy?" Mark asked.

"If the title sticks," Steven winked.

"Shut up," Mark laughed.

The big baby didn't let Steven up for a good five minutes but when she did and Steven could stand to get his things in through the entryway, she still walked around his legs looking up at him, her pink tongue hanging out of her mouth and her tail beating against Steven's denim clad legs.

"Good to have you home, brother," Mark said embracing him.

"Good to be home," Steven answered.

"I was just about to put a pizza in the oven for lunch, want some?"

"Love some, I'm gonna hit the shower, then change out of this, wore it on the plane. I'll be right out."

"Sounds good," Mark replied heading back to the kitchen. Ada looked between her masters and barked.

"Oh, come on, girl," Steven finally said and hit his thigh. Ada barked again and bounded over to him.

———

Steven came back to the living room fifteen minutes later, Ada close beside him. Grabbing a beer from the fridge, he collapsed on the sofa and beckoned his German Shepherd up beside him. The pup jumped and wiggled her way under his arm letting out a huff. Absently stroking the pup's head, Steven grabbed the remote and called to his brother watching the pizza in the oven.

"Mind if I change the channel? After everything, a war story isn't exactly what I want to see."

"Yeah sure," Mark called back. "I wasn't even really watching it."

"Thanks," Steve said and turned the channel.

"So how did the mission go?"

"Didn't end well," Steven answered.

"Does it ever?" Mark asked.

"No," he admitted. "But I did my job and it's over. The terrorist is dead and millions of people are safe. That's what matters." He didn't need to tell his brother that the woman he used to get into the terrorist cell cried she loved him just before her brother pulled the trigger in an honor killing right in front of him.

"The last thing you need is a war movie," Mark replied.

"Right?" Steven laughed humorlessly.

"Oh, I've got some news for you," Mark said taking the pizza out of the oven and cutting it into slices.

"Yeah?" Steven asked. "What is it?"

"Kim and Scott are engaged," Mark said as he walked back out with the pizza.

"What?" he questioned. "What do you mean engaged?"

"Like engaged to be married," Mark clarified handing him a plate with three slices and some potato chips.

"When did this happen?" Steven asked.

"Well, she told me they were together in Ireland, but I couldn't talk to you," he explained.

"That was like two weeks ago. How did it go from dating to marriage in two weeks?"

"They've known each other for nearly twenty years so that's how," Mark said sitting in the Lazy Boy next to the sofa. "What do you want to do about it?"

"I need more information first."

"Apparently, it was all so romantic. Though how a proposal in the hospital could be romantic, I have no idea."

"Who's in the hospital?" Steven questioned.

"Oh yeah, I forgot to tell you," Mark answered. "Scott was shot."

"Okay, you're gonna have to begin again," Steven said allowing Ada to grab a potato chip off his plate.

"You keep feeding her like that and she'll get fat," Mark scolded.

"I'll take her for a run later," Steven promised. "I'm waiting, talk."

Mark filled Steven in on what had happened during the three months he had been undercover. He finally got to the part where Beth had called him earlier that day to tell him about Kim's engagement.

"Have you talked to Scott?"

"No," Mark answered. "I was going to go a little later today."

"Have you talked to Kim?"

"Not about Scott since Ireland," Mark said.

"Did she sound happy?" Steven asked.

"Yeah, she really did."

"What about Jon?"

"Haven't talked to him yet, but I have news about him and Mom too," Mark said softly.

"Oh shit," he said. "What?"

"They're back together," Mark said.

Steven closed his eyes and a four-letter word slipped through his lips.

Chapter Forty-Nine

Courtney woke with a splitting headache and the sirens screaming didn't help. Ryan and several nurses worked around her, his face ashen and his expression grim.

"Doctor," one of the nurses called to him when she saw her waking.

"Ryan?" Courtney's throat felt like shards of glass were scraping away.

He looked up sharply. "Oh, thank God," he replied coming closer to her. "Don't move."

"What happened?" she asked.

"Someone tried to kill you both," he replied, his eyes skating to her side.

"Where's Jon?" she asked.

Ryan motioned with his chin. She turned slowly to see a group of nurses around Jon. His neck was in a brace, blood spattered his face and chest but his eyes were still closed.

"Is he okay?" she asked. Ryan didn't answer. "Dammit, Ryan answer me."

"He's alive," he answered. "But that's all I know."

"I have to get to the precinct," she tried to get up but the nurses held her shoulder down.

"You're not going anywhere until I get my tests run," Ryan stated.

"Ryan," she said.

"No," he replied firmly. "Not going to happen. Now let's get you on a gurney."

———※———

After Ryan ran his tests, Courtney still hadn't heard about Jon. When another nurse walked in, she decided enough was enough.

"I need to know how my partner is doing," she said.

"I can check for you, miss," the nurse answered. "What's their name?"

"Lieutenant Jonathan Greene," she replied. "I haven't heard anything since I was brought in about two hours ago and if I wasn't tied up with all these tubes, I would be going out there myself."

"Let me see what I can find out," she said.

"Thank you," Courtney huffed. Her mother patted her hand to calm her.

"It'll be all right, sweetheart," she said.

"No, it's not all right," she answered. "I need to know if he's even alive."

"I'm sure if something bad had happened Ryan would tell you," Isabella replied.

"I need to make sure he's okay, Mama," Courtney said. "Seeing him like that…"

"I know," she answered tightly. "Getting the call from Ryan, I felt the same."

"We all know the risks," Courtney went on. "But I know it doesn't help."

"It doesn't," her mom replied. "But it's your choice and I am so proud of you."

The nurse came back in and smiled.

"Lieutenant Greene is still unconscious," she said. "They're taking him for an MRI to make sure there's no brain swelling. He has a nasty crack on the head but he's alive and all vitals are normal."

Courtney fell back into the hospital bed. "Thank God," she breathed. "And when can I leave here? My fiancé is just being over cautious."

"Dr. Marcellino has ordered you upstairs for the night."

"I am not staying overnight," she shook her head. "I have a job to do. As it is, the evidence is being collected and I can't be there."

"Miss, please, we need to monitor you. There could be a concussion," the nurse said.

"Is there any legal reason to keep me here?"

"Well… no, but the doctor's orders are—"

"If the doctor wants to keep this ring on my finger, he better let me check myself out and get back to work," Courtney said.

"Sweetie, Ryan's just concerned for you," her mother said.

"No, there's concern and then there's over-protective," she replied. "And right now, he's over-protective and I hate it. Now nurse, could you please unhook me so I may discharge myself?"

"I… I need to speak with the doctor," she said and before Courtney could say anything she hurried out of the room.

Courtney growled and leaned back in the bed.

"You should listen to the doctor, sweetheart," her mother said. "I understand you want to get back out there, you always did. You fell off your bike, you didn't even let me put a Band-Aid on before you were back on. But, this was a very serious injury. Jon's still unconscious. That could have been you."

"And if it were, Jon would be doing the exact same thing as I am right now."

"Very possibly," Fred's voice came from the door. Ryan's

mentor and head doctor walked in.

"Fred, thank God," Courtney said. "The reasonable one. Tell me I can leave."

"Ryan is concerned about you, Courtney," Fred replied. "But I will say, if you were my patient, I would have let you go by now. There is no sign of internal bleeding and you are awake and causing havoc as usual," he winked. "But you're not marrying me."

"Don't I know it," she answered. "So sign the discharge papers and let me out of here. I'll deal with any backlash from Ryan."

"Ryan can speak for himself," Ryan's voice came from the doorway. Courtney groaned and rolled her eyes.

"Listen, mister," Courtney said as Ryan walked in. "Don't you have other patients who need you? I am fine. Now please let me get out of here."

"Courtney, you have had a serious injury and if something were to happen to you that I could have prevented I will never forgive myself."

"Nothing is going to happen to me," Courtney replied.

Ryan looked to Fred then Isabella. "Could we have a moment, please?"

Courtney's mom and Fred left the room and Ryan walked around the hospital bed. Courtney moved her legs so he could sit on the side and take her hand. He didn't say anything for a little while and Courtney let him think. After a moment, he looked up at her and sighed.

"When I saw you lying there," he broke off and looked away. Clearing his throat, he finally went on. "I have never been so scared. I thought I had lost you."

"But you didn't," she answered.

"I know that now, but the risks are still there," he replied. "What if I didn't run that one test and I let you leave?"

"Then you let me leave," she said. "Because I want to and

if something happens it is not on you. You would not have been the one at fault."

"But I could have prevented it."

"Not always," she replied. "You aren't Superman. You're a doctor but you can't tell the future."

"I just want to keep you here away from the madman who tried to kill you," he looked away. Courtney pulled him back to look at her.

"You can't protect me, Ryan," she said. "Love me, yes, help me, absolutely, but you can't protect me. I love you. I want to be your wife more than anything but I have to be me. I have to do my job. Don't take that away from me." Ryan took a deep breath. Without another word, he stood and took her chart. Looking it over once more, he took the pen out of his coat pocket and scrawled his name.

"You're free to go," he replied.

Smiling at him softly, she stood and took her IV over to him. As gently as he could, he took out the small tube and covered the puncture with a Band-Aid. Kissing it when he was done, he looked into her eyes. Grabbing his coat lapels, she pulled him to her and kissed him deeply.

"I love you," she said when she pulled away. "And I promise you, I will text you as much as I can and if I feel anything weird, I will call you."

Nodding, he wrapped his arms around her and hugged her as tightly as he allowed himself. After a bit, he straightened and stroked her cheek.

"I'll get your mom to help you get dressed," he said softly. Courtney kissed him one more time before letting him go.

Courtney dialed a number as soon as she was in her mom's car. "Hello?" the person answered on the third ring.

"It's me," she replied.

"Courtney?" he asked. "What's going on?"

"I need you to meet me."

"Okay," he replied. "When and where?"

"My office, I assume you know the way, Black King."

He paused and just before he hung up he said, "I'm on my way."

As soon as her mom dropped her off at the precinct, Courtney headed up the elevator. Some of the officers stopped her to ask how she and Jon were doing. After a brief update, she reached her office and closed the door. Immediately going to her desk, she logged in and, hating everything about what she was typing, keyed in a background search on Jonathan Mitchell Greene, Carolina Bernardo-Greene, and Scott Charles Greene.

Chapter
Fifty

"Courtney," Dave called as soon as he walked into the office. Jumping at his voice, she looked over at him and stood. "What the hell happened?" He crossed the room in four long strides and reached out to hold her. She backed up, tired of being coddled. Clenching his fingers, he lowered his arms. "Are you all right?"

"I'm fine," she answered.

"You know then," Dave said thrusting his hands through his salt and pepper, more salt than pepper, military buzz cut.

"That's not why I called you, but yes, I do," she replied. "Thank you for getting me partnered with Jon."

Dave blinked. "That's not what I expected you to say."

"That's beside the point," she said. "Right now, I need help."

"Where's Jon?"

"We were in an accident," she explained what had happened shortly before. "He's still in the hospital."

"Are you all right?"

"I'm fine," she replied. "Now are you going to help me or not?"

"How do you know about Black King?"

"Because Jon said his CO in Vietnam was known as Black King and you were his CO in Vietnam. It's not rocket science."

Dave took a deep breath, "It's been a while since I've been called that."

"But that's your name," she replied. "Now, will you help?"

"Of course," he answered. "What do you need?"

"I need a CCTV camera warrant and facial rec within a few hours. And I need the file of a psych patient."

"Consider it done," Dave replied. "Let me make some calls and I'll need access to a computer."

"I'll log you in to Jon's," Courtney said.

Scott had finally fallen asleep again after the doctors approved a low dose of painkiller. Kim sat beside him, watching TV. His face contorted in pain and he opened his eyes to look at her.

"Hey," he whispered.

"Hi," she replied leaning forward. "How do you feel?"

"I've been better," he answered. "Why aren't you here?" he patted the spot beside him on the bed.

"Because the doctors won't let me," she said. "They say we need to watch you."

"I can't sleep without you," he replied.

"I love you for saying that, but I won't lie there. Incentive for you to get better soon."

"Very soon," he breathed. "What are you watching?"

"Nothing really," she said. "Do you need anything?"

"Yeah," he answered.

"What?" she stood and leaned over him. "What can I get you?"

"A kiss?"

She smiled and leaned down further. "I think I can do that."

They didn't pull back until someone in the doorway cleared their throat.

"Steven!" Kim smiled as she turned from Scott.

"Hey, baby sis," he said. They met halfway and hugged tightly.

"It's so good to see you. When did you get home?"

"Earlier this morning," he answered.

"What are you guys doing here?" she asked looking over at her other big brother, Mark.

"Mark told me what had happened. I wanted to make sure you were okay, Scott," Steven said looking around her.

"Thanks, man," Scott said. "I appreciate it. I'm all right. Still recovering."

"Your vitals look good," Mark, a pediatrician by trade, said as he looked at the monitor.

"I also heard you two were engaged," Steven said. At Kim's questioning face, he went on. "Mom told Mark who told me."

"Sorry, was it supposed to be a secret?" Mark asked looking back at her.

"I would have liked to have told my brothers but no, no secret," Kim answered walking back to Scott who had raised the bed with his control so he could sit up.

"Can we see the ring?" Mark asked.

Kim proudly displayed it for them to inspect.

"That's gorgeous," Steven said visibly impressed.

"It was my mother's," Scott explained.

"It's absolutely beautiful," Kim replied as she stroked Scott's hair off his forehead.

"Hey, baby sis," Mark said. "Would you mind getting me something to drink? I'm parched."

"The canteen is in the basement," she replied.

"I think they want to talk to me alone, baby," Scott said.

"No way," Kim stated. "Scott is recovering from nearly being killed twice. I'm not going to let you guys bully him. I'm happy, I love him and, besides I'm not a kid anymore."

"We know that, but it's a brother's prerogative to talk to the guy his sister's gonna marry," Mark said.

"I'm not leaving," Kim crossed her arms over her chest.

"Babe, I'll be fine," Scott reassured her. "And if they start beating me up I'll call a nurse."

"I'm not going any further than right outside. If you need me, you shout."

"I won't need you, but I will call for you," Scott said.

"You hurt him," she looked at her big brothers. "And you'll have deal with me."

"Understood, baby sis," Steven answered trying but failing to hide his grin. "We just want to talk. That's all."

Kim walked to the door and turned. "Oh, and if you want to talk about respecting me until the wedding, save your breath, we've already slept together and I don't see that stopping anytime soon."

Seeing Steven's jaw drop and Mark's grimace as they thought of their baby sister sleeping with Scott, she smiled and walked out of the room.

———

Nearly two hours later, Courtney and Dave were reviewing the CCTV camera from the hospital for the sixth time. Zooming in on the face of Dan Howard, Courtney was certain she had never seen him before. Dave was checking for an update on facial recognition when Jon stalked into the office.

"Jon!" Courtney cried standing and rushing to him. "Thank God you're okay."

"Don't," Jon replied holding up a hand.

"If you're going to be all alpha male then you can go ahead and leave now," Courtney said. "I don't have time or energy to fight you."

"You should have stayed at the hospital," Jon spat.

"Oh, get over it. Really, you overreact and I'm not going to give up on this case just because someone tried to kill me. If they want me to stop, they should not try to kill me. That just makes me angry. Now are we going to work together? Or do I need to fight you some more?"

Taking a deep breath, Jon sighed. "Fine," he said. "But don't think that just because we stopped talking about this we're finished discussing it."

"We're finished discussing it, Jon," she replied. "I'm not a child. I make my own decisions."

"What have you found?" he asked.

"Do you know this man?" Dave showed him a printout of Dan Howard's face looking up at the security camera.

Jon studied it for a moment but shook his head slowly. "No, though like Rick, I have a feeling I've seen him before."

"I don't know him," Dave answered. "So it's no one in the military. And I've cross referenced the info you asked me for, the list of those who had been rejected or dishonorably discharged from the corps who wanted to be a sniper as well as cross referencing them with fallen veterans at the Offensive. Nothing came up. The faces don't match."

Jon walked around the office and froze when he stood next to Courtney's desk. "What is this?" He tapped the three files.

"I ran a background check," she said.

"On me?" he demanded.

"Yes," she replied.

"And my wife and son?" his eyes shot daggers at her.

"This man," she grabbed the picture from him and held it up so he could see. "Is after you. You're telling me you wouldn't have done it if our places were reversed? Come on, Jon, be a cop. If we have a victim being attacked, you would do a background check to see what could have triggered it."

"Have you thought about asking me?" He demanded.

"Gee, good idea, but would you have allowed it? Especially Carol?" Courtney replied.

"Dammit, Courtney," he cursed. "This isn't something you should have done without asking me."

"Next time we have a homicidal lunatic coming after you, I'll be sure to ask first, but until then, man up and let's solve this," she said.

Gritting his teeth, Jon turned away from her. "Dare I ask if there is anything we can use?"

"No, but that doesn't mean it was a waste."

"That's exactly what it means," Jon replied. "Next time why don't you talk to me first."

"Fine, next time I will, but I couldn't. If you don't recall, you were unconscious for hours."

Dave gave a shrill whistle and they stopped. "Right, now, I pulled some strings and got the file on Hannah Turner," Dave said. "Courtney and I were studying it just before you arrived."

"What did you find?"

Dave opened the file and began reading. "'Hospitalized for intense mental instability. Suffering from vivid illusions that her brother was murdered in Vietnam, specifically the Easter Offensive. Claims her brother comes to her telling her to avenge his death. Schizophrenic, delusional, and capable of great strength and apathy. Considered to be a high flight risk and extremely dangerous.'"

"Seriously Mat you do know how to pick them," Jon mumbled.

"But a couple months later, the notes change," Dave revealed. "'Hannah has shown great improvement the past week. She no longer speaks of her brother constantly. She has been allowed out of isolation and into the main area with the others.

While under constant supervision, she has shown an ability to converse pleasantly with others. With this new prescribed medicine, she may be released by the end of the month.' We all know how that turned out."

"She shot at Ryan," Courtney supplied.

"Exactly," Dave answered.

"Were you debriefed on the case?" Jon asked.

"Of course," Dave replied. "I think we all were as soon as it was known. Is there a file?"

"We found one in Mat's safe," Jon said. "Only Courtney knows I have it. Any luck in tracking Mat's phone? We need to see if there's a Lexus LX in the area."

"Where are the security videos from the hospital parking lot?" Courtney rummaged on Jon's desk.

"Here," Dave found them. Putting the DVD in the player, she fast forwarded until they saw Dan Howard walk out of the hospital. He disappeared for a few minutes and they saw him walking to a car. Courtney huffed when he got into a sedan.

"I was sure," she said.

"It might not be his car," Jon replied. "The LX could be Hannah's."

"We need to find the captain's phone. Maybe find a way to bug it."

"This is where I need to leave," Dave said. "I can't know you're bugging a US Citizen's phone. But I will tell you," he pulled out his phone, "GPS puts him on I-465."

"Thank you, Dave," Courtney said. "I really appreciate your help."

"You know I always help my friends," he smiled at her.

"Before you go," Jon called. "White Queen's Bishop to Black King's Knight four."

Dave froze and looked up at him. "Jesus." He exhaled. "I haven't heard that in thirty years."

"I need to know," Jon said. "October twentieth. What happened?"

"You were there," Dave replied. "You saw it."

"I don't remember," Jon admitted.

"Turner," Dave said. "Sergeant First Class." Jon's brows furrowed in confusion. "I need to go. But don't forget, Gunny," he said to Jon over his shoulder. "How did we used to communicate when we didn't want anyone else to know?"

"What did he mean?" Courtney asked when he left. "And who is Sergeant First Class Turner?"

"He meant invisible ink," Jon replied pulling out the file and a lighter from his desk. "As for Turner, I don't remember. I'll keep thinking. But let's do this first." He held the lighter up behind the first page. "You remember what Scott said the dividers of sixty were?" he asked.

"I don't remember all of them," she said. "But the logical ones; one, two, three, five, ten, twenty, and sixty," she replied.

"What was it that I just said? The date I mentioned?" Jon prompted.

"October twentieth," Courtney supplied.

"Which numerically is?"

"Ten-Twenty," Courtney answered. "I don't know how the captain could have orchestrated all of this so quickly. How did he know?"

"He knew after Billy was shot," Jon replied. "He got involved for a reason. We need to figure out why and clear his name."

"That may be impossible with how deep he is already."

"Possibly," Jon said. "But until it is completely impossible, I will keep trying."

"And as your partner and friend, I will be by your side," she promised. Jon looked over at her and only then did she realize his face was still scraped and he had two white bandages holding a nasty gash on his forehead together. "Are you all right," she passed a hand over his face.

"I have a bloody terrible headache, but I'm all right," he promised leaning over kissing her cheek. She rested her head on his shoulder only to pull away when he flinched. "Landed on my bad shoulder wrong. I'm fine," he replied. She nodded. All of the sudden the terror of what they had been through together hit her and she began to shake. Jon set the paper and lighter down and took her into his arms. "Shh, it's okay."

"Ugh, I hate it," she replied. "I'm a cop, I shouldn't be like this."

"Like what? Brilliant? Brave? Stubborn?"

"Scared," she admitted.

"Welcome to the club," he replied. "I'm scared. It's human nature. Don't build a wall around your emotions, that's what makes mistakes. Embrace them and move on. You are allowed ten seconds to embrace the fear and then nothing. Okay?" She nodded into his chest and let the panic hit her. After ten seconds, Jon snapped his fingers and forced her back from him. "Enough," he replied. She nodded and took a deep breath. "You are safe, you are alive, we both are."

"Thank you. We've been through hell recently, haven't we?" she said softly.

"There isn't anyone else I would rather have had by my side," he replied.

"Me either," she said. "Let's get back to work."

Jon agreed and picked up the paper and lighter again, holding the heat behind the sheet to bring out the inviable ink. Words began to form on the page and once it was clear, Jon spoke low. "Do you have your phone? Could you take a picture?"

Grabbing her phone from her pocket, she took a snap of the words and read them.

Jon,

I pray you figure this out and find this message. If not, I'm a dead man. If that's the case, you know who I need you to talk to and what to say to them. But listen, her name is Hannah Turner, and she had a brother. Christopher was in the army and died on October 20, 1972 during the Easter Offensive under friendly fire. She has made it her mission to kill everyone who was there. That includes you, me, and Dave among many others. She has a partner; Aeron. I don't know who he is, but I have heard he hates you, something to do with Ireland and the land. Please be careful. I have gone undercover to try to get as much information as I can, but we both know what this could do. This guy has known you since he was a boy and he's now mid-thirties, dirty blonde, five-ten, green eyes, pale skin. I don't think he's alone in this either. I heard Hannah ask him about Rob. I don't know who Rob is, but I'm hoping to figure it out soon. I'll get a message to you as soon as I can. Watch your back, Black King's Knight. Please know whatever happens, whatever I say or do, just know it is to keep you safe.

I love you, brother.

Mat

"Aeron again... Aeron... spelled A-e-r-o-n," Courtney said. "What does it mean?"

"It's the name of a Celtic god," Jon explained.

"Who is this Rob?" Courtney asked. "Do you know a Rob?"

"I know several Roberts but none go by the name Rob."

"He's the mastermind?" Courtney asked. "He's the one Aeron was to report back to?"

"Apparently," Jon replied. "We need to figure out who this guy is."

"Okay," Courtney stated. "How?"

"Let's get that trace on Mat's cell phone from Dave, see where he is. Grab the cameras from that area and see what we can."

"Who's more important? Rob or Aeron?"

"Right now? Aeron," Jon replied. "He's the one who tried to kill you, me and Scott."

"Okay, I'm on it," she said sitting at her desk and logging back into her computer.

———

Courtney walked through the precinct with two cups of coffee. When the pain of being thrown from the explosion caught up with them, their bodies started lagging. She needed caffeine and the weak precinct coffee wasn't going to work.

Just before she left, Jon told her he would call in Officer Callen, one of the police techies to help with tracing Mat's phone. As she entered the office, she saw Jon standing behind his desk chair, the young officer seated typing furiously. She offered Jon his coffee and asked what she had missed.

"Callen has Mat's phone GPS pinging off a tower up near the Fashion Mall on Keystone Avenue."

"They're going shopping?" Courtney teased.

"Doubtful, Detective," Callen replied focused on the computer. "They're traveling around sixty miles an hour."

"Sixty?" Courtney questioned. Callen nodded and looked between them.

"Is that important?"

"It's just a theory," Jon replied. "Please keep a track on them and if you can, see if there are any security cameras in the area."

"Jon," Courtney whispered and they walked to the other side of the room. "Are you sure you want to know?"

"I need to know where they are, Courtney," he replied. "I

need to find them. Could you run a trace on Sergeant First Class Christopher Turner?"

"Already running it before I went to get coffee. I'll check the status," she said heading over to her computer.

"Got him," Callen called. "They stopped at a light and I found their car. It's a Lexus LX 2007 model." Callen showed Jon the image on the screen.

Jon looked over at Courtney and they locked eyes.

"Could you set up a tap on his phone? If he makes any calls I want to know about them."

"Sure, yeah," Callen answered.

"You're probably wondering why we're doing this. Especially considering the captain's recent… issues."

"That's not for me to know, sir," Callen replied. "Let me set this up and I'll be on my way. Is there anything else you will need?"

"No, Callen, thank you," Jon said.

"Jon," Courtney called to him. Leaving Callen to set up the tap on Mat's phone, Jon walked over to his partner's desk. "The trace came back. Sergeant First Class Christopher Turner, born November 16, 1952, Chicago. Enlisted in the army in 1970. Deployed to Vietnam in 1971. Killed in action 1972. Survived by his younger sister, Hannah and parents now both deceased. There's a picture."

"Dear God," Jon breathed as the face on the screen flashed in his mind. The scene unfolded before him. For a moment, he could smell the humid putrid smell of the Vietnam jungle, the sweat trickling down his temple from the fifty pounds of gear on his back, the irritating strap under his chin from his helmet and the feel of his M40 rifle in his hands. Looking to the left, he saw Mat's face, and to the right Commander Albert led his troops through the muck to surround the enemy. Billy locked eyes with him and nodded.

"Jon?" Courtney's voice snapped him out of his memories. "What is it?"

"I knew him," Jon said. "How I don't know... It's like something is right there but I just can't remember." Jon weaved for a moment as the pain in his head increased and he grasped the back of Courtney's chair.

"Jon?" Courtney called but her voice sounded so far away. He reached for her but he couldn't hold himself up. "Jon!"

The world spun and darkness took him.

Chapter Fifty-One

"Gunny," Dave's voice was faint. Jon opened his eyes to see his commander standing over him in full camouflage. "Get up, it was only a small explosion."

"Sir?" Jon asked.

"Get up," he offered his hand.

"Land mine," Mat's voice came next as he walked up to him. "We need to tread carefully."

"Who got it?" Jon asked.

"The Turner kid," Dave said. "Come on, let's get moving. I don't like being out in the open like this."

"Where's the body?" Jon asked. "Let's take him home."

"There isn't a body left, Jon," Mat replied.

"Jon," Billy called to him. He turned. "You gotta take care of this."

"Take care of what?" Jon asked.

"Turner," he said. "He fell onto the land mine but he wasn't killed by it."

"What happened?"

"Don't you remember?" Billy asked. "He was shot." His eyes drifted to Albert. "By friendly fire."

"Damn fool," Albert was saying as he looked down. "Shot

off his gun right next to my ear. I reacted."

"You didn't mean to kill him, Albert," Dave said.

"But I shot him," he sat down. "Poor kid. What am I going to tell his family?"

"That he died saving us. He discovered the mine field and sacrificed himself for us," Dave said.

"But that's not what happened," Jon replied.

"No, but do you really want to drag a good soldier down?" Dave demanded. "What happened was terrible, yes but it would be an even bigger tragedy to sully a good man's name."

"Jon," Billy called and his image blurred. He was standing one second then in a wheelchair the next. "He died but there was no body, no closure. Help the family. White Queen's Bishop to Black King's Knight four. Help Hannah."

———

"Jon!" Courtney shook him awake. He opened his eyes and looked up from where he had fallen. "Jon, can you hear me?"

"Aye, I can hear you," Jon replied. "I also remember what happened to Sergeant First Class Christopher Turner and I know where they're going."

"Where?" Courtney asked as she helped him up.

His eyes flashed to the map hanging on the wall. Pulling out a sharpie from his desk drawer, he went over to the map and drew eight lines evenly down the image and then eight lines across. Counting the spaces, he paused on one space and put an X in the box then circled something.

"What is that?" She asked. "What's there?"

"It's the warehouse where Carol was killed." Just as Courtney looked over at the square, Jon's phone rang the trumpet fanfare for a Spanish Bullfight. "It's Mat."

———

"Hello, Mat," Jon answered the phone and put it on

speaker after asking Callen to leave the room.

"Jon, I need you to meet me," Mat said, his voice strained.

"I know what's going on," Jon replied.

"It doesn't matter," his voice cracked. "I need you to meet me."

"The warehouse?" Jon asked.

"You know then," Mat said then immediately groaned.

"Are you all right?"

"I have to stay on point," Mat said. "Meet me at the warehouse where Carol died. We have things to discuss." The line ended abruptly.

"Jon," Courtney started. "You know it's a trap."

"Yes, but that doesn't stop me from needing to help him."

"You're not going alone," she said.

"I'm not having you come with me," he replied. "It's too dangerous."

"Like hell it is," she answered. "I'm your partner, we're together in this as in all things. I'm not going to let you go alone. If you think I'm kidding then you don't know me."

"I do know you, Courtney," he said. "But I'm not letting you come with me."

"Then I'll come on my own," she replied. "You cannot stop me from being with my partner."

"Let me do this alone," he stated. "I need to do this alone."

"Why?"

"Because it's my past coming forward."

"And you think I would not want to be with you if I knew?"

"Somethings? Yeah, there are somethings in everyone's past they don't want anyone to know. And this is something I need to do on my own."

"This is bollocks, to steal a term from you," Courtney

replied. "You think I would change my opinion of you if I knew something you did in your past? Does that mean I should think you would change your opinion of me? Come on, Jon we're partners and partners stick together no matter what."

"Fine, Jaysus, woman," he snarled. "Get your gun and your coat."

"Promise me one thing," she said as she grabbed her side arm from the desk drawer. "If it comes down to you or him, you won't hesitate, because he won't." When Jon didn't answer she went on. "You have a family who loves you. Don't fill that plot next to your wife too soon."

Nodding once, he agreed but pulled out his phone. "I have a call to make." They walked to the elevators and down to the parking garage. Once they were alone in his car, Jon dialed the number.

Rick stepped outside Scott's hospital room to answer his cell phone. Jon was calling him and when he answered, the tone in his brother's voice made him pause. Listening for a while as Jon explained what was going on, his hand clenched in a fist but his voice remained light.

"Just be careful," Rick said and when Steven walked out of the room to see what was going on, he spoke again. "I'm glad Courtney is going with you. You take care of each other. We'll hold the fort down over here. Be careful, Jon." After a beat, he hung up and looked over at Steven.

"Is there a problem?" Steven asked.

"No," Rick lied. "Nothin' to worry about. Just Jon letting me know he's doing something."

Steven's eyes narrowed as he scrutinized him. "Do you know what it is I do, Patrick?"

Rick looked at him. "Not exactly, but I have an idea," he answered.

"You know who I work for?" Steven asked.

"Three initials symbolizing three very large words," Rick replied.

"And do you know what they pay me to do?" he asked.

"You know when I'm lying," Rick stated.

"Yes, you're lying," Steven answered. "So since you know that, why don't you tell me the truth?"

"It's nothing for you to worry about," Rick said. "Jon is following up on a lead. The case is coming to a head and he wanted me to know what was going on in case it goes south which it very easily could."

"Dammit, don't you realize that man could be my father?" Steven demanded.

Rick put a hand on his shoulder. "Aye, I do and you need to know something. Jon would be honored to be your father. He told me himself."

"He's never taken an interest in me, why should he start now?" Steven demanded.

"That's not true. Next to Scott and Ryan, you're the person he talks about the most," Rick replied.

"I don't believe that," he said.

"You can tell when I'm lying you just told me so, so tell me, am I lying?"

"If you know so much about me, then tell me this. What happened to my girlfriend; Chrissie?"

Rick was quiet for a moment. "Jon told me she was in the north tower on September eleventh. He said you were on the phone with her and couldn't save her. That you haven't forgiven yourself even though it was your handler who wouldn't help you. I'm so sorry," Rick replied.

Steven said nothing for a time but finally he locked eyes with Rick and determination shone brightly. "Tell me what is going on."

Chapter
Fifty-Two

Since the Escalade was rubble, Jon pulled the Ferrari into the gravel driveway of the warehouse. The Lexus LX sat near the entrance. His stomach twisted as he heard Courtney dismantle and reassemble her gun beside him. Looking over at her, she didn't smile, she merely nodded and reached for the door handle. They had a plan, he would go inside through the front and she would go around back, cutting off their escape.

"I'm going to call Scott," he said. "Five minutes."

Courtney nodded and got out of the car, ducked and hurried around the side of the warehouse. Pulling out his phone, he called Beth.

"Hey," she answered. "How are things going?"

"Not great," Jon replied. "Baby, listen to me. I love you and I need you to do something for me."

"What's going on, Jon?" she asked.

"Please promise me you will take care of Scott for me."

"You're scaring me, what's going on?" she demanded.

"I don't know what's going to happen," he answered. "But I need you to know I love you. And please let me talk to Scott for a moment."

He heard her gasp and whimper as if holding back tears

but she said only one more thing before she handed the phone to Scott. "I love you, Jon."

"Dad? What's going on?" Scott asked.

"Scott, listen to me, I love you and I need you to know I would do anything for you."

"What are you saying?" he asked.

"Nothing," Jon replied. "I just need you to know I have always loved you and your mom. No matter what happens, I'll always be there for you. You know that, right?"

"Dad, you're scaring me," Scott said.

"Just know that," Jon replied. "I have to go now."

"Dad? Dad! Wait. Please!" Scott's voice was so desperate.

"Scott, I have to," Jon said.

"Just wait one damn minute," Scott replied. "I know you have always loved me and no matter what happens I love you, dad. Thank you for everything you've done. But you damn well better be back here in one piece. Understand? I'll let your little goodbye call go for now, but you stay alive. Do you hear me?"

Jon let out a single laugh releasing some of the tension that surrounded him. "Yeah, Scottie, I hear you. And I will."

"Good, now go kill that son-of-a-bitch," Scott said.

"I intend to," Jon replied.

———◦———

"I don't know if this is a good idea, Steven," Rick was saying as he drove. "I mean, I'm a businessman and a pacifist."

"That's all right we can't all be perfect," Steven replied dismantling his gun, blowing in the barrel and putting the gun back together.

"I'm serious," Rick said.

Steven looked over at him. "So am I." Rick finally looked back to the road and nodded. "Just stay behind me and don't get in my way."

Chapter
Fifty-Three

The smell that hit Jon as he opened the door to the warehouse was a mixture of dust and musk and brought with it the painful memories of what happened the last time he was there. As soon as his eyes adjusted to the darkness, the florescent lights flipped on, blinding him for a moment.

"So," he heard a familiar voice say. "You've come. Alone."

Once Jon's eyes adjusted to the lights, he could see Mat standing before him.

"What is it, Mat?" Jon asked. "Why did you ask me here?"

"Because he had no choice," another voice said from the shadows.

Jon peered into the shadows. "Aeron, I presume?" Jon called.

The man laughed. "Always had a way with words, didn't you, Jon?" the voice asked.

"I have, yeah," Jon replied. "But not as good as the way you have, eluding me. Come out of the shadows, Dan Howard."

"I wondered how long it would take you to figure that out."

"Only one part," Jon admitted. "I'm man enough to say I still don't know who you really are."

"Oh, but you do," the voice said. "You know my whole family. We go way back."

Jon listened to the voice and strained his mind to try to remember it. It did sound vaguely familiar, but he couldn't place it.

"Do we?" Jon asked. "Well, forgive me. You'll have to remind me who you are."

"All in good time, Jon," the voice said.

"What is it that you want from me?" Jon asked, still trying to peer into the darkness at the man standing there.

The man chuckled. "Well, you know, there is this little thing that I've had my eye on for a while, but that's beside the point. You know Hannah over here... baby? Where are you?" the man called.

"Here," she said from the opposite side and walked out of the shadows.

"Hannah here has a complaint to file with the US Military. Go ahead, babe."

"I was nine when my brother died in Vietnam. I remember how it destroyed my parents," she started. "I've been told by countless people I obsess over it, I'm delusional, psychotic. Well, I'm not. What I am is a threat to the function of this military. I know things, things they don't want me to know, things you all did."

As she spoke, Jon wondered why Mat merely stood there. He didn't look bound.

"We did nothing," Jon replied. Mat closed his eyes for a moment as Hannah pulled out a gun and aimed it at Jon. "I know this man has used your fixation on your brother's death as fuel for his fire."

"You don't know anything," she shouted.

"I know you are his pawn. He's using you, Hannah don't you get it? He doesn't care about you, you're merely a piece he can move on his human chessboard. He has been telling you false information about us. But tell me something." Jon took a step closer. "Do you really believe that Mat would have told you the truth? He may be an idiot on some things, but this? I think he would have told you the truth."

"The truth according to whom?" she asked.

"You want the truth?" Jon asked tired of the game. "The man you should be talking to is your brother's CO. You're right, I did see your brother get shot."

Mat looked over at him, eyes wide.

"On October 20, 1972, I saw Commander George Albert, your doctor at Northwestern Hospital, your brother's CO, the man Aeron shot and killed after killing Billy, turn around and shoot your brother dead. Aeron killed him without telling you the history I bet, without giving you the satisfaction of killing him yourself. Did Mat or I pull the trigger on your brother? No. We didn't know what we saw. In the heat of battle, there is no way to know what exactly we saw. But there were whispers. 'Thank God someone got rid of Chris Turner. That kid was insane.' He died because he was stupid enough to sneak up behind his CO and fire a gun right beside him. Albert reacted and we didn't prosecute him because your brother was wrong. He knew what to do but chose to ignore it. Thank God he's dead."

Hannah screamed and cocked the gun. Mat shoved her as she pulled the trigger. Courtney ran in from the back and aimed her gun. Mat raced toward Jon tackling him to the ground as two shots were fired, one from Hannah and one from Courtney. Mat groaned but didn't move. Jon pushed him off and saw the blood on his arm.

"Mat," Jon checked him.

"I'm okay," he answered holding his arm with his other hand.

"Jon?" Courtney called.

"We're clear," Jon shouted.

"She's down," Courtney said. "Freeze!" Courtney yelled, gun poised as she saw Aeron running to the side door.

Aeron stopped short, his back to them as he raised his hands in surrender.

"Turn slowly," Courtney ordered as the man was standing in the light now. Jon stood and, knowing his friend was all right, went to his partner, gun in hand.

"Turn around," Jon commanded when he hadn't moved.

"Really?" the man asked. "Are you sure you really want to know who I am?"

"I said turn around," Jon replied.

"Oh, I heard what you said. You're starting to sound too much like my father." The man turned around and shocked registered on Jon's face as he slowly lowered his gun. "Good to see you again, Jon."

Chapter
Fifty-Four

Keelan O'Grady hung up the phone again after leaving another message for Jon. He dropped his head in his hands after he stared at the wire transfer information glaring on the screen. How one million euros had been transferred out of the estate's fund, he had no explanation for.

Someone knew all the information in order to approve the transfer. But who?

"Keelan," Kathleen's voice came from the doorway. "What is it?"

"It's nothing," he replied.

"You're a lousy liar," she said, walking over to the desk and sitting down in the seat opposite him. "Tell me what's going on, lad."

"I can't get a hold of Jon," he said.

"Do you have to?" she asked.

"I need to talk to him. Something has happened and I need to know what to do."

"What is it?" she asked.

"I'm not sure, but it affects us all," he said, his eyes turning toward the graveyard that held his son, Riley's body.

Iollan grabbed his phone and answered before it woke his girlfriend.

"Da'," he asked. "Is everythin' all right?"

"I'm sorry to call you this late, lad," his dad said. "But I need to ask you something."

"What is it?" Iollan leaned back in his chair where he was studying for his exam.

"I need to know, have you heard from your brothers, Colman, Sean or Brendan?"

Iollan's eyebrows furrowed. Colman though several years older than Iollan was his closest brother in age.

"No," he replied. "I haven't heard from Brendan in years, not since Riley died. Colman sent me a letter about three months ago, but that's it. Why?"

"I just heard from one of them. I don't know which, but... he's stolen a large sum of money and transferred it to an offshore account in the Caymans."

"How large is large?" Iollan asked.

"A million euro," his father said.

"How did the banks allow this to happen? Aren't there safety measures in place?"

"I thought so, but you lads are the only ones who know the details of the funds."

"But I don't even know all of them," Iollan said. "You've kept them all from us so this sort of thing doesn't happen. Have you talked to his lordship?"

"I can't get a hold of him," he answered.

"Why do you think it's one of the brothers?" Iollan asked. "Could the system have been hacked?"

"It's possible, but I received an e-mail from one of them unsigned, saying, 'Thanks for teaching me about the ins and outs of financial records, Dad. It has really come in handy these last few years. Don't think of this as a robbery; it's just compensation.'"

"'Compensation'?" Iollan asked.

"That's what it said," Keelan replied.

"Da'," Iollan said softly. "Am I crazy or does that sound like..."

"It can't be," Jon breathed. Aeron smirked. "You're dead."

"Who?" Courtney asked.

"Tragic ceremony, I'm sure," Aeron said without answering Courtney. "Boating accidents are always a tragedy. My mother must have cried her eyes out and my father... well, he was probably too busy to attend."

"You son-of-a-bitch," Jon shouted. "Your father loved you!"

"Oh, I'm sure," he said. "But when I failed his test to be the next steward and that... that child was chosen over me, oh that was it."

"And Mat and Hannah?" Jon asked.

"Who could I get that was close enough to you so you would see your whole world, your aspirations, your life, crash down around you like mine had?" he asked. "Hannah was just crazy enough to be played, for me to incite that anger. And with her desires to take down your friends, it fell into my plan perfectly."

"Who shot Scott?" Jon demanded.

"That was me and I have to say shooting Scott was the best feeling in the world. Of course now I will have to kill him and Kim, she could be carrying his bastard."

"You messed with his meds?" Jon replied.

"Of course," he answered. "It was easy. Everyone trusts a man in a lab coat who's confident in what he does. Dan Howard, RN, well, he was good, wasn't he? I enjoyed you calling me, Courtney, asking me for my alibi for Hannah's disappearance. But you know the one I liked was the FedEx driver. You looked right at me and didn't even recognize me."

For a moment, Jon remembered the day Billy died. He was at Courtney's apartment and had answered the door for the delivery. There was something about him Jon did not like, apparently, even then, somewhere in the back of his mind, he knew who he was.

"It was rather fun, don't you think?" he asked. "I stole the old M40 rifle from Mat's house while he was busy with Hannah upstairs. I used it for every murder and recorded it…" He reached for the something in his pocket.

Jon and Courtney raised their guns and warned him to stop.

"Whoa, easy, Grandpa. Just showing you this," he showed the black book. "I record everything in here and I think some people would be very interested in your comings and goings. And Mat's activities would be of great interest to his government."

"That's my government too," Jon said.

"When are you going to wake up and realize you don't belong here, Jon?" Aeron's Irish accent showing through strongly. "Your government is across the ocean, a government you turned your back on."

"What are you talking about?" Jon asked.

"Don't you remember?" Aeron replied. "They remember you."

Jon froze. "You're on a vendetta for the IRA?" Jon asked.

"Eamonn O'Malley sends his regards," Aeron said.

Jon's face drained of color as he stared at the man before him. "You're lying," Jon finally said.

"Would I?" Aeron asked. "Eamonn wasn't the original man I worked for. But Rob let me down. After he went off on his own, I sought out the man I knew would remember you."

"Who is this Rob character?" Courtney demanded. Aeron

didn't even look at her.

"Why don't you go on outside and play, Courtney? Daddy and I need to talk."

"Hey," Courtney raised her gun. "Don't think I won't shoot you, asshole."

"Such ladylike language," Aeron replied.

"Just tell me one thing, why?" Jon asked.

"Because you and your stupid family traditions ruined my life!" he yelled.

"Who the hell are you?" Courtney demanded.

"Are you going to tell her or should I?" Aeron asked.

"This is Riley O'Grady, Keelan's son and Iollan's brother," Jon said.

"You're dead," Courtney stated.

"Riley is dead. I'm not Riley anymore," Aeron replied. "Riley was a feckless drifter, a dreamer. I have purpose. I am Aeron, Celtic god of war and death, carnage, and slaughter."

"Wow," Jon breathed. "And I thought Hannah was crazy." Courtney grinned.

"You think that's funny?" Riley's eyes snapped to Courtney.

"A bit, yeah," she replied.

"Maybe this will wipe that grin off your face," in one swift move, Riley had pulled out a gun from his back pocket and aimed it at Courtney.

Jon and Courtney both fired wounding him, but when he raised the gun again, aiming it at Jon, a third gunshot rang out. Riley weaved and looked down. Blood seeped out of his chest. Dropping the gun, he collapsed on the floor.

"No!" Courtney shouted. Looking back to see who had shot him, Steven ran up to Jon, gun in hand. Rick was close behind him. "Why did you kill him?" She demanded.

"He was going to kill Jon," Steven replied.

"Wound him," she shouted. "He could have information."

"That's not my job," Steven answered.

"And who invited you here?" she demanded.

"Stop," Jon shouted and, after kicking the gun away, he knelt. "Riley, just tell me why."

"You stole my birthright just like you stole his," Riley said, looking over at Rick. "You should understand... you're firstborn... you deserve it all... like I do."

"You are not the firstborn, Riley," Rick said. "And I think I'll take my chances with my brother. Blood is thicker than water, after all."

"Blood?" he scoffed. "Blood is nothing."

"Your father has cried to me because he thinks he's to blame. Your mother can't even bring herself to go to your grave because she faints every time she sees your name on that stone. Your brothers have all told me they miss you more than you could ever imagine," Jon revealed.

"Not all of them," he grinned, blood coating his teeth. "Brendan hasn't said anything for a long time."

"What have you done? Where is he?" Jon asked.

"They should change the name on that tombstone."

"You and Brendan went out on the boat together?" Jon stated.

"Bravo, Sherlock."

"What happened?" Jon asked.

"You work it out, genius," Riley said choking. *"Erin go bragh."* After a moment, Riley let out a breath and his eyes stared off into the distance.

When he was sure Riley was gone, Jon made the sign of the cross on himself and stood from the body, looking over at Courtney.

"He wouldn't have broken even if we had a chance," Jon said.

"You don't know that," Courtney replied.

"Call it in," Jon stated. "Let's get forensics out here." Courtney stared at him for a bit then pulled out her cell phone and called dispatch.

Jon turned to Steven and Rick. "Rick told me what you were doing," Steven said. "I couldn't let you go alone."

Jon put a hand on Steven's shoulder. "Thank you," he said and pulled him into a hug.

"As much as I enjoy happy endings, I am bleeding over here," Mat's voice called.

"Courtney's calling it in," Jon replied. Steven walked over to Hannah to make sure she wouldn't move. Courtney's shot had incapacitated her but hadn't killed her.

Jon walked over to Mat and offered a hand. Once he was upright, Mat looked over at his best friend. "I'm sorry," he said.

"I know why you did it. You were protecting us."

"I honestly thought she wanted to kill us all," Mat said.

"I honestly think she did," Jon replied.

"I didn't know Riley was behind this. I didn't know who he was," Mat revealed.

"I know," Jon replied and smacked his good arm. Mat groaned in pain. "Sorry."

"Don't worry, Gunny," Mat said. "I've been through worse than this. It'll take more than just a bullet to stop me. Besides, you're bleeding too."

Jon looked at his arm and shrugged. "It's a graze," he said.

Mat looked over at Hannah. "You know what I have to do?" Mat sobered.

"Yeah," Jon nodded. "Where will you go?"

"I don't know," Mat answered. "Home?"

"Texas?" Jon asked.

Mat shook his head. "Madrid," he replied.

"I'll miss you," he said.

"I'll miss you too," Mat replied. "I'll make sure to at least write when I think it's safe."

"How long will you be away?" Jon asked.

"As long as it takes," Mat said.

"Courtney and I will work to clear your name," he said.

"I know," Mat answered. "She's good for you, Jon. Keep her safe."

Jon looked over at Courtney still on the phone with dispatch. Glancing over to him, she smiled slightly.

"Yeah, she's something special," he said. Then before he thought anymore about her or where they were, he turned back to his friend. "You'll miss Scott's wedding."

"Are you shitting me?" Mat grinned. "It's about time."

Jon looked down but spoke low. "Beth and I are together now."

"Good," Mat answered. Jon looked up surprised. "It's about damn time, brother. Look, I know you'll always love my sister, but you can't be alone. You don't deserve to be alone. I know she'd be happy. So, I am too. And when the time comes that you marry, be sure to let me know. I stood up with you the first time. I'm not missing it a second."

Jon smiled slightly and nodded as they heard sirens blaring in the distance.

Chapter
Fifty-Five

Jon knocked on Scott's hospital room door. The laughter and conversation continued and Scott called for him to come in. As soon as the door opened, Scott grinned.

"What took you so bloody long?" he asked.

"Sorry, you know these criminals, no sense of punctuality," Jon answered and walked over to his son giving him a hug.

"Thank God," Scott mumbled into his dad's shoulder and gripping him tighter for a moment. "Who was it?"

"Later," Jon answered. "Right now, I need to go snog my girlfriend," Jon winked at Beth.

"Get a room," Scott laughed.

"Not a bad idea," Jon teased. But before he went to Beth, he locked eyes with his son. "How are you doing?"

"The doctor said I should be able to head out of here soon," Scott said. "All my tests came back without a problem and as long as I take it easy, I can head home tonight."

"Fantastic," Jon replied. "We'll get some food and watch a movie."

"My thoughts exactly," Scott answered.

"Now if you'll excuse us," he said leaving his son's side and grabbing Beth by the hand leading her out of the room.

———————

After properly greeting his girlfriend, Jon found Steven, Rick and Courtney standing together.

"Everything good with the local cops?" Jon asked.

Courtney nodded. "They got forensics out there. Hannah has been taken into custody and Riley's body is in the morgue."

"Thank you," Jon said. She nodded but when his eyes drifted to Steven, she stepped back and made an excuse of needing to get some lunch. Rick agreed and they walked to the canteen together.

"Thank you," Jon said to Steven. Steven nodded but didn't say anything more. "Can I ask you something?"

"Yeah," Steven answered.

"I asked your mom about you," Jon replied. Steven's eyes twitched but he said nothing. "I hope you want to know as much as I do."

"Know what?" Steven asked.

"No need to play dumb, Steven," Jon replied. "I need to know if you are my son."

"Considering the other option is to be the product of a man who brutally raped my mother for over an hour at a party, I can see some good in finding out," Steven answered.

"You know?" Jon asked.

"When I first was hired by the company," Steven revealed. "I looked up my dad and mom. Buried, was an old police report by someone named Olga about a rape she wanted to report but did not witness. It was buried because when confronted, both parties denied it. But their names were clear as day; Paul Anderson and Elizabeth Nixon."

"I don't want you to know if you are Paul Anderson's, I want to know if you are mine," Jon answered.

"And there's a distinction?" he asked.

"A great distinction," he replied. "I don't ask this to tear you down. I ask this to see if you are my son. Paul doesn't deserve you…" Jon looked down, placed his hands on his hips and looked up at him. "And neither do I."

"At least I know with you, Mom was happy," Steven answered. "What are you asking?"

"I want to know if you would consent to a paternity test."

Steven was silent for a while but when he answered, his voice was strong. "When Rick told me what was going on, the only thing I could think of was I had to help you. Not for Mom's sake, not for Scott's sake or Kim's but for mine. In that moment, I knew I needed to get to you. Then Rick told me something that solidified my feelings."

"Can I ask what it is he said?" Jon asked.

"He told me you talk about me. Next to Scott and Ryan, I'm the one you talk about the most. I tested him. I said if he really knew me he would know the answer to one question. What happened to Chrissie?" Steven took a deep breath. "When he answered, I knew what he said was true. You care enough to tell your brother things about me. Not in a way that would invade my privacy but so he was informed about… your sons. I've been angry at you for too long and I didn't know why. I realize now, I was running from the fact I have always wanted a father. Not just a father, I wanted a dad. Paul Anderson was never a dad. Though in my heart I know I am his child, I am your son."

"Always, Steve," Jon answered. "Always. Never think any differently. You are my son. Even if you aren't blood."

Grabbing his shoulder, Jon pulled him into a hug.

———

Jon snuck into Mat's room after making plans with Steven. They needed to get Mat out of there and soon. "How are you feeling?" Jon asked as Courtney helped Mat stand from the hospital bed.

"Like I got shot," Mat replied. "But I've been through worse. I'm fine, thanks to Detective Shields." Courtney smiled and made sure he was upright before she let go of him to retrieve his shirt. "How's Scott?" Mat asked.

"Better, they're releasing him tonight," Jon replied helping Courtney get Mat's Oxford shirt over his bandages.

"You sure you won't get in trouble for this?" Mat asked looking at Courtney.

"We have the Mayor on our side," she shrugged as she helped button his shirt. "But we have to get you out of here soon. I've heard the Mayor can't hold off the Deputy Chief any longer. He's hell bent on arresting you."

"Did you by chance find the key that was taped under the Remington?" Mat asked. Jon fished it out of his pocket and handed it to him. "Thank you."

"I have to ask," Jon said. "What's it to?"

"A locker with some liquidated assets," Mat replied. "How long do I have?"

"Ten minutes, if that," Courtney replied.

"Jon," Mat said stopping him. "I don't have time to say goodbye to Scott. But, I want to give him something. Could you go to my house and find that loose floorboard in the kitchen? Inside is something I've kept for a while. Carol would want him to have it."

"Sure," Jon answered. "When do you want me to give it to him?"

"On his wedding day," he replied. "In case I can't be with him."

"Okay," Jon confirmed. "I will. But now we have to get you out of here."

Courtney went to the door and peeked out. Motioning them through, they bustled him to the meeting place where Steven pulled up in his car.

"Make no stops," Steven said walking over and handing Mat the keys.

"I have to," Mat replied. "But I won't be long."

"Their names are Zoe and Cliff," Steven explained. "They're waiting for you at the airport."

Mat nodded and thanked them. Turning back to Jon, he gave a small smile

"Write," Jon said.

"I will," Mat replied. "Take care, brother."

"And you," he hugged him tightly.

Mat turned to Courtney. "Take care of him for me?"

"Promise," she said. "It was an honor working with you, Captain."

"I owe Dave a lot," Mat replied. "He knew we needed you in our midst. You've helped more than you know. Take care of yourself, Shields."

"I will," she answered. "And you, sir."

"You gotta go," Steven stated. "Now."

———◦———

Later that day, Scott was wheeled out of his room to the reception area.

"I can walk," Scott said, turning to look at the nurse pushing the wheelchair.

"Hospital regulations, Mr. Greene," she smiled.

As they arrived at the reception area, Scott stood to sign the release form and the nurse behind the counter spoke, "Thank you very much, Mr. Greene. I hope you had an enjoyable stay. Don't take this the wrong way, but we'd rather not see you back here."

"Oh, trust me. I don't want to be back here for a long time," Scott replied.

"Good," she answered.

As they turned to leave, the deputy chief and four armed

policemen walked out of the elevator.

"Lieutenant," the DC called to Jon. "Which room is the former captain in?"

"Room 251," he said.

"Dad!" Scott cried. The look in Jon's eyes silenced him.

The DC motioned to the four policemen for them to fan out and cover the exits. Jon watched the DC walk down the hallway then gripped his son's elbow gently but firmly and motioned for Kim and Beth to walk with him.

"Let's go," he urged. Rick and Steven waited for them at the main doorway. Jon passed Scott's duffel to Steven and touched his arm, letting him know he would be right back.

Heading to the Emergency area of the hospital, he found Ryan exiting one of the rooms and called to him.

"Hey," Ryan replied. "Scott get out all right."

"Yeah, but I need you to stay away from DC Andrews," Jon said. "He's here and he's looking for Mat. I don't think he knows you're my nephew, but just in case, go out for a coffee if he calls for you. Okay?"

"Yeah. Sure, Uncle Jon," Ryan replied. "Where is Uncle Mat?"

"Better you didn't know," he said. "Oh and another thing," he lifted an evidence bag with two other bags inside it. "I need you to run a test for me."

"Okay," Ryan answered, taking the bag. "And what exactly am I testing for?"

"Are these two people related?" he stated.

Ryan nodded slowly. "Sure," he said. "It shouldn't take long."

"Will you let me know when the results come in?" Jon asked.

"Absolutely," he said.

"And," Jon started. "This stays between us."

"That's my job."

"Good," he said. Seeing the elevator doors open and DC Andrews barrel out with two other police officers frantically looking for Mat, Jon slipped past and met Steven just outside the main doors. "Any news?" Jon asked.

"Safe and sound," Steven replied. "He'll be in the air in twenty minutes."

"Thank you," Jon said.

"No worries," Steven replied. "I hear Madrid is beautiful this time of year. What about our other thing?"

"Should get the results soon," Jon said.

"Will you call me?"

"As soon as I know," Jon confirmed.

"Thanks," he said. "I've received another assignment. I'll be leaving Thursday. I don't know how long this one will take."

"Be careful?" Jon urged.

"Always am," he answered.

"Will I be able to call you?" Jon asked.

"Should," he answered. "I'll still be in town."

"There's a terrorist cell in Indiana?" Jon dropped his voice.

"That's what I'm going to find out," Steven replied. "If I don't answer, leave me a message. I'll call when I can."

"Take care of yourself," Jon said.

"Hey, I'm Casanova. What's the worst that could happen?" Steven asked.

Epilogue

A man sat at a table in the outside Café Gijon in Madrid, Spain, listening to the live music that played. His face had been altered by a closely trimmed goatee. His hair, usually dyed dark brown, was now naturally salt and pepper.

Watching the tourists as they walked by, he thought of the events that led him there. The storm had finally calmed and, as he sat drinking espresso, he finally relaxed.

He checked the time and looked around the square. His date was late. Ordering another espresso and another Magdalena, a Spanish pastry that he had missed since he had been in America, he recognized one of the songs the band in the square began to play and smiled.

It had been a long time since he had been home, and he missed the sights, the sounds and the smells. Everything was so vivid, so beautiful. Even the birds sounded differently there. He was home, but he didn't have a home. His family's villa was about ten miles south of the city, but he could not go there. That could be a place the people looking for him would look. The sudden realization he was homeless was a little disorienting.

He had made three phone calls when he landed to let his family know he was safe. His mother cried and his father told him to take care of himself. His best friend was glad to hear from him. The last call was to a local number. It had been far too long, he wasn't sure she would recognize him. He would know her anywhere. He had relived their summer romance every time he heard their song. No one knew about her.

"Mateo?" he heard from behind him.

Closing his eyes briefly, he smiled. Turning they locked eyes, she still took his breath away.

"Connie."

To be continued...

Acknowledgements

Hello! Thank you for reading! I have loved Jon and Courtney ever since I thought them up in 2005. They will always be near and dear to me and to be able to revisit their first book was a real treat! I hope you enjoyed their story as much as I did and don't miss the next installment in the Greene & Shields Files series, Once Upon a Midnight Dreary available now! Jon and Courtney find themselves entrenched in murder, mystery and Edgar Allan Poe. Remember Rob? He's back for more. Nevermore, that is.

The third and final installment in the series, Old Sins Cast Long Shadows should be out in 2017! See how this trilogy is completed. Eamonn O'Malley, leader of the IRA joins the fun. Jon's old sins cast long shadows… Enjoy!

The Greene and Shields Files

Book Two

ONCE UPON A MIDNIGHT DREARY

M. KATHERINE CLARK

CHAPTER ONE

Detective Courtney Shields looked up from the bloody mess at her feet when she heard her partner's car drive up. Lieutenant Jonathan Greene stepped out of his black Escalade and straightened his suit jacket around his gun. His black wavy hair, greying at the temples, lent to the dominance of his image. His deep, mesmerizing green eyes, rivaled the Irish countryside where he called home. Standing a few inches over six feet, Jon was built like the rugby player he was; broad shoulders tapering to a slender waist with a physique men half his age envied.

But that day, Courtney saw dark circles under his eyes, a tightness around his mouth and a stiffness in his movements. Hoping his insomnia had nothing to do with their previous case involving his own family and more to do with his girlfriend, Beth keeping him awake at night, Courtney watched as he walked toward the crime scene.

———◦◦◦———

Jon always kept everyone at arm's length, keeping his emotions in check and letting only those he allowed in, recently Courtney had been able to sneak her way past his defenses. She was able to read him more and more each day. Schooling his reactions, he knew his most valiant efforts were thwarted by the heaviness in his eyes. It's not that he didn't want to tell anyone what he was feeling, it's just there were times he swore he saw *his* face… a dead man. Riley O'Grady, the man who was haunting him.

Pushing all thoughts aside, he knew nothing was as important as solving the case before him. Still walking over to his partner, he ducked under the police tape and nodded at her.

"What've we got, partner?" He asked.

Courtney smiled at him and accepted the coffee he handed her.

"Hey," she greeted. "Better ask the doc."

"Mornin', Grace," Jon smiled addressing the deputy coroner, Dr. Grace O'Malley. "What've we got?"

"Nothing like a gruesome murder to make you hate Mondays even more," she responded. "And where's my coffee?" she asked eyeing him.

"Another time," he answered, his eyes dancing as he gazed at her over the rim of the coffee cup and gave a wink.

"Uh huh," she answered, but he saw the slight pink color of her cheeks as she looked down. "All we really know for certain is that he is a Caucasian male, late 50s early 60s." O'Malley answered.

"Who found him?" Jon asked.

"Street artist came out early in the morning before the unis were on patrol," Courtney replied. She motioned to the young man standing beside the cop cars talking to a uniformed officer.

"All right, Grace, show me," Jon said.

"It's a little weird," Grace said turning back to the tarp. "Prepare yourself."

Jon gave a quick nod to the doctor and she lifted the

sheet.

"Jesus," Jon breathed crouching down. "What could've done that? A dog?"

"The worst kind of dog… a man," O'Malley answered.

"Not funny, Grace," he said looking over at her. "How could a man do that?"

"Not my territory, I'm afraid," she answered covering the victim back up. "The heart has been completely removed through the chest cavity."

"Have you located it, yet?" Jon asked.

"Not yet," she answered. "But it is possible the killer took it with him."

"Could it have been a woman?" Courtney asked.

"More than likely not," O'Malley said. "It would take a great deal of sheer force to break open a man's rib cage. It is not something I would say a woman would be able to do unaided."

"What about with the use of rib cutters or something a little more crude?" Courtney asked.

"No sign of any instrument," Grace answered. "But I won't know for certain until I get him back to the lab. It looks like the ribs were pulled and broken like one would break a wishbone from a turkey."

"Was he alive or dead at that time?" Jon asked.

"Dead," she confirmed. "It looks like he was struck on the back of the head roughly two to four hours ago."

"Making it between 5 and 7 this morning," Courtney stated.

"Can I take him now?" Grace asked.

"Let us know what you find out," Jon replied and turned to go. Before he took three steps, Courtney grabbed his arm.

"Wait," she said. Turning her head as if listening for something, she went on. "Do you hear that?"

"What?" He replied.

"Hey guys, quiet down for a second," she called out. No one was listening. Jon gave a shrill whistle that got everyone's attention.

"Everyone silent!" He shouted. Everyone in the area went quiet. After a moment, Courtney spoke.

"There," she whispered. "Hear it?"

A faint metallic heartbeat was coming from somewhere nearby. Grace looked around.

"It's near me," she whispered. Jon took a step closer to her and Courtney walked around to the other side of the pallets the body was laying on.

"Jon," Grace said. "It's directly under the body."

Jon beckoned her to come toward him. Taking his outstretched hand, she let him pull her forward and pushed her behind him. Taking a step closer, Courtney was opposite him. Jon held his hand up telling her to wait. Crouching, he gently pulled the tarp from covering the body.

The wooden pallets the body was on came into view and the sound seemed to be coming from directly below the victim and it was getting louder. Courtney nodded at her partner and reached beneath the wood, pulling out a small recorder. The sound of the heart beat played loudly on it by then.

"What kind of a sick joke?" Courtney asked Jon. He shook his head and looked back under the pallets.

"Grace," he called. "I think we found the heart."

O'Malley went up to him and bent low. Reaching for it with her gloved hands, she pulled the bloodied organ out from under the wooden slats.

"Looks like it," she answered. "And there's something attached to it. Looks like paper."

"It's too badly stained for us to read," Courtney answered, taking a look at it. "I'll send it to forensics, maybe they can retrieve something."

"This is very odd," Jon said. "I'm going to go talk to the witness." The uniform nodded as Jon and Courtney walked up. "Thank you, Harper," Jon greeted the officer before turning his attention to the young man. "My name is Lieutenant Greene, this is my partner Detective Shields, Mister—?"

"That dude was just lying there. I mean he was just lying there and I saw all the blood and I don't remember—"

"It's all right, my partner and I are just trying to understand what happened here," Jon said. "Can you tell us what you saw?"

"The dude's dead!" His voice cracked as it went higher. "I mean his chest and the blood and did they say his heart was missing?"

"Yes," Jon said. "It was a very brutal attack and you are the only one who can tell us what happened before we arrived. What's your name?"

The young man looked at him suspiciously. "John," he answered.

"Is that your real name?" Jon asked. The street artist swallowed and his eyes drifted to his bag of graffiti tools. "We're not here for your street art," Jon said. "We don't care about that. Just tell us what happened."

He looked past Jon to the body being pulled onto the gurney in the coroner's body bag.

"I was walkin' through here," he said. "And I looked over and saw this guy lyin' on the ground and I see he ain't movin'. So I call out to him, and he doesn't answer. So I go a little closer, and I call out again, then I see he's definitely not movin' so I go a little closer and I see the blood and his chest and I – I think I scream or somethin'. I see one of the cop cars and I take off running toward them!"

"Did you see anyone else around the body?" Jon asked.

"Nah man! It was just him. He was lying there all cut up,"

he cried.

"Thank you, now I will need you to go with the officers to the precinct and get your statement in writing," Jon said indicating the police officers.

Courtney waited until the patrol car was driving away before she turned to Jon.

"You don't think he did it, do you?" she asked. Jon shook his head. "Yeah, me neither," she answered. "That heartbeat was some kind of sick joke."

"Let's get that letter down to forensics see if they can recover anything and have them try to lift a print off of the recorder," Jon said.

CHAPTER TWO

"What are you doing?" Bradley Henderson asked his brother, Quinn as he pulled one of the drapes closed.

"We gotta lay low," Quinn said tugging the other one and bathing them both in muted light. "Things gotta cool off. There's dozens of troopers looking for us."

"How long are we staying here?" Brad complained looking around the hotel room. "It's no better than prison."

"We're free that's what matters," Quinn said.

"Not for very long," Brad replied.

"I know what you're thinking and the answer is no," Quinn answered. "We have to lay low and wait for it all to pass."

They may have been only a few minutes apart with Quinn being the eldest but they thought the same.

"You know I'll look after you," Quinn went on. "Didn't I while we were upstate?"

"I'm tired of running," Brad replied. "I thought giving them what they wanted would give us free reign."

"Free reign?" Quinn replied. "Shit, what are you, an idiot? What did you think would happen? A full pardon? Clean slate? A medal? C'mon man," Quinn reasoned. "We're cop killers."

"That was over ten years ago," Brad said.

"Do you think that matters?" Quinn demanded.

"We didn't pull the damn trigger!" Brad defended.

"What do you—" Quinn was interrupted by a knock at the door. Putting a finger to his lips, Quinn motioned his brother to be quiet.

"Who is it?" Quinn called out.

"Come now, Quinn," a voice from their past surprised them. "Open the door like a good little criminal and let me in."

Quinn locked eyes with Brad. Suppressing his nervous swallow, Quinn took a deep breath and opened the door.

"Paul?" Quinn questioned, not recognizing the man before him.

"Tsk, tsk, tsk, you boys have been bad," Paul said. "And by the way… it's Rob from now on." Pushing past the much taller man, Paul stepped into the hotel room. "Nice place you've got here," he said looking around.

"Yeah they don't exactly allow escaped felons into the Ritz," Quinn countered, bolting and chaining the door.

"How have you been, Bradley?" Rob asked. Brad shrugged. "And you Quinn?" Rob turned to him. "You look thinner than last time."

"Prison food will do that to you," Quinn answered.

"How about a nice steak dinner? On me, of course," Rob offered.

"We can't be seen out and about, half the state is looking for us," Quinn answered.

"Ah no, see, Quinn and Bradley Henderson cannot be seen out and about," Rob unbolted the door and removed the chain. "But two nephews come to visit me? No one will bat an eyelash. But we need to clean you up." Opening the door, Rob let three women into the room carrying dry cleaning and one backpack each.

"Enjoy, boys," Rob said. "They're already paid for. Meet

me at this location when you're finished," he handed them a folded piece of paper. "Take your time, though. Ladies," Rob called to them. "Take *good* care of them. They've been locked up far too long and have probably missed a woman's touch. Enjoy!"

<hr/>

There was a knock at Jon's and Courtney's office door and a moment later Officer Callen walked in.

"Excuse me, Sir, Ma'am," he said. "The forensics came back. John Doe is not in the system and the recorder had traces of latex. The paper had a couple words that forensics *were* able to make out but the entirety of the note was unreadable."

Callen handed Courtney the file and once he left, Courtney looked over at Jon.

"Listen to this," she started. "The three readable words were 'deed' 'planks' 'hideous'."

"Very interesting," Jon thought a moment. "And rather old language. Who really says *hideous* any more or *planks* for that matter?"

"Something about this whole thing seems strangely familiar," Courtney replied. "Almost like I've read about it," intrigued, she turned to the computer. "I need to check something." Typing into her search bar, Jon stood near her waiting for the search. Finally the results she was expecting popped up. "Ha! That's why it seemed familiar! It's from *Tell Tale Heart* by Poe," she explained.

"It's been a while for me, love," Jon said. "It's been since Primary School since I've read a Poe. Remind me about that one?"

Just as Courtney started to speak, Jon's cell phone rang. "Hey, Ryan," Jon answered.

"Hey, Uncle Jon," Ryan replied. "Sorry for the delay, the lab was backed up but I have those paternity test results you asked me for when Uncle Mat was in the hospital a couple weeks ago."

Jon's stomach twisted and he felt himself go pale. It had finally come. The moment he had been waiting for, for the past thirty-six years had finally come. The answer to the question; was Steven Anderson, Beth's eldest son, his son too?

"Do you want me to meet you, or do you want me to just tell you?" Ryan asked.

Jon debated for a second.

"Courtney, could you give me a second?" He asked. Nodding, she grabbed her water bottle and left the room. "Just tell me…" Jon finally said.

Steven took a big risk joining Jon for lunch just before he went off on another assignment. But as he remembered their conversation, he knew it was worth it. Jon's words echoed in Steven's ears as he drove.

"As much as I wish this to be false… it looks like I am *not* your father," Jon said.

"You're saying that Paul Anderson is my father?" Steven demanded. When Jon nodded, Steven cursed angrily and stood.

He had always known. But now that it was fact, he wished he never agreed to that damn test in the first place. Was it better not knowing and… hoping? Three words escaped his lips before any others.

"Don't tell mom," he had said softly.

CHAPTER THREE

After Jon and Steven parted ways, Jon called Dave and Courtney and cashed in a favor. He couldn't go back to work, not now, not after everything. Maybe it was a mistake to go home but Jon needed a good glass of whiskey, some alone time and a long run to clear his head. Dropping his keys on the washroom ledge, he took off his shoes, tie and suit jacket and walked through the house to the living room.

Gazing at Scott's picture, he was relieved. He only had one son, and that's all he wanted. He enjoyed being a father *figure* to any man who asked, but he would only ever have one son.

Unbuttoning his collar, Jon went to the bar and poured a glass of whiskey. He breathed in the scent of the golden liquor and took a gulp reveling in the slow burn of the alcohol. Even though he was relieved, a part of him still hurt, especially for Steven. The man had just realized that he was the product of Paul Anderson's brutal rape of his mother. Jon knew, even before Steven had asked him not to, he could never tell Beth, it would tear her apart.

Knowing he needed to speak with someone about the thoughts whirling around his brain, he pulled out his phone and dialed a well-remembered number.

"Dr. Hinkle's office, how may I assist you?" the receptionist answered.

"Dr. Hinkle, please," Jon said.

"May I ask who is calling?" she asked pleasantly.

"Jonathan Greene," he answered.

"Thank you, Mr. Greene, one moment please."

"Jon?" The doctor answered a moment later.

"Hiya, Doc, got me on the *high priority* list, eh?" Jon asked.

"Off the *suicide watch*, that's as far as you're getting," the doctor chuckled. "You outta be happy you're only on my *immediate answer* list for now."

Jon had to laugh but there was no humor in it. The doctor had been on the receiving end of Jon's suicidal rants more than once.

"Are you busy?" Jon asked.

"I have a patient coming in ten minutes. What's up?" Hinkle asked.

"I finally found out about Steven," Jon said.

The doctor was silent for a moment.

"Give me a second," he finally said. Putting his side on mute, Hinkle told his secretary to cancel his day's appointments.

———⋙◦⋘———

Quinn: He called his shrink.

Rob had to smile as he read Quinn's text report. Jon was cracking.

Rob: What was the theme?

Quinn: Mostly that he isn't some guy's father.

Rob smirked.

Rob: Who's?

Quinn: Some guy named Steven.

Rob laughed in triumph.

"Oh Beth, all those times you tried to use that against me... I could've told ya he wasn't Jon's. Just look at him," Rob chuckled. Taking his phone, he texted Bradley.

Rob: Keep Steven in your sights. Report back to me what he's doing.

Brad: He passed the airport, heading to his hotel. I'm following. What does this guy do?

Rob: He's CIA.

Rob looking up at his computer screen at one of the pictures of Steven and Jon from their lunch earlier that day. "And he's mine."

⸺⸻◦◦⸻⸺

Steven found the hotel programed into his GPS off to a left of the divided highway. As he waited for oncoming traffic to break, his eyes consciously drifted up to his rearview mirror.

Car: Toyota, sedan, tan, lightly tinted windows, 2004 model.

Driver: late 30s, blonde, shaggy hair, sunglasses, Colt's hat, clean-shaven, alone.

Following: not so well, since the Indianapolis airport.

Amateur, Steven shook his head.

Pulling into the first parking spot he saw, Steven paused before getting out. He spied his handler's car. Knowing the code if something was wrong, Steven pulled out his phone and shouldered it, pretending to have a conversation as he walked around his car to the trunk. Pulling out his suitcase and hooking his computer bag over his neck, Steven walked into the hotel.

"Good afternoon," the desk clerk greeted Steven cheerily as he lowered his phone from his ear.

"Hey, how ya doing?" He asked quickly. "Checking in."

"Absolutely, what name is the reservation under, Sir?" She asked typing something into the computer.

"Craig Stevens," he answered.

"Do you have your driver's license on you, Mr. Stevens?" she asked.

"Yeah absolutely," he pulled out his wallet and handed her the fake, government issued ID. Looking down at his phone as it buzzed in his hand,

Flash: I'm shipping up to Boston.

Steven was glad to see his handler's code letting him know everyone was in position. Stealthily glancing around the room, he saw the man who had followed him for the past hour looking nonchalantly at magazines at the entryway table.

"Welcome Mr. Stevens," the hotel receptionist went on. "We have your room ready for you. Will this be on the same card you reserved with us?"

"Yes," he answered. The desk clerk handed him the paperwork and he looked it over.

"Damn," he said teasingly. "Didn't know I'd be signing my life away."

She giggled causing him to glance up at her through his rectangular framed glasses and smirk. He knew he looked good. Ralph Lauren would have been proud. It was his job to always look sexy.

"All set," he replied after signing his name.

"Here's your key, Mr. Stevens. You'll be in room 208. I hope you have a pleasant stay." She said.

"It's been pretty great so far," he answered winking at her.

She grinned at him. "If there's anything else I can do, please don't hesitate to let me know," she said suggestively.

"You'll be the first," he replied.

Turning, he looked around for the signs to the stairwell. Waiting on the second landing for a couple minutes, he listened. No one followed him. Exiting the stairs, he saw Zoe, one of his colleagues, dressed as a hotel maid and another agent, Cliff dressed in pool attire with a towel draped over his shoulders. He nodded at Steven as they passed each other and Cliff went into the elevator.

Once Steven reached room 208, he slid in the keycard into the lock and the smell of cinnamon filled the air.

"You're late," he heard from the other side of the wall. Gordon stepped into his view.

"Dammit, Flash, give me a second to put my bags down," Steven said, using Gordon's code name as he walked over to the TV and set his computer bag on the desk beside it.

"What was the business downstairs?" Gordon asked chewing his signature cinnamon chewing gum. "Should I tell them to stand down?"

Steven pulled off his leather jacket and draped it over the back of the desk chair.

"I don't know," he answered. "Tell them to keep an eye out." Steven described the tail as he walked over to Gordon and pointed out the sedan in the parking lot. Gordon gave the announcement over the walkie. He read off the driver's license for Mac, their techie, to run.

"So, any change to the plan?" Steven asked sitting in the oversized chair in the corner.

<hr>

Bradley got a room on the ground floor directly below Steven's room. He sat on the bed and pulled out his phone.

Brad: He just checked into his hotel. I couldn't get anywhere near his room. Too many guys with earwigs.

As he waited, he pulled off his jacket and shirt. His phone buzzed on the bed.

Rob: I warned you already. Don't get too close.

"Yeah I know," he muttered harshly. Going to the bathroom, he ran the shower. It was nice to have his own room, his own bathroom, his own space. After ten years in prison, he reveled in taking a shower without anyone watching him.